# People
## of the
# Songtrail

## BY W. MICHAEL GEAR AND KATHLEEN O'NEAL GEAR
## FROM TOM DOHERTY ASSOCIATES

### NORTH AMERICA'S FORGOTTEN PAST SERIES

People of the Wolf

People of the Fire

People of the Earth

People of the River

People of the Sea

People of the Lakes

People of the Lightning

People of the Silence

People of the Mist

People of the Masks

People of the Owl

People of the Raven

People of the Moon

People of the Nightland

People of the Weeping Eye

People of the Thunder

People of the Longhouse

The Dawn Country: A People of the Longhouse Novel

The Broken Land: A People of the Longhouse Novel

People of the Black Sun: A People of the Longhouse Novel

People of the Morning Star

### THE ANASAZI MYSTERY SERIES

The Visitant

Bone Walker

The Summoning God

### BY KATHLEEN O'NEAL GEAR

Thin Moon and Cold Mist

Sand in the Wind

This Widowed Land

It Sleeps in Me

It Wakes in Me

It Dreams in Me

### BY W. MICHAEL GEAR

Long Ride Home

Big Horn Legacy

Coyote Summer

The Athena Factor

The Morning River

### OTHER TITLES BY W. MICHAEL GEAR AND KATHLEEN O'NEAL GEAR

The Betrayal

Dark Inheritance

Raising Abel

Children of the Dawnland

Coming of the Storm

Fire the Sky

A Searing Wind

www.Gear-Gear.com

www.gear-books.com

# People
## of the
# Songtrail

### A NOVEL OF NORTH AMERICA'S FORGOTTEN PAST

# W. Michael Gear and
# Kathleen O'Neal Gear

TOR®

A TOM DOHERTY ASSOCIATES BOOK · NEW YORK

PEOPLE OF THE SONGTRAIL

Maps and illustrations by Ellisa Mitchell

A Tor Book
Published by Tom Doherty Associates, LLC
175 Fifth Avenue
New York, NY 10010

www.tor-forge.com

Tor® is a registered trademark of Tom Doherty Associates, LLC.

The Library of Congress Cataloging-in-Publication Data is available upon request.

ISBN 978-0-7653-3725-2 (hardcover)
ISBN 978-1-4668-3230-5 (e-book)

Tor books may be purchased for educational, business, or promotional use. For information on bulk purchases, please contact the Macmillan Corporate and Premium Sales Department at 1-800-221-7945, extension 5442, or write to specialmarkets@macmillan.com.

First Edition: May 2015

Printed in the United States of America

0  9  8  7  6  5  4  3  2  1

*To the Hot Springs County Library in Thermopolis, Wyoming*

*We work with many rare printed resources that are only available—even in the digital age—through exhaustive library searches. Over the years, we have asked the outstanding staff at the Hot Springs County Library to find us some of the most obscure, out-of-print anthropological and historical resources on earth. To our amazement, they've almost always come through for us.*

*We sincerely thank you for all your hard work to help us write better books. We send special thanks to Tracey Kinnaman.*

# B.C.

| 13,000 | 10,000 | 6,000 | 3,000 | 1,500 |
|--------|--------|-------|-------|-------|

PEOPLE *of the* WOLF
Alaska & Canadian
Northwest

PEOPLE *of the* EARTH
Northern Plains & Basins

PEOPLE *of the* NIGHTLAND
Ontario & New York &
Pennsylvania

PEOPLE *of*
*the* OWL

Lower
Mississippi
Valley

PEOPLE *of the* SEA
Pacific Coast & Arizona

PEOPLE *of the* RAVEN
Pacific Northwest &
British Columbia

PEOPLE *of the* LIGHTNING
Florida

PEOPLE *of the* FIRE
Central Rockies &
Great Plains

# A.D.

| 0 | 200 | 1,000 | 1,100 | 1,300 | 1,400 |
|---|-----|-------|-------|-------|-------|

**PEOPLE *of the* LAKES**
East-Central Woodlands & Great Lakes

**PEOPLE *of the* WEEPING EYE**
Mississippi Valley & Tennessee

**PEOPLE *of the* MASKS**
Ontario & Upstate New York

**PEOPLE *of the* THUNDER**
Alabama & Mississippi

**PEOPLE *of the* RIVER**
Mississippi Valley

**PEOPLE *of the* LONGHOUSE**
New York & New England

**PEOPLE *of the* MORNING STAR**
Central Mississippi Valley

**PEOPLE *of the* SILENCE**
Southwest Anasazi

**The DAWN COUNTRY**

**The BROKEN LAND**

**PEOPLE *of the* MOON**
Northwest New Mexico & Southwest Colorado

**PEOPLE *of the* MIST**
Chesapeake Bay

**PEOPLE *of the* BLACK SUN**

1994 E. MITCHELL

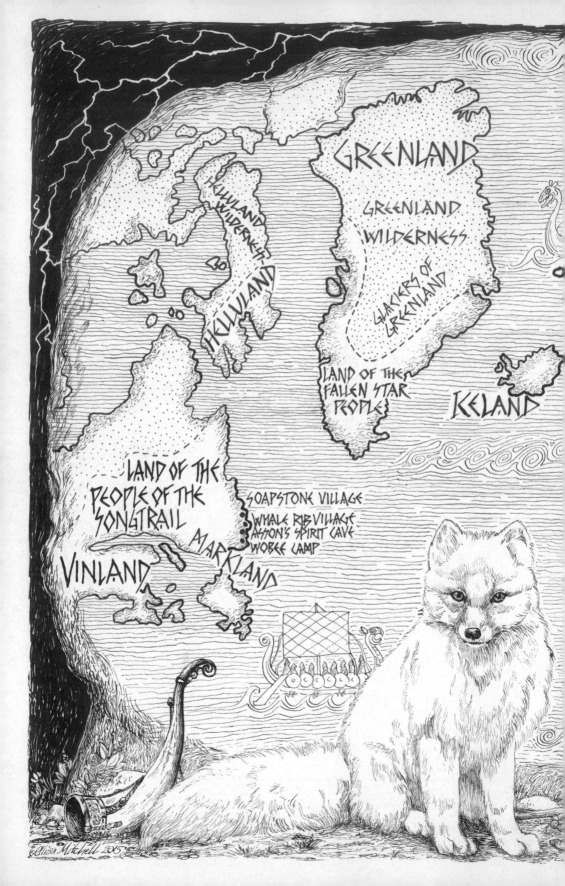

# Nonfiction Introduction

A.D. 900–1200 was a spectacular period of exploration in the history of the Northern Hemisphere, largely made possible by what climatologists call the Medieval Warm Period. This was a time of unusual warmth in the North Atlantic. As sea ice retreated, it opened previously unavailable sea routes, which resulted in a vast expansion of the Viking world. In a process known as *landnám*, or land taking, Norse explorers searched much of the globe for new regions to colonize. We also know from written records that sailing the North Atlantic at this time was perilous.

On his first voyage to Greenland in A.D. 986, Eirikr Thorvaldsson, better known as Erik the Red, left Iceland with twenty-five ships and around five hundred colonists. Only fourteen ships survived the journey. The arctic was melting rapidly. As both glaciers and ice sheets collapsed, they spawned massive ice islands, chunks of ice weighing billions of tons that drifted out to sea, where they broke up into smaller but still gigantic ice islands. In addition, as ocean and surface temperatures climbed, arctic fog seems to have become particularly brutal.

Three things were going on in Europe that made these dangerous voyages attractive: war, religious persecution, and the spreading myth of a paradise that lay across the seas far to the west.

## War

Beginning with the murder of King Edward the Martyr in A.D. 978 and the crowning of the new king, Aethelred the Unready, England saw increasing wealth, trade, and population growth. Aethelred's thirty-eight-year reign was notable because of this prosperity but also because of the wars that resulted. If you have nothing, there's little reason for invaders to attack you. But as wealth grows, so does the avarice of your neighbors. England saw escalating coastal raiding and large-scale incursions from Scandinavia, including conquests in 1014 by Danish king Sweyn Forkbeard and his son, King

Cnut, in 1017. In addition, a civil war raged within England from 1014 to 1016 while Aethelred battled his own son, Edmund, for rule. Of particular note in these series of wars was the St. Brice Day Massacre, the slaughter of the Danelaw, England's Danish population, in A.D. 1002, which prompted Sweyn Forkbeard to wage war against England from 1003 to 1005.

## Religious Persecution

Christianity was spreading across Europe, sparking religious upheavals. A relevant example here is Iceland (Stromback, 1997), where the first inhabitants were Irish Anchorites. They were called Anchorites because they preferred the symbol of the anchor (for the Fisherman) to that of the cross. Ninth-century Christendom was heavily influenced by the eremitical traditions of Christians in Asia Minor and Egypt, the early heart of the monastic movement, which placed great value on the virtue of solitude as a kind of penitential exile.

Ari mentions Anchorites in his *Íslendingabók*, written sometime between 1122 and 1133, and says that when Norsemen first arrived in Iceland they found Irish monks already living there, but the monks left because they would not stay in the presence of heathens. In his excellent study, *The Conversion of Iceland*, Dag Stromback writes that monks who refused to be persecuted or to live with heathens ". . . once more set sail over the wide ocean, perhaps seeking fresh isolation in Greenland or perhaps setting course to the south, back to the lands they had left." We would add here that they may also have set their sights farther west, on the shores of North America; hence we have the story of Saint Brendan and his legendary visit to America.

For Anchorites who did stay, life was not pleasant. The account of Asolfr Alskik in the *Landnámabók* is a case in point. He is recorded as having been a peace-loving man of deep faith, a Celt by birth, who came to Iceland. He was shunned by the local populace and driven from one location to another. During the tenth century Christianity was not powerful enough in Iceland to defeat the native Scandinavian religious traditions, particularly the highly magical Seidur religion, which included the worship of Thor, Odin, Freya, and other spirits and deities. Seidur practices and rituals were woven into the very fabric of Old Norse society. Concepts of the soul, afterlife, social structure, personal rank, and power were founded in the Seidur tradition. In fact, we would argue that one cannot understand *landnám,* Viking warfare, or the conflict with Christianity, without an understanding of Seidur.

Around A.D. 1000, Christianity's power dramatically increased.

While early Christians in both Iceland and Greenland were persecuted, the reverse is also true. As Christianity gained more of a foothold, entire countries were ordered to convert, as was the case with Iceland in A.D. 999 or 1000. Those who refused to abandon their cherished Seidur traditions fled, seeking religious freedom elsewhere. Interestingly, that same year Erik the Red's son and wife, Leif and Thjodhild, sailed from Greenland to Norway and spent the winter in the court of the Anchorite king, Olaf, where they adopted Christianity. When they returned to Greenland, Thjodhild asked Eirikr if she could build a small chapel on their farm. He granted permission, providing that she built it out of his sight. He remained true to his Seidur faith to his dying day in A.D. 1001.

## The Myth of Paradise

The promise of paradise has played a significant role in world history, driving exploration and colonization, and this was particularly true during the Medieval Warm Period.

Settlers who traveled to Greenland and on to North America at the end of the tenth century came, for the most part, from western Iceland near the Breidafjord area and were the descendants of Gaelic and British emigrants who were steeped in magical tales of a wondrous land that lay beyond the sea to the west. Celtic sources refer to this land as Tir na Bh-Fear BhFionn. The Norse called it Hvitramannaland. It is also mentioned in Latin sources as Albania-Land. Similar in many respects to the Norse story of the Odainsvellir, the Fields of the Undying, it was said that those who managed to get there had no way back.

Yet this far western land was the reason many brave men and women dared the dangerous journey across iceberg-ridden seas, through blinding arctic fog that left them lost for many days with no idea of where they were sailing, and storms so monstrous an unknown number of vessels were sunk or crushed upon distant shores.

Losing ships was so common that official expeditions were established to comb the wild regions in search of the bodies or skeletal remains of shipwrecked mariners and bring them back for proper burial. As in *The Tale of Tosti*, the men who completed these bleak tasks were referred to as *lig-lodin*, meaning "corpse-lodin."

Ancient vellum manuscripts, called *The Book of Settlements*, record these journeys. There are five extant versions of this book, the oldest of which is the *Sturlubók*, translated by Sturla Thordarson between A.D.

1275 and 1280. The *Sturlubók* records that among those with Erik the Red on that first journey to Greenland in 986 was an Anchorite from the Hebrides. As well, *Eirikr the Red's Saga* documents that on Karlsefni's journey to North America in 1003 he carried Anchorite slaves from Scotland. These Celtic Christians were steeped in the lore of Tir na BhFear BhFionn. The place where they would make landfall bore striking resemblance to these legends. It was a promised land of trees and grapevines and a wealth of animals. A paradise . . . with one exception.

All of the names for this land, Hvitramannaland, Albania-Land, and Tir na BhFear BhFionn, meant "the Land of the White Men."

But the phrase had nothing to do with skin color. In Old Norse the term *white* had a negative and fearful connotation. A clearer Norse meaning would be "the Land of Evil Men" or "the Land of Dangerous Men."

As mapmakers had done for centuries, they might as well have written: "There be dragons."

What was this strange, mystical paradise that so many were willing to risk death to find? What wonders and mysteries awaited them? The peoples who met them on the eastern shores of North America—the ancestors of the Iroquois, Algonquians, and Inuit (Eskimo)—already knew.

And they were willing to protect it with their lives.

# People
## of the
# Songtrail

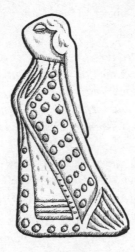

# One

## Thyra

*F*irelight fills the room. I hear murmuring echoes that seem to come from great distances, voices I almost recognize. One voice is velvet soft: "Thyra, you must let them go. You'll hurt them."

I don't know where I am. England maybe. But I think I'm two or three. Mother's beautiful face swims out of the night, smiling down at me. She appears annoyed, as though I've failed some test of humanity. Behind her, firelight dances over the log walls, and I remember that all morning I've been crawling around, gathering the fluttering orange wings on the floor and trying to scoop them up. They've been talking to me, scolding me for trying to catch them. I don't understand why I can't grasp the half-transparent butterflies in my hands.

"Here." Mother reaches up to clutch her silver pendant. "Hold my hand and help me release them."

I place my small hand in hers. As a flood of warmth fills me, the orange wings flutter upward and disperse in a hypnotic dance across the ceiling. I watch them with my mouth ajar. They are so beautiful.

Mother's necklace dangles in front of my eyes. She sees me looking at it. "Someday you will be a great seeress and this will be yours. You will be able to walk in and out of our Helgafell as though no door existed at all."

Helgafell. I don't know what that is.

Mother bends, picks me up, and carries me to the fire-warmed wisent hide spread before the stone hearth. Hanging on the wall beside the hearth is a metal staff and a glittering sword etched with runes. The sword's name is Hel. Over *and over Mother has told me the story written upon her shining blade. The runes tell of the giant goddess of the underworld, after whom the sword is named. The goddess, Hel, is half-black and half-white and lives in the hall of Eliudnir, the hall "sprayed with snowstorms," in Helheim. Her bed has a name, Sick Bed, and her bed curtains are Gleaming Disaster. Her dish is Hunger, her knife Famine.*

*My empty stomach squeals when I look at the sword. Hel sings me to sleep at night, her voice sweet and high, like wind through standing stones.*

*An iron cooking kettle hangs just above the hearth flames, but I smell only the mineral scent of steam rising. Mother is bundled like a dying skeleton, in a ragged blue cloak with a gray wool blanket wrapped around her shoulders. The angles of her cheeks are sharp as lance blades.*

*Even now, when I think of her, I am filled with a tremendous sadness for which I can find no reason. I remember that she could change into a deer. I saw her do it. I remember her long ivory hair and the gentleness of her hands. And I remember screams that day. Her screams? I've been trying to remember all my life.*

*A knock comes at the door.*

*Mother turns. Brightness crosses her face like summer sunlight striking the glaciers, breathtaking and fragile. "Oh, thank the gods, your father is home. I'm sure he caught a bird or fish to throw in the stew pot."*

*A man enters—not Father—whispers something to Mother, and a panicked expression creases her face. She grabs the man's arm. "Are you certain of this? But why? Why would he do this?"*

*"When Pallig defected to join the raiders ravaging the south coast, the king heard rumors that the Danes were about to kill him and his councilors, then take his kingdom. He decided to act first."*

*"Is Pallig—"*

*"No one know for certain, but Sweyn fears for your life and your daughter's."*

*Shouts outside. Three men run past the open door. The man talking with Mother whirls to look, then licks his lips. "The traitor wants Eyr badly. We can't let him get his filthy hands on her."*

*Mother hesitates for an instant before she grabs an iron rod from the pegs above the door and shoves it into his extended hands. Then she strips her necklace from her throat and gives it to him. "Give these to Avaldamon. He will need them. And, Baldur, I know you're an accomplished Seidur practitioner, but don't use Eyr unless you must. And never use the pendant and Eyr together! It's too dangerous. I can barely control them. You—"*

*"I'm so sorry, Veth—"*

*"No time for regrets. Go! I'll be behind you."*

*I seem to have gone blind, or perhaps I've fallen asleep, as children do in the midst of the most dire things. I see nothing now . . . but I hear Mother's footsteps hurry toward the rear of the room, then she gasps as another door squeaks open on rusty hinges. The room is drowned in darkness, though the firelight continues to shine at the edges; the roof and walls appear to be a mosaic of amber shards.*

*From out of the dark, Mother's eyes appear—just her eyes—filled with tears, staring at me with enough love to last me a lifetime.*

*A man orders, "Quickly! She's a* myrkrida, *a darkness-rider. Don't let her touch her sword or staff. Grab them from the wall. And make no mistake, he wants her alive."*

*. . . then the screams. Voices tangle. I've never heard Mother scream before. Is it Mother?*

*Hard hands grab me and swing me up into muscular arms. I see no faces, but I smell smoke, hear people running and children sobbing.*

*Outside, my vision returns. Ashes, white as snow, bathe the air with brilliance. The man carrying me mounts a horse.*

*As we gallop away, the town is a dream born of moonlight, sculpted in icicles, dying in fire.*

*. . . That's the last thing I remember. Ice and flames.*

*My next memory is of a new family, a new home, a place where ghosts haunt the hidden crevices in the floor. I live in Denmark now. I have a baby brother. I'm happy. I am loved.*

*Are my dreams of that other mother, that other home, just the fanciful creations of a child's mind?*

*Possibly.*

*I don't know why it matters any longer.*

*Except that sometimes at night I hear that other mother calling me as though she's still trying to find me.*

*And I desperately long to go to her.*

# TWO

**Thirteen years later . . .**

Ealdorman Uhtred of Northumbria paced the small candlelit room with his hands clasped behind his back. His black woolen cloak fell to the tops of his goathide boots, and was fastened over his right shoulder with two oval brooches, exquisitely crafted into the golden shapes of roaring dragons. Shoulder-length auburn hair swayed around his tanned face as he moved. Despite the peat fire burning in the hearth, the air was icy and dank.

Another man, taller, stood before the single window with his back to Uhtred. He stared fixedly out at the foggy coast of northern England where dusk settled over the rolling hills like veils of smoke-colored silk. Even silent and still, he projected authority. He'd pulled his brown hood up to shield his pale, patrician face. A silly precaution, in Uhtred's mind, because the short chieftain from Greenland, Gunnar the Skoggangur, who stood near the door, undoubtedly knew his royal identity.

Uhtred shifted to study Gunnar. Blond and skinny, the Skoggangur always chose to stand near the door in case he had to make a hasty exit. As he folded his arms across his chest, his burly arm muscles bulged beneath his faded green cape. His skills as a ship's captain were the stuff of legend.

Uhtred said, "The civil war does not go well, Gunnar. We stand upon a precipice that, I assure you, falls away into oblivion for the Danelaw. We cannot lose. Do you understand the grave nature of the task we've placed before you?"

"Dozens of my relatives still live in the Danelaw, and dozens died during the slaughter thirteen years ago. Of course I understand."

The Danelaw, the portion of northern England inhabited by Danes, lived in terror that King Aethelred planned to repeat the St. Brice Day Massacre—the slaughter of thirteen years ago. Gunnar's relatives must have impressed that fear upon him. His wrinkled face had set into hard lines.

"Very well. The gold is there at the end of the table." Uhtred extended his hand to the bronze box.

Gunnar reached down to pick it up. "And what if I don't find the Prophetess?"

"Then the contents belong to you. Given what we've already paid you, it should be more than sufficient to account for your efforts."

The Skoggangur hefted the box, judging the weight of the gold within, and the act caused the tall man at the window to heave a disgruntled breath, as though annoyed at the pusillanimous chieftain's avarice.

Gunnar gave him a brief glance. He had little respect for those who had lived pampered lives, particularly royalty, and probably especially King Aethelred's own son. Gunnar had spent much of his forty-seven years in flight from the law, which, if truth be told, is precisely why Uhtred had chosen him. Quick-witted, the wiry little man had seen it all and feared nothing. Plus, the Skoggangur was uncommonly loyal to his family in the Danelaw. During the worst of times, Gunnar had braved enemy fleets to bring them food and needed supplies. No matter the risks, the Skoggangur would do his best to protect his relatives.

"Are you satisfied?" Uhtred inquired.

"You're certain you want me to include Thorlak the Lawspeaker and his strange apprentice, Thyra, in the colonizing effort? Seems very ill-advised to me. Given Thorlak's past, especially his former rivalry with the Prophetess, if he discovers what I'm up to—"

Uhtred interrupted, "We know from reliable sources that he's eager to find Hvitramannaland and, apparently, some great treasure there. Let's oblige him by providing the funds. I'm sure neither Cnut nor Aethelred would seek out his talents, but we want to remove that temptation from their minds. We need him out of the way. How much more out-of-the-way can he be than if he's in Vinland with a group of colonists seeking religious freedom?"

Gunnar's gaze sharpened. "What is this great treasure he seeks in Hvitramannaland?"

"That's just the sort of thing I'd expect you to ask, you old thief. How would I know? You've spent far more time around him in Greenland than I. Have you heard anything?"

Grinding teeth moved beneath Gunnar's bearded jaw. "Not even a whiff, which means he's been keeping it to himself well. How do you know about it?"

The glint in the little man's brown eyes annoyed Uhtred. Gunnar, naturally, would want the treasure for himself.

"My friend, I have many sources you do not."

"Well, that's an unpleasant surprise." Finally, Gunnar added, "And you'll bear all costs of my transporting the Prophetess safely back to England?"

"Certainly."

The Skoggangur nodded but still seemed to be contemplating the difficulties ahead. He clasped his hands behind his back and started pacing. "Before I go, let's discuss the bald facts, shall we? I assume we are all aware that neither King Aethelred nor King Cnut will be happy if I find her. If she's alive, and either king suspects for an instant that she may be coming home to support the aethling Edmund"—he glanced pointedly at the man before the window—"each will want her dead, and will do everything in his power to stop me, including the murder of everyone in the colonizing expedition."

"Why do you think the Danelaw hired the likes of you, Gunnar? We expect discretion and complete secrecy."

"Not to mention courage. She was the most feared Prophetess on earth." A cynical humor touched Gunnar's voice. "What if she doesn't wish to return with me?"

"Convince her, Skoggangur."

Gunnar's blond brows plunged down in an evil manner. "Well . . . I'll do my best. Personally, I think she's dead, but—"

"Just do your job," the hooded man replied in heavily accented Danish.

Gunnar squinted at the man's broad back. "I was only making sure we understand each other."

"We do," the man said.

"Well enough, then." Gunnar tucked the bronze box inside his green cape. The hooded man couldn't see it, but Gunnar gave him an elegant bow. As he straightened, he said, "I'll send word if I find her, and apprise you of her approximate arrival time."

"The sooner the better, Gunnar. We are in dire straits here."

The Skoggangur turned on his heel and left, gently closing the door behind him.

Uhtred ran a hand through his auburn hair and shook his head. "Well, he's off. May Thor help him."

The hooded man turned. He looked very much like his father, with an oval face, long nose, and eyes perpetually narrowed as if nothing ever pleased him.

"His name, Skoggangur, means 'forest-walking,' doesn't it? Meaning that at some point in his life he was ejected from civilized society and forced to live in the wild, little better than an animal himself. He's a criminal."

"Oh, indeed he is. For many years, Gunnar's troop of scoundrels cut a wide swath across Iceland. But wealth can transform society's opinion of even the lowliest men. After he managed to kill enough men and steal enough brocades, precious stones, wines, cattle, and thralls, he could afford to pay one thousand marks of gold for a cargo vessel named *Thor's Dragon*."

"One thousand marks? A foolish sum for a mere cargo vessel."

"Perhaps, but overpaying brought him to the attention of the finest families, and allowed him to join the highest ranks of the realm, the *godar*, the men responsible for maintaining Greenland's religious and judicial organizations." Uhtred paused. "That was a long time ago. He is now renowned for his charity and justice. Gunnar maintains a religious hall on his farm that is open to all members of the Seidur faith."

"Hardly the sort of man I would have expected you to hire to carry out so critical a mission."

"He is also a master of navigation, Highness. He's sailed *Thor's Dragon* to the Hebrides, Rome, the great city of Mikligardur, and all the way to Alexandria in the Black Land, and many places in between. This trip, however, will be his first to the Land of the One-Legged Skraeling barbarians."

The hooded man's jaw clenched. "You're telling me that we just hired an outright murderer because he's a good sailor?"

Uhtred gave him a grim smile. "Partly. Gunnar's greatest asset, however, is that he can be bought. Most men in similar circumstances would eventually yield to their conscience or patriotism, or any other justification that allowed them to weasel out of the agreement. I assure you, Gunnar the Skoggangur has no conscience or sense of loyalty, except to his family, or that which he sells to the highest bidder."

"Can we rely upon the fact that he will not sell us out to someone who offers him more?"

Uhtred spread his arms in a placating gesture. "Once he sells his services, he scrupulously honors the agreement. That's how he and his forest-walkers survived. A man could count on them."

Edmund walked over to stare down into Uhtred's tight eyes. "We desperately need that woman. My father and Eadric, the despicable ealdorman of Mercia, are massing their forces as we speak, and King Cnut is just waiting for his opportunity to attack England and take everything we hope for." His nostrils flared with a breath.

"I'm well aware of that, Your Grace."

"Are you, Uhtred? Well, let's be certain we understand the same things. When Sweyn the Forkbeard last attacked England, he attributed all of his triumphs to his Prophetess. He said it was her Seidur witchery that allowed him to ravage and burn anywhere he pleased, until no naval or land force dared to stand against him. He became so powerful that wherever his army marched, people threw down their weapons and fell to their knees to pledge allegiance to him. If we have King Sweyn Forkbeard's renowned Prophetess on our side, it will terrify Cnut and my father. Perhaps even into submission."

Edmund—the man who would be king—softly added, "I *must* have her."

He strode for the door and exited with his plain brown cape swaying about his long legs.

Uhtred exhaled the breath he'd been holding. Great Odin, he knew far better than Edmund what was at stake. If the Prophetess had been here thirteen years ago, King Aethelred's slaughter of the Danelaw would have failed and many members of Uhtred's family—and Gunnar's family—would be alive today.

Uhtred stared at the empty doorway for a few moments, remembering loved ones long gone, then grabbed his hat from the peg on the wall and followed Edmund into the luminous twilight.

# Three

*Hafvilla*

Darkness veiled the misty sea.

Gunnar the Skoggangur hung on to the prow scroll of *Thor's Dragon* with one hand while he extended the whale-oil lamp with his other hand, trying to see the icebergs that floated like white mountains through the glistening arctic fog.

Gunnar would not tell his crew or passengers, but he had no idea where they were, or even what direction they were headed. For all he knew, they could be sailing out into the midst of the vast southern ocean where there was no land, just water that went on forever to the edges of the earth. And doom.

He shook wet blond hair out of his eyes and expelled a shaky breath. How could he, the great navigator, have gotten so lost? Each day he took readings with his sunstone and shadow compass and aimed the vessel accordingly. West. Due west.

Gunnar squinted into the lamplit fog, trying to fathom what he'd done wrong.

Sunstones, crystals of feldspar, could be held up even on foggy days and would tell a man the location of the sun, for the stone flared brighter when moved over the face of Sol. Or Gunnar could usually orient himself with his shadow compass. The compass was a disk of wood with notches cut around the edge, and a hole in the middle for the sighting pin. To keep it level, the compass floated in a bowl of water. The arc of shadow cast by the pin would be measured against the notches. On a westerly course, a shadow that was too long would indicate the ship had veered too far north, or a shadow arc too short meant he was too far south.

Gunnar had done everything he could to keep them on course. What had happened?

The ship rocked beneath him, riding the black swells. They should have made landfall in Vinland eight days ago. Instead, he'd been wallowing in this unnatural fog for twelve days. Had the other seven ships of colonists made it? Or were they also suffering *hafvilla*, the curse of being lost at sea?

Lightning flickered through the mist, then the low roll of thunder echoed. Gunnar noted that the swells had started coming closer together. Somewhere out there, a storm raged. They must be right on the edge of it.

His fourteen oarsmen knew it, too. They mumbled darkly to one another and tugged to tighten the ropes around their waists. The ropes tied them to the mast to keep them from being swept overboard if the seas grew rough. The scent of their fear sweat almost overpowered the sea's salty fragrance.

Gunnar turned and called to his tiller, "Bjarni, what do you see out there?"

From the aft steerbord side, Bjarni called back, "Not one thing, Godi!"

"We barely missed that last iceberg. Best keep your eyes wide open."

"Yes, Godi."

Through the misty halo of lamplight, he could just barely see Bjarni. The twenty-six-year-old redhead appeared as only a vaguely darker splotch on the right side of the ship toward the rear. As the tiller, Bjarni was in charge of the rudder, the big oar fixed to the hull and moved by rotating the attached arm. It required a quick-witted man who was willing to pit his strength against the storm and defy it. Bjarni the Deep-minded was the only man Gunnar trusted there.

The groans of struggling oarsmen filled the air. They were all tired beyond any—

"Ice!" someone yelled.

Gunnar saw the massive white mountain slide out of the mist right in front of them. "*Laddebord, Bjarni! Laddebord!*"

The ship veered sharply left, and the iceberg slipped away into the foggy darkness like a glistening phantom.

Gunnar wiped his eyes on his sheepskin sleeve. Spray ran from his protruding forehead, and filled the deep wrinkles of his face. Gods, he'd been a fool to agree to this secret mission for Edmund. The man was no more competent to rule England than his father, King Aethelred. Worse, King Cnut was just biding his time, waiting for the civil war in England to weaken both sides, before he sailed in with his army and reconquered England once and for all. . . . But Edmund was the best chance Gunnar's relatives had. Maybe their only chance.

Gunnar sucked in a deep breath and held it for a moment. Horrifying images flickered behind his eyes. The leaders of the Danelaw had already begun preparing for the inevitable moment when armies would come marching in, hence their alliance with Edmund. In exchange for food, weapons, and soldiers, Edmund vowed to use his army to protect the Danelaw from all attackers—be they from Aethelred or Cnut, or some currently unknown opportunist.

Gunnar wasn't sure Edmund could even protect his own hide, let alone the hides of others. Edmund must feel the same way.

And so . . . the Prophetess. *Vethild the Darkness-rider.*

Gunnar expelled a shaky breath. This business of hunting legends gave him a stomachache. No one really knew what had happened to her after the St. Brice Day Massacre. Some said she'd been murdered by her enemy and chief rival, Thorlak. Others claimed she'd been kidnapped and hauled off in chains to a mythical place called Hvitramannaland, the Land of the White Men. The Angles called it Albania-Land. Vethild's husband, Avaldamon, spent years trying to find her. In the process, he himself had vanished, never to be heard from again.

Were Gunnar a superstitious man, he'd suspect Vethild was responsible for their current situation. She'd reputedly been a master of the weather, creating massive storms with the wave of her hand, or whirlpools that swallowed entire fleets. Was she trying to stop him from finding her? Or was she driving *Thor's Dragon* toward her like a whipped stallion? Gunnar liked neither possibility.

He shook off the premonition. Gods, a man couldn't afford to think like that. It was unnerving.

Gunnar tightened his hold on the prow scroll when waves suddenly slapped the bow. *Thor's Dragon* rode up on a big swell, then plunged down the other side.

Gunnar shouted, "Steer into that wave, Bjarni! It seems the storm is upon us."

One of the young oarsmen, Kiran the Kristni, roared, "Rolf, you oaf, stop chopping at the water and pull!"

"Shout your mouth, blasphemer, or I'll use my oar to gut you! If we sink, it's because you're aboard, you Anchorite bastard!"

A massive wave tossed *Thor's Dragon* skyward. Gunnar grinned in senseless euphoria. Rolf the Cod-biter was pretty worthless, but Kiran had proven himself a true asset, despite the fact that Rolf was right. Kiran, a big, black-haired sixteen-year-old, was a devotee of the Monk's Tester, Lord of the Peak's Pane, whom he called the Christ. If Gunnar had any wits, he'd publicly condemn Kiran as a blasphemer, and thereby ease the worries of both his crew and the colonists, most of whom did not take kindly to having an Anchorite aboard. They were afraid of Anchorites, and for good reason.

Just a few short years ago, the entire country of Iceland had been ordered to be baptized. Those who'd refused to convert had packed up and sailed for Greenland. But then Eirikr the Red's own wife and son had become Anchorite missionaries. Those who held fast to their Seidur faith were afraid the same thing was about to happen in Greenland. They'd had no choice but to flee.

Every time something had gone wrong on this voyage, it had been blamed on Kiran. The colonists, in fact, had urged Gunnar to throw him overboard.

*The fools.*

They needed Kiran. Gunnar had purchased Kiran and a Skraeling boy, Elrik, along with a girl named Kapusa, from a Hebrides merchant who claimed the Skraeling children had come from Vinland. Kiran was fluent in the Skraeling tongue, and he—

"Dear God, pull!" Kiran roared.

A sudden gust of wind ripped the lamp from Gunnar's hand and slammed him back against the prow, filling his lungs with so much air that he could not exhale. Strangling on wind, he watched helplessly as *Thor's Dragon* wallowed broadside and a huge wave swelled far above Gunnar's head. *Great Thor* . . .

Too late Gunnar managed to turn his head sideways, gulp air, and yell, "Bjarni! Steerbord!"

The wave overcurled the ship. Gunnar stared straight up into it, watching thunderbolts flicker through the roof of foaming water. As the ship drove deeper, the weight of the wave crushed the air from his lungs. Gunnar's evil deeds, every one of them, flashed before his eyes.

When he emerged from the water, Gunnar gulped air and yelled, "Keep her to the steerbord, boys, or we're going down!"

Bjarni steered the ship left into a massive wave that tossed them high into the air. As *Thor's Dragon* ascended the wall of water, Gunnar wrapped both arms around the prow and hugged it to his breast. The ship crested the wave and hurtled down the other side into a boiling trough of foam.

For a terrifying instant, Gunnar thought he was a lost soul. The bow plunged into the water. Gunnar held his breath until the ship lunged up again; then he shook soaked blond hair away from his face and shouted, "Steerbord, Bjarni!"

Gunnar rode the ship down as it dove into the next black trough. The descent felt weightless. When they hit bottom, the mast let out an agonized groan. Gunnar spun to look at the oaken timber. They'd lowered the sodden sail hours ago. It lay rolled and tied to the base of the mast, but it had shifted, and was now pointing toward the hold, funneling all the water on the deck. . . .

*Gods, help me; how much water has flooded into the hold?*

The *Dragon* had a second deck and enough trusses that it could withstand heavy seas, plus the extra deck provided shelter for their cattle, goats, cargo, and thralls, not to mention the twenty colonists who must be green and heaving by now.

He shouted, "Sokkolf? Grab hold of your tether rope and pull yourself back to the mast, then untie and get below! See how much water has flooded into the hold. Organize bailers if need be!"

"Yes, Godi!"

Sokkolf, a muscular twenty-year-old, pulled his oar into the ship, secured it, and tugged himself along the rope on his belly.

Gunnar watched him disappear into the hold.

A few moments later, *Thor's Dragon* shot straight upward, rising so high that Gunnar could see above the fog and out across the rain-lashed ocean where lightning danced. As the ship crested the wave, the *Dragon*'s bow upended and stood almost over her stern. She seemed to hang in midair before plummeting into the yawning valley below.

Gunnar blinked at the darkness. Without the lamp, he seemed to see more clearly. At least he could distinguish the black water from the foaming crests of the waves.

A few instants later, a halo of lamplight swelled from the hold, and the fog glistened like gold dust when Thyra emerged. Tall for her fifteen years, long ivory hair whipped around her narrow shoulders. The girl was Thorlak's apprentice, studying Seidur magic at his feet, and for that reason alone Gunnar did not trust her.

As she lifted her lamp to study the violent sea, Gunnar could see the freckles that sprinkled her fair-skinned face. She wore a long white tunic sewn with the black image of Sleipnir, the eight-legged horse that Odin rode on his spirit travels to other worlds. A Seidur sword hung upon Thyra's hip. He'd heard tales that she could change herself into different kinds of dogs, wolves, or foxes and use her new form to spy upon others, or to tear them to pieces with fangs and claws. He didn't believe it, but it didn't pay to be too skeptical about such things.

"Thyra!" Gunnar shouted against the wind. "Get below. It's too dangerous on deck!"

She held her lamp higher, saw Gunnar lashed to the prow, and smiled. Her teeth were etched with black runes. "I've come to do battle with Thor, Godi."

Thor was the god of storms, and the fates of sailors.

"We don't need your help. Get below!"

Gunnar's stomach lurched as *Thor's Dragon* plowed into the next wave, the prow cutting so deep that Gunnar found himself submerged in the black water for a full three seconds. Just before the bow swung upward, he heard a sudden thunderous crack and, through the wall of water, glimpsed the mast tilt. It wobbled for an instant, as though fighting to stand straight again, then the timber let out an earsplitting shriek and toppled to the steerbord, flinging the rolled sail up like child's toy, then unfurling it across the deck.

Three oarsmen dove overboard before they were crushed. He could see them dangling by the ropes around their waists. Two men had vanished. Were they trapped beneath the timber or heap of woolen sail?

When the torrent of water receded from the deck, Thyra laughed.

Gunner couldn't see her behind the tangled pile of rigging and sail. Frightened, he waited until *Thor's Dragon* surged upward again, then he tore loose from his lashings and careened across the slippery deck toward the broken mast. He had to cut the ropes and shove the cracked timber overboard before the weight capsized them. Just as the ship crested the monstrous wave, Gunnar grabbed hold of the sail and held on as the steep descent began.

Ten feet away, Thyra stood up with a strip of sail tied around her waist and her Seidur sword clutched in both hands. Reeling, she cried out and lifted her sword to the heavens. As Gunnar staggered, fighting to stay upright, he stared in astonishment. Did she truly plan to do battle with Thor himself? Not a healthy idea.

A brilliant flash lit the air around Gunnar. At the same time, thunder almost knocked him from his feet. His eyes widened when the air started to sparkle.

Thyra shouted, "*Godi, watch!*"

Gunnar tore his gaze from the sea.

The tip of her upraised sword burst into blue-violet flame, then a conflagration encased her entire body. The phosphorescent halo turned her pale skin and white tunic an unearthly shade of purple. Ecstasy twisted her beautiful face.

*Thor's fire . . .*

Gasps and shouts erupted across the deck.

Thyra let out a deep-throated roar. As she thrust her sword higher into the storm, violet fire streamed down her arms, then spilled across the ship in glowing rivulets, flickering, dancing, sheathing every object and person with shimmering splendor. The tangled sail seemed to burst into blue flame. Just as the ship dove down another wave, a distinct hissing sound filled the fog, and the tips of every pointed object in sight blazed so brilliantly that Gunnar let out an incoherent cry. An immense number of minute sparks darted though the air around him.

Bjarni's attention must have wavered, for a wave broadsided *Thor's Dragon*. The wall of water flooded over the top of Gunnar. He clutched the torn sail with all his might as the wave lifted him high above the deck. Holding his breath, he continued to see glowing points of blue-violet flame.

*Where's Thyra? What of my crew? Are we sinking?*

An odd, long-buried memory flashed . . . he and his troop of forest-walkers, reeling drunk, beating a merchant to death for not bringing their mead with enough haste. *Gods, what sort of men would do something like that?*

He felt empty, his bones as hollow as a sparrow's. Had he done enough good in his later years to make up for his youth? Not likely. Some things, like killing the merchant, were not redeemable. If he had one more chance, he . . .

High above him a miracle spun to life. A fluorescent rainbow arched across the sky. The magnificent colors seemed too beautiful to be of this world. Was it the Rainbow Bridge that went from Asgard, the City of the Gods, to Midgard, the World of Men?

He tried to shift to see if the bridge also extended from Asgard to the roots of Yggdrassil, the sacred tree. Yggdrassil connected the worlds below to the worlds above. That bridge was reputed to be even more magnificent, and rarely seen by men, except at death.

When his ship swooped out of the sea, Gunnar's body slammed to the deck like a hurled rock. He gasped a breath into his starving lungs and rolled to his back. The ship heaved and pitched beneath him, but patches of gray predawn sky shone through the clouds. As though being swept away by a huge hand, the arctic fog started to shred and thin.

Groans filled the air.

Gunnar blinked in disbelief and sat up.

The waves, still formidable, were no longer monstrous. As the terror drained from his muscles, amazement set in. He felt light-headed.

"*Somebody help me!*" Bjarni shouted. "Help me pull Kiran aboard!"

Gunnar scrambled to his knees, saw Bjarni leaning over the steerbord side gripping a rope in his fists, and straining until his bulging muscles seemed about to fray.

Gunnar slipped and slid his way across the wet deck, grabbed hold of the rope and, hand over hand, helped Bjarni pull Kiran aboard. The big youth was half-drowned, spitting up water and gasping. His shoulder-length black curls straggled around his bearded face. His green eyes had gone huge.

Gunnar slapped him on the back, and as he did, he lost his footing. He felt himself tilting, falling, and he let out a yell just as he toppled over the side.

A granite hand grabbed his arm as he fell, and Gunnar's body pounded the hull so hard it knocked the wind out of him.

"Kiran, help me!" Bjarni shouted.

Kiran scrambled to the edge, gripped a handful of Gunnar's shirt, and helped Bjarni drag him aboard.

Gunnar gasped, "Gods, that was a close one, boys. Thank you!"

Kiran turned to vomit up a flood. When he could finally breathe, he rasped, "Godi, I've never seen Thor's fire like that."

"Nor have I. Now get yourself together. I need every man. Start looking for others who might have been swept overboard."

Kiran coughed. "Yes, Godi."

Gunnar, Bjarni, and Kiran dragged men aboard. Two were gone, swallowed by the sea. The empty loops that had been tied around their waists dangled from ropes over the side.

When he had eleven oarsmen and Bjarni back at their posts, rowing to keep the ship steady, Gunnar stumbled to the broken stump that remained of the mast and slipped his arm around it to look for Thyra, or others, who might be flailing out among the waves. He'd no idea how he'd rescue them, but he'd find a way.

"Thyra?" he shouted. "*Rolf? Sokkolf? Where are you?*"

Fog drifted around Gunnar in tufts, but a narrow band of ocean had opened up beneath the fog, revealing water for quite a distance. Where the waves reflected the sky, they had a pink sheen. Sol's appearance on the eastern horizon couldn't be far away.

The change in the weather had been so sudden Gunnar still couldn't believe it. Had Thyra's bold willingness to do battle with Thor softened the Old Redbeard's heart?

The toppled mast, ropes, and torn sail created a tangled mass that stretched across the deck, and floated upon the sea to the steerbord. There he saw a strange lump. Thyra had wrapped the sail over her head and shoulders, wearing it like a burial shroud as she floated in the icy water. Only her pale face showed in the midst of the white fabric. Her crystalline blue eyes seemed to peer through Gunnar to his bones. If he hadn't known better, he'd think that gaze still flamed with Thor's phosphorescent fire.

"Thyra! Are you alive?"

She threw her head back and laughed with what sounded like wild exultation. "I'm more alive that I have ever been!"

Weak with disbelief, Gunnar shouted, "Kiran, pull Thyra aboard! Bjarni, once she's aboard, you need to help me cut the broken mast loose. We're not safe yet."

Kiran scrambled to extend a hand to help Thyra as she crawled across the extended mast, and when the young woman at last stood on the deck she walked straight to Gunnar. The storm had soaked her thin white tunic so that it clung to her young body like a second skin, outlining her small breasts. He smelled the perfume of her body. Mingled scents of sea and young womanhood, and something pungent, perhaps left over by the blue flames that had swallowed her whole. Drenched ivory locks sleeked down her sides and back. The dark runes on her teeth flashed with her smile as she extended an arm and pointed to something over his shoulder. "Behold the reward, Godi Gunnar."

Gunnar spun around.

A silver line etched the shape of the foaming water where it dashed itself against towering black cliffs. Smoke rose from what might be a village, but whether those fires belonged to their fellow colonists or the Unipeds he could not say.

Every crew member cheered.

Gunnar ran a hand over his face. "Stop gaping and get back to work! Kiran, keep searching the sea for Rolf and Sokkolf. They may still be alive out there."

# Four

### *The Moon When Seabirds Lay Eggs*

As Chief Badisut neared the crest of the grassy hill that sloped down to the beach, he propped the butt of his lance on the ground and shoved windblown gray hair away from his dark eyes. The dawn air had a bite today. He flipped up his collar and shivered inside his knee-length wolf-hide coat. In the distance, icebergs drifted across the ocean, appearing and disappearing in the fog, their peaks shimmering with snowy brilliance.

He turned to look at the line of people coming up the caribou trail behind him. Eighteen men, the hunters, carried lances. Eleven women and six children wore packs.

His wife, Kannabush, walked at the head of the group of women and children. She'd tied her graying black hair back with a leather cord; it made her brown eyes all the more beautiful. She'd given him eight children in the past two tens of winters, though only four had lived. Two beautiful daughters, Shebin and Washgeesh, and two sons, Camtac and Ewinon. Or three sons, if his kidnapped boy, Elrik, remained alive.

While the men hunted the seals that sunned themselves on the rocky shoals below, the women and children would set up work areas for skinning, cleaning, and packing the meat for transport back to Whale Rib Village.

Their village, Whale Rib Village, perched on the top of a sea cliff to the north, surrounded by forest. It was three hands of time to get home. If they wished to arrive before dark, they needed to get to work.

He lifted his hand to wave his people forward but stopped when he saw trotting up from the west the scout he'd sent to learn the whereabouts of the seals. Gower had seen just seven-and-ten winters, but he'd proven himself a clever hunter. Sweat glistened on his oversized ears where they stuck out through his shoulder-length jet hair.

Once Badisut knew how the seals were beached, he could plan the hunt. Gower stopped in the rear of the line and spoke with Badisut's youngest son, Camtac, and seemed to be waiting for someone. Both youths kept glancing over their shoulders. At what or whom?

When old Asson labored up the hillside, breathing hard, murmurs eddied through his people. The elder had shoulder-length black hair and a stern oval face with a long nose that reminded Badisut of a seagull's beak. Asson had seen forty-five summers but looked far older. Deep wrinkles crisscrossed his sun-bronzed face.

Asson was the single Kutsitualit in the land, and a pathetic one at that. The Kutsitualit were a special kind of holy people reputed to have only one hip bone, which allowed them to change into legless creatures like snakes and fish and swim to Adlivun and Adliparmiut, the Lands of the Dead beneath the sea.

At one time, tens of Kutsitualits had filled People of the Songtrail lands, but now only Asson remained. Badisut suspected it must be a hard life. The Kutsitualits lived alone, mostly in sea caves, pursuing Spirit journeys that frightened him even to contemplate. Still, it annoyed him that they'd been cursed with the likes of old Asson. Half of his predictions were wrong, and the other half were questionable. Worse, Asson only came out of his sea cave—which lay a short distance from Whale Rib Village—to bring bad news.

Camtac called, "Father?" and sprinted toward him with his lance in his hand. Gower and Asson followed him.

Small and skinny for his age, Camtac had seen four-and-ten winters. His wide cheekbones angled down to his pointed chin, giving his face a triangular shape, which accentuated the thinness of his nose and the upward slant of his eyes. Camtac stopped before Badisut. "Gower says that Elder Asson stopped him and wouldn't let him go to Seal Cove. The elder says there are strange boats in the cove and they've scared away all the seals."

"Canoes? Kayaks? Umiaks? What kind of—"

"They're Wobee, Badisut," Asson panted the words, as though he'd run all the way. "The boats are long and curved."

Badisut gripped Asson's arm in surprise. *"Are you sure?"*

"I'm sorry to bring you such news, but there's no doubt."

"How many boats?"

"Two. So far."

A thread of panic had begun to twine through Badisut. "Did you see people? How many are there?"

"I was too far away to count," Asson said, "but I think—"

"Come with me." Badisut grabbed Asson's arm and strode toward the crest of the hill where they could look down into Seal Cove. Camtac and Gower trailed behind them.

When the rest of the line started to follow, Badisut held up a hand and called, "No! Stay there for now. You will scare the seals." More softly, he said to Gower and Camtac, "We must do nothing to strike fear into our people's hearts."

Curious muttering began, but the line stopped. Kannabush gave Badisut a questioning look, to which he made a "be calm" gesture.

He strode to a high point and looked down into Seal Cove. At the sight of the ships, his fist clenched around his lance.

Camtac stared at the ships, then looked at Badisut. "What are they doing here, Father?"

Badisut studied the ships. Ten winters ago, when they'd stolen his young son, Elrik, the ships had been different, longer, with more oar holes in the shallow hulls. These ships were wider and possessed higher sides. He watched in growing fear as the Wobee led animals up from inside the ship's belly, onto the deck, then across a plank bridge they'd built to the shore. Iron bells clanked as the animals trotted beside their masters. Odd mooing and bleating rose.

"Father?" Camtac repeated. "Why are they—"

"The last time they came they wanted to kidnap children. They took your older brother, Elrik, and Matron Metabeet's daughter, Kapusa. I don't know why they've returned."

Badisut's eyes narrowed. He needed to confer with the Council of Elders on this matter. A trading mission loaded with prime furs might be the least threatening method to approach them. The Wobee had a tendency to loose arrows whenever they glimpsed the People of the Songtrail.

Badisut turned to Camtac. "My son, please tell your mother that we will not hunt seals today. We're must return home and meet with the Council of Elders. Do *not* tell her that the Wobee have returned. Some will wish to gawk at the newcomers, or even go down to speak with them. We can't take that risk. We'll tell the whole story when we get back to Whale Rib Village. The Council will decide our course of action. Gower, please help him to pass the word down the line."

"Yes, Chief."

As the youths trotted away, Badisut moved to stand at Asson's side. Badisut said, "Do you think these are the same Wobee who stole Elrik and Kapusa?"

Asson shrugged. "It's possible."

"What if they're here to steal more children for slaves?"

Asson's bushy black brows lowered. He turned to look at Badisut. "We must stop them."

Elrik's five-winters-old face welled in Badisut's memories. Gods, he had loved that boy, but Badisut's anguish had been trifling compared to Kannabush's. For two winters after they'd lost Elrik, she'd alternately raged and fallen into deep, dark pits of despair where she couldn't stop weeping. The only thing that had saved her was the birth of their twin daughters eight winters ago. Having new babies to love seemed to have lessened her grief. How would Kannabush react when she found out the slavers had returned to their country? Badisut suspected her first response would be to plead for the Council to organize the surrounding villages, attack the Wobee, and kill them all.

Asson turned to look at their people, then gazed back at Badisut. "Chief? Your hunting party is ready to return home."

Badisut spent a few more moments watching the Wobee. A large man with ivory-colored hair and a bushy beard strode off the ship and began shouting orders. People scurried to obey.

*Their chief?*

A short time later, a very tall man with bushy red hair and a beard walked down the plank bridge toward the large man. When he reached the rocky shoals at the foot of the bridge, the tall man lifted his head and gazed right at Badisut and Asson.

A prickle flushed Badisut's body. His pulse sped up until it thundered in his ears.

Badisut lifted his chin and studied the stranger. After ten heartbeats, he knew. *That is the man to be reckoned with. The others don't matter.*

Asson affirmed Badisut's fears. "You should be afraid of that man, Badisut. Spirit Power fills the air around him."

As Badisut watched, another boat appeared out of the fog and sailed toward the ships anchored in Seal Cove. The people on shore started pointing and cheering.

"Blessed gods," Badisut whispered. "How many more boats do they have waiting out there in the fog?"

Asson shook his head. "I don't know. What do you need me to do?"

Badisut's thoughts veered down frightening paths that ran far into the future. "Why don't you use your Spirit Powers to make them go away?"

Asson blanched. "I—I've already tried."

"And failed. As usual," Badisut exhaled the words.

"Chief, perhaps we should—"

"I don't need your pitiful insights, Asson. However, if everything goes wrong, there is one thing you can do to help. I want you to run to Soapstone Village and convince Drona to help us fight them."

Apparently unoffended by Badisut's comment, the aged Kutsitualit replied, "I will. I give you my oath."

Badisut trotted back to the group of people who stood talking in dire tones. "There are no seals today, so we're going home. Follow me!"

As Badisut trotted past Kannabush, he ignored her worried gaze.

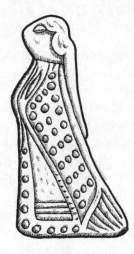

# Five

## *Thyra*

**W**hen *Thor's Dragon* neared the fog-shrouded cliffs, the ship lurched beneath Thyra's feet, forcing her to wrap an arm around the prow scroll to hang on. The bow plunged down, then rode the wave upward. The view from the top stunned her. Trees covered the countryside for as far as she could see and, in the distance, jagged mountains raked the belly of the sky. Was this Vinland? Markland? Slabs of rocks covered the lowlands, which made her think it might be Helluland. No matter, she hadn't expected this grandeur. Nor had she expected the strange voices that called to her.

*Blessed Odin, the Spirits who guard this shore are strong.*

She closed her eyes to listen. Howls filled the wind. Unearthly beautiful, the notes lingered, then flew upward to be joined by thumps and wingbeats. Wavering yips filled the silences between the beats. Though she was a thrall, freedom coursed through her veins and, for the first time in nine months, since her family died, she could get a full breath into her lungs.

She turned when she heard Kiran's steps behind her.

He smiled at her with his whole heart in his green eyes. He was tall for sixteen, and his curly black hair whipped around his bearded face. "Take care, Thyra. Godi Gunnar says the currents near shore are liable to be fierce. He's worried about you standing out here so close to the edge."

She reached a hand to him, and when he took it she pulled him closer. "Do you hear them, Kiran?"

He gave her a puzzled look.

"The voices of the shore Spirits. They're singing to us."

As a slight frown lined his forehead, reflections off the ocean sprinkled his tanned face with shards of light. She knew it worried him when she heard such things. He was an Anchorite and didn't understand.

Thyra squeezed his hand. "My mother called to me in my dreams all night long. She pulled our ship here, Kiran. I know she did."

Thyra felt the familiar strength of his arm go around her, holding her against him. "Take your time with this, Thyra. You don't even know she's real. She could just be spun from a thrall's wishes and loneliness."

Despite his gentle tone, her chest ached. Since the deaths of her family in Denmark, the only thing that kept her sane was the belief that her Other Mother was real.

"The Lawspeaker believes me, Kiran. He asks about my Other Mother all the time. He believes she's here, too. That's why he's been training me in the Seidur arts. He says that if we combine our powers, we can find her. He wants to help me."

Kiran tenderly brushed beads of water from her white sleeve. "I'm sorry, Thrya. I know how important it is to have dreams; I just—"

"That's why the Lawspeaker ordered me to travel aboard *Thor's Dragon*. He said Godi Gunnar was the best navigator and the most likely to survive the journey. The Lawspeaker wanted to keep me safe."

Kiran hesitated before he said, "I'm sure he did. Forgive me?"

She wiped her eyes on her sleeve. "I love you. Of course I forgive you. But you must have dreams, too, Kiran. Now that we are here in this strange land, what do you hope to find?"

Thyra looked up into his face, aware of his body against hers, of the dampness of his woolen shirt on her arm.

"I've already found what I want. You."

Thyra hugged him hard. "It breaks my heart when you speak that way, Kiran. You know it can never be."

"I will find a way, Thyra."

He bowed his head and seemed to be studying the deck. Thralls could not marry without their owner's permission, and even if Godi Gunnar was willing to sell Kiran to Thyra's owner, Lawspeaker Thorlak, her master would never agree to buy him. Thorlak despised the Anchorite faith, which Kiran had told her he would never disavow. The Lord of the Peak's Pane meant everything to him.

Kiran smoothed his fingers down her cheek. "Well, the fog's shredding.

Let me just stand here for a few more moments and watch the land with you. Do you think the other seven ships are waiting just beyond the fog?"

Thyra gazed out at the morning sun shimmering through the veils of mist. For a time, she listened to the rhythm of waves against the bow.

"I hope so, Kiran."

# Six

Chieftain Dag the Ice-fist glared at the incoming ship, then back at the crest of the hill where the Skraeling barbarians had stood. A mixture of disgust and exultation filled him. The hide-clad people had disappeared from the hilltop as suddenly as they'd appeared, leaving the green terrace overlooking the beach adorned only with drifting fog. A large blond man, full-bearded, Dag shook his head. "One-Leggeds."

"We are not in the Land of the One-Leggeds in Vinland. Why do you still call them that?" Thorlak the Lawspeaker asked.

Dag shrugged. "I like the sound of it. Should we go after them?"

The Lawspeaker didn't respond. His amber eyes remained focused on the hilltop. No expression crossed his starved and bony face. He had bushy red hair and a beard that had just begun to possess a few silver threads. Thorlak wore a long black cloak over his shirt and trousers, both woven from the finest red wool. He favored red above all colors.

"Did you hear me, Thorlak? They're probably coming back." Dag reached to pull his sword from its scabbard, just in case.

The Lawspeaker's hand shot out, clasped Dag's sword, and shoved it down hard, back into the scabbard. "Don't touch your sword."

Dag swung around to glare at Thorlak. The Lawspeaker's eyes seemed to enlarge. He had the inhuman gaze of a lion. They sucked at a man's breath, as though through his gaze alone the Lawspeaker could siphon off a soul and send it wailing into the dark abyss.

Dag swallowed hard. A smart man never showed fear before the Law-speaker. "What's the matter with you? They're Skraeling barbarians. In years past, they've killed many of our colonists. We must be prepared. Until we can set up traps to catch—"

"Prepared, yes. Provoke them, no."

Thorlak's hand, which remained around Dag's sword hilt, let go with a shove that made Dag stagger sideways.

The Lawspeaker drew his long fingers back and clutched them to a fist at his side, then turned to look again at the hilltop. In the blue sky above the fog, storm clouds trailed streamers of rain.

"Well." Dag cast a sidelong glance at Thorlak. "If we're not going after them, we should get booths set up. Looks like there's a storm coming."

As young Snorri and Alfdis the Lig-lodin strode by carrying heavy boxes, helping to unload the ship, Dag called, "You two. Come over here."

"Yes, Godi." Alfdis, twenty-two, gestured to Snorri, who'd just passed his fifteenth year. They both bent at the knees to set their loads upon the sand.

Dag glared at them. Alfdis had gotten the name Lig-lodin because in recompense for youthful crimes he'd sailed the coastlines and brought back for burial the remains of the deceased, usually the victims of shipwrecks but sometimes those who had not survived the brutal winters. To Dag, such penance would never make up for the fact that Alfdis was a thief. If the rogue were a slave, Dag would turn him over to Thorlak for "training." Thorlak was a genius at breaking thralls.

As they rose, Alfdis said something soft to Snorri, who nodded, then Alfdis wiped his hands on his faded blue cape before glancing—as he should—at Dag. Despite his discomfort, Alfdis led the way forward with his broad shoulders squared. Snorri had milk-blond hair and a youth's wispy beard. Alfdis was a black-haired, blue-eyed scoundrel never to be trusted. What a collection of colonists the Lawspeaker had amassed! Not that Dag cared. He made his fortune finding and selling unique thralls. Midnight-skinned babes from the Black Land and red-haired maids from the Heb-rides had brought him most of his wealth. He was here for the one truly rare and valuable thing that could be found in this alien land: Skraeling children. They brought a fortune in Frisia and Saxony. Most people did not think they were human, but rather a strange *humanlike* creature, pos-sibly even a new, previously unknown troll, or maybe half troll and half dwarf, for they were small of stature compared to human beings.

As Alfdis and Snorri approached, Dag lifted his chin in a superior manner and demanded to know, "What did you see up there on the ter-race?"

Snorri's mouth gaped. "I—I didn't . . . Nothing, Godi. My eyes aren't so good—"

Alfdis interrupted him. "I saw two Skraeling men. Both elders from the looks of them. . . . Sir," he added as an afterthought.

"Yes, you did. Now get back to the ship and tell the other colonists that they must be prepared to protect themselves. I want you to find the crates of weapons and organize them for easy access—"

The Lawspeaker's voice broke in, feather soft: "Belay that order, Alfdis the Lig-lodin."

"Sir?"

Only Thorlak's eyes moved. He shifted them from the hilltop to Alfdis. "I have another task for you."

Before Alfdis could answer, Dag said, "How dare you contradict one of my orders!"

Dag's hands suddenly twitched. Flitting images of blood and sunken eyes flashed before him, and the scent of decaying flesh was so strong in his nostrils that he almost gagged. Then *something* reached into Dag's chest and squeezed his heart. It started to labor, beating like a pounding hammer.

Startled, Dag managed to whisper, "Of c-course, I realize that you and Godi Gunnar organized this colonizing effort." The pain in his chest eased a little, and he added, "My apologies, Thorlak. I was just upset by the sight of the One-Leggeds."

Without taking his gaze from Dag, the Lawspeaker said, "Alfdis, I would appreciate it if you and Snorri could assemble some of our trade goods on the terrace where we saw the Skraelings. It's a good distance above high tide. We should be prepared to be congenial when the Skraelings return."

"Will they return, Lawspeaker?" Alfdis asked. "If I were them—"

"They will return. By dusk at the latest."

Alfdis bowed. "Then Snorri and I will be quick about getting the goods laid out on tables on the terrace."

"Good. Now leave me to speak with Godi Dag."

"Yes, Lawspeaker."

With visible relief, Alfdis and Snorri hurried away, trotting back toward where the ships were being unloaded.

Dag reached up to tug at his collar. It had grown unbearably tight. "What do you wish to speak with me about?"

Thorlak squinted out at the ocean. "What ship do you think that is? Can you tell?"

"No, it's too far away. But that makes three ships that survived the storm. Thank the gods for that. Though five are still missing."

"The sail looks too large to be the Skoggangur's cargo vessel."

Dag smirked. "You're praying he sank, aren't you? I know you two don't get along. I don't like him, either, but he did fund our quest for religious free—"

"Do you really think I would have assigned my talented young apprentice to sail with him if I wanted *Thor's Dragon* to sink? Hardly. But Gunnar *will* be a hindrance to that which we seek."

"If that which we seek even exists, which I doubt."

When a ray of sunlight broke through the clouds and bathed the beach, Dag frowned. An unnatural circle of shadow wavered around Thorlak. Dag spent a few instants trying to fathom what trick of light could cause such a thing. The deepest part of the shadow pooled around Thorlak's feet. It resembled a pit that dropped away into the blackest underworld of the Norns, the supernatural women who held the fates of both gods and men in their hands.

Thorlak's thin lips twisted into a smile, as if he'd read Dag's bewilderment. "Her daughter, Thyra, believes she's here. She told me so herself. In fact, I think Vethild drew us to this very spot. And when we find her, we will also find the key."

Dag rolled his eyes. "Thyra is just a heartsick girl, Thorlak. How could she know anything? For the life of me, I've never understood your obsession with the girl."

"She's critical to us."

"Oh, please, if she's so important, why did you abandon her after the massacre thirteen years ago? Instead of raising her yourself you spent years paying others to—"

Thorlak's icy voice cut him off: "Perhaps you've forgotten that I was a hunted man? A traitor, in the eyes of some. I couldn't afford to drag a child around with me while I fled across five countries. Besides, too many people knew what the child looked like."

"Better to hide her away, eh? Until she'd grown up enough that no one would recognize her?"

The Lawspeaker stared out at the sea as though he saw some faint enigma out there.

"What if the girl turns out to be as powerful as her mother, Thorlak? What if all you've done is create a pretty little monster? Aren't you afraid—"

"She's not as powerful as her mother. Everything she knows she learned from me. And with the skills I've taught her, Thyra is going to lead me to her mother like a dog sniffing out a trail."

Dag stared at him. "Be careful, Thorlak. Arrogance has been the downfall of many a man. When you finally decide to discard her—"

"Your opinions are irrelevant to me."

The threat in the man's voice made Dag stiffen. "Well, then. I should be about my duties. Once everything is in order here for my settlers, I'll take my crew and sail south to examine the territory there."

"To capture more thralls?"

"Of course. We need them for the new colony. There's considerable work to be done. You don't think I'm going to do it, do you? I'll return in two or three days."

Thorlak flipped up his black hood and, without a word, walked to the game trail that cut across the hill, heading up the slope.

Dag expelled the breath. "Great Odin, I hate that man. If I didn't need him to help me find the treasure, I swear I'd have him murdered in his sleep."

Dag's gaze clung to Thorlak. The Lawspeaker's movements exuded an aura of restrained power, like a man always keeping his strength under tight rein. No one really knew what he was capable of.

It worried Dag that it wasn't physical strength Thorlak kept at rein but something far more frightening. Dag had heard wild stories about the Lawspeaker's supernatural powers. Most were ludicrous, of course.

Dag reached down to adjust his sword belt, which had slipped to an uncomfortable position around his waist. When his grip tightened on the sword's iron hilt, it cracked off in his hand, having broken just below the guard.

"What!" he gasped.

Reddish flakes powdered his trouser leg and scattered the ground at Dag's feet. Stunned, he turned the broken sword up to look at it. The interior of the blade had a solid core of rust. How could that have happened?

*That's where he touched my sword.*

Dag's gaze lifted.

The Lawspeaker had climbed to the top of the grassy terrace and stood with his back to Dag. Thorlak seemed to be looking off to the northeast. His midnight cape flapped around his tall body like unnatural wings.

Alfdis the Lig-lodin cast a glance over his shoulder as he moved down the passage, past twenty or more empty livestock stalls in the hold of Godi Dag's ship, and stopped before the heavy oaken door. He'd seen

Dag striding for the ship, and knew he had little time. The door's iron hinges and lock plate gleamed, oiled by the godi's thralls. The only light that streamed into the hold came from the open cargo port above. Voices carried, men laughing as they worked on deck. Alfdis listened for a few moments, judging their positions, then placed his hand upon the latch. The door *snicked* as he opened it and slipped inside.

Dark, the chamber smelled of oiled leather and freshly washed wool. Fragrant, despite many days at sea. To his right, Alfdis could make out a large metal chest, and a smaller wooden box beside it. The chest sported a massive lock—he'd never be able to break it without making considerable noise, and attracting attention—but the box was not locked. It had only a hinged wooden lid.

Alfdis went to the box, lifted the lid, and began rifling through the objects inside.

# Seven

## *Thyra*

Thyra sat on the deck with her knees drawn up, watching the dark cliffs pass, but she kept glancing at Godi Gunnar, who stood in the rear speaking with Bjarni the Deep-minded. She could hear Gunnar's voice above the waves and surf but couldn't make out any words, perhaps because she was too tired to concentrate. No one had slept well last night, least of all Thyra, who'd spent the night tormented by such hopeful dreams they'd left her restless.

She hugged her knees to her chest. As *Thor's Dragon* skimmed across the waves, squealing seabirds fluttered around her.

They'd called her an odd child, for she'd seen and heard many curious things as she'd grown up. The strange stories of Vinland had fascinated her most of all. Some said it was inhabited by giants and dwarfs, even by trolls: little people who lived underground and had no iron at all. They made arrowheads of walrus tusk and used sharp stones for knives. Other stories claimed they had great prophets, shamans with only one hip bone, who could change shape at will and fly to the stars, or just as easily swim to the underworlds of the dead. Much as Seidur magicians could.

She heaved a sigh. Maybe if she just closed her eyes for a short time, she'd feel better.

Stretching out on her stomach on the cool deck, she pillowed her head on her arm so that she could still see the beautiful cliffs while she drifted into haunted dreams . . .

*I'm sitting on a bear hide with my redheaded brother, Thord. I am fourteen. Thord is ten. We both have flotillas of tiny ships, carved from oak, placed amid the swells of the rumpled bear hide. They look pale against the black hair of the make-believe ocean. Thord's face is contemplative. He's fixed his fierce blue eyes on my lead ships.*

*While he considers his next move, my gaze drifts around the house. It's autumn in the fjord and the scent of dry grass blows in through the open door. Outside, I see Mother and Father standing with their arms around each other. Father has blond hair and bright blue eyes. Mother's hair is a deep, dark red. They look westward across the snow-veined mountains, and I know they are waiting for someone. A messenger arrived yesterday to tell them to prepare for the exalted visitor's arrival. Mother spent all night and all morning cleaning and baking. The table is covered with fresh bread, wine, and cheese. A roast cooks in the iron pot sitting at the edges of the coals in the hearth. I heard Father whisper that the visitor is an ealdorman, but I don't know what that is.*

*Thord taps a finger authoritatively on the bear hide. "Your warships are scattered all over the ocean, Thyra. You have no head for strategy. I'm going to crush your fleet."*

*"Why do I have to be Sweden?" I say plaintively. "Can't I be England?"*

*Thord's young brow wrinkles, and he gives me a look like I'm dim-witted beyond words. "King Sweyn Forkbeard rules all of Denmark, and England. If I'm Denmark and you're England it means England has risen up against the true king. There will be civil war. Is that what you want?"*

*"I don't want war. I just don't want to be Sweden. Can I be Iceland?"*

*"Why would you want to? It's a frozen rock."*

*As though to emphasize his words, Thord moves his warship across the swells of the hide and whacks my lead ship, sending it cartwheeling across the plank floor.*

*Morose, I rise to my feet and trot across the room to fetch it. Just as I reach down and grasp the toy, the clatter of hooves on stones sounds outside. I run to the door to see the men riding up the fjord. There must be twenty riders, but the man in the lead is the most grand. He wears shining chain mail and carries a sword on his hip. The hilt is inlaid with gold and crusted with jewels. He has black hair and a braided beard. Even before he dismounts, his gaze fixes upon me and remains for a long time. He has eyes so blue they could be polished azure coins.*

*"Ealdorman," Father says with a bow. "You're looking well. Please share our midday meal with us."*

*Four of the riders closest to the ealdorman dismount first and stride forward, pushing past me to search our home. Thord leaps to his feet with a cry, then they proceed around back and reappear on the other side of the house.*

*"Just the two children, my lord," one of the men says. He's a red-faced man, running with sweat, as though he's fevered. His eyes have a glazed look.*

*Thord rushes to stand beside me in the doorway. He whispers, "They're from England, probably servants of King Sweyn Forkbeard."*

*The ealdorman dismounts from his horse, straightens his heavy chain mail, and walks to extend his hands to Father. Father takes them in tight grips, and in accented Danish the dark-haired man says, "So much has happened since last we spoke, Norm, I don't know where to begin . . . except to say the Forkbeard is dead."*

*Father appears shocked. He swallows hard. "When?"*

*"Months ago. The snows were too deep to send you a message in the winter, and the summer was too tumultuous. He was buried in the Roskilde Church."*

*Father hesitates. "Is that what he wished?"*

*"I doubt it. But his wants were no longer of any concern. His Anchorite son, Harald, made the decision. Harald could have cared less about his father's Seidur faith." The man shakes his head, "Though, God knows, the Forkbeard built enough churches. He was quite the politician."*

*Father's voice is urgent. "And the succession, my lord? Who rules now?"*

*"Harald succeeded him, but the Danish fleet proclaimed his older half brother, Cnut, king. In the confusion, Aethelred the Unready marched back from his exile in Normandy and drove Cnut out of England. Aethelred rules England now and Harald is the Danish king, though Cnut asked Harald to share the kingship with him."*

*"Will he?"*

*The man laughs bitterly. "No. But, trust me, Cnut will be king soon anyway. Harald cannot stand against him."*

*Father glances at me, and a chill climbs my spine.*

*Thord leans sideways to whisper, "Why did Father look at you?"*

*"I don't know." But a black bubble is swelling in my chest. When it bursts . . .*

*"Cnut's army is mending ships. He's marshaling his forces to return to reconquer England."*

*Mother turns her back to us, and I watch her long red curls blow across her shoulders in the cool breeze. She's whispering to Father, but his tight eyes have fixed upon me and Thord. Father nods and turns back to the ealdorman.*

*"And what of our charge, sir?"*

*The ealdorman pulls a jangling bag from his belt and hands it to Father. "Personally, I think it's a cruel myth, but if not, the girl may be useful to keep her mother in line. Besides, she is apparently the only one who can identify it—or so her benefactor believes. Keep her safe."*

*The girl . . .*

*Me?*

*Father holds the bag. The strings tug at his fingers, as though it's heavy.*

"Why does he think the Prophetess survived the massacre? That was thirteen years ago. I heard she died in the flames."

The man's chain mail clinks as he shifts position. "Just rumors. There are those who say that at the height of the chaos, when every Dane in England was being slaughtered, Aethelred had her spirited away aboard a Norse ship headed for Albania-land."

"And is it a myth?"

The ealdorman glances over his shoulder to make sure his men can't hear him. "It doesn't matter what I think. Edmund is committed to finding her, which means Cnut is even more committed."

Father expels a breath. "I think it's a waste of effort."

The man chuckles. "Then you are the only one who does. Think on this, Norm. Less than a month ago, on Michaelmas Eve, a great tide rose up from the sea, higher than any tide known before, and flooded England. Many villages were submerged and washed out to sea. Countless people perished. It was a terrible sight. Bodies washed up onshore for days."

Father shifts. "Do they imagine the Prophetess is responsible?"

"Of course. No matter where she is, if she's alive she will be using all of her powers to destroy King Aethelred."

My knees have started to shake, and I don't know why. Thord grips my arm hard, helping to support me.

He hisses, "What wrong with you, Thyra?"

His red hair and freckled face gleam in the sunlight pouring from the sky.

"That name—Albania-Land—I've heard it before."

"I've never heard it. Where did you hear it?"

I don't answer.

. . . Because on the long cold nights of winter, my Other Mother comes to me in my dreams, holds me tightly, and whispers Albania-Land lullabies to me. The words seep up from inside my heart and lilt around my skull. She tells me she's been there a long time, living in a cave by the sea with one of the strange Skraelings who inhabit that faraway land. Once, she told me she'd gotten word that my real father was alive and that he was coming for her.

I have no memories of my real father.

The ealdorman claps Father on the shoulder. "Keep your solemn oath, Norm the Black, and even if the Apocalypse comes, your family will be well." He strides to his horse.

As he canters away down the fjord trail, his soldiers fall into line behind him. The clacking of hooves on stone slowly fades.

Father kisses Mother's red curls. "We're all right," he says. "For now. We're all right."

*"You didn't tell him about her gift. You said you would. Her benefactor's messengers ask almost every time they come if she's showing signs of having inherited her mother's talents."*

*"When he needs to know, I will tell him."*

*Mother touches Father's cheek, then steps away, and hurries toward the house to take me in her arms. She hugs me so hard it drives the air from my lungs.*

*Almost ill with despair, I weep. . . .*

Thyra felt a hand, large but very light of touch, gently stroking her hair, and heard Kiran's deep voice, calling, "It's just a dream. All is well, Thyra. Wake up. It's just a dream."

When she opened her eyes, she found Kiran kneeling on the deck beside her, anxiously studying her face. The breeze flapped his black curls around his worried green eyes. "You were sobbing. Are you all right?"

She sat up and smoothed long ivory hair away from her wet cheeks. She would have liked to hold him, to blurt out the confused fears that wracked her and talk with him for hours, but knew it wasn't the time. So, she only nodded in answer. "I'm fine. Really."

Kiran sat down on the deck, and considered her gravely for several moments. "Are these bad dreams of your Other Mother? This is the third time this week I've found you—"

"This is Hvitramannaland, Kiran. I'm sure of it. And she's here, waiting for me." She shook her head and turned to gaze at the passing cliffs, where gulls fluttered and perched. "She needs me. I'm worried that she's in danger."

He tenderly laid a hand against Thyra's cheek, and tried to smile away her fears. "Well, as I understand it from Godi Gunnar, Vinland is a dangerous place. We're liable to encounter knob-nosed trolls, and giants with walrus tusks for teeth, and half-human beasts the size of rats screaming like wild banshees."

Thyra smiled despite herself. "That's not what Elrik says awaits us."

Kiran gazed at her with such love in his eyes, it soothed her fears. "No. The way he tells it, the People of the Songtrail are just like us, though wiser and happier, because they live in a land of plenty, filled with towering trees. He says giant herds of animals cover the land like moving clouds and Spirit Power breathes in every blade of grass. He says strange woolly cattle crowd the interior and when flocks of birds begin migrating they darken the skies for days. I can't imagine—"

"I miss Elrik. Why didn't Godi Gunnar bring him? Elrik knows the language much better than you or I."

Kiran heaved a sigh. "Because he was afraid Elrik would escape back to his people. But I wish he was here, too. And Kapusa, as well. They would be deliriously happy to see their homeland."

"I've heard that Kapusa has a new baby, and a husband who loves her. I doubt she would have wished to return. She's made a home for herself and her children in Iceland."

Kiran reached down to twine Thyra's fingers with his. "I know, but it broke Elrik's spirit when Godi Gunnar sold Kapusa. I wish she'd had the chance to decide for herself."

Thyra noticed that the few colonists who stood around the deck were glowering at them. Some of them despised Thyra, a Seidur seer, for associating with an Anchorite blasphemer such as Kiran. Two of the men kept whispering to each other and glaring at her.

When Thyra clamped her jaw, she felt the familiar strength of Kiran's arm go around her back, shielding her against the chill wind, and she felt safe for the first time in days.

"Thank you for waking me, Kiran. That's not a moment I like reliving."

He paused before asking, "Do you want to tell me about it?"

"No, Kiran." Then she softly added, "Someday. But not today." She tipped her chin to the glowering settlers.

Kiran turned around and saw them. "I wish they'd just leave us alone. I don't interfere with their religion. Why can't they—"

"That's fear in their eyes, Kiran. Not hatred. They're afraid of Anchorites. Your priests want to kill the thing they hold most dear. Their faith."

Kiran held her closer and whispered in her ear, "I don't want to kill anything, Thyra. I just want to be with you."

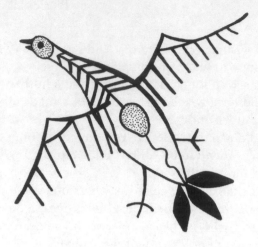

# Eight

Thunderbird's ageless gleam wavered through the veils of rain that fell across the rolling hills.

As Asson forced his shaking legs down the slope, wind whipped the hood of his seal-gut slicker around his face. In the distance, Soapstone Village nestled on the shoreline, its nine hide lodges surrounding the longhouse. From this angle, the longhouse's sod roof resembled a low grassy mound.

He hurried.

*Blessed Spirits, how many are dead at Whale Rib Village? Did they win the battle or lose?*

He panted as he trudged down the slope.

In the winter the People of the Songtrail rolled up their bark and hide lodge covers and moved into the longhouse for warmth, but during the summers the longhouse served as a central gathering place for council meetings or celebratory feasts. Today, it was a feast. The lodges stood empty, their hide door flaps swaying in the wind, but the sound of laughter and scent of roasting seals carried. He could imagine the people sitting around the fires with children on their laps, talking about the day's worries, unaware of the strange ship anchored a short distance to the north.

Asson's path converged with a caribou trail that wound over the hillside, which made walking easier on his aching left hip.

Far below, a man stepped from the longhouse and stared out at the sea. He wore tailored caribouhide clothing. He had turned his tall collar up against the wind that fluttered his long black hair. Even from this distance, Asson recognized Chief Badisut's son Ewinon.

Asson's head hung as he resolutely marched toward the man.

# Nine

The salty fragrance of morning mixed with the scents of spring grasses and wildflowers. Ewinon filled his lungs. As his broad, muscular chest expanded, a sensation of contentment filled him. He lived for days like this, beautiful cool days filled with fresh seal meat and the happy voices of his people gathered in the longhouse, delighting in the bounty.

Ewinon gazed out at the fog that clung to the twinkling ocean. Light rain continued to fall, but Mother Sun's warm light had begun to tear the mist to gauzelike strips, revealing sunlit waves and diving seabirds.

He walked toward the woodpile stacked two tens of paces from the longhouse. To the west, towering spruce trees, larches, and poplars dotted the forest. The leaves had just unfurled on the shorter alders and brush, creating a green haze across the uplands. Soon, the berries would blossom and hungry bears would begin to haunt the thickets.

Just the thought of giant bears caused his hand to lower to the iron knife tied to his belt. The People of the Songtrail collected Fallen Star People from the far north and worked the iron with stone hammers to fashion knives, harpoon blades, and tools for working bone and ivory. In some ways iron blades were inferior to good chert knives—he hated rust— but Fallen Star blades had advantages, as well. For one thing, they didn't shatter as easily.

He slapped a mosquito. Every exposed patch of skin on his body—and the body of everyone in the village—bore a coating of red ochre mixed with grease and spruce pitch to keep the insects away.

As Ewinon bent to the woodpile and started loading broken branches into the crook of his left arm, laughter rose from the longhouse. He looked back.

Through the four holes in the roof, smoke curled into the blustery air. The tang of burning spruce and the richness of roasting seals rode the wind.

Mapet's sweet laughter erupted. Ewinon smiled. Gods, she was a miracle. They'd joined one winter ago, and had a two-moons-old infant son. Ewinon no longer wished to imagine life without them.

He piled more branches in his left arm. Because Mapet was an only child, her father, Chief Drona, had asked Ewinon to leave his home in Whale Rib Village and move here to live with her family. Usually, it worked in reverse, but he'd loved Mapet so much, Ewinon had begged his father to allow it. Ewinon missed his family, especially his younger brother, Camtac, who'd only seen four-and-ten winters. He wished he could be there to teach Camtac the lessons of manhood: how to hunt and fight. In Ewinon's absence, his best friend, Gower, had promised to take care of Camtac.

Ewinon chuckled. Gower was so honorable, he would, of course, carry it to extremes. By now, Camtac must consider Gower more of a brother than Ewinon.

He tested the weight of his armload of wood, decided he could carry no more, and rose to his feet.

Just as he turned back for the longhouse, he sighted the man coming down the hill. The stranger wore a seal-gut rain slicker over a heavy moose-hide coat and pants. His blue-painted leggings came up to his knees. He'd pulled his hood down over his face and held it against the wind, which made it impossible to see his features. Despite the black hair that whipped around the edges of his hood, he moved like an old man, perhaps five tens of winters. Tall, he stood about Ewinon's height, one-and-ten hands. A small pack rode his back, and pouches crowded his belt. Ewinon saw no weapons.

The man lifted a hand to Ewinon. He waved back.

It would have been rude to continue toward the longhouse without greeting their guest first, so Ewinon dumped his armload of wood beside the longhouse door and walked out across the wildflower-strewn meadow to meet the stranger.

Ewinon stopped dead in his tracks. *Asson.*

Ewinon swallowed hard and called, "Elder Asson, it's a joy to see you again! What brings you here?"

In fact, no one was *ever* glad to see Asson, and the old man must know it. He was constantly rushing into the village to bring them prophecies that never came true, or report that massive Spirit beasts were approaching, beasts that no one but Asson could see.

Asson panted, "Good morning . . . Ewinon . . . son of Badisut. How old are you now?"

"Ten-and-six winters, Elder. Why?"

"You aren't . . . carrying your lance."

Ewinon gestured to the woodpile he'd just dropped. "Because I came out for wood."

"If I were an enemy warrior, I'd have already spilled your guts."

"Er, well, I suppose."

"From now on, I want you to carry your lance with you wherever you go."

"Yes, Asson."

The elders in Whale Rib Village joked that Asson had never married because no woman could bear it, but in truth everyone knew that the love of Asson's life had died from a fever when he'd seen barely two-and-ten winters. After that, the boy had become moody and withdrawn. He'd gone off to study the ways of the Kutsitualit with the legendary Neechwa, and had never returned to the world of ordinary men.

While most people thought Asson was a pitiful excuse for a Kutsitualit, many winters ago Asson had displayed great Power. He had stilled terrible storms with the wave of his walking stick and caused flocks of birds to fall from the sky like hail. Twice, when the people were hungry, he had asked whales to beach themselves to provide food for starving children. And the whales had come.

A few respected Elders, however, had always maintained that these great feats had not belonged to Asson but to a half-deer half-woman Spirit he had secreted away in some distant cave. The Spirit, they said, had been the source of his earlier Power. But at some point the Spirit Helper had left him and his Powers had vanished.

As Asson came closer, Ewinon grimaced at the different-colored pouches on his belt. They probably contained magical Healing herbs, or even more disturbing things, like enchanted amulets made from white bear snouts, or the powdered bones of the Inugagulligait, the mysterious dwarfs who roamed the hidden reaches of Earth Mother.

Asson wobbled up to Ewinon, gave him an uneasy smile, and slipped his arm through Ewinon's. "May I hold your arm while you escort me to see Odjet and Chief Drona?"

"Of course, blessed Elder."

Odjet was the shaman of Soapstone Village. Two tens of winters old, his *inua* was so powerful he could just as easily change into an eagle as he could a salmon.

Inuas were independent humanlike creatures that allowed transformation. All living things possessed an inua, including plants and animals, but also mountains, lakes, and the air itself. If an inua was powerful enough, a human could take on any form he wished. And animals could become human, or change into other animals.

Asson stumbled and grabbed Ewinon's arm hard as they descended the slope toward the longhouse.

"Forgive me," Asson apologized.

"Are you all right, Elder?"

"Just weary. I haven't slept in two days."

"Two days? Did you run straight here from your cave near Whale Rib Village?"

"Yes."

Ewinon continued walking, but worry constricted his heart. "Why have you come, Elder? Did you take a Spirit journey to Adlivun?"

Asson glanced sidelong at Ewinon, and his heart stopped beating. The elder's eyes were wide and shiny. Ewinon could see all the way through the brown orbs and down into the deep dread that tormented Asson. "You don't have to answer, Elder. I was just talking."

Asson tore his gaze away and fixed it upon the caribouhide curtain that draped the longhouse door. "Let's get inside away from prying eyes, then I'll explain my mission."

"Yes, Elder."

As he guided the old man toward the door, Ewinon glanced around. He saw no people, so Asson meant "other" eyes. Ewinon now noticed every bird that flew, or insect that darted above the wildflowers, wondering if they were humans who'd transformed into animals to get close enough to hear his and Asson's conversation.

Sounds of laughter and happy voices wafted from the longhouse, along with the delicious aroma of seal fat crackling over the fire.

Ewinon pulled the door curtain aside and held it for the Kutsitualit to enter. When the old man ducked inside, groans filled the longhouse. Several people leaped to their feet, preparing to leave. Those still seated seemed frozen in place with chunks of meat, or cups of warm seal blood lifted halfway to their ajar mouths. During the Long Days of summer, the People wore simple leather shirts, pants, and dresses, some decorated with painted beads or shells.

Mapet gave Ewinon a horrified look, as though he'd escorted a demented skunk into their midst. Long black hair streamed over her shoulders, framing her beautiful face. Their infant son lay on the floor beside her, sleeping in a nest of arctic fox furs. Ewinon gave her a sheepish smile.

Benches, piled with hide bags of dried blackberries, crowberries, and trout or char, lined both long walls. Sealskin bags of oil and whalebone boxes rested beneath the benches. The boxes held personal items. Lances and harpoons leaned in the corner to Ewinon's left. To Ewinon's right, coils of musk ox hair cordage, ropes made of spruce roots, and caribou sinew hung from pegs on the wall.

Ewinon stepped forward. "Look who I found outside. The Blessed Asson has come for a visit."

Faces pinched in disgust.

Ewinon glanced at Asson and saw the old man look away, as though hurt by the greeting.

"F-forgive us, Blessed Asson," Chief Drona stammered. He placed his chunk of seal meat in his wooden bowl. As he rose to his feet, long black hair swayed across the front of his white-painted hide shirt. Three-tens-and-eight-winters old, the chief had slanting eyes and a flat nose. Handsome, he had a boyish charm that made him so attractive to women it had brought him four wives. Red ochre covered his entire face, except for the white rings painted around his eyes—which marked him as the village chief. "We had no warning that you were coming." Drona cast an annoyed look at Odjet, as though the young shaman should have foreseen such a calamity.

Odjet sat two fires away with his wife and three daughters. He looked as surprised and dismayed as everyone else. He took one last gulp from his wooden cup, then rose and came toward Asson with a strained smile. When Odjet was a child, the other boys had nicknamed him Weasel-Mouth because of the narrow and pointed shape of his face. "Elder, we are honored by your presence. Will you join us for breakfast? We hunted seals yesterday, and our best lance throwers harvested several."

"Please, Asson, sit at my fire." Chief Drona gestured to the spaces on the hides between his wives. "Odjet and Ewinon, you, too."

"I accept your gracious hospitality, Chief, though I have very little time," Asson answered.

As the Kutsitualit walked forward, three of Drona's wives rose, excused themselves, and scurried from the longhouse. At least ten other people followed. Asson pretended not to notice. He sat down in front of the flames and pulled his seal-gut rain slicker over his head, shook it out, then placed it at his side.

"You're looking pale, Asson. Are you well?" Drona's first wife, Lathun, commented. She smoothed graying black hair away from her ugly face and gave Asson a warm smile. She'd been captured by the Masks People once. They'd tortured her until all that remained of her face was a criss-crossing mass of scars. But she had kind eyes.

"No, Lathun, I'm not." The heat of the longhouse must have begun to seep into his bones, for Asson untied the front of his moosehide coat, revealing a soot-streaked shirt beneath. Bars of ribs stuck out through the leather.

Lathun seemed to be examining his skinny frame. She used a caribou-antler spoon to scoop steaming meat into a wooden bowl, then handed it to Asson. "Would you like a cup of seal blood, too?"

"I'd be grateful for water. I thank you."

Lathun picked up a cup and held it out to Ewinon. "Son-in-law, would you pour the elder a cup of water from the gut bag, please?"

Ewinon took the cup to the rainwater bag hanging upon the wall near the door. As he filled it, seven more people ducked outside. Mapet strode forward with their son cradled in her arms. Before leaving, she gave Ewinon a worried smile, and whispered, "Don't let him touch you with any dried-up white bear snouts."

"I won't."

"I'll be waiting for you in our lodge. I can't wait to hear the story."

He smiled. "I'll be there soon."

She touched him gently before she ducked outside, and a gust of cold wind assaulted Ewinon.

He glanced down the longhouse. Those who'd been kind enough to remain had risen and stood with their shoulders leaned against the walls, muttering to one another.

Ewinon placed the cup before Asson, then sat down between Odjet and Lathun. The old shaman shoveled seal meat into his mouth as though he hadn't eaten in days—which he hadn't, not if he'd marched day and night to get here. Grease shone around his mouth and coated his fingers.

Chief Drona watched Asson with narrowed eyes, concerned that the aged shaman seemed to be starving.

"Asson?" Drona inquired. "My relatives in Whale Rib Village still bring you offerings during the Long Nights, don't they?"

"Yes. Forgive me; once I've eaten, I'll tell you why I'm here."

Asson gobbled another bite of seal.

Everyone around the fire leaned forward to watch him. Asson seemed oblivious. He continued shoveling seal meat into his mouth as fast as he could.

Asson at last set the empty wooden bowl aside and heaved a deep sigh. "I'm sorry I couldn't answer sooner. I've just been so hungry." Relief twisted his wrinkled face. No one broke the silence until the old shaman said, "I have something to say."

Drona sat back on the hide and gritted his teeth, waiting for what he knew must be a dread announcement. "Let us hear."

Murmurs passed through the onlookers, and the tangy scent of burning spruce suddenly smelled powerful.

"Drona, I regret to tell you that your relatives in Whale Rib Village are under attack. They've been under attack for two days. Badisut asks your help to fight them off."

*"What?"* Ewinon blurted. "My family—!"

Drona lifted a hand to silence Ewinon's outburst, but his gaze remained locked with Asson's. "Who does this thing? The Masks People?"

Odjet's eyes reflected the flickering flames like polished obsidian.

"No, old friend. The Masks People are far south hunting deer in the butternut forests. An old enemy has returned. The Wobee. Three of their ships anchored in Seal Cove three days ago to the south of Whale Rib Village, and another ship arrived just yesterday—which makes four Wobee ships. One of them is anchored just north of Soapstone Village in Gull Inlet."

Surprised voices filled the house.

Drona's mouth seemed to have gone dry. The white painted rings around his eyes changed shape as he squinted. "Blessed Ancestors, I won't have enough warriors to guard this village if I send men to fight for Whale—"

"But you must, Drona," Asson said. "Badisut is desperate—"

"Chief?" Ewinon interrupted. A man did not interrupt a blessed Kutsitualit, but Ewinon had started shaking. He stumbled to his feet. "I beg your indulgence, Elder Asson, but no matter what Chief Drona decides, I must fight for my home village. I—"

"Sit down, Ewinon."

"But you don't understand! I have to—"

*"Sit down!"* Drona ordered. When Ewinon sank to his knees, Drona said, "You would leave Mapet and your son here without your protection, Son-in-law? What if the ship to the north attacks us while you are gone? Could you live with their deaths?"

The rage drained from Ewinon's muscles, leaving him sick to his stomach. "No, Chief, I couldn't. But I won't be able to live with myself if my family in Whale Rib Village is slaughtered, either."

The people who'd been leaning against the walls muttered and came forward to encircle Drona's fire. Almost everyone had a relative in Whale Rib Village.

The firelight cast Asson's deep wrinkles into shadow, making it appear as though his face were netted with thick black webs. "Drona, please listen to me. Even if it means the destruction of your own village, you must help Badisut. If we cannot create an alliance of villages to fight them, I fear they will steal our land, kidnap our children, and more and more will come here thinking it's safe." Through a long exhalation, he added, "And now, I must head back. I—"

"But you're exhausted, Asson," Lathun said. "Please stay overnight and rest before you—"

"There is no time for rest. I thank you for sharing your morning meal with me."

"You must stay, Asson. The Village Council will wish to hear your words," Drona said.

"Everyone here has heard them and can repeat them. The facts are simple: Whale Rib Village is being attacked by the Wobee. Your relatives need your help. The Council must decide quickly."

Asson grunted to his feet. "Ewinon, don't take too long making your decision. Fate awaits."

"What decision?"

Asson slipped his seal-gut rain slicker over his head, bowed to the chief and Lathun, then turned and let his gaze drift over the faces of the people who'd been shifting ominously. He stared so long that Ewinon thought Asson might be trying to memorize each troubled face.

Asson said, "It would help me to get back to the battle if I had a canoe."

Drona pointed to the east. "Take the one down on the beach that's painted with blue whales. That's my personal canoe. But first tell me—"

"You are a good chief, Drona." Asson dipped his head in gratitude. "And a good friend. Place your trust in Odjet. Listen to him."

Asson ducked beneath the door curtain and disappeared.

For ten heartbeats, no one made a sound, then pandemonium broke loose. People rushed forward, shouting questions.

"Chief, why have the Wobee come?"

"What should we do?"

"Are they going to attack us?"

Ewinon shouldered through the crowd. He had to speak with Asson.

When he stepped outside into the sunlight, Ewinon called, "Elder?"

The old shaman stood on the low rise ten paces to the east, facing the most beautiful arctic fox Ewinon had ever seen. The animal had just started to change color, losing her white coat and replacing it with dark gray hairs, but it remained mostly white. Her eyes were so blue they seemed bits of fallen sky.

Ewinon let his hand fall to rest on the knife at his belt. The fox must have smelled their feast of seal meat and come to investigate. The magnificent animal lifted its muzzle, and its nostrils flared as it judged Asson. Arctic fox was delicious. If Ewinon could get close enough, he might be able to run her down.

One cautious step at a time, he walked up behind Asson.

"Elder, if you'll distract it, I—"

"Shh! Can't you hear her, you fool?"

Ewinon listened but heard only the faint voices of his relatives in their lodges and North Wind Man's whispering through the wildflowers. "No, Elder."

Asson didn't reply for a long time; he kept his gaze riveted on the fox.

The animal lifted one front paw, cocked her head, then trotted over the hill and loped away, headed northward.

Asson lifted a hand to massage his forehead. "Forgive me for speaking harshly to you, Ewinon. You're worried and grieving in your heart. I shouldn't have expected you to understand."

"What did you hear, Elder?"

Asson turned halfway around, and his seal-gut rain slicker rattled in the wind like ghosts walking on dry bones. The old man squinted one brown eye. "You must go to Mapet this instant and make your plans. Then meet me at the chief's canoe on the beach. If you wish to save any of your family, we must leave in less than one-half hand of time."

Ewinon went pale as the ramifications sank in. "Gods, Elder, I'll be right there."

# Ten

When Gunnar saw Thyra walking down the grassy knoll along a caribou trail, he straightened and used his sleeve to shove blond hair away from his wrinkled face. *Where has she been?* She wore a long gray cloak over her white chemise. Her thick ivory hair spilled from the hood like a torrent of frost. Gunnar needed to speak with her. She didn't understand the dangers that lurked in this new land. If he let anything happen to Thorlak's favorite thrall, Gunnar's world would suddenly be even more unpleasant.

He turned, spied Bjarni, and called, "I'll return shortly. You can get started building the booths."

"I will, Godi!"

They'd weighed anchor just after dawn. As soon as the tide had dropped and Gunnar laid out the gangplank to begin unloading, Thyra had disappeared into the hills. He'd thought, perhaps, she had taken the opportunity to escape her master and fled. To Gunnar's relief, she had not.

He strode down the rocky shore toward her. To the north, numerous bays scalloped the coastline, rimmed by rocky shoals, scrubbed by white surf. Beyond them, green hills gave way to forests. The air smelled of sea mixed with wet aspens, birches, and wildflowers.

As he closed on Thyra, her blue eyes drifted out to the horizon where swells washed against massive icebergs. The bergs resembled snow-clad mountains thrusting up through patches of light fog.

"Thyra?" Gunnar called.

Her gaze made him straighten. Gunnar wore a faded green shirt that had been mended in many places, and plain brown trousers. Oh, he could dress in splendor, and did when he held court on his farm. Today, it was impossible to tell him from his thralls. He liked it that way. When he'd been a forest-walker he'd commanded respect through deeds, not wealth.

He called, "Your booth will be ready by nightfall. You wanted it up on the high point, didn't you?"

Thyra turned to look. While half his thralls worked to repair the ship, the other half had spent the day cutting poles for booths—the temporary houses where they'd live until *Thor's Dragon* could sail in search of the other ships. The settlers continued to carry packs and oaken boxes off the ship and to stack them along the shoreline above high tide. As they worked, children raced up and down the beach, laughing.

"Yes, that high point"—she gestured—"if it's possible to build up there." Sunlight flickered through her long ivory hair.

"Well, it's a rocky promontory, but we'll try."

Building booths involved laying out poles, nailing cross braces to secure them into panels eight feet long, then setting them upright, lashing them together, and roofing the structures with canvas. In these temporary shelters, canvas hangings served for doors.

Gunnar stopped in front of Thyra and gave her a curious appraisal. Saying that her eyes were blue was like calling the deep heart of a glacier blue—a ridiculous statement that could not possibly convey the shifting azure depths or unearthly luster. "I spent half the morning looking for you. Where were you?"

As if she felt his male gaze, she tucked a stray lock of her tumbled hair behind her ear and straightened her cloak about her narrow shoulders. "I was out exploring. I wanted to see the land."

"I'd rather you didn't do that. We've no idea what troubles await us here. If I've figured my maps right, we're not even close to Vinland. The storm blew us far to the north."

"Then are we in Helluland? That would explain all the stone slabs that cover the uplands."

"My guess is we made landfall farther south in Markland." Gunnar's dark eyes narrowed as he surveyed the steep cliffs to the southeast. "But I could be wrong. I need to get the settlers situated before I can work it through. You're not going to be wandering off again, are you? Kiran was especially concerned about you this morning."

A smile touched her lips as warmth filled her eyes. The black magical

runes etched into her teeth flashed in the sunlight. "Tell him that I was
out searching for Elrik's people. He'll understand."

Gunnar's blond brows knitted. "It may soothe him, but it does not
soothe me. A lone woman should not be out looking for One-Leggeds.
They're liable to skewer your liver before you can explain your noble
cause."

"I promised Elrik I'd try to find his family and tell them he is well."

Gunnar propped his hands on his hips. He worried more about what
would happen to her before the One-Leggeds killed her. Men were men, no
matter where they came from. "That's fine, but I'd take it kindly if you
refrained from searching out danger until we've constructed a solid pali-
saded village. What are your plans for the rest of the day?"

She inhaled a deep breath, and Gunnar had to struggle to keep his
gaze off her small breasts. He couldn't help himself. She was still very
young, but someday she would become a magnificent woman. She told
him: "I might ride Odin's steed, Sleipnir, into the underworld in search of
Rolf and Sokkolf. Their souls may want to come back."

Gunnar suppressed the shiver that ran up his spine. Many gods, and a
few human beings, borrowed Sleipnir to descend into Helheim to find lost
souls and bring them back, but it was dangerous business for Seidur seers.
Gunnar had known three women who'd fallen dead as stones trying to
ride through the deep, dark valleys to reach the gold-paved bridge of
Gjaller. Beyond it lay Helheim, and the land of the long dead, where
battles go on forever.

"Well, if you're serious, first off, I'd like to have Sokkolf back, but you
shouldn't waste your time on Rolf the Cod-biter. He was about as worthless as they come. Second, if you're going into a trance, I want you aboard
ship where I can have my maidservant, Arnora, keep an eye on you."

Thyra gave him a little laugh. "You shouldn't worry about me. I can
care for myself."

"I know your magic is strong, but what happens if you go curl up on a
hilltop to fall into your Seidur trance, and I can't find you when the time
comes to leave? I'll make a sincere search, but if necessary, I'll set sail
without you."

She gave him a chiding look. "Would you, Godi?"

"Yes, I would."

"If it worries you, I'll return to the ship before I mount the sacred
steed."

"I've your word on that?"

"You do."

"Good. Now let's return to this business of finding Elrik's people." Gunnar narrowed his right eye at her. "What do you think the One-Leggeds will do when they see a beautiful young woman standing alone and vulnerable in their village?" She opened her mouth, but he cut her off. "Let me answer my own question, because I know men far better than you ever will, Thyra. I'll not have you raped, cut apart, or sacrificed in some bizarre ritual to their alien gods. I do not want you out searching for Elrik's people."

Thyra turned slightly away and appeared to be gazing out at the vast sea. "I will not appear to them as a vulnerable young woman, Godi."

Gunnar wondered what she meant, but he said, "Well, I can't stop you, but—"

"I'll be careful. Don't worry about me."

He heaved a disgruntled breath. "Very well. I'll see you later."

"You may see my *body* later, but I won't be there, Godi."

"I understand."

As Gunnar strode back toward the stack of poles, he studied *Thor's Dragon*. This country had fierce thirty-foot tides. At low tide, the ship rested canted at an angle on the sand close to shore, which meant they could extend a gangplank for ease of unloading. But as soon as the tide rushed back in, *Thor's Dragon* would be lifted upon the flood.

He cast a nervous glance over his shoulder. Thyra gave him an odd smile. Rather than making him feel better, her smile sent a shiver up his spine. All day long, he'd had the feeling of impending doom. Once, he'd thought he glimpsed a hooded figure standing just over his shoulder. It vanished the instant he looked, but that did nothing to convince him it wasn't there. As a boy, he'd seen *draugar*, living ghosts, sneaking around grave mounds in Iceland. They surely existed here, as well.

To reassure himself, he reached up, grasped the golden pendant of Mjölnir that rested over his heart, and uttered a soft prayer to Thor.

# Eleven

Thunderbirds shook the longhouse. The scent of fear was so strong it nauseated Camtac. He forced a swallow down his aching throat.

"You must aim carefully now," Father said as he shoved gray hair away from his wrinkled face. "We have just four lances left. Don't forget to drop after we cast."

Camtac blinked sweat from his eyes. The longhouse had been constructed of saplings woven together with brush, then covered with bark and sod. After being assaulted with hammers and arrows, most of the sod had crumbled and fallen into the house, leaving the sapling frame exposed like the ribs of a fine winnowing basket. The weave created a lattice less than two hands away from Camtac's head. Light rain fell through it, dappling the dusty hide clothing of the people huddled inside.

Gower stood by the barricaded longhouse door with his lance clutched in tight fists. His wife and children had been killed two days ago. Grief seemed to seep from his pores and drag at his muscles like heavy hands. His movements were sluggish. Rain painted zigzagging lines over his cheeks.

Camtac let his head fall forward. All around him, collapsed portions of the roof littered the floor. Over the past three days, they had created trails through the debris. Everything that had been hanging from the roof poles had fallen: shattered whale-oil lamps, digging sticks made from caribou shoulder blades, whole grapevines with the shriveled fruit attached. When the precious bags filled with walnuts, pecans, and butternuts had hit the floor, they'd burst and scattered. Walking was treacherous.

Camtac tried to force his thoughts to congeal. He was so tired, he'd begun seeing things. At the edge of his vision, the starlit wings of *tunghaks*, evil Spirits, fluttered, and half-visible inua peered at him from the deepest shadows. He had the overpowering urge to sleep.

*Not now. Not in these last moments.*

Another volley of arrows slashed through the roof gaps. Camtac threw up his arm to shield his head from the thatch and dirt that tumbled down.

His relatives stared at one another with blank expressions, waiting for the end. Ten of them were left. Four days ago, Whale Rib Village had contained three-tens-and-nine people.

Two women and three children huddled in the rear next to the pile of corpses. Camtac's mother and two sisters lay there. He couldn't look at them, or grief suffocated him.

The village sat at the edge of a sheer cliff that rose two hundred handlengths from the crashing water. Thick stands of mountain maple and alder surrounded the village on three sides. They should have been safe here, but the Wobee carried strange bows. Bows that, if stood on the ground, stretched two or three hands longer than Camtac's people were tall. It was a powerful weapon that shot great distances.

"Get ready now," Father said.

Camtac lowered his arm, and his gaze fixed on the gap in the bark wall. Outside, dead bodies and dropped lances and clubs covered the plaza, people who had perished in the fight before they'd reached the "safety" of the longhouse. Bloated bellies appeared huge. Some had been there for three days. Seagulls, ravens, and insects scavenged the corpses. Yesterday, Camtac could still recognize the faces of his relatives. But not today.

At the northern edge of the plaza, enemy warriors moved among the bodies, tearing away fur cloaks and jewelry, tucking each cherished item into a sack to carry back to their evil leader. He must be some kind of chief. Camtac had heard him called Thorlak. The warriors' laughter resembled the yelping of wolves.

When a horn blew, the enemy warriors started back for the trees.

Father said, "That's the closest they will get."

Camtac gripped his lance and studied the gap in the wall. *Draw back the shaft, aim high, hold my breath.*

"Cast!"

Camtac hurled his lance with all his strength and dropped flat. No death cries rose. Instead, the responding volley from the Wobee whistled into the longhouse, showering them with clods of dirt and puncturing the roof and walls in dozens of new places. The strange iron-tipped arrows quivered where they stuck in the opposite wall, creating an unnatural hum that almost sounded like words.

Father brushed dirt from his shoulders before he peered through the gap to see what was happening. After five heartbeats, he hung his head. Gray hair tumbled around his face in filthy locks. "We are out of arrows and lances. Best draw your knives."

"But we can use their arrows, Chief," the young warrior Talawk said. He had a narrow, flat-nosed face and short black hair. His knee-length hide shirt was filthy from the long fight. "If we break them to the proper length—"

"I've tried it," Camtac said. "They don't work right when you cast them; they just careen through the air."

"We don't have to cast them. We can—"

Father said, "Talawk is right, my son. We can use the long arrows as spears when the time comes."

Camtac exhaled hard. He should have thought of that. His soul was just so tired he could no longer reason things out.

Talawk straightened at Father's praise and picked up one of the arrows to use as a thrusting spear when the enemy broke into the longhouse for the final kill.

In the lull, men and women raised up. Worried whispers eddied through the longhouse.

Father's expression rended Camtac's heart. He must be thinking that if he'd just led them out into the forest, a few may have escaped. They knew these forests much better than Wobee did. Instead, Father had ordered everyone to run to the longhouse, and trapped them in a chamber of death. But how could he have known about the enemy's bows? As a last resort, villagers always ran to the longhouse when attacks came.

Camtac put a hand on Father's shoulder. "We're not done, not yet."

Father whispered, "I fear you are the single person who thinks so. When I follow the Songtrail to the skyworld to Dance with our ancestors in the green lights, I expect our great-grandfathers to call me before the sacred council fire and demand to know why I killed our people. I will have no words to explain."

From where he kept watch, Gower said, "Chief Badisut, they're stepping out of the trees."

Through the gap, Camtac saw the bright capes and glittering metal that now decorated the edges of the forest.

Father said, "They may think we're all dead. But they will be cautious. Expect another volley."

The old warrior named CrookedBoy slumped to the floor and began breathing in rapid bursts as though he couldn't get air. "I can't take . . . any more. Gods, I can't!"

Father glanced at him, then turned around to look at the people in the house. Pride seemed to swell his chest. "We put up a glorious fight. We lasted three days against eighty Wobee warriors with longbows. No people anywhere could have done better or fought more bravely. But if we see these beasts in the afterlife, we'll rip their red heads from their scrawny necks and play ball with them."

CrookedBoy and Gower laughed. That was something, at least: evoking laughter in the face of the worst defeat they would ever know.

"Are we giving up, Chief?" Talawk asked.

Gower looked away. Gower, of course, would never give up. *Would he?*

Father sagged against the wall, pretending he was bending to assess the situation through the gap in the wall. In truth, the sight of the enemy must have stopped his heart and frozen his blood.

"It's over, Talawk. Death one way, slavery the other."

Through the pole lattice overhead, Camtac watched the Cloud People moving across the lavender sky. They seemed to have all the time in the world. For a few precious instants, he allowed himself to think of tomorrow morning, of the dew that would cover the meadow, and the scent of hickory smoke that would rise from breakfast fires. Gower and Camtac would share a hot cup of spruce-needle tea and laugh about Ewinon having to move to his wife's village instead of Mapet moving here. It had never occurred to either of them that they would lose their dearest friend to marriage.

Howls erupted as the enemy marched forward behind a line of painted shields. Camtac watched them come on. Some carried the longbows; others swung iron swords, or axes. Father said that ten winters ago there had been Traders who spoke fragments of the invaders' tongue. They said that each weapon had a name, phrases that sounded curious to Camtac's ears, like Odin's Gleaming Fire or The Ice of the Red Rims. Camtac wondered if Odin was a Spirit, or if the icy Red Rims were a magical country.

Stout leather jerkins protected their bodies, along with shirts, breeches, and shaggy woolen or fur cloaks. The average warrior wore a cap made of heavy hide, but the elders had conical metal helmets with strips of metal that hung down over their noses. A few of the helmets were carved and ornamented with inlaid gold and silver. Chief Thorlak literally glittered. He wore red braided silk—a strange slippery fabric— adorned with golden threads that flashed in the sunlight. He sported many upper arm rings, and three golden brooches pinned back his fox-fur cloak so that it draped his right shoulder in folds. In truth, he looked magnificent. He stood on the hill behind his war party, hands on his hips. His teeth were clenched tight, his bushy beard like a red ring around his face.

Hatred warmed Camtac. Three days ago, the Council decided that Father should take a small group of people to the Wobee Village and try to Trade furs for iron blades, axes, and red cloth—all items the elders had handled more than ten winters ago. Father had also wanted to ask about Elrik, to see if he was still alive. He'd hoped to buy Elrik and Kapusa back.

The trip had been futile. Neither group knew the other's tongue, and the Wobee were ignorant of Trade sign language. Still, they managed to point and smile at things they wanted, and the Wobee held up fingers saying how many pelts they would take for the object. The Trading was uneventful until the last fifty heartbeats, when the red-haired chief, Thorlak, told his people not to Trade any iron weapons or tools. Instead, Thorlak had taken their prime ermine and beaver pelts and given them milk and a handful of thin strips of red cloth. Not a fair exchange. In the middle of the incomprehensible argument, Old Woman Obosheen had picked up a string of beads to look at them, and the big ice-haired chief had roared and chopped off her hand with a sword. Screams of outrage erupted on both sides. Swords flashed and lances were cast . . . eight Whale Rib Village warriors died, along with five Wobee warriors. When Father ordered them to run, the Wobee had followed.

Outside, the enemy warriors halted thirty paces away to draw back their longbows and let fly. The arrows glistened like slender flames as they leaped into the air and plunged down toward Camtac.

"Get down!" Father ordered.

People dove for the floor. The steady *shish-crack* of arrows splitting the fragile roof poles seemed louder than before. The far wall prickled with humming shafts.

Father propped his elbows on his knees, and dropped his head in his hands. Camtac studied the jerking body of Talawk. An arrow impaled his head. Camtac stroked his friend's bloody hair until the movements stopped.

"Father?"

Father reached over and pulled one of the long arrows from the floor. While he cradled it across his lap, he fingered the iron tip, as though mystified by it. "How do they do this? How do they make iron so hard? Our people have been using iron from Fallen Star People since before memory, but nothing we do hardens it like this."

Camtac stared at him. What did it matter now? "This is not your fault, Father."

More arrows battered the roof, and dirt cascaded down upon them.

Father chuckled. It sounded insane, given the circumstances. "Perhaps the Kutsitualits will protect us, eh? Like they did in the old days? Maybe they will leave their sacred caves and fight as warriors on our side? Their great magic would surely blind our enemies. Or maybe they will just change us all into polar bears, and we'll be able to rip the invaders to pieces."

Camtac clamped his jaw to keep tears at bay.

As a boy, he'd longed to be a Kutsitualit. The story of Alarana had been his favorite. Alarana was a girl who'd been killed and eaten by wolves. After they'd cleaned the meat from her bones, the wolves had carried them to an ancient inua she-wolf who draped the bones with caribouhide and Sang them back to life again. Afterward, Alarana could change into a caribou at will.

Sometimes Camtac swore he saw her running wild and free across the tundra and such longing filled him that he could not stand it. If only he had been allowed to study with old Asson, his life would have taken a different path. He would not be here now.

Gower crawled over and knelt before Father. His round face ran with sweat. "Chief? Please, tell us what to do. The People need to hear your voice."

Father cocked his head in a birdlike manner. "Do?"

"Yes, Chief. Tell us to fight."

Father closed his eyes and shook his head.

Camtac exchanged a look with Gower, then tipped his head back against the wall to stare up at the Cloud People. With the coming of night, they had turned an ominous bruised shade. Each time Camtac blinked, the world went blurry.

When the fiercest volley yet battered the walls, Gower threw his body on top of Father, protecting him. Curses and screams of sheer terror wavered through the house.

"Will they never run out of arrows?" Gower rolled away from Father and lunged to his feet to peer through the gap.

Camtac got on his knees to look. As they came on, Thor's warriors playfully leaped rocks and kicked corpses.

Father inhaled a deep breath and through a long exhalation said, "We are out of time."

"Gods, please," CrookedBoy choked out. "I don't want to die."

"Let's run!" ShiHolder cried. "If we run some of us will—"

"We sound like mewling cubs!" Gower roared. "Get on your feet and fight!"

A few people stood up on shaking legs and reached for enemy arrows.

Gower pounded his breast with a knotted fist. "We are the People of the Songtrail! Never forget that! I need someone to help me cover the roof. If they climb up there to look inside the house, we can kill at least a few of them! Someone help me!"

"It's too late, Gower." Father shook his head.

Camtac picked up an arrow to use as a spear. As he squared his narrow shoulders, he looked up at Gower as though he were the reborn Spirit of an ancient legendary warrior.

Gower met his adoring gaze, and said, "Ewinon would be very proud of you."

"I wish he was here."

"So do I."

"Do you think Thor's warriors attacked Soapstone Village?"

Gower wiped his forehead with his sleeve and blinked sweat from his dark, worried eyes. "If they did, he gave them a good fight."

Camtac nodded. If he died in a few heartbeats, just being able to stand beside Gower for the last battle would have been worth it.

Father wiped his mouth with the back of his hand and grinned at Gower. "I suspect, if you don't foul it up, you're going to become a legend today."

"Legends arc all dcad men. I refuse to die." He whirled around to stare into the tear-bright eyes of his relatives. "If we keep fighting, we will live!"

Gower's confidence seemed to have shaken Father back to his senses. He reached for his war club where it rested against the wall. "We need one more person to help us guard the roof! Who will—"

"I—I'll try." CrookedBoy crawled across the floor with his white hair dangling around his wrinkled face, and jerked one of the long arrows from the mats. When he stood up with the makeshift spear, his knees shook.

Gower playfully bumped Camtac's shoulder and gave him a huge smile. "We're going to live. I promise you we are."

Gower's leering grin seemed so bizarre under the circumstances that Camtac laughed. "I'm trying hard to believe you."

The Cloud People must have parted, for the evening gleam poured through the roof weave and fell across people's upturned faces in purple streaks. Everyone stared at Father and Gower, awaiting instructions.

Father said, "When they climb onto the roof to shoot down at us, we must strike quickly. ShiHolder and Duthoon, protect the children as best you can. Even if they are taken captive, a few may survive. If they force us outside, and you can run, run hard for the Shaman's Trail. They'd be crazy to follow you."

The trail, little more than a jagged ledge, spread just three hand-lengths wide. It was called the Shaman's Trail because it took magical talents to survive it.

Ten-winters-old Podebeek yelled, "I don't want to be a captive! They'll take me away to the Fallen Star People lands, just like they did Elrik and Kapusa. They'll make me a slave! I wish to be a warrior!"

His mother, ShiHolder, Camtac's aunt, pulled Podebeek back to the floor beside her infant daughter, and murmured something that seemed to calm the boy.

Father said, "Live. Anyone who can. Just . . . *live*."

Outside, voices called questions in the strange guttural Wobee tongue. Camtac understood one word, "Badisut."

"There are too many!" CrookedBoy moaned. "This is useless! We're beaten!"

"You're beaten, not the rest of us!" Gower replied. "Don't listen to him. We're going to live!"

Father put a hand on Gower's broad shoulder. "Gower, when they climb onto the roof, I want you to skewer the man on the left. Crooked-Boy, thrust your arrow into anyone you can. Camtac, your arms are short. Take the man on the far right where the roof slopes lower. He'll have to straddle the weave to get into shooting position. Drive your arrow through the inside of his thigh . . . that big artery. We won't have long to kill them."

CrookedBoy broke down in tears. "We're *done*, Badisut. Can't you see that? Let's surrender! They may show us mercy."

Feet thudded on the skeletal roof poles and four men with drawn bows aimed down into the house. The evening gleam shone in their brilliant red and white-gold hair.

Before Father could give the order to let fly, CrookedBoy cast his spear aside and yelled, "We give up!" He staggered back with his arms wide open. "We surrender!"

"Now!" Father ordered.

Gower and Camtac lunged at the same time. Gower's spear sliced through one man's groin. He cried out and lurched to get away. Camtac speared his opponent's left thigh. The man roared in pain but let fly into the house before he jumped off the roof poles. Another man lost his balance and crashed through the skeletal weave to the floor. Father leaped upon him with his war club already in full swing, cracking his skull. The man flopped senselessly. Enraged cries rose outside.

Ten heartbeats later, Father said, "Where are they?" His gaze searched the roof weave. "Why haven't they sent more warriors?"

Gower stumbled over debris to peer through the gap in the wall. His black hair and clothing were coated with roof fall, turning him into a stocky gray apparition. "They're just standing out there talking."

Heartbeats thumped past.

Then a raw voice cut the evening: "Badisut, come out! Chief Thorlak says he will allow everyone to live if you yield."

Gower jerked around to stare at Father. "Is that Matron Metabeet?"

"Doesn't sound like her, but if she's been screaming for days, who knows?"

Camtac, too stunned by hearing her voice to feel either relief or fear, stared up at Gower. "I thought the Matron was dead."

"It can't be Matron Metabeet," ShiHolder said as she bounced her infant in her arms. "I saw her shot just after the battle started. She was running away from her house, trying to get to the forest, and an arrow lanced clean through her."

Gower added, "Matron Metabeet does not speak their tongue. How could she understand anything Thorlak said? Does Thorlak finally have someone out there who knows our language? One of the far north Traders?"

Father batted dust from his sleeves, and frowned. "If that's Matron Metabeet, she may just be saying what she thinks he wants her to."

Gower shifted his gaze to the interior of the house. Dust filled the air. "Do you believe her?"

From where he huddled on the floor, CrookedBoy wept, "Why not? Perhaps if we walk out with our hands open, Thorlak will let all of us live. What do we have to lose?"

Gower's eyes narrowed. "I don't believe Thorlak."

"I tell you, he might!" CrookedBoy flung out an arm to point at Father. "We must surrender! If we all die in here, it will be your fault, Badisut!"

"I don't know *how* to surrender," Gower replied.

"Die if you wish to, but I say the rest of us should surrender!"

Camtac glared at the old warrior. "I'm staying at Gower's side. I will fight until the end."

"You'd rather die?" CrookedBoy wailed. "You have your whole life ahead of you!"

"The rest of you can walk out." Gower tucked a lock of soaked black hair behind his oversized ear. "But Camtac and I won't. They're going to have to come in here and kill us."

CrookedBoy blurted, "I just can't stand this any longer! I'll take the chance that Thorlak is telling the truth."

The old warrior charged for the door, cast aside the locking plank, and bolted outside with his hands open, crying, "I'm unarmed. Look!"

Dove-colored evening light streamed into the longhouse. No screams erupted. No bows sang.

Duthoon rose from the rear and walked forward, dragging her five-summers-old daughter by the hand. The child's mouth was wide open, shrieking without making a sound. "I have to think of my girl. I—I'm sorry, Chief Badisut. I'm leaving."

"I'm going, too!" ShiHolder pushed forward with her baby in her arms. Podebeek trotted at her side with one hand twisted in her skirt. Both women had seen less than two-tens-and-five winters. "I'm sorry, Badisut. I want it over, even if they kill me when I walk out that door." ShiHolder shouldered past Gower and strode outside with her back stiff and her head held high, dragging her son behind her.

Outside, the unmistakable sound of orders being given was followed by the clanking of armored men getting into position.

Camtac braced a hand against the wall, closed his eyes, and prayed.

There was a long pause.

Camtac had to spread his feet to keep standing. "What . . ."

Three paces to his left, a beautiful white fox stepped out of the shadows and wavered as though it were a reflection cast upon the wall by Brother Moon's first gleam. It cocked its head and stared straight at Camtac, its mouth moving, as though trying to speak to him.

"I—I don't hear you."

"What are you talking about?" Father asked.

"Father, I see—"

Matron Metabeet's shout broke in: "Badisut, stop this! Thorlak has not killed anyone who's come out, but he says if you do not surrender, he will slaughter us all!"

Gower tugged one of the long arrows from the wall and wrapped his sweaty hands around it. "He's going to slaughter us anyway, Chief. You know it as well as I do."

Father bowed his head. "Probably. But if we stay in here, it is also certain death."

Camtac felt weightless, see-through, a man made of air. He just stared at the fox. The animal seemed to shine with an inner light. Was it a tung-hak? A Kutsitualit? The Spirit animal seemed to be assessing Camtac's courage.

He faced the fox and lifted his chin in defiance. "I'm not leaving."

Father must have thought Camtac was speaking to him, for he smiled. "You're very brave, my son. But I must go. I may be able to negotiate for our People."

Father picked up one of the broken arrows and slipped it up his sleeve. "On the other hand, if Thorlak breaks his promise, perhaps I can kill him before I die."

Camtac's gaze darted back and forth between Father and the fox. He stammered, "I-I love you, Father. If you see Mother or Sisters, or my brother, Elrik—"

The fox jerked as though struck. Its glistening eyes flared.

"I will." Father took a few precious moments to stroke Camtac's dusty hair. "They loved you very much, you know?"

Camtac fought the tears that burned his eyes. "Save our People."

"Yes, if I can." Father headed for the door and lifted his hands before he walked outside.

*The fox melts to a pool of white upon the floor, then seems to evaporate in darkness.*

"Come on!" Gower grabbed Camtac by the arm and hauled him to the gap in the wall where they could see what was happening in the meadow outside.

Father stopped beside CrookedBoy, and the women and children.

"Gower," Camtac whispered, "I just . . . I saw . . . something."

"If it wasn't Chief Thorlak, it doesn't concern me. Tell me later."

Chief Thorlak, surrounded by guards, stalked toward Father. Matron Metabeet trailed a few paces behind him. Despite her thirty-eight summers, she was still a handsome woman, tall, with an oval face; her doe-hide dress clung to her body, outlining her perfect female form. Even from this distance, Camtac could see her legs trembling.

As Thorlak strode closer, Gower gripped Camtac's shoulder hard and spun him around to stare hard into his eyes. "Look at me. Just look at me."

"Why?"

Sweat beaded Gower's turned-up nose. He smelled of blood. "Don't ask any questions. Just do exactly as I say. Do you hear me? We are finished here. We're going to have to run."

"But I thought you said we would fight until—"

"*Badisut!*" The odd rasping voice of Chief Thorlak made Camtac tear loose from Gower's grip to look outside again. Sword in hand, the enemy chief gestured for his warriors to close the circle around Father's group.

ShiHolder seemed to be the first to understand. She thrust her baby out to the closest warrior. "Please, I beg you. Take my baby. Take both of my children as your slaves! My son is a hard worker!"

"Take mine, too!" Duthoon cried.

A tall ice-haired man called out to Chief Thorlak, and they argued back and forth. Several other men joined the argument. Finally, Thorlak nodded, and Ice Hair strode forward, making a "give-them-to-me" gesture with his hands.

ShiHolder clutched the baby against her as she dragged Podebeek toward Ice Hair. Duthoon was right behind her. Podebeek let out a bloodcurdling cry of rage and terror, and fought against her grip. *"No, Mother! No!"*

Ice Hair grabbed Podebeek's hand in the hurtful grip of a careless stranger, then gestured for the infants in ShiHolder's and Duthoon's arms, as though desperate to have little girls.

Gower spun around. "We're going to run right now." He tugged Camtac away from the gap in the wall and toward the doorway.

A long-drawn-out moan went up from his relatives outside.

"What's happening out there, Gower?"

"Don't think about it. Just do as I tell you to."

Shouts and cries rose outside.

Through the doorway Camtac saw a white fox break from the trees and streak toward Thorlak with its fangs bared, snarling and barking insanely. *I must be dreaming.* Several warriors drew back their bows to kill the little animal.

ShiHolder and Matron Metabeet took the opportunity and ran for the trees.

"Follow me! Now!" Gower gripped Camtac's hand and ducked into the growing darkness, sprinting hard for the Shaman's Trail.

In the meadow behind them, wavering cries, too shrill to be human, pierced the night. Moments of ungodly brilliance splitting open along a silver edge of iron.

When they reached the trail, Gower yelled, "Run hard, harder than you have ever run, my brother!"

War cries erupted, accompanied by the clatter of metal weapons.

Over the edge of the cliff, down the narrow ledge trail, they pounded along the cliff face, fleeing like spooked caribou. Far below, dark waves battered the cliffs.

# Twelve

Gunnar had enough light to see, but just barely. He sat on the sandy shore with the torn sail spread across his lap. A ball of thick woolen twine rested beside him. Evening had settled upon the beach like a sparkling veil of silver dust, and the starlight was stunning. Every grain of sand shimmered.

Gunnar trusted no one else to mend his sails. He'd seen men and women take stitches as long as his arm, stitches he had to pull out and redo himself. As he ran the needle through the wool, he scrutinized the small, tight stitches he'd made. His careful workmanship would assure that the sail held, at least until the settlers could get the spinning workshop set up and weave a new sail for *Thor's Dragon*.

Milk cows lowed from the grassy terrace above the beach.

The settlers had already built a sod fence around the cows, goats, and sheep, and put their iron sickles to good use, cutting hay for the animals. Haystacks created fragrant humps. For supper, they'd shared freshly hunted caribou haunches and fine aged cheese. As soon as they found the other seven ships—*if any had survived the storm*—they'd head south for Vinland. For now, however, they'd erected temporary booths with pole walls and cloth roofs. Small altars dotted the areas around each booth. Most were dedicated to Thor, Odin, Frey, and Freya, and a variety of other gods and goddesses, but many also honored *fylgjur*, each family's guardian spirits, called fetches. Fetches took various forms, sometimes appearing in the shapes of animals.

Porkell the Elder knelt in front of the altar to his fetch, a wolf, quietly praying, as he did every morning and evening, even aboard ship.

Gunnar tugged a stitch tight. If Greenland became an Anchorite nation, all these cherished altars and beliefs would be labeled demonic and forbidden. And every settler knew it. Whether or not he succeeded in finding the Prophetess, when his obligations to his relatives in the Danelaw were done he would go home to his beloved wife and farm in Greenland. It worried him that Greenland might be ordered to convert to the Anchorite faith, as Iceland had. Gunnar didn't want to live in a world without these small shrines.

He frowned out at the sea while he considered the problem. While he supported the goals of the colonists, so far as he could tell fleeing to a new land would not solve the problem—or would only solve it for a short time. The only way Gunnar knew to truly guarantee religious freedom was by accumulating and wielding wealth. Wealth, after all, was power.

As Gunnar watched the wall of dark clouds pushing toward the shore, his thoughts drifted to Thorlak's "treasure." What was it? Legends said that Hvitramannaland overflowed with gold and jewels, but somehow Gunnar doubted that would draw Thorlak. He was already rich beyond most people's imaginings. It had to be something more than ordinary wealth. Something stunning. What?

Gunnar took another stitch and grimaced at the damp wool. Sand clung to the fabric. He absently brushed it off. Thorlak was motivated by just one thing: personal prestige. He wanted people to look up at him with awe in their eyes.

Which was mostly why Gunnar despised him.

When Kiran marched up the beach toward him, Gunnar set his sail aside. The youth had been working his heart out, unloading the ship, caring for the animals, sharpening the metal tools, and helping bail water from the belly of *Thor's Dragon*. Kiran's shoulder-length black hair hung in thick curls. He wore a filthy white shirt and tan woolen breeches. A large iron pendant in the shape of an anchor hung over his barrel chest.

"You're looking bedraggled, Kiran. Did you get enough to eat?"

Kiran gave him a tired smile. "I ate more than my fill of the *kosweet*, Godi. I've never tasted deer as rich and delicious."

"Kosweet, eh? Did Elrik teach you that word?"

Kiran crouched at Gunnar's side. "Yes. He said that I would love eating kosweet as much as I would love watching the animals run free and wild through the country." While most of Kiran's oval face hid beneath his black beard, his straight, patrician nose belied his position as a thrall. He had a regal face, the angles perfectly balanced.

"I'm glad to have you along, Kiran, to speak with the One-Leggeds. If we ever meet them."

"It might have been wiser, Godi, to have brought Elrik. I fear that when we meet his people—"

"I fear it, too." Gunnar had not brought Elrik because the thrall would have bolted into the wilderness the instant they made landfall and Gunnar knew it. Because, if the situation had been reversed, it's what he would have done.

"What did Elrik tell you about his people? How many warriors do they have?"

Kiran shifted to a more comfortable position. "It's not the warriors we'll need to worry about, Godi. It's the Kutsitualits. Magicians with only one hip bone. Elrik said we must befriend them because they can change into any shape they wish to deceive us, or call up the ocean itself to drown us."

"One hip bone? One-Legged? Perhaps earlier expeditions tangled with these Kutsitualits, eh?"

"Since none of our earlier expeditions succeeded, I'd say that's probable."

Gunnar took another stitch and pulled it tight. The talk of One-Legged magicians made him think of Seidur magic. "What of Thyra? Is she still in her trance?"

"Yes, Godi. That's what I came to tell you. She's curled up down below in the milk cows' hay."

"Is she breathing?"

Kiran nodded. "But I can't find a heartbeat."

"Well, that's common enough for Seidur seers. I pray she finds Sokkolf and returns in good health."

"I've been praying for her to come back to me." Tenderness touched Kiran's voice.

Gunnar smiled. The whole crew knew that Kiran was enamored of Thyra. Sometimes after supper on the ship, the two of them spent all night talking and smiling at each other. Kiran had been teaching her the One-Legged tongue. Gunnar had no idea how Thyra felt about Kiran's attentions, but a marriage would never be. The Lawspeaker openly declared that he wanted all Anchorites dead or in chains.

Which reminded Gunnar of something he should have done yesterday.

He pinned his needle in the sail and rose to his feet. His wet leather jerkin creaked with his movements. "Kiran, I'd be grateful if you'd gather all the other thralls and bring them to my fire."

"Yes, Godi." He cast a glance over his broad shoulder at the thrall's fire, situated ten paces from the colonists' booths. "They are all deep in their cups of wine, though."

"Good. They deserve the reward. Without them, none of us would be alive. My gratitude extends especially to you, Kiran the Kristni."

"Thank you, Godi, but I lost my oar in the storm. I'm not worthy of your praise." He rose to his feet. "I'll return with the thralls momentarily." He strode away with his muscular shoulders swinging.

Gunnar walked down the beach, thinking about Kiran's sense of honor. The one law of the sea—which Gunnar had beaten into the skulls of his thralls—was that you held on to your oar no matter what. In heavy seas there was no time to go and fetch another, and with an oar position empty the ship moved like a fish with a fin missing. But Kiran's loss had nothing to do with negligence. The man and his oar had been swept overboard.

As the darkness intensified, the light of the campfires turned brilliant, burnishing the shore with flickering gold.

The booths stood in a ring on the terrace above high tide. Though each booth also had its own small cook fire just outside the door, most people had gathered around the large central fire on the beach.

Gunnar had erected his booth closest to the beach. If anyone was going to get flooded when a high tide surprised them some night, he wanted it to be him, rather than some poor cold child.

Five women continued to wash dishes down by the sea. Their soft conversations buoyed his spirits. He kept telling himself that all was well, that they'd find the other ships. But, truthfully, they might have sunk in the storm. Great Thor, that would be a travesty. If Gunnar and his settlers were the only Greenlanders who'd survived, life here would be even more of a struggle than he'd anticipated. And as for finding Edmund's Prophetess . . .

Four boys and three girls raced past Gunnar, laughing in a game of chase. He smiled. They ranged in age from four to nine.

Around the central fire, a few colonists looked up at him. They had dour faces. Gunnar lifted a hand and two men did the same in response. The others appeared angry. They blamed Gunnar for allowing an Anchorite aboard his ship, which they believed had brought them bad luck. They also blamed Gunnar for making landfall before he'd sighted the other ships.

Of course, if he hadn't, given his snapped mast and shredded sail, they might all be dead. The colonists were farmers, not sailors, and didn't grasp that fact, though he'd endeavored to explain it.

The fire outside Gunnar's door, to the credit of his thralls, burned brightly. A pile of driftwood rested nearby. He walked up and began throwing a few more sticks onto the flames.

Kiran led the group of thralls toward Gunnar's fire, walking steady as a rock. Several men behind him were reeling on their feet, laughing too loudly as they told what must have been rollicking good stories, for they had every other thrall in guffaws.

Gunnar counted them. He had twelve sailors left. In addition, he'd brought three women: a weaver, a potter, and a maidservant who handled his personal needs, including washing his clothes, cleaning his house, and fixing his meals.

Owning thralls had been a sign of his ascendance, up from the depths of forest-walking and into the ranks of the godar. Men without thralls were considered poor and of lower status.

As his thralls gathered around him, Gunnar studied their faces. Finnbogi the Skull-splitter was a large fellow with a block of chin that made up half his face. He wore his black hair tied back with a piece of rope. He was as handy with an ax as he was at *knattleikur*, a traditional game of bat and ball.

Standing beside Finnbogi was Arnora, Gunnar's maidservant. A pretty thing with long reddish-brown hair, she had the gentle eyes of a lamb. She cooked the finest fish stews Gunnar had ever eaten. Not only that, she also had a knack for chess, which Gunnar appreciated on long sea voyages. Arnora had been three years old when Gunnar purchased her from her worthless cur of a father. Gunnar had watched her grow up. She was more of a daughter than a thrall.

Gunnar forced a smile and lifted both hands to get their attention. "I've called you all together this evening to make an important announcement."

Most went quiet, listening, though two very drunk oarsmen, Sigmund and Ingolf, kept whispering and snickering in the rear of the group.

Gunnar raised his voice. "Kiran and Bjarni, please step forward. Each of you has served me well. You've been loyal and honorable, but when I fell over the side just after the storm, the two of you saved my life. In partial payment of the debt I owe you, as of this instant, I free you from your bondage, adopt you into my own family, and set you loose to find your fate as you will. If you ever need anything, come to me and I—"

Gasps and stunned cries rose. Even the drunks pushed forward to stare, wide-eyed, at Gunnar.

Gunnar continued, "But I will not free you to live in poverty. You're my family now, and you will need a stake in the new world. Tomorrow morning, first light, I will reward you with enough wealth, I think, to keep you safe until you can establish yourselves in this new world."

As a din of shocked voices rose, Gunnar lifted his hands higher. "I'll ask you to listen for just a short while longer." The ruckus died down. "Should either of you wish to stay in his current position as a hired laborer, I would welcome it, and I promise to pay you well."

As Gunnar lowered his hands, Bjarni looked up with huge eyes. His red hair had an amber gleam in the firelight. When he broke down in sobs, Gunnar's chest felt hollow.

"Now, go on and enjoy the night, but be here at first light to receive your stake."

For a time, each *leysingi*, or freed thrall, just stood in shock, as though he'd been struck an unexpected blow. As the realization sank in, the other thralls started hugging them and weeping. Sigmund let out a yowl and broke into a drunken dance.

To Gunnar's surprise, Bjarni rushed forward and threw himself at Gunnar's feet to kiss his boots. "Thank you, thank you, Godi."

"Bjarni, get up, please. You're a free man now. You must never kiss another man's boots for as long as you live." Gunnar had kissed more boots than he could count, and he'd hated it.

Bjarni rose and wiped his tears on his tan sleeve. "I would like to work for you as tiller, Godi, if you're sure you want me."

"Of course I want you. You're my right arm on the ship. But will you do me the favor of considering the matter for at least one night? You have, I suspect, more hopes and dreams than you've ever realized. If you still want the job a few days from now, it's yours."

Bjarni swallowed hard and nodded. "Yes, Godi, I—I will. I'll see you in the morning."

Rather than returning to the revelry, Bjarni walked off to the north, heading up the beach sheathed in Máni's silver gleam. He must need time alone.

Throughout Gunnar's speech, Kiran had stood off to the side, at the very edge of the firelight. As the thralls walked back to their fire, Kiran came forward.

For a time, he just stood in front of Gunnar staring at him with his green eyes half-squinted. "Godi, I'm sorry I lost your oar."

"I'd rather have you breathing than the oar, Kiran. Think no more of it."

Kiran's brow furrowed.

"What is it, Kiran?"

The Kristni lifted his gaze to meet Gunnar's. "I don't know if I want to work for you, Godi."

"Well," Gunnar exhaled the word. "I'll be sad to lose you, but if I were a man of your skills, I wouldn't work for another man. I'd carve my own future from the land."

"As you did?"

Gunnar's head waffled. "Well, in my own way, yes. Though I doubt many would view my methods as honorable."

Kiran licked his lips. "I know it sounds foolish, using your own wealth to pay you back, but after you give us our stake in the morning, I would like to pay you for the oar, Godi."

The earnestness in Kiran's voice made Gunnar smile. "That will be acceptable, Kiran. That way you owe me nothing. You can start your new life beholden to no man. Very wise."

Kiran bowed. "Thank you, Godi. Good evening to you."

"Good evening."

Kiran walked away toward where the thralls stood jabbering excitedly, but his steps were slow and methodic, as though he were counting each step he took into freedom.

The colonists had all turned to watch Gunnar, perhaps wondering what he was up to. He could hear them muttering among themselves. Despite his promises that he would go searching for the other ships as soon as ship repairs were completed, they were not happy.

Young Helgi the Stout rose from the fire, frowned as he watched the thralls dancing and weeping; then he made some proclamation and excused himself from the settlers' fire to stalk toward Gunnar. Twenty-four, Helgi was a hothead who complained every time he opened his mouth. Worse, he had no vices. The man didn't imbibe, or gamble, or chase women, which struck Gunnar as unnatural. Truth be told, it made Gunnar suspicious of him. Helgi's long black cloak dragged on the ground, as though he'd borrowed it for this journey.

When Helgi stopped before Gunnar, he spread his feet, bracing for a fight. "What just happened?"

"I'll thank you to be more civil, Helgi the Stout. I don't like your tone."

Helgi glared back at him. "Your thralls are celebrating. Why?"

"I just freed two of them: Kiran and Bjarni."

Helgi's mouth gaped, showing his missing front teeth. "*What!* Who will sail the ship and load the—"

"I've offered each a job. They may accept. They may not. But in any case, it's none of your concern. Are you afraid of a little hard work?" The last words had come low and threatening, in Gunnar's best forest-walking voice.

Helgi's fat face reddened. "We'll see what the other godar and the Lawspeaker have to say about your impudence. I—"

"If they're alive. Keep in mind, I may be the last godi in the new world." Gunnar gave Helgi a friendly smile that never touched his eyes. "That will leave you in an odd position, won't it?"

Given Gunnar's criminal past—which every colonist knew by heart—Helgi must realize that setting himself up as Gunnar's enemy might not be the healthiest idea. Particularly if Gunnar *was* the only godi—the only law—in the land.

It took a few moments for Helgi to grasp his predicament. When he did, he swallowed his pride, and said, "I was just surprised, that's all, Godi. They are your property. Of course you have the right to dispose of them as you see fit."

"I thought you might see it my way. Good evening to you, Helgi."

The big man stood staring at Gunnar for a few moments longer, then strode back to his fire. As his gums started flapping, shocked voices rose. A man angrily shouted, *"He freed the filthy Kristni?"*

Gunnar exhaled hard. He'd seen Helgi's type before, all bluster with no backbone. A troublemaker, pure and simple. If someone didn't slap the man down hard in the near future, the colony would have no end of troubles with him.

Gunnar lifted his gaze to the moonlit uplands where dark forests rolled across the hills. Máni's face dazzled tonight. Every wet rock reflected her sparkling gleam.

His worries turned to Thyra. She'd been in her trance a long time. Had she gotten lost on her journey to Helheim?

Gunnar offered a prayer to his family's fetch, and said, "Come back, Thyra. It's dangerous out there. Do you hear me? Rolf and Sokkolf aren't worth your life."

# Thirteen

"Are they coming after us, Gower?"

Rain blew down from the edge of the storm, slanting through the starlight in misty veils. Soaked, Camtac had been shivering for at least two hands of time as he followed behind Gower on the cliff ledge.

Gower didn't even slow his brutal pace, he just cast over his shoulder, "They are."

The roar of the ocean filled the darkness. Breakers boomed and savaged the cliff below their perilous trail.

Camtac braced a hand against the wet rock to his right and took a moment to steady his shaking legs. The water sheeting from the rocks had turned the narrow ledge into a creek.

Camtac looked down at the ribbons of moonlit foam crashing against the cliff below. South Wind Woman flipped his long black hair around his triangular face. Camtac shook it aside and picked up the pace, trying to catch up with Gower, who'd gotten too far ahead. His sealhide boots splashed water with every step.

All night long, Camtac had longed to weep. Every time he'd almost broken down, Gower had ordered him to focus on the trail, or his empty belly, or what he would do to avenge their relatives. Not that Camtac needed the instruction: He could think of nothing but his family. The worst part was not knowing if they were alive or dead. *Someone* must *have lived.*

Camtac stumbled. He was so tired. He longed to sleep. Deep inside, he knew in his heart that he'd wake in bright sunlight to find himself home again. It would be two summers ago, and he'd be walking behind Ewinon, laughing as they set off on some new adventure.

"Watch the trail, Camtac! I heard your foot slip!"

"I—I'm trying."

Camtac's gaze fixed on Gower's hide boots. He stepped when Gower did. Moved when Gower did. The one thing that kept Camtac anchored in this world was his friend's broad back swaying in front of him.

This was an ancient trail used by shamans seeking visions. They shouldn't even be down here. It was considered too dangerous for anyone without very powerful Spirit Helpers. Portions of the ledge often cracked off, leaving the path jagged and unpredictable.

"Are you all right?" Gower asked over his shoulder.

"They can't be after us, Gower. We haven't seen anyone since we dropped onto the Shaman's Trail."

"They're right behind us, Camtac. Believe me."

"Are you telling me that to scare me? So I won't ask to sleep again?"

"I'm telling you because *they're right behind us*! We can't afford even a small mistake. Do you understand? One mistake and we will be—"

"I understand! You've told me ten tens of times."

Gower expelled a frustrated breath and stared up at the cliff rim high over their heads.

Camtac followed Gower's gaze, craning his neck to peer upward. Star People frosted the rocky rim as the last of the storm moved out to sea.

Camtac had been worrying that Thor's warriors were behind them on the ledge. Now he understood Gower's dread. Thor's warriors might not be on the Shaman's Trail but watching their movements from the rim above. They could drop stones, or bide their time, waiting for Gower and Camtac to climb up again. Which they would have to do, unless they found some unknown trail that led to the water below.

"Gower? Where are we going?"

"Just follow me, Camtac. We're going to be all right."

Each time the trail bent back toward him, Camtac could see Gower's rebellious expression. Gower wasn't going to let Wobee warriors beat him, no matter what it took or cost.

"Gower, please, I need to know."

Shoulder-length hair whipped around Gower's face. "My grandfather once told me that if you took the main ledge across the cliff face it would lead you to Asson's forbidden Spirit Cave. It's not the cave where he lives, but a sacred place where he communes with dangerous Spirits. Grandfather said there are two Spirits there who can kill a man with lightning bolts. I'm trying to find a safe place to sleep. We're both stumbling and stupid."

"So you're taking us to a place where the Spirits will kill us with lightning bolts?"

"I suspect they're more our friends than the Wobee."

Camtac studied the crisscrossing ledges formed by the jutting layers of limestone. There were tens of possible paths.

"Your grandfather know which was the right path?"

"He didn't. He found it by accident. But he said a man had to follow the main ledge that cut across the cliff. He also said that when you found the cave, you'd know it."

"But . . . wasn't that many winters ago? What if the ledge he followed spalled off?"

Gower turned to give Camtac a disgruntled look. "Have you always been so negative, my brother?"

"Yes."

"Well, I'm telling you, we're on the right path, and the cave isn't far away."

Camtac thought about it. "But what if—"

"Just walk!"

As they veered around a wide curve in the trail, Camtac saw dozens of sea caves dotting the black wall ahead. His eyes widened. Inside the caves, birds perched. When they heard Gower and Camtac approaching, they woke, and the caves filled with glowing eyes. On occasion chirps erupted, but usually the birds remained quiet, just watching them.

"Could I stop for a few moments to catch my breath, Gower?"

"No."

Gower climbed over a chunk of stone that blocked the ledge, and Camtac lost sight of him. Panic seared his veins. He rushed forward to clamber up the wet stone. When his sealskin boots slipped, he felt himself leaning out over the edge, about to topple to the jagged rocks below.

*"Camtac!"* Gower caught his flailing arm and jerked him backward hard, slamming Camtac against the cliff. *"Dear Spirits, what were you doing?"*

Camtac flattened his chest against the stone, panting while his fingers grabbed for handholds. "That was close."

Gower half-shouted, "I don't care how tired you are! If you fall, I will find your bloody corpse and beat you to a pulp for stupidity. Do *not* take your eyes from your feet!"

"I'm sorry."

Gower's angry expression melted. "Forgive me, brother. I know you're numb, but I'm *sure* it isn't much farther. Just stay with me." Gower released Camtac's arm. "I want you to hold on to the back of my coat with your left hand and place your right hand against the cliff to steady your knees. Then watch where you're stepping."

Camtac nodded shakily.

"Grab hold now."

Camtac grabbed a fistful of Gower's coat, and kept his right hand on the cliff while he carefully placed his boots.

Another full hand of time later, the cliff curved inward and Camtac saw a gigantic rockshelter. The water had undercut the cliff, scooping out what resembled a rough-hewn black bowl around five tens of body-lengths across.

"Is this Spirit Hollow?"

"I think so."

Camtac glanced up at the rim again. There was a lake nearby, Bull Lake, where Spirit caribou lived beneath the water, grazing on the grasses that grew along the bottom.

Gower stopped.

"What's wrong?"

He didn't answer for a time. "I can't see the trail."

"What?" Camtac strained to see around Gower's broad shoulders.

Gower searched every possible ledge. "Oh, I can't believe it! We'll have to find another way."

"But how? Where?"

Gower frowned at the cliff above them. After several long moments, he shook his head. Then he looked down. The endless freeze-thaw cycles of winters and summers had sent huge chunks of cliff falling to the waves below. Camtac could see massive blocks canted at angles in the boiling surf.

His heart battered his ribs while he waited for Gower to make a decision.

Bravely, Gower sank his fingers into a crevice and leaned out over the edge to see better. Black hair whipped over his round face. "Blessed Ancestors, *I—I think that's it.*"

"What?"

"There's a crack in the cliff right beneath us that looks like the entry to a cave. Stay here while I climb down to see."

Without waiting for an answer, Gower got down on his hands and knees and extended one leg over the edge, seemed to find a foothold, and climbed down.

Camtac crouched on the ledge and leaned forward, watching his friend as he descended the precipice one handhold at a time. Two body-lengths below, the crevice resembled a gaping maw just wide enough to allow a human body to slip through. Camtac sniffed. Fragrances of moss and water rose from the crevice. Gower lowered himself into the dark opening and vanished.

Camtac frowned up at the cliff overhead, and blinked. He wiped rain from his eyes before looking again. Dark silhouettes rumpled the rim. Brush? *Men?* They didn't seem to be moving.

He returned his gaze to the sea. Far out in the distance, a black wall of arctic fog was pushing toward them. As the temperature continued to drop with the night, the fog would thicken and swallow the coastline. He and Gower needed to be off this cliff before that happened.

Gower called, "It is a cave!" In an awestruck voice, he added, "Blessed Spirits, Camtac, you have to come down and see this."

"I'm coming."

Camtac grimaced at the dark silhouettes on the rim again, then swung his legs over the edge, studied the wet rocks, and found a foothold. As he began the descent, fear prickled his chest. He'd spent his whole life climbing rock faces like this, but never after a rainstorm when the ledges dripped water. He had to dig his fingers into crevices and wedge the toes of his boots to keep from tumbling over the edge, but his feet kept slipping.

When he stood with his feet braced on the lip of the maw, a yellow gleam burst to life. Gower stood forty hands below, an oil lamp in his raised hand, looking straight up. His round face had an amber gleam.

"Camtac, once you step into the crevice, you'll see a stairway to your left. But it's slippery. Be careful."

"Where did you get the oil lamp?"

"It was sitting in the handhold when I entered the crack, along with a soapstone box of warm coals to light it. All I had to do was touch the bark wick to the coals and blow."

"*Warm* coals?"

"Yes. Don't think I'm not worried about that. I know Asson hasn't been here for at least two days."

*Do Spirits need lamps to see?*

Camtac lowered himself into the crevice, spied the stairs that had been cut into the rock, and stepped onto them. From what little he could see, the cave was deep, nine or ten body-lengths, and twice as wide. Gower seemed to be standing on a rocky protrusion that jutted out into the middle of the cave, obscuring the view of the bottom. Keeping his arms out for balance, Camtac descended the wet steps.

About halfway down, he saw two red hands painted upon the wall to his right. The People of the Songtrail believed that hands connected the human world to the world where the inua lived.

"Gower? Do you think this is Asson's Spirit Cave?"

Gower held his lamp higher to see Camtac, who still stood high above him. His eyes flared golden.

"What else could it be? Grandfather said that he once saw a Spirit caribou rise up from Bull Lake, shake water from its coat, and follow the Shaman's Trail to Asson's Spirit Cave. He told me the story when I'd seen ten winters. He said there's a tunnel that leads out of this cave and down to the water."

"How did the caribou squeeze through that crack?"

"It was a *Spirit* caribou. I don't know, but he said the caribou trotted to the bottom of the cave and entered the tunnel. He lost sight of it, but he tracked it down to the sea ice where the hoofprints changed into the slide of a gigantic tail."

"A tail?"

Gower's voice turned reverent. "Grandfather swore it was a killer whale hunting the land in the shape of a caribou and it had the eyes of his third wife, who'd run off winters before."

On trembling legs, Camtac hurried down the rest of the steps and walked out onto the lamplit rock to stand beside Gower. In the flickering gleam, the cave seemed to expand around him. Green mossy ledges created a beautiful mosaic. "I've heard Asson say that after the inua give you the Power to change shapes, you never want to go back to being an ordinary human. The enchantment is too strong. It's like a flock of red-eyed terns soaring through your veins."

"Grandfather agreed. He believed that once his wife became a killer whale, she never wanted to be human again."

Camtac edged across the protruding rock and peered down into the darkness where the lamplight cast faint reflections. He blinked in exhaustion, then froze when he thought he glimpsed antler tines moving in the very bottom of the cave. A curious shape crept through the shadows. But as it moved, its ears turned to spruce needles, its long tail to twigs, its brown coat to bark. . . .

"Gower? I think . . . I think there's a tree down there."

"What? Where?" Gower walked out to extend the lamp over the edge. "Blessed Ancestors, that's the strangest spruce I've ever seen. Look at those drooping needles. How can it grow in here?"

Camtac put a hand to his heart. "Thank the Spirits it's a tree. I thought for a moment that one of the cave's Spirits was walking around down there."

Gower gave him a worried look. "Come on, let's climb down the remaining stairs and find a soft place to get some rest."

As they descended, the scent of water grew more pungent and the lamp reflected from an odd white pool. About four body-lengths across, the pool filled the hollow in the bottom of the cave. The spruce grew right at the edge of the water.

"What's that?" Gower asked as he lifted his lamp.

"Where?"

"At the edges of the pool. White rocks?" Gower stepped across the moss-covered floor and squinted. "Blessed Sea Woman, Camtac, they're skulls. And the pool is filled with bones and small bits of metal. Come look at this."

"Bones?" Camtac couldn't take his eyes from the skulls. They'd been arranged in an eyeball shape. He walked closer and looked down into the water. His reflection overlaid the bones like a ghostly image. His face seemed more triangular, his thin nose sharper, his dark eyes as large as black moons. "They're all human bones, Gower."

"How did they get here? You don't think . . . Oh, gods, did your grandfather say the Spirits killed humans and ate them?"

"No." Gower tipped his head back to look up at the opening high above them. "I suspect they fell through that crack in the roof."

Water trickled down the walls, sending tens of rivulets flowing, like golden braids, into the pool. As Gower moved his lamp around, sparks flickered among the bones, shining from pieces of metal. When the lamp's gleam illuminated the walls, Camtac gasped.

Gower whispered, "Blessed Ancestors . . ."

Curious images had been carved into the stones. There were ten tens of running caribou, whales spouting, and seals slapping their tails. Those pictures Camtac understood, but he didn't grasp the strange squiggles that trailed across the walls in dark lines. "What are those pictures, Gower?"

Gower's bushy black brows pulled together. "I'm not sure, but . . . do you remember when we were in the Wobee camp? They wore iron pendants with symbols like that."

Camtac just stared for a time. "They look old. Do you think Wobee lived here long ago?"

Gower seemed to see something interesting, then walked across the springy moss floor. Camtac, stumbling with fatigue, followed.

At the base of the protruding rock was a scooped-out place almost as tall as a man and two body-lengths deep. Camtac could see two rolled hides, soapstone pots, and baskets stashed in the rear. A variety of walking sticks leaned against the cave wall within easy reach of a sleeping person. Why did Asson need so many? Constructed of willow, alder, iron, and birch, maybe each had a different purpose?

Gower set his lamp on a rock, and ducked inside. "This must be where Asson sleeps when he comes here."

Camtac couldn't take his eyes from the curious symbols, wondering if they had Spirit Power. Some were beautiful. One flat rock face was covered with them, some higher than a man could reach. Many of the lines had been carved on top of older images. Beneath one line, Camtac could make out two stick-figure men with lances chasing a bearded seal. Another line had almost obliterated an earlier image of Sea Woman.

Camtac glanced back at the bones in the pool. The People of the Songtrail buried their dead beneath the ground. Did the Wobee bury their dead beneath water? Were the symbols testaments to cherished ancestors?

"There are dried fish in these baskets," Gower called. "And paints in the soapstone pots."

Unlike Gower, Camtac didn't have to duck to enter the hollow. He just walked inside and watched as Gower moved through the flickering lamplight, lifting the lids of baskets and pots, seeing what each contained. At last, Gower pulled strips of dried fish from a large basket, and handed several to Camtac.

"Let's eat, little brother, and then we'll roll up in the hides and sleep."

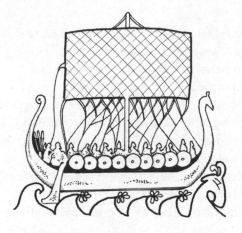

# Fourteen

Kiran carried his whale-oil lamp cupped in his left hand as he descended the wooden stairs into the belly of *Thor's Dragon*. When he stepped off into the livestock stalls, the faint scent of manure rose. After the animals had been off-loaded, the crew had bailed out the flooded hold, but it took time for pungent odors to fade. The air held other scents, too, the richness of wet wood and the clean scent of freshly cut hay.

He lifted his lamp and searched the animal-chewed stalls. Those that had not held animals brimmed with stacked barrels of wine and mead, looms, boxes filled with sewing needles, glass beads, ringed pins and brooches, knives, iron strikes-a-lights, and nested wooden pails for holding urine needed for bleaching and dying wool. The recently dried-out bolts of fabric smelled like the sea breeze. More valuable items, like books, gold, and precious stones, were stored in locked boxes on high shelves inside Godi Gunnar's personal chamber, which occupied the triangular portion of the ship's bow, just behind the hay stall.

Kiran walked the five paces to the stall, where he found Thyra lying curled in the middle of the fresh grass cut from the meadows.

Seeing her eased his fears.

He stopped outside and lifted his lamp to study her. She'd pulled her hood up, then wrapped her gray cloak around her slender body like a blanket. Long ivory hair fell from her hood and spread across the hay like strands of spun silver. He just stood for a time with his arms braced on the stall, looking down. Her beautiful face, sprinkled with freckles, looked so pale it struck at his heart. His body seemed too frail a vessel to hold all the love he felt for her.

Barely audible, he said, "It's me, Thyra."

A safe distance from the hay, he set his lamp on the wooden plank floor, and went to kneel beside her. She looked dead. Her eyelids didn't move. Her nostrils didn't flare. Worst of all, her skin had a waxy yellow sheen, as though drained of life's blood.

Kiran gently stroked her hair where it spread across the hay. "I'm worried about you. Are you all right?"

He'd give her his entire heart if he could, though she was a mystery to him. At times, she seemed like a creature of the glaciers, born of blue silence and blinding reflections. When she told stories about ancient kingdoms populated by giants and dwarfs, it was as though she'd been to those places, and it filled him with a fear of demons and ghosts.

Some nights after their tasks were done they'd just sit outside, shivering in the shine of the northern lights, and she'd tell him about Odin and Thor, and the magnificent golden halls of Asgard. In return, Kiran told her about the simple fisherman who died in shame only to rise in glory. They never argued. Sometimes Kiran thought she might secretly believe in the Lord of the Peak's Pane, or at least long to, and it gave him hope. Above all, they listened to each other. Kiran never wanted to live without the sound of her voice.

"I thought I'd come to tell you that we got the booths set up today. The colonists have moved in and seem a little happier, though nothing will keep Helgi the Stout from his constant complaining. He tormented the godi throughout the day. He's a whiner, that one."

In Kiran's mind he could see Thyra smiling, and it made him smile in return. "And Bjarni's been working like a fiend to get *Thor's Dragon* repaired so we can be off to find the other ships. The godi took a shadow compass reading at noon and sunset. He thinks we're six or seven days north of Vinland. After we cut a new mast, and get it installed, we'll be headed south."

Thyra's nostrils flared with a deep breath, as though maybe she'd heard Kiran.

He stroked her hair again. "I've been a little . . . lost. Godi Gunnar freed me, Thyra." He took a deep breath, trying to believe it. "But I don't know what to do with my newfound freedom. I still wait around for Godi Gunnar to tell me what to do, just as I have for most of my life."

Thyra's lips twitched with a faint smile.

"Can you hear me?" He sat down beside her. "The worst parts are the sudden bouts of exultation that drop away into bone-deep fear. It's as though I'm afraid of being free. That sounds silly, doesn't it? I ought to just—"

Boots padded on the stairs behind Kiran. He turned to see Godi Gunnar coming down the steps. He wore his tan cloak over his long green shirt and mud-spattered brown trousers. Blond hair clung to his wrinkled cheeks. Was it raining again? Drops glistened on his turned-up nose.

"Good evening, Godi."

"How is she, Kiran?"

"I don't know how to tell. She hasn't moved. Is that normal?"

The godi propped his forearms on the top rail of the stall and looked down. Lamplight flickered in his brown eyes. "I've witnessed Seidur seers lie in trance and not move a muscle for up to three days. I swore they were dead. . . . Until they woke up, of course."

Kiran returned his attention to Thyra's slack face. The freckles that sprinkled her nose looked darker in the lamp's gleam. "All she's ever wanted is to understand the ways of Seidur magic. She said the Lawspeaker trained her in the art."

"Yes, Thorlak told me that's why he bought her nine months ago. He said he knew that with the proper instruction she would become his greatest asset, his 'perfect tool.'" Gunnar laced his tanned fingers together and propped them on the top rail. "I don't know much about her. Do you? Why would he take it upon himself to train a thrall in the ways of Seidur magic?"

Kiran shifted to sit cross-legged on the wooden floor at Thyra's side. "I think she's told me every detail of her life in Greenland these past nine months, but she's told me almost nothing of her childhood—except that she grew up on a farm in Denmark."

Gunnar scratched his bearded cheek. "Have you specifically asked her about her early life?"

"I have. She won't tell me."

"Then leave it be, Kiran. People with a past like to keep it bottled. When you tell another human being your worst moments, you forever see those times in the way they look at you. Brings back things you're trying hard to forget."

Kiran wasn't sure he understood. In his sixteen years, he'd found that to make friends you had to share the darkest details of your life. But maybe, given Godi Gunnar's almost legendary past, Kiran had no idea how dark such details could get.

"You don't want to disturb her overly much, Kiran. I've heard that if Seidur seers get distracted while riding through the underworlds, they can be kidnapped by malevolent entities. Or just lose their way and never get back."

Godi Gunnar turned to leave, and Kiran asked, "Godi? Can she hear me?"

Gunnar cocked his head. "Thorlak told me a curious story on that subject once. He said that right after he began training Thyra, one of his other thralls, a man named Ari, had fallen through the ice. When four thralls hauled him to Thorlak's house, poor Ari was dead as a hammered rat. Thorlak had started preparing to bury him when Thyra asked him if she could try to ride into Helheim and bring Ari's soul back. Thorlak gave her permission. I think he was curious to see if she could do it. After many hours, Thorlak was sure Thyra was dead. He shook her and slapped her and shouted curses at her . . . nothing worked. Right at the end, he started burial preparations for both Ari and Thyra. That, of course, is when Ari sucked in a sudden breath and sat up. Thyra awoke a short while later, and Thorlak said she was very perturbed with him. She repeated every curse he'd uttered word for word. So . . ." Gunnar waved a hand uncertainly. "Maybe when they're close to getting back they can hear you? When she wakes, ask her."

"Thank you, Godi. I will." Kiran's voice sounded worried even to him.

"She *is* going to wake, Kiran." Godi Gunnar gave him a confident nod.

"But what happens to her body if her soul is attacked in the underworlds?"

Gunnar made an airy gesture with his hand. "You're stretching my knowledge of Seidur magic. I know that when seers change into other forms, like bears or wolves, if they're killed in that form, their human bodies die. But as to what happens to a seeress who's sent her soul into the underworlds aboard Odin's magical steed? That I don't know. I'm a Thor worshiper, and not much acquainted with this new fascination for the one-eyed war god."

Kiran reached up to clasp the iron anchor that hung to the middle of his chest. His lips moved in a silent prayer, trying to ward off the evil one-eyed war god, Odin.

Gunnar paused and narrowed an eye at Kiran. "What does your Monk's Tester say about all this, Kiran? My guess is you're supposed to keep far away from such doings."

Kiran bowed his head. "My priest told me the entire Seidur faith is demon worship."

"Did he?" Gunnar asked with exaggerated politeness. "Well, I'm not a man to pass judgment on another's beliefs. I'm committed to the notion that men ought to be able to believe whatever tripe they want to. Including me. In fact, there's quite a lot of tripe I hold dear."

There was a smile in his voice that made Kiran look up. The godi's eyes sparkled.

"Thank you, Godi."

"Don't worry about her, Kiran. Not yet. And don't let it slip your mind that we've an early morning tomorrow. I've hired you for the day. I need you rested."

"I'm going to find my sleeping sack very soon."

"Good." Godi Gunnar lifted a hand to him, turned away, and climbed the stairs, disappearing out of Kiran's sight. He heard Gunnar's boots thudding across the deck above him.

Kiran reached out to gently touch Thyra's slender fingers where they rested on the green hay. "I'm waiting for you to come home to me."

He rose and walked over to pick up his lamp. Before he left, he took one last long look at her beautiful face.

How did a newly liberated man convince someone like the Lawspeaker to sell his prize thrall to an Anchorite?

# Fifteen

Thick clouds obscured the night sky, blotting out the starlight.

Alfdis the Lig-lodin pulled up his hood when rain began to fall from the stygian darkness. He continued through the burned village toward the Lawspeaker's camp at the edge of the trees. All around Alfdis, heaps of debris smoldered. When the wind gusted, red patches flared amid the wreckage, providing enough light to keep him from tripping. Gouts of smoke drifted across his path.

He rubbed the sting from his blue eyes. He had tied his black hair back with a cord, but it had come loose and straggled around his face.

Alfdis gritted his teeth in preparation. He was not looking forward to facing the Chieftains' Council and delivering the news that he and Snorri had lost their Skraeling quarry.

Alfdis squinted at the three men sitting around the fire. Even from a distance, a man would know they were the godar. The chieftains' jewels and cloaks—embroidered with silver and golden threads—flashed in the firelight. They must be in council or they wouldn't be wearing their best coats. Flushed with victory over destroying the village, they wore exultant expressions. Out in the trees, more than seventy warriors lay curled in their sleeping sacks, far from the sights and smells of the battlefield. Alfdis hoped to be out there soon himself, once he'd delivered his report.

Childish laughter drew Alfdis' attention.

A pole cage, imprisoning a Skraeling boy, stood fifteen paces away. Four laughing Norse boys surrounded the cage: Godi Dag's sons. The little tormentors thrust long sticks through the bars and howled in triumph when they drew blood from the captive child. In response, the Skraeling stormed the bars and raged at them, gnashing his teeth like a wild dog, grabbing at their sticks, trying to wrestle them away from the larger boys. The tussles sent the Norse youths into breathless paroxysms of laughter.

The sight sickened Alfdis. He truly hated those little boys. They were too much like their father.

And Alfdis was too much like his mother. Like her, he could hear ghosts. On this rainy night, enraged alien voices whispered all around him, barely audible. The Lawspeaker should have moved their camp back to the shoreline. No one with sense taunted the draugar, the living ghosts. They could appear as a slip of moonlight, or a breath of wind. They were best known for wrapping their strong hands around a sleeping man's throat and choking the life out of him before he woke.

As the storm moved southward, moonlight spilled upon the earth, and the cloud shadows seemed to dance in wild gyrations. Alfdis shuddered as he veered wide around two sprawled corpses.

The woman's body—Metabeet had been her name—lay on its back, her brightly painted blue-and-yellow dress dark with old blood. Her head had been hacked to mush by war axes. One of Metabeet's broken legs twisted at an angle, and the splintered bone shone in the moonglow. *She shouldn't have tried to run when the bizarre white fox appeared.* He couldn't take his eyes from Metabeet's mutilated skull. He'd been feeling numb since yesterday, and he knew it was deep shock.

With the exception of three awful years, Alfdis had spent much of his life as a farmer. When necessary for the defense of his village, he'd taken up his sword and ax, but battle was not something he relished, as some men did. Especially not over a grievance such as the one that had provoked this slaughter—an old woman lifting a string of glass beads. It seemed ridiculous. He longed to return to the small tree-lined cove where they'd dropped anchor and finish setting up their booths. Anything to get away from here.

As he approached the godar's fire, men turned to look at him. Each had his hood up against the light rain. The Lawspeaker put aside the knife he'd been sharpening on a whetstone. His black cloak fell over his shirt, obscuring the fine crimson silk. He was tall, with bushy red hair and beard; the hollows of his cheeks were shadowed. His eyes resembled holes in his face. The sword hanging at his side swayed. Skyrmir, Thorlak's sword, was named after the Giant King of Utgard. The sight of it affected Alfdis like the icy quiet that descended in deepest winter, when it hurt to breathe or move. The sword was powerful; of that he was certain. The Lawspeaker always kept it sheathed. Legends said that no one alive had ever seen Thorlak bare the blade. Because anyone who had was dead.

"Alfdis!" Thorlak called, and extended a hand to him. "Join us. Tell us of the fates of the Skraeling runaways."

Alfdis bowed to the powerful godar. None of them had participated in the killing part of the battle, so their splendid cloaks remained clean and unsullied. Hooded blond and red heads dipped to acknowledge Alfdis' arrival.

To his right, the young tormentors must have grown tired of shoving sticks into the cage. As the boys began to wander off, the Skraeling child sank to the floor, covered his face with an arm, and his shoulders heaved in silent misery.

Alfdis fixed his gaze upon Godi Dag, then moved to Thorlak. "I regret to inform you, Lawspeaker, that we did not capture them. They scurried down a sheer cliff and vanished into thin air."

Godi Dag snapped, "What?" A large blond man, full bearded and blue-eyed, he had a reputation for cruelty that had made him very unpopular in Greenland. "How could you lose them? What happened? Don't you realize they will trot to the nearest village and scream the story of their destruction? Your pathetic failure may well endanger the lives of our people, and even our whole colonizing mission! Thorlak, I told you he was unreliable."

Godi Ketil the Fair-hair nodded. "You know it's true, Lawspeaker. We should have dispatched a man with a warrior's soul. Alfdis is a coward."

Thorlak rose to his feet and stood, as though no longer human but a carved stone statue. His stillness was eerie. When he smiled at Alfdis with perfect white teeth, Alfdis swallowed hard. The face might have been conjured from a nightmare.

Alfdis held his tongue. Making excuses would surely doom him.

"What of the boy that went with you?" Thorlak's too-soft voice asked.

Alfdis hesitated. A man had to take care what he said before a Lawspeaker—especially this man. Spine-tingling stories were spun about Thorlak. It was said that if the Lawspeaker spent too long at a farm the crops withered in the fields, and if he touched a man's knife or ax it rusted to dust in a matter of moments.

"The Lawspeaker asked you a question. Where is Snorri? Why isn't he here with you?" Godi Dag demanded to know.

"I sent him to find his sleeping sack. He's just fifteen; I didn't think it was necessary for him to—"

Godi Dag growled, "I wished to question both of you. You have no authority to make such decisions. In the fut—"

"Your *arrogance* is beginning to displease me, Godi." Thorlak's voice lingered on the word *arrogance*, as if it took effort not to use a stronger word. "Alfdis did as the godar instructed. He is blameless."

The sharp angles of Godi Dag's face tensed. "What? I'll remind you that the man spent three years in banishment for thievery. My farm was in the Life-ring Enclosure in Iceland. He's a no-good, Thorlak. I don't grasp why you allowed him to take passage with us."

"It was not Alfdis who chopped off the Skraeling woman's hand and started this slaughter, Godi Dag; it was you."

"She was trying to *steal* a string of red beads!"

Alfdis stared straight ahead where wind rustled the starlit alder leaves, but shame coursed through him. The "Life-ring" referred to the silver ring a man guilty of lesser outlawry had to pay the godi in order to save his life. The "Enclosure" described the three homes, no more than one day apart, where the outlaw was permitted to stay while he arranged passage out of Iceland. Beyond that enclosure, the outlaw was fair game. Anyone could murder him without punishment. Alfdis had fled to Greenland in exile, and once there he'd begun a new life, working his own farm and, on occasion, for Godi Gunnar.

Thorlak folded his arms across his chest, turned his back to the godar, and walked out to the edge of the firelight. He seemed to be staring at the darkness as though he saw something out there. His long cloak flapped around him. "You stole a goat, is that right, Alfdis?"

"Yes, Lawspeaker, to feed my sick wife and son."

"Both died?"

"They did, yes. Plague." Though he'd lost Aud and Runolf seven years ago, Alfdis' insides still twisted at the memory. Would that wound never heal? The image of Aud's loving smile welled behind his eyes, and he hurt.

Thorlak shifted. His cape swayed.

Godi Ketil said, "The youth, Snorri, has bad vision, doesn't he?" Ketil used a hand to smooth his blond beard, as he did habitually, to the annoyance of anyone who had to spend much time in his presence. "How did he perform on the search?"

Alfdis felt uncomfortable answering that question. If the godar knew the boy had bad eyes why did they assign him the task? "He had some difficulty after full dark. But it wasn't his fault that he lost sight of the—"

"So it was Snorri who let the runaways escape?"

Alfdis straightened. "No, Godi. The fault was mine. We saw the runaways go over the edge of the cliff and tried to follow them, but the path was far too treacherous in the storm, so *I* decided we would track the Skraelings from the rim above. As the cliff trail rose and fell, however, we lost sight of them." Alfdis took care wording his next sentence: "It was *my* decision to send Snorri southward to search ahead while I waited at the last place I'd seen the runaways."

"Stop trying to protect the worthless orphan. Clearly, it was Snorri who lost the Skraeling beasts," Godi Ketil said.

Dag nodded. "The boy *must* be punished. Where is his sleeping sack? Run off and fetch him." Dag shooed Alfdis with both hands. "Go on. Be quick about it."

Alfdis started to turn.

"Stand your ground, Alfdis the Lig-lodin."

Wrapped in flickering light on the outskirts of the fire, shadows pooled around the Lawspeaker's tall body as he half-turned. Alfdis could just make out the dark profile inside the Lawspeaker's hood, which seemed cut from the blackest black cloth. "Do you mete out judgments, Godi Dag?"

"I have a say in the matter, Lawspeaker," the godi snapped.

"Perhaps you wish I was not here, so that you alone could judge and punish without hindrance, as you did on your farm in Greenland?"

"We didn't have a Lawspeaker for three days' ride! I had to make my own judgments."

"Yes. *Unfortunate.*" The word held deadly patience. The shadowed figure turned slightly more, so that firelight sheathed his bony face and reflected in his amber eyes, but he was not facing the godar when he added, "So long as I am Lawspeaker, the laws will be obeyed."

The Lawspeaker turned full around and fixed his nightmare eyes upon Godi Dag. As Thorlak moved, the shadows around him seemed alive, stepping with him, but an instant later.

Godi Dag straightened. He made an airy gesture with his hand and laughed. "It wasn't my intention to start a quarrel. I'm relieved you're here, Thorlak. We need a specialist in the law." He turned to Alfdis. "If I offended you, Alfdis, my sincere regrets."

"Accepted, Godi," Alfdis responded.

The chieftains glanced at Thorlak, then pretended to have found something fascinating on the toes of their boots.

As Thorlak walked back to the fire, the runes on Skyrmir's hilt glittered in time to his stride. A pale, elegant weapon, it seemed to reach into Alfdis' chest with a ghostly hand and squeeze his lungs. When a man's gaze rested upon that sword, it was hard to breathe.

The Lawspeaker stopped before the fire, lifted his bearded chin, and surveyed the assembled godar. "I pray you all sleep well."

The godar glanced at one another, took the hint, and rose to leave.

"Pleasant evening to you, Lawspeaker," Godi Dag said.

He led Godi Ketil out into the forest where their sleeping sacks must be waiting in the midst of their private armies.

When Alfdis started to leave, the Lawspeaker's deep voice stopped him. "Remain, Alfdis."

He turned back. "Of course, Lawspeaker."

Thorlak tilted his head, as though listening to a song he couldn't quite identify.

"You hear them, don't you?"

"Hear what, sir?"

"The Skraeling draugar that whisper all around us."

Fear galloped through Alfdis' veins as he tried to figure out how the Lawspeaker could use such information against him. "I-I sometimes think I hear such voices, Lawspeaker, but I'm a simple man—"

"No, you're not." Thorlak stared unblinking at Alfdis, as though searching for some deep, dark secret. "I'm just beginning to see that."

When the Lawspeaker dropped his gaze and walked around the fire to sit down in his previous position, Alfdis let out the breath he'd been holding.

Thorlak picked up his knife and whetstone, and began taking long, rasping strokes. "Seidur magic rides the winds, Alfdis. Go with care this night."

"Y-yes, Lawspeaker."

Alfdis bowed and walked away, trying not to appear as though he was rushing to put as much distance between himself and Thorlak as possible. But Alfdis had barely gone five steps when a commotion broke out in the trees. Men gasped and lunged from their sleeping sacks to run down the hill. Shocked conversations erupted.

Alfdis halted, trying to see what had caused the commotion. While he searched the darkness, the Lawspeaker walked up to stand beside him; the man still carried his knife and whetstone.

In a dreadful voice, Thorlak said, *"Dear Odin, what's he doing here?"*

"Who? I don't see . . ."

Alfdis' voice faded when he glimpsed a man staggering in the midst of the crowd of stunned onlookers. As he made his way up the hill, Alfdis noted that the man was dripping wet. Had he just dragged himself out of the depths of the sea? Drenched hair plastered his gaunt cheeks. His expression was death haunted, confused, as though he did not know where he was or how he'd gotten here.

Alfdis gasped, "That's Sokkolf! He was aboard *Thor's Dragon!*"

Alfdis lunged into a dead run. All he could think of was that Godi Gunnar's ship must have sunk and somehow Sokkolf had managed to swim to shore.

As Alfdis passed the Skraeling boy's cage, he heard choked weeping.

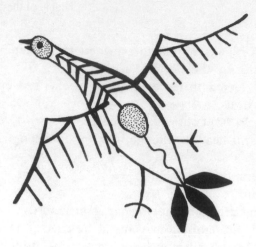

# Sixteen

Fog surged and retreated with the motions of the surf. It appeared as a phosphorescent gleam at the edges of Asson's fire. He watched it to keep his gaze off Ewinon where he stalked back and forth near their beached canoe. Beads of moisture glistened on the youth's rain slicker, and coated his odd triangular face—the hallmark of Badisut's children.

As the mist thickened they'd been forced to stop and make camp on the strip of sand that ran along the base of the towering cliff. Asson wasn't sure where they were, but he thought they might be near the Spirit Cave. If he could discern the shape of the cliff, or the patterns of the limestone, he'd know. In the darkness, all he could see was a mist-shrouded black wall. When the tide came back in, it would rise to swallow half that wall.

Mother Ocean had quieted. Asson added another piece of driftwood to the fire. "You may as well stop pacing and sit down. We can't leave."

Ewinon ignored him and continued pacing. Inside his seal-gut hood, soaked black hair clung to his cheeks. "Elder Asson, my relatives could be dying. I can't stay here!"

"No sane man canoes through fog like this. The chances of striking reefs or being overturned by waves you never saw coming are too great. You can be carried out to sea on thunderous currents and lost forever. You won't be able to help anyone if you're dead."

Asson gestured to the soapstone teapot resting at the edge of the coals. "Have a cup of tea. It will calm your stomach."

Ewinon strode to the fire and slumped down across from Asson. The youth closed his eyes to massage his temples. "Tell me you've had a vision, Asson. Tell me you know what's happening in my village."

"I wish I could have visions on command, but I can't."

Ewinon squinted at him with one skeptical eye. "You really are a poor Kutsitualit, aren't you?"

Asson reached for Ewinon's pack, and drew out the youth's wooden cup. "My talents are meager at best. Old Neechwa, now there was a great Kutsitualit. She's been gone for ten-and-seven summers, but I still miss her." As he dipped the cup into the teapot, the sweetness of dried crowberries rose with the steam. "How's your brain ache?"

"The tunghaks have made me so sick to my stomach—"

"If you will agree to sleep afterward, I'll drive the tunghaks out of your head. But you have to do as I say."

"I *can't* sleep, Elder. As soon as the Fog Spirits thin out, we must—"

"As soon as the Fog Spirits start to leave, I'll wake you, and we'll be on our way. But right now, you need to let me help you."

The youth had been suffering since midday to the point that any light brought him agony.

"All right, Elder. I'd be grateful."

Asson set the teacup on the sand before him and pulled open the ties on the red and the yellow Spirit pouches hanging from his belt. He took two pinches of powdered willow bark from the red pouch, dropped them into Ewinon's teacup, then added one single leaf of water hemlock plucked from the yellow pouch he had acquired from Traders in the south. During the spring, the tender leaves of the hemlock could be placed inside boots and worn under the feet for those who suffered from unabated brain aches but had to be changed daily. As Asson stirred the concoction with a sliver of driftwood, the sickly sweet scent of raw parsnip wafted up. "Drink all of this, then roll up in your caribou hide."

He handed the cup to Ewinon, knowing full well that the youth would have no choice but to sleep. The Spirit of the water hemlock would force it upon him.

Frustration lined the youth's face as he took the cup in both hands. "Asson, forgive my anger. I just feel so helpless."

"If Sea Woman has chosen to delay us by sending Fog Spirits, there is a good reason for her decision. Perhaps we are not supposed to arrive until tomorrow."

"But you told me we had to leave Soapstone Village that instant if I wanted to help my family—"

"Sea Woman must have seen something that forced her to change her mind."

Ewinon's mouth puckered with distaste. "Your Spirit Helper is fickle."

"She can be."

Ewinon took a long drink of the bitter liquid and wrinkled his nose. "What a dreadful brew."

"Indeed." Asson frowned at the mist. The Fog Spirits were closing in around them like a dark, protective wall. "When it's time for us to leave, Sea Woman will call the Fog Spirits back to her cave beneath the sea, and release us. But for now, you must close your eyes and allow the Spirits of the sacred plants to help you."

Ewinon tipped the cup all the way up and drained every swallow; then he stuffed the cup back in his pack. Veils of fog swayed around him. "My sisters are eight. And Camtac is just ten-and-four winters old. They must be terrified. Gods, I wish I was there."

At the guilt on Ewinon's face, Asson's heart constricted. A mentor's task was to point out the path and the pitfalls, but the sojourner had to find his own way through the darkness. And he always walked alone. If a sojourner was fortunate, in the last moments he would discover a lamp to light the path. Most never did.

Of course, Asson made a clumsy teacher. He never seemed able to explain the intricacies of Spirit Power, and when he did, his students ran away like scared rabbits.

When his thoughts began to turn to the great Kutsitualits and Lightning Spirits who'd taught him, he was assaulted by feelings of inadequacy. He frowned at Ewinon. "Do you regret that you moved to Soapstone Village to join with Mapet?"

"No, of course not. I love her with all my heart, but—"

"But you wish she'd moved to your village, as women traditionally do, which means you would be there right now fighting alongside your father and Gower."

Ewinon hung his head and stared at the sand. Wet black hair fell around his face. He appeared to be considering the matter, but the answer was clear on his tormented face.

"Ewinon, stop peering into your own souls, and sit here with me in this world for a few instants."

Ewinon's frown lessened as he looked up. "I'm here, Elder."

"I don't think so. I think your souls are occupied killing Wobee."

Ewinon sat back on the sand and blinked. "Well . . . yes."

"You don't even know that your family is dead, but already you're will-ing to kill every ice-haired man, woman, and child—"

"I will *not* kill a child."

Asson stabbed a finger at the two caribou hides that lay rolled, warming, beside the fire. "I want you to go to your hides, and try to sleep without killing anyone in your dreams."

"That's impossible, Elder. Once my souls are freed in sleep I'm going to hunt them down—"

"If you don't stop, it will sap the strength you're going to need tomorrow."

Ewinon stared out at the glistening night, and his jaw clenched. The waves behind him washed the shore in smooth, gentle strokes, though Asson couldn't see the water now, just dense fog.

"I'll sleep, but not for long."

"Agreed."

The youth reached over, rolled out his caribouhide, and pulled it around him. He flopped onto his left side with his back to Asson.

*Finally.*

Asson took a long drink from his teacup and watched the Fog Spirits eddying in the firelight. The crackling of the driftwood fire mingled with the surging waves, reminding him of the Spirit Cave. He longed to be sleeping on his soft bearhide, surrounded by the fragrances of damp moss and spruce needles while he spoke with old friends.

"What do the Wobee want, Asson?"

He frowned. "I thought you were asleep?"

"Not yet."

"Are you asking why they attacked Whale Rib Village?"

"No, I mean why are they here in our lands?"

Asson wrapped both hands around his warm cup. "When I last saw them, ten winters ago, they wanted furs, slaves, and timber. Perhaps they want the same things now."

Ewinon tugged the hide about his tall body. "If anything has happened to my family, I—"

"No man, even one unplagued with a brain ache, could have canoed faster than you did today. Now forgive yourself and sleep."

Ewinon vented a deep sigh and rolled to his back. In less than three-tens of heartbeats, his breathing had gone deep with sleep.

Asson sipped his tea. The tart sweetness eased some of the tension in his shoulders. He didn't blame Ewinon, but the youth's intense emotions affected Asson like a beating with a stick. They made it hard to concen-trate on the important things.

He peered down into his plum-colored tea. In the firelight, he could see his reflection. His shoulder-length black hair hung in stringy locks, and his nose resembled a long, pointed beak protruding from a nest of wrinkles. The scent of crowberries rose from the cup. He loved crowberries. Every summer he collected them from the uplands above his cave where they grew in wild profusion. He dried basketfuls on sunny rocks for winter storage, then added them to everything from fish stews to . . .

At the edge of his vision, Asson caught a glitter. It crept closer but with agonizing slowness. He didn't wish to alarm Ewinon, so he said nothing while he kept an eye on the movement. It was low to the ground, like something crawling toward them.

Amid the white glitter a black spot appeared. Asson's eyes narrowed. He set his cup down and rose to his feet.

Cautious, Asson walked toward it. When he got closer, a faint whimper sounded. He continued one step at a time, hoping not to frighten it. A grayish-white head and black nose appeared. Asson stopped. The fox's eyes had slitted against pain. Shallow breaths puffed its chest.

He circled wide to try to understand what he was seeing. He traced the animal's path. The fox had hopped on three legs for as long as it could, then it had dropped to its belly and dragged itself toward their camp with one wounded front leg flopping. Part of an arrow, about two hands long, still jutted from its right shoulder. Blood soaked the animal's side and belly.

"What is it?" Ewinon propped himself up on his elbows.

"Go back to sleep."

Ewinon started to rise, and Asson held out a hand to halt him. "Stay where you are. It's a wounded animal."

"What kind of animal?"

"An injured . . . fox. I think."

As Asson walked closer, the fox closed its eyes. It breathed in swift pants. "It turns out that I do need your help, Ewinon. Please bring me a bowl of water."

Ewinon threw off his hide, yawned, and reached for the water bladder beside the teapot.

While the young man found a bowl to fill, Asson sat down beside the fox and pulled its soft head onto his lap. At his touch, the fox trembled. Its paws jerked, as though trying to run with no more strength than a dying rabbit.

He whispered, "Did you come looking for me? Why?"

The fox's muzzle fell open, and he could see the sharp teeth that lined the jaws.

"Look how small it is!" Ewinon said. "At most that fox is two hand-lengths tall at the shoulder, and five long. Is it dying? Are we going to eat it? Is that why you're—"

"Bring me the water." Asson held out a hand.

Ewinon approached and extended the bowl. "That's a lot of blood. It's a wonder it's still alive."

Asson dipped his fingers into the bowl and trickled water into the beautiful creature's mouth. A relieved groan came from the fox's throat as it swallowed the droplets. When the bowl was half-empty, Asson opened the blue Spirit pouch hanging from his belt and added a pinch of crushed marsh laurel. A powerful sedative, people often used it to destroy themselves. He tipped the fox's head up and trickled the rest of the laurel-infused water onto the animal's tongue. It watched him with wet eyes, as though terrified to trust him.

Softly, he said, "I'm going to pull out the arrow and bandage your wound. You're going to be all right."

The fox licked the water from its muzzle, and closed its eyes again.

Ewinon knelt beside Asson to study the fox. "It is a fox . . . correct?"

Asson made an offhand gesture. "I need my pack from the canoe. Could you get it for me?"

Ewinon rose. "Don't think I failed to notice that you didn't answer my question." He went to the canoe but kept casting glances back over his shoulder. As he pulled Asson's wolfhide pack from the bow, he called, "Do you need the whole thing, or do you wish me bring you something specific?"

"Bring the entire pack. I'm not sure what I'll need."

Asson searched the fox's fur for other wounds that might not be so apparent. He discovered she was female but found no other injuries. The weapon had passed through her shoulder and lodged against her chest wall. With every step the fox had taken, the metal arrow point had sliced back and forth. Shredded muscle quivered beneath his probing fingers. The pain must be excruciating.

When Asson thought the marsh laurel had stunned the fox's senses, he gripped the bloody shaft and carefully worked it from the animal's flesh. Snarls rumbled the animal's throat, but the cries were faint and senseless.

Asson examined the bloody point. He wiped it on his hide pants and then stuck his tongue to it. "This is Wobee iron. It tastes of having been melted."

"They *melt* iron?"

"Yes. I've seen them do it. When I was a boy."

"Asson?" Ewinon asked in a worried voice. His dark eyes glanced from the fox to Asson and back. "That's not the same fox we saw outside of Soapstone Village, is it?"

"I honestly don't know."

"Really? Or are you just saying that to keep me calm?"

Asson petted the fox's back. So soft. She'd just started to change color, losing her snowy winter fur and growing grayer, though her belly was still pure white where it wasn't soaked with blood. "I'm not sure what she is. But I want you to go back to sleep and leave me to my task. I don't need your help to bandage her wounds."

South Wind Woman sniffed around the fox, ruffling the white tufts of her ears, then drifted to Ewinon and rattled his seal-gut hood.

Ewinon glared at the fox for a long time before he said, "After you bandage her wound, what are you going to do with her?"

"Do with her?"

"Don't pretend you're befuddled. You know exactly what I'm asking."

Asson's bushy brows plunged down. "Let me ask you a question?"

"What?"

"How was the world created?"

Ewinon scowled at him as though he knew Asson was engaged in lesson teaching and it annoyed him. "Why? Have you forgotten? The world was created when Raven harpooned land from his canoe. He kept pulling on his harpoon, and more and more land kept coming up."

"Yes. In the same way, you've harpooned this fox with your fear. If you keep pulling, there's no telling what will emerge."

"What does that mean?"

"Just what I said."

The Fog Spirits blew around Ewinon. He squinted through them at Asson. He returned to his former question. "What are you going to do with the fox?"

Asson sighed. "I'm going to let her go."

"Is that the truth, or are you just trying to get me to go away?"

"I'm trying to get you to go away. But it's also the truth."

Ewinon heaved an exhausted breath. The Spirit of the water hemlock should be running with his blood by now. "Very well, I'll go, but first promise me you'll tie her up before you fall asleep. I don't want to wake with her teeth embedded in my windpipe."

"Don't worry, great warrior. I won't let this tiny half-dead fox kill you. I give you my oath."

Ewinon shook his head at the slight and marched back to his hide. This time, he lay down facing Asson and the hurt arctic fox. Ewinon kept opening one eye to glance at them, until sleep overwhelmed him.

Asson untied the laces on his pack, drew out a tuft of moss, along with several strips of seal leather, and set about creating a poultice for the arrow wound.

Barely audibly, Asson whispered, "Are you a fox, little one?"

When Kiran tiptoed down into the hold around midnight, he found Thyra asleep next to one of the goats, her head pillowed on one arm. The sound of his footsteps woke the goat; it lifted its black head and nibbled hay as it watched him.

Kiran stood for some time staring at Thyra. What a painting this would make: the sleeping woman, her ivory hair tumbling over the hay, the black goat with shining eyes lying beside her, the monstrous leaping shadows cast over the walls by the lamp he carried. He smiled. Thyra looked so young and innocent, and very beautiful.

He walked over and looked down at her. Softly, he said, "I just needed to see you, Thyra."

He sat down cross-legged and set his lamp to one side. In the flickering gleam, he noticed that her hands and feet were twitching, like the paws of a dreaming dog. That was new. Was she dreaming, or was she still riding Sleipnir to the dark underworlds to find the souls of Rolf and Sokkolf? He had no idea.

Kiran heaved a sigh and glanced around at the boxes, crates, and wine barrels that filled the hold. Deep down in his soul, Thyra's magic worried him. He struggled constantly with his priest's warning: *All such magic comes from the great adversary, Satan. Have nothing to do with it, or you risk damning your soul to eternal flames.*

What would Thyra do if she knew that Kiran suspected her magical journey was wicked, something orchestrated by Satan himself? Kiran knew only that it would hurt her and it was very important to him never to hurt her. She was such a strange mystical creature, at times he wasn't sure how to treat her or what to say to her. He had not expected to be so drawn to the magical apprentice of the man he considered to be the very embodiment of Satan on earth: the Lawspeaker.

Kiran lightly stroked her arm. The skin felt silken.

He felt certain that if she were the tool of Satan he would not love her so much. It wasn't possible. Somehow, he would sense the evil and his feelings would vanish. Instead, every day his love for her grew stronger.

Kiran let his gaze move from her face down her white throat and to the swells of her breasts visible beneath her white chemise. He so longed to run his hands over every curve of her body. Sometimes, like now, the need was a physical ache.

He drew his fingers down her arm to where her hand rested upon the hay. "You're not lost down there, are you, Thyra? Godi Gunnar said he'd heard of Seidur seers getting lost on their underworld journeys. That's what woke me up out of a sound sleep. I heard you calling my name, and you were crying."

Her hand twitched beneath his fingers.

Kiran stretched out in the hay beside her. The goat watched him as it chewed its cud. He could hear the hay crunching in its mouth. When she felt him beside her, Thyra's hands and feet stopped twitching. He gently lifted her hand and pressed her fingers to his lips. They were so cold. "I'm just going to put my arm around you, Thyra, to warm you up. You're freezing."

As he moved closer to her, the ache intensified until it was almost unbearable. He stretched his arm across her and held her close for such a long time that when the pink light of dawn streamed into the hold it surprised him. He sat up and rubbed his eyes.

The goat had wandered off and curled up five paces distant. The animal was sound asleep.

"I have to go, Thyra. The godi is expecting me at first light. I pray I'm not late already."

Tenderly, he leaned over and kissed her lips. She didn't move. He petted her long hair, letting the silken feel of the strands seep into his soul; then he rose to his feet.

His lamp had burned out sometime in the night. As he walked over to pick it up, he whispered, "You've been gone too long, Thyra. Something's wrong. I know it. Forget about Rolf and Sokkolf. Come home. Please. Just come home."

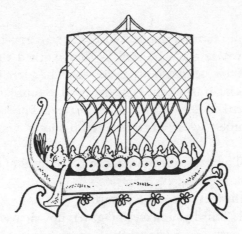

# Seventeen

The sweetness of trampled spring grasses suffused the dawn air. The fog had thinned to a faint mist.

Kiran took a deep breath and listened to the colonists laugh and scold their children as they carried their packed belongings to the gangplank that extended from *Thor's Dragon* to the shore. They had to get loaded with haste; the tide would be rolling in soon to swallow this shore. The booths had been dismantled and the poles bundled for the voyage. The bundles rested in stacks a short distance from the gangplank. Everyone seemed eager to find the other seven ships and begin building the lives they'd hoped for.

In the distance, a large herd of kosweet ran like the wind over the rolling hills. The sight unchained something in Kiran's soul, something he never knew existed. He couldn't help but long to be out there dashing through the wilderness with them.

Kiran wiped his sweating brow on his tan sleeve. Early that morning, they'd hauled a heavy spruce timber up the gangplank and onto the deck, then affixed three towlines to it, one to step the timber into the mast position, and ease it through the hole in the deck, and the other two to keep it steady during the process. Once the mast had been lowered into its framing, Godi Gunnar would clamp an iron bracket around it, hammer in the locking pin, and secure the bracket to the deck, while Vilfil and Finnbogi did the same below.

To prepare, Godi Gunnar had asked Kiran to carry Thyra's limp body to his quarters, where she'd be safe as they worked the new mast into place. The feel of her slender body in his arms had left Kiran longing for so much more. As he grasped the rope, he tried to reorganize his thoughts.

"Ready?" Bjarni called to the three teams. The redhead's wedge-shaped face streamed sweat. He'd braided his long, wavy hair to keep it out of the way.

"Yes, ready!" The calls went down the three lines and men took good grips on their ropes. "Ready!"

Kiran braced his feet to pull back hard.

Bjarni shouted, "Gird yourselves! Tighten up! Heave!"

Kiran heaved with all his strength. Groans erupted down the line as men labored against the weight of the spruce timber. Backing up a step at a time, they slid the new mast through the hole in the deck and pulled the spruce timber into position amidships on *Thor's Dragon*. The other lines stretched taut, keeping it stable while Godi Gunnar and Vilfil worked like fiends, clamping down the brackets and hammering in the locking pins.

Kiran's muscles went rock hard beneath the swaying weight.

"Ho!" Godi Gunnar called as he stood up with one fist raised in success. "We're sitting lovely now! She'll hold through ten more storms. Good work, all. Bjarni, if you'll see that the sail is hoisted and secured, we'll be on our way with the tide. Kiran, may I see you, please?"

Kiran released his grip on the rope and strode across the rocking deck to meet Godi Gunnar halfway. The godi looked thinner today, and more careworn. The settlers had been at him all morning, uttering one complaint after another. Blond hair hung about the godi's shoulders, and his deep wrinkles seemed sculpted of dark brown leather.

Godi Gunnar said, "I can pay you for your work in gold if you like, Kiran, but—"

"I'd rather have red cloth, Godi, if that's all right? Elrik said his people believe that all blood-colored things have life in them. They value life."

"You're a born merchant, Kristni. You're going to do just fine out here in the business of trade." Gunnar lifted a hand to his maidservant. "Arnora, could you fetch an arm's length of red cloth for Kiran?"

"Yes, Godi."

Arnora's long reddish-brown hair bounced as she trotted down the stairway to the lower deck.

Kiran wiped his brow on his dirty sleeve. The colonists had already hauled their packs to the gangplank, and waited for Godi Gunnar's invitation to board. The strongest men held the tethers of the livestock a short distance away. The cattle, sheep, and goats would come up last and be tethered on deck until they anchored for the night; then they'd be off-loaded and taken out to graze.

"How may I serve you, Godi?"

"You're not serving me, Kiran, you're working for me, and you can call me Gunnar. You don't have to—"

"You've been Godi to me since I was a boy. I'm not sure I can change that."

Godi Gunnar smiled. "Well enough, then. Can you help get the settlers aboard and secure them below?"

"I can, yes."

Arnora trotted up the stairs clutching the piece of red cloth. "Here it is, Kiran."

"Thank you, Arnora." Kiran folded the cloth and tucked it inside his shirt.

Arnora gave him a heartbreaking look. "I know you'll soon traipse off on your own adventure, and I want you to know I'm going to miss you. We all are."

"I will miss you more. You're my family, and have been for almost longer than I can remember. I . . . I don't know what I'll do without you."

"When we all earn our freedom, maybe you'll hire us for your trading company?"

"I will, Arnora. Anyone who wants to come with me will be welcome. But you'll see me often until that time comes."

She stood on her tiptoes to kiss his cheek, said, "Then this is just good-bye for now," and left to attend to her duties.

Kiran gazed at the waiting colonists. The children raced up and down the sand, laughing and throwing seashells at one another, while the adults swatted at the huge cloud of iridescent black flies that swarmed them. The little beasts had nasty bites. Kiran wondered what Elrik's people, the People of the Songtrail, used to keep them away. He hadn't thought to ask before he'd left.

Kiran took a deep breath and held it in his lungs, feeling the air, before he let it go. He'd just started to dream of what life as a free man might mean. He didn't want big things. Just small moments. He wanted to bring Elrik home and set him free, and he longed to marry Thyra. Though he knew that so long as she belonged to the Lawspeaker that was impossible.

*Thor's Dragon* swayed beneath Kiran's feet, reminding him of his work. He strode to the gangplank and trotted onto it to start gathering up the settlers. Halfway down, his heart caught in his throat.

He stopped dead, staring at the line of armed warriors who'd just crested the hill fifty paces behind the settlers. Because of the angle of the hill, the settlers couldn't see them yet. If something wasn't done, the colonists would panic and arrows would be loosed before anyone knew why the Skraelings had come.

Kiran turned and called, "*Godi?*"

Godi Gunnar straightened from where he'd been kneeling beside Bjarni and stared at Kiran. Kiran lifted a hand toward the Skraelings. The godi's eyes widened. He quickly surmised that the settlers couldn't yet see their strange guests. When surprised voices erupted from the crew, the godi lifted both hands for silence.

Godi Gunnar strode to the middle of the gangplank to stand beside Kiran and examine the line of men. "They're armed."

"Why wouldn't they be, Godi? They were probably out hunting kosweet when they saw us."

Godi Gunnar exchanged a glance with Kiran, and nodded. "Will you act as translator?"

"I will."

"Then it's just you and me, and I want no blustering. Let's see if we can get the settlers to grasp this situation before we've got more trouble than we can handle."

Godi Gunnar strode down the plank, and went straight to the big farmer, Porkell the Elder, who'd become the unofficial leader of the settlers. Porkell stood behind the main group, holding the tether of two milk cows. In his fifty-seventh year, he towered over the other settlers, and stood slightly taller even than Kiran. Red-faced, like all those in his family, he had white hair and a scraggly beard. A slow-talking, ominous man, Porkell was perhaps the most beloved elder. He always spoke his mind, but in low, direct tones that generated deep respect from others. Dressed in an old gray cloak that had been mended in dozens of places, his sharp green eyes missed nothing. He'd already started glancing over his shoulder at the hill and frowning, as though he knew they saw something he did not.

Before they reached him, Porkell handed the reins of his milk cows off to another settler and walked out to meet Godi Gunnar and Kiran. "What's afoot, Godi? I can see from your face that we're in trouble."

"No, we're not. Not yet, and we won't be if you'll listen to me."

Porkell's brow furrowed. "What is it?"

"Kiran and I are going to speak with the strangers who just appeared on the hill behind you. They've shown no signs of malice, and until they do, I won't have anyone reaching for a weapon. You understand what I'm saying, Porkell?"

Porkell's white head dipped in a single nod. "They are Skraelings, I suppose?"

"They are. If you can do it without appearing to be in a rush, I think we should get the women and children on board quick as possible. Then everyone else, and last the livestock. Will you handle that? Call for Bjarni if you need assistance."

Porkell searched the hills again, saw nothing, and his piercing gaze returned to Godi Gunnar. "I'll get them aboard and keep a firm hand while you're gone, but hurry. We've some young men with fiery blood, as you well know. Helgi's likely to be troublesome."

"I know, Porkell. We'll return soon as we can. Let's be about it, Kiran."

Gunnar led the way up the grassy hill at an unhurried but purposeful pace. Fifty men had lined up on the rocky crest of the ridge. All were painted red, and bristled with weapons. Quivers stuffed with arrows draped shoulders, knives and hatchets hung from belts, and almost every man carried a lance and bow. Gunnar had been in worse situations, but not many.

He smiled, which he figured was a universal symbol of good faith, but as they got closer the dour expressions of the warriors made his stomach knot up. "Hold your hands out, Kiran. Just so they know we mean no harm."

"Godi, when we've made another ten paces, could I take the lead?"

Gunnar turned to frown at the youth. Kiran might be sixteen, but he was a man with the heart of a lion. "I always strive to put myself between others and harm, but if you think that's best, I—"

"I do, Godi."

They climbed through a fragrant patch of wildflowers to reach the crest of the hill; then Kiran stepped out in front of Gunnar, and stopped. For just a few moments, Kiran's green eyes scanned the men. He walked straight toward a boyishly handsome fellow with long black hair and a flat nose.

Gunnar followed two paces behind, his gaze darting over the curious faces of the warriors. With the warmth today, many wore only hide aprons. He found it striking that they'd coated their skin, their lances, and even their shell jewelry with what appeared to be a mix of red ochre and grease, which meant iron deposits existed close by. The fellow Kiran approached had white rings painted around his eyes, and red ochre over the rest of his face and hair.

Kiran held his hands wider, said, "*Datyun*," and walked forward to kneel before the man. Kiran spoke respectfully to him. Surprised that Kiran spoke his tongue, the man rattled off a string of questions. Kiran answered back several times.

When the man gestured for Kiran to stand, he did. Kiran was a good two heads taller, and his shoulders spread twice as wide. The man said something harsh.

Kiran turned and gestured to Gunnar. It must have been an introduction, for Gunnar heard his name amid the other sounds.

The man stared unblinking at Gunnar, sizing him up. He asked Kiran something.

Kiran turned to Gunnar. "This is Chief Drona of Soapstone Village, which sits a short distance to the south. He asked why we've come to their lands. I told him we wished to trade with them. The chief responded that he didn't believe me. He thinks we've come to make war upon them."

Gunnar knew the stories of previous Norse voyages to Markland and Vinland where both sides had killed the other. Was that where Drona had gotten the notion?

Gunnar frowned. "Kiran, please tell the chief that we are a peaceful people." Gunnar extended a hand to his ship. "I brought a shipload of goods to trade. War is the last thing I want."

Kiran relayed the message. Chief Drona vented a disbelieving laugh and rapid words passed down the line of warriors. Expressions turned hostile. Several of the warriors took new grips on their lances, as though preparing to slaughter Kiran and Gunnar.

"What's happening, Kiran?"

"I'm not sure yet, Godi. Apparently one of their villages was just attacked." Kiran's handsome face slackened as he listened to their conversations. "Godi . . . the village was attacked by Wobee, which is what they call us."

The surge of panic that rushed through Gunnar left him feeling ill. *Our people. It must be.* "How many ships have they seen?"

Kiran asked the chief and the man answered in a voice that could have cut glass.

"Four, Godi, including our ship."

"Four out of eight. I wonder which ones survived?"

Chief Drona kept eyeing Gunnar like a slab of meat he longed to carve up for his warriors.

"How far away are the other ships?" Gunnar glanced down the hill at *Thor's Dragon.* The settlers had all boarded, and Bjarni—*Thank the gods for Bjarni*—had hoisted the sail, set the rigging, and gotten all the oarsmen into position. Porkell had just commenced leading the mooing milk cows up the gangplank and onto the deck.

Kiran spoke for a considerable time with Chief Drona. The chief sounded upset, and Kiran was trying to calm him in a low, soothing voice. They spoke for such a long time that Gunnar became worried about their topic. These people may have blood feuds, same as the Greenlanders did. If Thorlak had murdered Drona's relatives, did that give Drona the right to take payment in the form of Wobee lives—even if Gunnar and his settlers had had nothing to do with the attack?

Finally, Kiran turned. Wind blew his black curls around his bearded face. "The village that was attacked is two days' run to the south. His people have been watching us, and when it appeared that we were readying our ship to sail away, Chief Drona came to make sure we left. He wants you to know that he'll be sending a war party to run along the shore, to parallel our course. If we weigh anchor and set foot anywhere in their lands, they will attack us."

"Well," Gunnar exhaled the word. "At least he's forthright about it."

Chief Drona's eyes kept shifting from Kiran to Gunnar. While he didn't understand their words, the man seemed to be a good judge of facial expressions. Gunnar took that to heart.

"Kiran, translate as I go, if you will?" Kiran nodded, and Gunnar lifted his gaze and looked Drona in the eyes with all the honesty he could muster. "Chief, I want only peace with your people. I don't know who the Wobee are that attacked your village, but I'm very angry about it."

Kiran translated, and Drona's eyes narrowed, listening, but skeptically.

Gunnar continued, "I am a judge in my country."

Kiran hesitated as though trying to decide how to translate that. When he had, Gunnar added, "*I give you my oath* that I will hold the people who did this responsible for their actions. I don't know how you settle such tragedies, but we will pay the wergild, the blood money, you demand. Within reason, of course."

"Godi," Kiran cautioned, "we don't know how many died. The wergild might be everything you own. I'm not sure you want to—"

"Just tell him. Either we find a way to befriend these people, or our colonizing effort is dead right now, Kiran. Tell him."

Drona studied Kiran through thoughtful eyes as he finished relaying the message.

After speaking, Kiran expelled a breath. Drona must have seen it as a sign that Kiran was disturbed by what Gunnar had said and even, perhaps, disagreed.

Drona's expression didn't change. He stared hard into Gunnar's eyes, evaluating his soul, it seemed. All up and down the line of warriors, men spoke in curious voices. When half shouts erupted from disbelieving men, Drona lifted a hand to quiet the commotion. As the voices died down, he blinked at Gunnar, then spoke to Kiran.

Kiran nodded and turned. "Chief Drona says that he agrees the proper Spirit balance must be returned to the world, but he wants to know if you understand their law of retribution?"

"Of course not. Do you, Kiran?"

"I think so, Godi. It's similar to our laws on the issue of blood feuds. Elrik said that in the case of murder, the victim's family had the right to claim goods, the life of the murderer, or someone in the murderer's family, as recompense."

"Well, if the family member is innocent, that will be tough to swallow, but perhaps we can negotiate the matter down to goods."

"The Lawspeaker—"

"Yes, if Thorlak is alive, he and I will be at each other's throats over this. Before we continue, ask Chief Drona if our understanding is correct."

Kiran spoke to Drona and the chief gave Gunnar a dour nod.

"Very well, then," Gunnar replied. "Explain to Chief Drona that our laws are very similar and, *as the judge in this matter,* I agree to those terms. Make sure he understands and agrees that I will act as judge."

Kiran and Drona spoke.

Kiran's brow furrowed. "Godi, he says that he cannot make such a decision alone. He must consult with the Village Council of elders, and with the survivors of Whale Rib Village."

Gunnar's head jerked in a nod. "I am agreeable to that. Where shall we convene court?"

Kiran and Drona exchanged several sentences, and Kiran turned back to Gunnar. "They wish to meet us at Whale Rib Village at midday tomorrow, and want some assurance that we will, in fact, be there."

Gunnar spread his arms. "What can we give them to guarantee our sincerity?"

"I don't . . ." Kiran blinked. Slowly, so as not to alarm anyone, he reached into his shirt and pulled out the folded length of red fabric, then bowed and presented it to Drona. For the first time, the chief's eyes flew wide in what appeared to be amazement.

"I'll replace that, Kiran."

"That's not necessary, Godi. It was my gift to him."

Drona unfolded the cloth and held it up to flap in the breeze while he showed it to his men. Several warriors came forward with their jaws gaping to examine the fine woolen fabric. Awed whispers rose. Drona ran his hand over the weave, then squinted at Kiran and asked a question.

Kiran bowed with what seemed to be deep reverence. When Kiran answered, shocked voices chattered, and Drona inhaled a breath, as if the words stunned him. Drona responded in a voice that sounded at once grievous and threatening. Kiran listened with a clamped jaw.

"Oh, no . . ."

"What is it?"

Kiran squeezed his eyes closed in obvious pain. Drona watched every nuance of his expression; then his gaze shifted to Gunnar, to evaluate Gunnar's response when Kiran explained: "Godi, the chief asked why I would give him such an extravagant gift, and I told him it was in honor of my friend Elrik, who'd been born among the People of the Songtrail. Then he told me that *they* are the People of the Songtrail. The village that was attacked by the Wobee is Elrik's home village."

"Gods above, I pray these are not Elrik's relatives."

"Drona's son-in-law is Elrik's brother, Ewinon, but the rest of his family was in Whale Rib Village. They may all be dead. He says that he fears their *tarneqs* are wandering the hills in rage."

"What's a tarneq?"

"The People of the Songtrail believe that each person has four souls. The tarneq is the visible ghost that is seen after death. Then there's the *puqlii*, the soul that keeps a person alive, the *yuuciq*, the personality, and the *avneq*, the voice. Powerful holy people can summon the avneq to speak with the long dead."

Gunnar massaged his forehead. He had enough trouble managing his one soul. He hated to imagine what sort of mess he could create with four. "Did you tell them that Elrik is my thrall?"

"No, Godi."

"Good. Let's keep that as a lever in case we require it. Kiran—if you can in good conscience—please tell the chief that I am a man of honor and will make sure that Elrik's relatives are fairly treated. Ask him for directions to Whale Rib Village, and tell him we'll meet him there two days from now to settle this matter, if that is acceptable. We want this done soon as possible."

As Kiran spoke, the tight lines at the corners of the chief's eyes relaxed. Kiran translated Drona's reply, "The chief agrees and will send canoes to guide our ship to the village, which sits upon a sea cliff to the south."

Gunnar hesitated. "One last thing, Kiran. Could you ask Chief Drona if he's ever heard of a chief named Avaldamon or a woman named Vethild?"

Kiran gave Gunnar a curious look but turned to Drona and relayed the question.

Drona shook his head. Without further discussion, Drona lifted his lance to his warriors and trotted away. The entire party followed him.

When they'd vanished over the crest of the hill, Gunnar heaved a shaky breath. "I don't know what would have happened without you, Kiran. You may have just saved the lives of everyone aboard *Thor's Dragon*. You're worth your weight in gold as a translator in this new land."

Kiran's bearded face was grim. "I can't believe this is how I first meet the People of the Songtrail. Thyra and I promised Elrik that we would find his family, and Kapusa's family, and tell them that he and Kapusa were well and still loved them."

Kiran's pained expression touched Gunnar. As children, Kiran, Kapusa, and Elrik had been inseparable, more like brothers and sister than best friends. "Well, let's see if we can repair some of the damage caused by—"

"Godi, I'm worried about what will happen if other members of the godar, or the Lawspeaker, are alive and do not agree with the terms you made today. If you can't keep your promises—"

"I *will* keep my promises to Drona." As Gunnar turned to give Kiran a stern look, wind whipped blond hair around his wrinkled face. "But, I'll admit, I'm already contriving a fallback plan."

They stared at each other. Behind Kiran's eyes Gunnar saw disturbing thoughts stirring.

"What is it, Kiran?"

"It's just . . . I must go with you, Godi. If I'm not there to translate—"

"Great gods," Gunnar blurted in relief, and clamped a hand on the youth's broad shoulder. "I'm desperately glad to hear you say that." After a brief hesitation, he added, "You weren't listening when I said you might be worth your weight in gold, were you?"

"I was, actually."

Gunnar chuckled. "All right, then."

"Godi . . ." Kiran hesitated. "If Thyra has not returned by the time we—"

"I'm worried about her, as well. I've seen Seidur magic go very wrong, killing those who wielded it. But I haven't given up hope, and you shouldn't, either."

"But what if her soul returns here and we're gone?"

"Thyra will find us no matter where we are. I've heard that the magical steed Sleipnir is guided by the location of the seer's body."

Kiran gazed out long and hard at the rolling green hills. "I pray you're right, Godi."

Gunnar gave him a sympathetic glance, and started down the slope through the wildflowers. Far out in the distance, he could see the water changing color. Bjarni must have seen it, too. He stood at the top of the gangplank with a worried expression. Wild red hair whipped around his head.

"Tide's coming in. We'd best hurry before we have to swim for it."

# Eighteen

## Thyra

You're safe. I'm here." *A man's disembodied voice drifts around me.* "I'm not leaving you."

*Is he real?*

*In my dreams, I'm fourteen and starving, stumbling along the deepest fjords in Denmark, using rocks to carve flesh from winter-killed carcasses, terrified every moment that bears or outlaws will find me. The malady struck so fast that I barely understand what happened. Just after the arrival of the ealdorman, Father fell ill.*

*I recall almost nothing. One afternoon Mother is soaking my hair with cool water to ease my fever, and the next time I wake she is gone. The house is cold. I find her body, along with my father and brother, all in the same bed, frozen beneath a mound of blankets.*

*I am suffering and so weak I can barely pull myself from my icy blankets. It's two days' walk to the next farm. I know I can't make it. In a daze, I wander about our home, eating everything there is left to eat, and shoving every stick of wood Father has chopped into the fireplace. When the scent of rotting bodies becomes too much to bear, I wrap Thord in a blanket and drag him outside into the snow. I try to drag Mother and Father, but they are so heavy, I collapse to the wood-plank floor in sobs.*

*My world is on fire with suffering and I'm sure the gods are on fire with me. Where is Jesus? After we converted, six months ago, Mother and I prayed to him every day. I do not understand the failure of gods.*

*Then . . .*

*I'm stumbling up the fjord. My head is too heavy to lift. When I see the men on horseback, I just stop and stare. They ride up the rocky trail toward me like sparkling visions. Tears streak my sunburned face. I lock my knees and wait for them.*

*The big man on the red stallion smiles. "Look at that wealth of ice-colored hair. No wonder he sent us to make sure the plague hadn't killed her. I guess it killed half the ealdorman's soldiers. She'll fetch a full mark of gold."*

*His friend just chuckles as he dismounts.*

*I say, "I have an uncle and aunt . . . in Uppsala. I need to get to them. Please, help me?"*

*They grab hold of my arms. "Oh, sure we will," the big man with rotten teeth says.*

*I feel my wounded body being lifted. I struggle.*

*"You're safe," the alien man speaks again in a soothing voice. "Don't waste your strength trying to run. Your arrow wound is fevered. Just sleep. I'll stand guard over you."*

*I feel my exhausted body lowered onto a soft hide and hear the roar of the ocean. Where am I? I try to open my eyes but can't. Heavy fog coats my face. The fragrant air is foreign, filled with the scent of wildflowers I do not know. It frightens me.*

*As sleep descends in quiet darkness, the memories of being held in chains aboard the ship to Greenland will not leave me alone. We thralls are crowded shoulder to shoulder. There isn't even enough space to lie down. The stench is suffocating. I can't stop crying.*

*The only thing that keeps me sane is the sound of my Other Mother's voice calling my name over and over. . . .*

Asson sank down beside the canoe and propped one arm on the gunwale. The wounded fox kept running in her sleep. Her legs jerked and faint yips and growls came from her throat. It worried him. The horrors that lay buried in her souls must have been stirred by her fever.

Asson hoped that she would find the place inside where those who struggled could rest. Tufts of mist drifted up the beach with feather-like slowness. But suspended far out above the lavender-hued ocean, the Fog Spirits curled in serpentine patterns. He sniffed the air. Mother Ocean was rising. They couldn't remain here for long.

The fox whimpered. Asson reached to pet her but stopped. His hand hovered above the bloody fur and twitching paws. He drew his hand back. If he touched her, he would just distract her from the journey.

His gaze moved to the fire where Ewinon flopped to his back. Ewinon awoke slowly, as though rebelling against the Spirit of the marsh laurel. Finally, Ewinon dragged himself upright and blinked around at the beach camp. His gaze lingered on the fresh driftwood burning in the fire and the six salmon, skewered on sticks, that canted at angles suspended over the flames. Asson had caught them at dawn. The delicious scent of bubbling fish skins filled the air. As Ewinon rubbed slumber from his eyes, he searched for Asson.

"I'm over here."

Ewinon swung around and saw Asson sitting beside the canoe with one elbow propped on the gunwale. Long, tangled black hair straggled down the youth's back. His brown eyes appeared swollen, as though he'd slept hard.

"It's dawn!" Ewinon jumped to his feet. "I told you to wake me as soon as the Fog Spirits left!"

"Yes, but I didn't want to disappoint you."

*"What?"*

Confused, Ewinon folded up his sleeping hide and stalked across the sand toward Asson to toss it into the canoe, apparently to hurry their departure.

Asson smiled at him, then his gaze moved to the two people trotting up the misty shore. Asson wasn't sure they, still far away, had spotted his camp yet.

"I can't believe you would just let me sleep! You know how important it is that we . . ." Just before Ewinon hurled the hides into the boat, he saw the arctic fox sleeping in the soft folds of Asson's wolfhide mantle. The animal lay stretched out on her left side with her black nose pointed toward the bow of the canoe. The dried blood that soaked her coat had matted. A leather bandage wrapped her right shoulder and encircled her chest. Tufts of moss protruded around the edges of the bandage.

"I'm surprised," Ewinon said, and some of his anger faded.

"Why is that?"

"It's still a fox."

"The strangest things surprise you. What did you expect it to be?"

Ewinon gave him a disgruntled look and eased his folded sleeping hide into the canoe's stern. "I thought you said you were going to let it go."

"It's comatose. You can't let a comatose animal go."

"You could just leave it on the beach."

"To be killed by bears or wolves, or have its eyes plucked out by birds before it wakes?"

Ewinon glared. "Maybe we should slit its throat and skin it. That way the fox won't have to worry about bears, wolves, or eagles and we'll have fresh meat for our trip."

Asson's brows drew together. He rose to his feet. "The quality of your various souls is genuinely disturbing."

Asson walked toward the fire. The delicious aroma of roasting salmon filled the morning air. The fish had begun to char, the skin shriveling and peeling back.

When he knelt to turn the salmon, he saw that the two people in the distance had started running. They must have seen Asson and Ewinon.

Ewinon, still oblivious, walked up behind Asson and stood with his hands propped on his hips. Light fog eddied around his young face. "Let's grab the fish and go. We can eat as we paddle."

"Really? You can paddle with one hand?"

Asson turned another fish and repropped the roasting stick, sinking the bottom into the sand to keep it at the right angle over the flames. The last fish, however, he picked up and carried back to the canoe. The fox wouldn't mind if it had a few raw spots.

"Asson? We need to leave here," Ewinon insisted.

"Yes, we certainly do."

Asson leaned the stick against the hull to cool, and let his gaze drift over the towering black cliff that ran the length of the beach for as far as he could see. Moisture dripped from the ledges and pattered upon the sand like raindrops. Blended with the rhythms of the waves, it was the purest music.

Ewinon crouched down beside the fire and jerked one of the sticks from the sand. As he rushed to chew the salmon off the stick he frowned and seemed absorbed in his thoughts. "The tide is coming in. Can't you hear it?"

"There's nothing wrong with my hearing, but yours worries me."

Ewinon scowled. "What?"

If North Wind Man were not carrying most of the sound away, the shouting of the runners would be obvious even to Ewinon. The stocky man kept waving his arms, trying to get Ewinon's attention, but Ewinon remained obtuse, seeing images inside his head rather than on the beach.

Asson climbed into the canoe and stepped around the packs to the fox's head. As he crouched beside her muzzle, he pulled the fish into the boat and rested it across the packs. Gingerly, he pulled off chunks of hot fish meat and arranged them around the fox's nose, hoping she would smell the salmon and open her eyes to eat.

While he waited, Asson checked her bandage. The wound had stopped oozing blood, but tunghaks had infested the torn muscles and, as they fed, the flesh swelled and filled with pus.

After she ate, he would cleanse her wounds and add a strong dose of the inner bark of tamarack to her moss poultice. If he couldn't drive away the feasting tunghaks, she would soon meet Anguta, who carries the dead to Adlivun, where they must sleep beside him for one full winter.

The fox's black nose wriggled. Her nostrils flared. Drowsily, one blue eye fluttered.

"You must eat." Asson picked up a chunk of salmon and held it in the palm of his hand before her mouth.

Her neck trembled when she tried to lift her head. She let it fall back to the wolfhide mantle, and stared up at him with glassy eyes.

"Let me help you." Asson sat down and shifted her body so that her head rested across his knees, then he held out the chunk of fish again, right beneath her nose.

A black-spotted tongue darted out, licked the salmon, and then her jaws weakly opened and she used her teeth to pull the meat into her mouth and swallowed it whole.

Asson held out another chunk, and another, until she'd consumed half the salmon. With a deep sigh, she fell fast asleep again.

Asson ate the rest of the delicious fish and wiped his greasy hands on his boots. The grease made them shed water better.

As he eased the fox's white head from his knees, and climbed out of the canoe, he lifted a hand and pointed.

"Look, Ewinon."

Around a mouthful of fish, the youth said, "Look at what?"

Asson gestured to the two people dashing down the shore toward them.

Ewinon lurched to his feet. "Blessed Ancestors, it's Camtac and Gower!"

Ewinon ran so hard to meet them that his boots kicked up spouts of sand. Surprised happy greetings rang out, followed by wild hugging when the people collided at the edge of the waves.

Asson frowned back at the fox, then cocked his head. He heard something strange on North Wind Man's cool breath: *A choking sound, as though a woman was suffocating on her own sobs. He recognized that voice. A jolt of fear went through him. Had something happened to her?*

Simultaneously, the fox let out a tortured whine. Asson's brows lowered, listening to the blended cries of the spectral woman and the fox.

Ewinon called out, "Asson, the Wobee destroyed Whale Rib Village! They—"

"Hurry it up and eat. We have to go," Asson ordered.

Ewinon looked stunned. He muttered to Camtac and Gower.

Asson marched back to the fire, and began rolling up his caribou sleeping hide.

"Good Morning, Blessed Elder," young Camtac called. Long black hair draped around his triangular face.

"Eat, don't talk." Asson gestured to the fish. "In a few heartbeats, we're going to be underwater."

"Yes, Elder. I—I know." Camtac knelt, pulled a roasting stick from the sand, and begin devouring the salmon.

The youth had a dazed look, as though his souls floated in shock. Asson looked at Gower. Short and stocky, muscles bulged through his caribouhide shirt. Grief rested like a cold mantle over his round face.

Asson said, "Eat, Gower."

Gower crouched and grabbed hold of a skewered fish as though to wring the life from it.

"Now, between bites, tell me how many captives they took."

As though he couldn't bear to think about it, Gower stared wet eyed at his salmon. "We don't know if anyone survived, Elder. We ran just before . . ." He glanced at Camtac and sympathy creased his forehead. "I think one of their leaders, a man with ice-colored hair, accepted both of ShiHolder's children, and probably took Duthoon's, as well."

"Accepted?"

Gower wiped the grease from his mouth on his sleeve. Mist had beaded on his broad nose and the curves of his ears where they stuck out through his jet hair. "When . . . when our relatives knew it was hopeless, they began to walk out of the longhouse. The Wobee warriors surrounded them. ShiHolder, she . . . she must have known—"

"She offered her children to the Wobee?"

Gower lowered his eyes and took another bite of salmon. As he chewed, he nodded. "Yes, Elder. And Wobee warriors may have captured others . . . when they tried to flee the battle."

Asson stuffed two moose antler spoons into his pack. Deep inside him, he could see it as though he'd been there. Badisut had probably hoped that by surrendering, he could buy the lives of some of his relatives. The children, at least.

"How old is Podebeek?"

"Ten winters, Elder." Gower ate his fish vengefully.

"Well, if they took captives, then, for the right price, we can buy them back," Asson said.

Ewinon glanced back and forth between his brother Camtac and his best friend, Gower. "You haven't told me what happened to—"

As though he wanted it out in the open, Gower blurted, "They're dead, my friend."

"Mother and Father . . . our sisters?" Ewinon looked at Camtac.

Camtac just ate faster, gobbling fish as though he couldn't get enough, but Asson suspected he was shoving down the sounds trying to come up his throat. He didn't seem able to answer.

Gower frowned. "I'm not positive about your father, but your mother and sisters are dead."

"What about your family? Your wife? Your three children?"

As Gower wiped his mouth on his sleeve again his hand shook. "My wife and children are gone."

Ewinon slumped to the sand as though the wind had been knocked out of him. "That can't be right," he insisted. "The Wobee killed almost our entire village? Didn't our warriors fight?"

"We fought like enraged bears, my friend," Gower said indignantly. "You've never faced their longbows. You don't understand. They can kill from great distances."

Ewinon seemed to come to his senses. He reached out to squeeze Gower's shoulder. "Forgive me. I didn't mean that the way it sounded. I know our warriors did everything they could to save our people."

"Someone always escapes," Asson said. "Didn't you see anyone run?"

"Some of our relatives may have escaped at the end, or even early in the battle. I don't know for sure. I did see ShiHolder and Matron Metabeet try to run. I don't know what happened after that. I dragged Camtac to the Shaman's Trail at a dead run. That's how we survived. They were afraid to follow us."

Ewinon gritted his teeth, which set his jaw askew. "On my ancestors' graves, I swear I'm going to kill them all."

Gower whispered, "*We*, my friend. We."

As Fog Spirits drifted through the dawn sky, pools of shadow moved over the beach and darkened the faces of the youths across the fire from Asson. Asleep, dead, ten tens of winters from now, Asson would see their hollow expressions in his nightmares.

He grasped his pack and got to his feet. "Come on. Grab your things; we're leaving."

Behind him, murmurs sounded. Someone kicked sand over the fire. Smoke rolled across the beach.

Asson eased his pack down in the stern of the canoe, and studied the fox. She hadn't moved a muscle. Now that Camtac and Gower were here, he could let them paddle while he cared for the fox's wounds.

He heard feet coming up behind him but almost leaped out of his skin when Camtac let out a bloodcurdling cry, stumbled backward, and fell to the sand.

"What's the matter with you?" Ewinon shouted.

Camtac lay propped on one elbow, staring wide-eyed at the canoe. "The fox. There's a—"

"I know there's a fox in the canoe. It's Asson's *pet*. Why did you scream like that? You almost scared my bladder from my body!"

Camtac dragged himself to his feet and eased forward to stand over the canoe peering wide-eyed down at the fox. "It . . . it's *her*."

Gower and Ewinon exchanged a confused look, but Asson stepped closer to Camtac. "You've seen this fox before?"

Camtac studied the sleeping animal. "I think it's the same fox. There was a fox. In the longhouse."

"There was no fox in the longhouse," Gower said. "What—"

"*Quiet!* Let him speak," Asson commanded.

Camtac glanced into each man's eyes before fixing his gaze upon Asson. "She tried to tell me something, but I didn't understand." He gulped hard. "At the very end, she launched herself from the trees and charged Chief Thorlak. I was sure she'd been killed. Every warrior had his bow aimed at her. That's why ShiHolder and Metabeet could run. The fox distracted them."

Asson's gaze turned to the wounded fox. Breath moved beneath the blood-matted fur of her chest. *Who are you?*

"I knew it!" Ewinon threw up his hands. "It isn't a fox." He glared at Asson.

Gower shifted his weight to his other foot. "Wh-what do you mean?"

"It's a Kutsitualit, Gower."

"But . . . how can that be? If she's a Kutsitualit, she'd change back into human form so we could take her back to her own village where her relatives would care for her."

Sternly, Asson said, "She's too weak to change back. Transformation takes great strength."

"Asson, is she really a Kutsitualit?" Camtac's young eyes suddenly glowed with reverence.

"I don't know yet."

"Gods, Father hoped the Kutsitualits would protect us. He prayed they would leave their sacred caves and fight as warriors on our side." He stared at the wounded fox in the canoe. "She *did* fight on our side."

Gower's mouth twisted in disbelief. "She probably just has the foaming-mouth disease. Did that occur to you? I saw her, too, when she broke from the trees. Her jaws slathered foam. Diseased animals do crazy—"

"Stop talking." Asson came to a difficult decision. "We're shoving the canoe into the ocean. Now."

"Y-yes, Asson."

They aligned on both sides of the boat. As they pushed it into the water, they jumped in. The slender birch-bark canoe bucked and dove in the waves until each of them had a paddle and could guide it away from the surf into deeper water.

Ewinon, who paddled in the bow, glanced back at Asson. Gower and Camtac paddled in the stern. "Where are we going, Elder?"

"Whale Rib Village."

Gower and Camtac went rigid. All eyes fixed on Asson. The ocean roared behind them as they rode the swells of the incoming tide.

"But, Elder, what if the Wobee are still there?"

"Do you want to bury your dead relatives, or not? They need to be able to find the Songtrail soon, before they become lost."

Asson looked down at the fox's torn body. Her muscles spasmed and shook. Still trying to run. Or perhaps she heard their voices. "Camtac, as we travel I want you to tell me *everything* you know about this fox."

# Nineteen

Podebeek huddled in the rear of the cage, watching the Tunghak Boys who sat around their breakfast fire pointing and hissing to one another while they stared at the strange man who sat nearby talking with Thorlak. Sokkolf. That's what Thorlak kept calling him. All day people had fluttered around the landing, asking Sokkolf questions, and appearing awed by the man's answers. Podebeek didn't understand their language, but the Wobee were apparently stunned to see Sokkolf.

Podebeek tugged his gaze away and looked out across his land at the ships rocking upon the waves.

The Wobee warriors had stripped Whale Rib Village bare. Baskets woven of arctic grasses sat in a line just beyond the trees, along with stacks of seal, caribou, and bear hides. In a separate location, near Chief Thorlak's fire, they'd gathered walrus tusks and soapstone pots of whale and seal oil.

Podebeek tried not to remember how Chief Badisut's body had lain sprawled on the ground, but he couldn't help it. Long hair had spread around the chief's crushed skull like a gray halo. He'd wanted the chief to get up. Wanted it badly. Sobs puffed Podebeek's chest, but no tears came. Where was his baby sister? Less than one hand of time ago, he'd seen Ice Hair march twelve other Whale Rib Village children into the largest ship, but Podebeek had seen no adult slaves.

He licked his bleeding lips. He hadn't had food or water since long before Mother had dragged him out of the longhouse. He didn't mind the lack of food so much, but without water his tongue and throat had swollen miserably. A smart and sensitive boy, he'd lived a pampered childhood. He was trying to be brave, but the realities of slavery had left him a quivering lump of fevered flesh. Had Elrik and Kapusa felt this way? Had they survived?

Podebeek wiped his running nose on his sleeve and fought to swallow down his inflamed throat.

With the passing of each hand of time, more and more wrath filled his skin and stretched his sinew tight as a drumhead. He glared at the Tunghak Boys with malevolence. The puncture wounds on his legs, belly, and chest had turned fiery. If he ever got out of this cage, they would never stab him with sharpened sticks again. He would steal a knife and rip them to pieces. Podebeek studied them with bloodshot eyes, dreaming their shrieks.

When the Wobee war party finished breakfast, and began preparing to leave, the Tunghak Boys rose from their fire and pointed at Podebeek's cage. All had flame-colored hair and hooked noses. Were they brothers? In a laughing horde they ran toward him, grabbing rocks as they came.

When Podebeek flung himself against the cage, yelling and shaking the poles, they hurled their stones. The first struck Podebeek in the shoulder, but the next hit him in the right eye and agony shot through him. He staggered, then lunged forward shoving his arms through the bars, growling like a rabid wolf, trying to get his hands on one of them.

The Tunghak Boys were startled. They stared at him for an instant, then the biggest boy barked at Podebeek, and all three began jumping around the cage, barking like dogs and snarling at him. The blow to Podebeek's pride made his agony all the worse. As a final insult, the boys circled his cage, untied their trousers, and urinated on Podebeek. This brought the boys especial glee. They laughed so hard they fell on the ground and kicked their heels in the air.

As he was dripping and fit to burst with rage, a sudden rush of strength flushed Podebeek's muscles. He lunged at the bars, roaring and frothing at the mouth, his eyes wild. He hit the bars over and over, leaping and slamming his shoulder against them until blood coursed down his face and blinded him. Then, shaking, he backed away.

The Tunghak Boys stared at him as though amazed. After a few shocked moments, they all smiled at one another, proud of themselves for drawing such a violent response.

From across the camp, Ice Hair shouted, and the Tunghak Boys uttered final barks at Podebeek, then raced away yelping with joy.

Podebeek wiped blood out of his eyes. He'd cut a gash across his forehead that wouldn't stop bleeding. Already it poured down the front of his urine-soaked shirt.

A man approached Podebeek's cage. His sky-colored eyes narrowed. He wore a long blue cloak, and an iron sword swung at his side as he walked. His black beard connected to the hair of his head at the temples, creating a great dark mask upon his face.

Podebeek readied himself to hit the bars again.

But the man approached holding one hand out in front of him, speaking to Podebeek in a low voice.

Though he didn't understand the guttural words, the man seemed to be trying to keep Podebeek calm while he came closer. He stopped a full two body-lengths away, and looked around to see if anyone was watching him; and then he spoke in a sympathetic voice. As though he realized Podebeek couldn't understand his words, the man pointed to the Tunghak Boys, then pointed at Podebeek, and finally aimed his finger at his own mouth and shook his head.

*He's telling me to be quiet when the Tunghak Boys torment me.*

Podebeek blinked. The man repeated the gesture. After a time, Podebeek nodded.

The man nodded back, gave him a warrior's uplifted fist sign, and strode away.

*He's the one who was in trouble last night. He's the one they called Alfdis.*

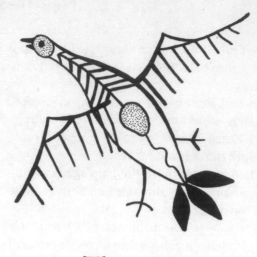

# Twenty

By late afternoon, the day had turned hot. Asson straightened from where he'd been scooping dirt with his bowl, and wiped the sweat from his wrinkled face. Ewinon, Camtac, and Gower continued their task of carrying soil. The burial mound was almost finished. Asson thought they'd covered the bodies well enough that wolves and other predators couldn't uncover them in search of food.

Asson watched his young friends as he caught his breath. Camtac was the shortest of the three. He worked with tears in his eyes. Gower's stocky body moved as though numb. Ewinon was the one Asson was worried about. His rage had been growing since midday when they'd finished digging the shallow pit in the soil, then begun carrying corpses and laying them inside. As they had Sung them to the Songtrail Ewinon's eyes had filled with such rage at the deaths of his relatives, Asson had feared the emotion might burst the youth's young heart. Every muscle in Ewinon's tall body strained against the weight of it. Though both Camtac and Gower had, on occasion, wept when they'd found loved ones, all day Ewinon's face betrayed only the emotion that gave him purpose: hatred.

Asson expelled a breath and looked around the village. The acrid scents of scorched hides and charred bark and the odd tang of burned whalebone boxes filled the air. Two lodges still smoldered, sending smoke rising before South Wind Woman swept it out over the ocean. The longhouse had not burned, but it had sustained the brunt of the battle.

A gust of wind tossed Asson's shoulder-length black hair over his brown eyes. As he shoved it away he listened to the dead. If he concentrated he could hear them moving, talking. Their voices were a soft, melodic drone. To his left, spectral feet kicked over a chunk of burned basket and sent it tumbling across the ground.

"Are you trying to get my attention?"

No response. Just the drone.

Asson knew from his Spirit journeys that the instant people called now was a place where both past and present were ahead as well as behind. The slaughtered villagers were both alive and dead. People from other nations did not understand this fact, and it was very hard to explain to outsiders. They thought the People of the Songtrail believed each person had two souls or four souls, or even more. No. A soul was not a thing; it was a *when*.

Asson heaved an exhausted breath and stared up at the blue afternoon sky strewn with drifting Cloud People. His own soul was already running the Songtrail, just as it was simultaneously being born. Anyone truly alive understood this. Every person had memories of dying and being born, and even memories before birth. Animals experienced *now* with a purity that far surpassed that of humans. They lived in the instant that was both ahead and behind at all times. They could only be caught if they allowed themselves to be, but they only allowed themselves to be captured because it didn't matter. They knew they were always free and always captured. That truth was perhaps the single greatest shock to the new Kutsitualit. When a shaman first learned to change shape to become an animal it was illumination. Time as a connected line of events ceased. There was no line. Never had been. There was just now. And now was both ahead and behind. Except in a person's dreams . . .

Asson turned to look at the fox. At noon, he'd arranged his coat atop a flat rock and placed the fox into the folds of the fur-lined hood. She often whimpered in her sleep. Sometimes her cries sounded more like muffled screams. He shook his head. When a soul was submerged in the ocean of suffering it became redemptive, but it wrung his heart. Whatever behind-and-ahead held her in its iron grasp, it was not pleasant. She must be stepping in both directions, neither there nor anywhere, trying to find a way back. If she would wake long enough for him to speak with her, he could help her.

"Elder Asson?" Ewinon called.

Asson turned to see the youth standing with his dirt-filled bowl in his hands. His perspiration-soaked doehide shirt clung to his muscular body. He'd pulled his black hair back and plaited it into a braid, which made his face appear as sharp angles. Ewinon tipped his chin to Camtac and Gower. Asson looked. Both men stood facing the water, their gazes glued like boiled pine pitch to the sailing ship gliding across the waves in the distance.

Asson frowned. "That's the ship I told you about, the one that was anchored to the north of Soapstone Village."

Ewinon stared at it with his jaw clenched. "There are more and more coming. We have to kill them before they fill our world, Elder."

Asson walked toward him. His hips hurt, as always after physical activity. When he stood beside Ewinon, he said, "Will you sit with me, for just a few moments? I want you to sit memory with me."

Ewinon turned to glare at him, still lost in hatred; then his expression softened. "Of course, Elder. But not for long. We should—"

"I won't take long." Asson gestured to the grass, and waited until Ewinon had sat down cross-legged. Then Asson lowered himself in front of the youth.

Ewinon clenched his fists and propped them on top of his knees, as though eager to have this over.

Asson lifted both open hands high over his head and let them fall as he said, "They sit in Adlivun, men and women long gone, with a feast arrayed before them. They are known as the Lost People. Anguta sits at the head of the feast, watching them. The delicious aromas of roasted grouse and kosweet fried in bear fat fill the room. But the people have snarled filthy hair and voices like knives, pitiful and angry, because hardened rawhide sleeves encase their arms so tightly that they cannot bend their elbows to comb their hair or bring food to their mouths. They have been starving for generations, and do not understand why the Spirits punish them so."

Ewinon fidgeted, as if annoyed and wondering why such a story could matter now, when the enemy was in sight. His gaze kept drifting away from Asson, back to the ship sailing southward. Dire murmurs passed between Camtac and Gower, and Ewinon strained to hear what they were discussing.

Asson made a sweeping gesture with both hands to get Ewinon's attention, and when he looked back Asson continued: "In the room next to the Lost People, men and women also sit before a feast. Their arms, too, are encased in hardened rawhide sleeves. But their voices are loving and happy. Their hair is clean and combed, and their bellies are full . . . because they have learned to feed one another, to care for one another."

Ewinon's black brows lowered as he studied Asson's face. "I understand, Elder."

"Do you?"

"Yes. You think I am walking the path of the Lost People."

Asson smiled and reached out to pat Ewinon's shoulder. "And I thought you weren't listening."

"Oh, I heard, all right, and I will gladly feed my enemies, Elder, if it means I can lure them to the feast so I can slit their throats."

"Now I'm back to thinking you weren't listening."

Ewinon leaped to his feet and flung out his arms in a wild gesture of frustration. "You want me to *help* them? After what they did? I would rather spend the rest of eternity with the Lost People in Adlivun!"

He turned his back on Asson, and tramped away to join Camtac and Gower.

Asson heaved a sigh.

With effort, he rose and stood stiffly, rubbing his aching right hip; then he headed over to check on the fox. As he approached, he saw that she was awake. Her head was up. Overwhelming relief filled him. She watched him approach with something akin to adoration in her glistening blue eyes.

Asson slumped down on the rock beside her and pulled the edge of the wolfhide up over the poultice on her wounded shoulder. It was healing fast. "Did you hear that disaster?"

The fox blinked up at him, just watching, not judging.

Asson stroked her side. "I've always been a poor Kutsitualit. I can't tell stories. I'm sure it's just that I use too many dramatic hand gestures. It unnerves listeners."

The fox stretched beneath his hand and let out a deep sigh.

"You were gone a long time, little fox. I feared you weren't coming back. I hope that soon you will show me who you are, so I can get you home to your worried relatives."

It took two tries, but the fox shoved up on her good elbow and looked out across the burned village. As her gaze drifted her breathing quickened, her chest rising and falling with shallow breaths. He thought he saw memories moving behind her eyes.

"Were you here? Camtac, that's the young man over there"—he pointed—"thinks he saw you here during the battle. He says you tried to help the People of the Songtrail, and because of you at least ShiHolder may have escaped. I have been wondering why you would risk your life for them. The Wobee almost killed you."

The fox licked her muzzle and swallowed hard.

"Are you thirsty?"

He pulled his pack up from where he'd stashed it behind the flat rock and drew it onto his lap. As he filled his wooden cup from his water bladder the fox's nostrils quivered.

Asson held the water beneath her nose. "Don't drink too fast," he cautioned. "Take your time."

Despite his warning, she lapped the liquid as though she couldn't get enough.

He frowned. "I'm sorry. I should have wakened you to drink. I thought you needed sleep more than water, but I may have been wrong."

The fox finally stopped drinking, and licked Asson's hand. She fell fast asleep with her chin propped on his forearm. She was so small he almost didn't feel the weight. South Wind Woman gently petted her fur. As the fox's sleep deepened, so did her breathing. It took ten tens of heartbeats before she started whimpering. The sounds were heartrending, like those of an imprisoned child. Tormented dreams drained a Kutsitualit's strength, which she needed to heal. If she was a Kutsitualit. He still wasn't certain of that.

"Just sleep, little fox. I will stand guard over you."

A single tear leaked from the corner of her eye and glittered on his forearm. Her whimpers and paw twitching stopped.

Asson didn't want to move his arm and risk waking her, so he continued sitting upon the rock, listening to the voices of the youths who watched the distant ship and plotted its destruction.

Like a wrathful hero from the old stories, Ewinon tramped across the burned village with Gower and Camtac following a few paces behind him. He'd obviously become the leader.

"Elder Asson," Ewinon announced, "we've been discussing it, and we've decided that we must send messengers to the surrounding villages to rally warriors to join us in attacking the Wobee. We must drive them from our lands, no matter the cost."

Asson rubbed his jaw with the back of his hand. "The other villages are probably already on their way here, Ewinon. They will have seen the smoke from the burning lodges."

"Then we'll meet them halfway." He turned to Gower, and said, "Go, my friend."

Gower gave him a stern nod. "I'll be back by noon tomorrow with as many warriors as I can gather." He loped toward the main trail that led through the forest to Dolphin Village and Mossy Grove Village.

"Elder," Ewinon said, "Camtac and I will run to Iron Blade Village. It's the largest village of the People of the Songtrail. We should be able to gather thirty or forty warriors there."

Asson asked, "Does it matter to you that the people on the ship you've been watching were not involved in the battle? Will you kill them anyway? According to the laws of our people, a man may not swear a blood feud for no reason."

Ewinon folded his arms over his broad chest. "According to our laws I may swear a blood feud against anyone who murdered a member of my family and I may kill every one of his relatives for as many generations as necessary to satisfy my claim against him."

"So, you think the people on the new ship are related to those who destroyed Whale Rib Village?"

"Maybe, but anyway—"

"What if they're not?"

Ewinon glared into Asson's eyes. The youth's sense of justice had been embedded early.

Asson said, "Surely the son of one of the greatest chiefs who ever lived would not wish to thoughtlessly kill innocent people? Do you think your father would approve of such an act?"

Grief flashed behind Ewinon's eyes. He looked away and the anger drained from his face. "No, he would not."

While Ewinon appeared to be considering Asson's words, young Camtac's head tilted to the side and his eyes fixed upon the sleeping fox with an intensity that made Asson stare at him.

"What's wrong, Camtac?"

"I . . . I *hear* her."

Asson swiveled around to look at his wolfhide coat where the fox lay curled up with her tail over her nose. "You mean her whimpers?"

"No, Elder, she's trying to speak to me." Camtac walked to the flat rock and look down at the hurt animal. He listened again. "I can't make out most of the words . . . but . . . I think she's saying Elrik's name."

Asson stiffened as though he'd just been slapped. "Are you telling me that she knows your lost brother, Elrik?"

"No, I-I'm just saying I hear her saying 'Elrik.' "

Ewinon's expression tightened. "Are you *certain* this is the same fox that charged Chief Thorlak during the battle?"

Camtac twisted to look up at his older brother. "I know it sounds bizarre . . . but I am certain."

"Well, if she remembers Elrik, she must be an elder from a neighboring village, someone who knew our brother as a boy. Asson, you should know her, especially if she's a Kutsitualit."

"I do not know her."

"How can you be sure? She's a fox now."

"Do you think I'm blind?"

"Don't Kutsitualits give off some kind of light, or stench, or—"

"What a dimwit you are."

Ewinon grimaced down at the fox, not sure what to make of her. The fox's chest rose and fell in the rhythms of deep sleep, but her paws were twitching, clawing for purchase in some desperate moment. "Why does she speak to Camtac when she's dreaming?"

Camtac licked his lips. "I don't know."

Asson said, "Probably because you're there with her."

A gout of acrid smoke blew over them. Asson closed his eyes until it passed. When he opened them he saw Ewinon grimace, disturbed by his comment.

"What do you mean, Elder? Camtac is standing right here beside me."

"Here is not the only 'when' she lives."

Ewinon squinted one eye. "I don't have time for riddles, Asson. We must be on our way to Iron Blade Village, or we'll never make it before nightfall. We will see you tomorrow, late morning."

Asson nodded in contrition and lifted a hand. "I pray Sea Woman protects you."

When they'd trotted away, leaving Asson alone at the edge of the burned village, he inhaled a deep breath. For a time, he stared down at the sleeping fox.

"Elrik?" he asked. At the sound of the name, the fox's eyes moved beneath her closed lids. "I'm beginning to think you and your Spirit Power are not of my world, little fox."

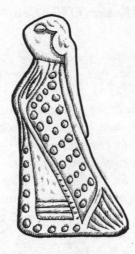

# Twenty-One

## Thyra

*T*he sound of ice thudding and crunching against the ship's hull wakes me, and the pain is stunning. Every muscle in my body screams at me to move. The hold is dark and freezing, despite the crush of bodies.

When awake, we slaves grant one another small privileges. We allow others to wiggle a foot along our side to relieve a cramping leg, or we shift our shoulders so that the person beside us can take a deep breath, but when we sleep those kindnesses cease and every square inch yielded by a sleeping person is ravenously stolen by others.

I groan, "Please, Frigga, I need to extend my leg."

Frigga doesn't spare the energy to answer, but she lifts her elbow, providing a small space for me to slip my foot through.

"Thank you, thank you, Frigga."

My hands are chained together, so I lift them as one and push tangles of ivory hair out of my eyes. It must be night. During the day light seeps into the hold and turns it gray. Now all is blackness. My world is little more than stench and sound. People breathe all around me. Some breathe deeply, still asleep. Others pant in pain. Near the prow, a man sobs. We've spent eleven days together in this dark sewer, listening to rumors fly. Some think we're going to a slave market in Iceland. But the trip from Bergen, Norway, to Iceland is only three days. So where are we going? Others say we have a wealthy owner and we're on our way to his farm in Greenland, not Iceland. One woman dared to say that

Denmark had been invaded and we were all the political prisoners of England and on our way to the gallows in London. After being pelted with feces, she shut up.

The rumor that has reached near gigantic proportions among the Anchorites is that our new owner is a demon straight from hell. A real demon, one of Satan's fallen angels. They say he has solid amber eyes, the hooves of a goat, and a tail that he cuts short to disguise his true nature.

When that rumor started, Frigga told me, "That's the worst one yet, isn't it? Slave markets want to make money, masters want thralls that work hard but eat little, and England wants revenge. We can all understand those things, but a demon? What will it want from us?"

For most of my life, my family worshiped Freya and Thor; then we converted to the Anchorite faith. I know little about the beliefs, but I wonder if demons need thralls to stoke the flames that burn forever?

Footsteps pound the deck over my head, and voices call orders.

"Thank the gods," a man says from my right. "They're dropping anchor. We've made landfall."

Every person seems to be holding his breath.

Soon, the cargo hatch is flung open and starlight streams over us. I squint at the ugly little man who trots down the stairs and calls, "On your feet, thralls! We're bringing you up on deck. One at a time! And no shoving or hurting each other or you'll get the club."

Few people can stand without help. It takes time before we can drag one another up and begin crowding for the stairs, climbing up and out into the fresh air on the deck.

As I emerge I gulp a lungful of the clean breeze; then a man grabs my bound hands and drags me over to a line of slaves that extends down the deck. He chains me beside Frigga. As each new thrall climbs up out of the hold, he or she is shackled to the line.

"Best make yourselves presentable!" the man shouts. "Some of you will be getting off here. Your new master is on the way to take a good look at you. I don't have to tell you what will happen if he doesn't like what he sees."

Murmurs pass through the thralls. Women try to comb their filthy locks with their fingers. Men square their shoulders and gaze straight ahead.

I stare out at the shoreline where smoke rises into the night sky. When the wind gusts right, the air smells of peat fires. In the distance, dark mountains rise, dotted here and there by lamplit farms.

A commotion breaks out as sailors rush to throw a rope ladder over the side. Twenty or more men climb up, but I see many vessels surrounding our ship, as though we've been taken prisoner by pirates.

A very tall man steps onto the deck. His guards flank him. The tall man ex-

*udes authority. He has his black hood pulled up, and his cape billows in the wind. The crew backs away from him like a pack of dogs at the sight of a larger, more dangerous predator.*

*The ship's captain, a burly man with a fat face, shoves his crew aside to hurry to the stranger, where he bows. "Lawspeaker, we had bad weather or we would not be late. I swear it. There's no need for this show of force. Did you think I'd . . ."*

*The Lawspeaker walks away from the captain, leaving him with his mouth still hanging open in midsentence, and strides to the head of the line of thralls. The captain follows two paces behind. I stand at about the middle of the line, watching the powerful Lawspeaker walk along. He is just a hooded figure to me. I can't see his face. The Lawspeaker examines each thrall as he moves down the line. Several grown men weep beneath his gaze. Women keep their heads bowed, refusing to look at him. The children don't know any better and stare up into his midnight eyes as though hypnotized by a deadly snake.*

*When the Lawspeaker nears me, I squeeze my eyes closed, and shake.*

*I hear him stop in front of me. After a few instants, he touches my hair, then extends a hand and lifts my chin. "Open your eyes."*

*The sound of his deep voice stuns me. I swear I've heard it before . . . where?*

*I obey, and stare into the amber eyes of Thorlak for the first time. Something like recognition fills his gaze. My lungs go still and cold. I do not see the face of a demon, but the face of a man who plans to kill angels.*

*The captain rushes to explain, "She's the one you wanted, isn't she? That's what your servants told me. She comes from Denmark. Her family died in the plague. Your men said her name—"*

*"I know her name, Captain," Thorlak says like one of the gods who know all things. "I knew her name before she was born."*

*A chill climbs my spine. I try to glance down to see if he has hooves, but he's still holding my chin to make me look at him.*

*Thorlak's voice drops so low I can barely hear him, and I'm standing closest to him*

*Thorlak says to the captain, "To whom do these other thralls belong?"*

*"Another godi. His farm is my next stop."*

*"Which godi?"*

*Uneasy, the captain replies, "I'm not at liberty to say."*

*"I see. Will you sell them to me?"*

*"Gods, no," the captain says with a shrug. "This particular godi is known for tracking down men who betray him and making the last moments of their life very unpleasant."*

*When Thorlak gazes down into the captain's eyes, the burly man winces. "You're sure you won't sell them? If you just passed by his farm, he would no* doubt think your ship had fallen prey to a storm or profiteers. I could make you a rich man today. My servant, the Greybeard, would discreetly handle the transaction." Thorlak lifts one finger. "But if I ever discover that you've cheated me by claiming more than your due—"

"I'd never do that to you, Lawspeaker!" The captain licks his lips. "To others, but not to you. But, sincerely, I can't sell them. He would find me. Trust me; I know him well."

Thorlak releases my chin and steps back. For several moments, he stares at the anchor pendant resting on my chest. "You will never mention the Monk's Tester or his teachings again, or you will be severely punished," he says sternly. "The true path has no anchors or fish. Instead, it's filled with sacred staffs, and gleaming swords, and hammers of immense power. I will teach you about the monstrous fire that lives in all things."

I'm shaking badly now. "I will learn anything you want me to, master."

"Yes," he says, "you will."

Thorlak turns to the captain. "Cut that necklace from her throat and throw it overboard, then unchain her."

The captain grabs the man closest to him and hisses in his face, "Do it right now!"

I'm free in moments, my pendant gone, and rubbing my sore wrists.

"Bring her." The Lawspeaker walks away, heading for the ladder.

Just before he climbs down, he says to the man holding my arm, "Capture the ship, sail it out to sea, burn it."

"Just the ship? Or everything?" His gaze pans over the thralls and crew.

"No one aboard this vessel who has seen the girl with me can live. Do you understand?"

"Yes."

Thorlak's face shows no emotion as he lifts a hand to another man, who instantly leaps forward awaiting instructions.

"Lawspeaker?"

"You are now in charge of the girl. See that no harm comes to her."

"Of course." He grabs my arm in the hard, careless grip of a stranger.

Thorlak climbs down to the small boat waiting below.

The guard forces me to climb down next. The wind is gusting. It isn't easy to hold tight to the rungs. As I struggle to hang on I keep saying to myself, "Frigga is going to die! I have to help her. I must do something!"

But I don't. I'm too frightened to even cry out a warning.

My throat aches with guilt as I step into the waiting boat.

# Twenty-Two

The afternoon wind had turned warm, blowing up from the south, and ruffling through the thick forests that covered the land to the west. Gunnar's chin-length blond hair, snarled and matted, stuck to his prominent brow, but on occasion it whipped loose and batted him in the eyes, which annoyed him to no end.

Where he stood beside the prow scroll in the bow of *Thor's Dragon* he could see Chief Drona's canoes slicing through the waves at the base of the dark, perpendicular wall of rock that created the coastline. The warriors moved with remarkable speed. Just ahead, around the next curve in the cliff, smoke rose. Off and on, for the past three hours, they'd seen people trotting along the crest of the cliff, paralleling their path. Gunnar assumed the party was composed of Drona and his warriors, but it could be other Skraelings, all headed toward the destroyed village.

Gunnar endeavored to put himself in their place. If the situation had been reversed, if a village in Greenland had been destroyed by German raiders, the news would have traveled like lightning. In less than one day, organized parties of men, carrying weapons, would have mounted horses and galloped away to find out what had happened. They'd be worried about lost relatives, and eager to hunt down the attackers.

Gunnar feared that when he reached the destroyed village tomorrow at noon, the village where Elrik's family had lived, he might discover both Drona and a mob of grieving Skraelings.

Kiran climbed up from the hold—where he'd probably been speaking with Thyra's sleeping body—and walked over to grip the rigging to steady himself while he gazed out across the green expanse of Markland. Black hair blew back from his bearded face, highlighting his straight, patrician nose and green eyes. The anchor pendant on his chest kept flipping over and over in the brisk wind.

Gunnar crossed the deck to stand beside Kiran. "How is she?" he asked as he gripped the rigging and spread his legs, allowing the ship to roll beneath his feet.

"The same. No change. I've been going down three or four times a day, talking to her, trying to get her to come home. I'm very worried, Godi."

"I am, as well, Kiran. When we find the Lawspeaker, he'll be able to tell us more. He knows a good deal about Seidur magic. He's been an Odin worshiper his whole life."

To the south, the naked rocks of an island thrust up above the waves. Just south of the island, the shore curved westward, and a narrow strait appeared between two landmasses. It looked to be some kind of inner sea passage. Drona's canoes headed for a small inlet. Gunnar squinted at the dark spots that had appeared upon the blue water. "Are those our ships?"

"Where?" Kiran's gaze searched the shore.

"In the inlet."

Kiran strained to see. After a few moments, he answered, "Yes, Godi. Two Norse ships."

"I thought Drona said there were three?"

"He did."

"I hope he wasn't mistaken. Perhaps one ship set sail to examine the southlands, trying to locate Vinland, same as we hope to do. But that means four were lost at sea."

Kiran didn't answer. He watched Drona's warriors drive their canoes up onto the sand far to the east of the two longships. With more than thirty-two oar positions and almost one hundred feet from prow to stern, the longships dwarfed *Thor's Dragon*. Each longship carried forty to fifty colonists, thirty or forty crewmen, and fifty warriors. Every godi had his own private army, but Dag and Ketil had brought several hired mercenaries, as well as thrall warriors.

"Should we anchor near the canoes, Godi, or—"

"No. We told Drona we'd meet him at the burned village tomorrow, and so we shall. Before that, we need to hear our people's side of the story."

"Of course."

As they sailed past the beached canoes and closer to the longships, Gunnar could identify them. He pointed. "The ship to the south is

Thorlak's vessel, *Logmadur*, and to the north is Godi Ketil the Fair-hair's ship, *Defense of Asgard*."

"I wonder what the third ship was?"

"We'll know soon enough. I'll try to meet with Thorlak as soon as we arrive."

Kiran turned to face Gunnar. "If he's still alive. He may have been swept overboard in the storm."

Gunnar experienced a brief moment of elation at the possibility, then sighed. "Oh, we will no doubt find him hale and hearty. My world is made of such trials."

Kiran suppressed a smile. "If you need my help—"

"I may. And may not. But if you're up to the task, I'd like you to accompany me to speak with Thorlak, though I'd ask you to wait a short distance away until I call for you. The Lawspeaker doesn't take well to people of your religion. His principal purpose in this new land is to avoid being forced to convert to the ways of the Kristni."

"I understand, Godi. I'll be close, but not too close."

Gunnar nodded and returned his gaze to the longships. As they got closer he saw that both vessels had lost masts and the *Logmadur* had a massive gash thirty feet long just below the gunwale. Both ships were undergoing repairs.

Kiran said, "Dear God, and I thought we'd been fortunate."

"Yes, the *Logmadur* must have raked an iceberg or a jutting rock. It's a plain miracle she didn't go down."

Gunnar's eyes narrowed. The removable dragon heads that decorated the prows of the longships remained attached, which surprised him. According to the Konungsbók, the legal code, dragon heads had to be removed from ships headed toward land, so as not to frighten off the nature Spirits that guarded the shorelines. Thorlak must have waived the code because he wanted to scare off the Skraeling Spirits. Interesting that the Lawspeaker would fear such things. Thorlak never seemed afraid of anything. He was the giver of fear, not the recipient.

When the people building booths on the terrace above the tide line sighted *Thor's Dragon* cries erupted and men, women, and children raced down to the rocky shoals. Hands waved. Gunnar thought he heard happy voices on the wind.

"I'll meet you here in one hour, Kiran. I need to speak with Bjarni about where to drop the anchor. We want to be close to the *Logmadur*, but not too close."

# Twenty-Three

As Thorlak's young thrall Jofrid the Foal's-brow strode across the green meadow, showing Gunnar and Kiran to the Lawspeaker's booth, her long blonde hair whipped about her shoulders. Thorlak had so many thralls, dozens, that Gunnar found it difficult to keep them straight. This young woman appeared to be around twenty, strong, with a maidservant's muscled arms, as though she'd spent her whole life scrubbing plank floors. Unattractive, with crooked overlapping teeth and a manly brow that thrust out over her blue eyes, she had a no-nonsense way about her.

Jofrid stopped four paces from Thorlak's booth and extended a hand. "This is it," she informed, and walked off, disappearing behind the booth.

As Gunnar studied the two silent guards who stood ten paces from the booth he called, "Thank you, Jofrid."

She didn't answer, but the muscular guards gave Gunnar a thorough appraisal.

Thorlak's booth stood on the high point overlooking the rest of the settlement and a good thirty paces from any other booth—a dangerous position if they were ever attacked, but it also projected power, which Thorlak would appreciate. Like all the booths here, Thorlak's was round and constructed of upright poles, with a pointed, conical roof, but the Lawspeaker's home was a third larger, spreading around twenty-five feet across. It intrigued Gunnar that the godar had allowed thatched roofs to be built, rather than the usual temporary canvas. They had repairs to complete, and wanted to stock up on food and freshwater, but soon they would all be headed south in search of Vinland. Permanent roofs seemed a waste of effort.

But as Gunnar looked north, it occurred to him that perhaps it wasn't such folly. In the distance, gray streamers of smoke stretched across the sky, thinning to nothingness over the blue ocean. The debris of burned homes continued to smolder for many days, which Gunnar knew from having burned so many. The godar were afraid—as well they should be. They must have built sturdy roofs because they were expecting a Skraeling attack.

Just behind his shoulder, Kiran said, "I'll wait here, Godi."

"I appreciate that, Kiran. Keep an eye on the guards."

"I understand."

Gunnar took a deep breath to prepare himself and strode headlong for the plank door. "Thorlak?" he called just outside.

From within, a deep rasping voice responded, "Godi Gunnar, I'm surprised you're not at the bottom of the sea. Enter."

Gunnar pulled the door open on squeaky leather hinges and stepped into the lamplit darkness. As he closed the door behind him he saw Thorlak standing in the rear, dressed in a bloodred shirt and trousers. The Lawspeaker bent over a table, lit by a whale-oil lamp. Sheets of parchment rested in stacks on the tabletop beside a quill and inkwell. What had he been writing?

Gunnar waited while his eyes adjusted. The lamp cast multiple reflections over the circular walls. There were few pieces of furniture—just the table and two chairs, which sat straight ahead of Gunnar, and a plank bed to Gunnar's left. Beneath the bed, wooden boxes sat in a neat line. To Gunnar's right a heavy oaken chest stood, carved with magical runes. He tried not to stare at it, but the huge iron lock made him wonder what it contained.

When Thorlak returned to the chair behind the table and took his seat, he gestured to the other chair. "Sit down, Gunnar. I'm pleased to see you alive. That means we have four ships now."

"The other four were lost to the storm? Are you certain?"

"If they aren't here by now, I suspect they're gone. Given the severity of the storm, we should consider ourselves lucky. How are the settlers you carried? Is my apprentice alive and well? How many did you lose?"

Thorlak's face looked cadaverous. All the bones stuck out, as though the moisture had been sucked out of the tissues, leaving the shrunken skin alone to cover the skull. The man had combed his wild red hair back and tied it with a cord, and trimmed his red beard. It created a perfect half-moon around the lower half of his face, which made his nose appear longer. It cast a fluttering shadow over his right cheek.

"I lost no colonists, and Thyra is alive, but two of my crew were swept overboard."

Thorlak gave him an eerie smile. "Only one, I think. Sokkolf dragged himself out of the ocean yesterday—"

"Dear gods! Sokkolf is alive?"

"Yes, indeed, and he's been telling a haunting story of how Thyra trotted into Helheim on the back of an eight-legged horse and brought him back from the dead."

Gunnar sat as if frozen. His mouth had gone dry. "Do you believe it?"

"Why wouldn't I? She is my student. I taught her how to ride into Helheim in search of lost souls."

Gunnar thought about it. It seemed impossible that Sokkolf could have been swept overboard, survived the storm, and managed to swim to shore. "Where is Sokkolf? I'd like to speak with him."

"I put him to work repairing my ship. I'll send him to you later."

After what seemed a long time, Gunnar said, "How many colonists did you lose?" *I had three good men aboard Thorlak's vessel.*

"Twelve drowned in the hold when my vessel struck the rocks just offshore and we took on water."

"I saw the gash in the *Logmadur's* side. I can't believe you survived. Thor and Odin must have protected you until you could make landfall." Gunnar dared not ask which settlers, lest Thorlak suspect he was concerned about particular passengers.

The booth felt too warm. Gunnar removed his leather jacket, walked to the chair, and draped it across the back before he sat down.

Gunnar gestured to the parchment sheets. One looked like an ancient parchment map, the scrawled lines brown with age. Another appeared to be a letter. "What have you been writing? A letter about our journey?"

Thorlak propped his elbows upon the sheets, leaned forward, and pinned Gunnar with those black pupil-less eyes. "No. I'm studying a treatise on magic."

"Magic? I'd think you had more pressing matters."

"What could be more pressing than understanding the nature of magic?"

"Well, to my mind, repairing my ship, finding food, staying warm, and the feel of a woman's silken flesh. I can think of lots of things I'd—"

"Do you believe that evil men can be redeemed, Gunnar?"

Gunnar blinked, trying to fathom the reason for this bizarre, irrelevant discussion. *Don't be a fool. Thorlak must have been informed when your ship was first sighted. He knew you'd be coming here. None of this is irrelevant. Not this discussion, and not the map on the table.* "That's an odd question, Thorlak, but I certainly hope so. What does that have to do with magic?"

"Most men believe that after death the gods will forgive them. It's a way of protecting themselves from truths they can't face. I, however, know that redemption can be had in this life."

"I presume you're trying to tell me something."

A faint smile turned the Lawspeaker's thin lips. "I've just been thinking about the dead, that's all."

Gunnar's wrinkles twisted into hard lines. The sensation of rising danger was almost overpowering, as though he breathed it in with the air around him. "Are you endeavoring to make some point, Thorlak? If so, do it. When you're finished, I have important things to discuss with you."

Thorlak smiled again, and it sent a tingle up Gunnar's spine. The man leaned back in his chair. "Do you recall the Prophetess, Vethild? She lived in the Danelaw—"

"Of course I recall her." A tendril of fear wound through Gunnar's belly. "Why?"

Thorlak tipped his bearded chin up and frowned at the conical thatched roof. The support poles spread like the spokes of a wheel. He seemed to be scrutinizing each one for flaws. "She had a *key*. Did you ever see it?"

"A key to what?"

Thorlak chuckled softly. "You wouldn't have to ask that question if you'd ever seen Eyr."

"Eyr is a key?"

"The key to Vethild's family Helgafell. Inside that sacred mountain is the chamber that holds the magical knowledge of the ages. Or so I've come to believe. No one really knows what her key was. But I think it was Eyr."

Gunnar stared at him.

After death, all souls traveled to their family's holy mountain, or Helgafell, where the door was swung open for them. Upon entry, the dead saw great fires blazing, heard the loud murmur of voices and the clatter of drinking horns. When their kinsmen spied them they rose to welcome the dead to the grand feast being held in their honor. Mead flowed like water at the banquet.

Gunnar shifted in his chair, irritated, and wondering what possible purpose this could have. "We need to discuss the events of the past few days, Thorlak. We can philosophize about Seidur trifles later. I've come about a matter of life or death—"

"Eyr is a matter of life or death. In fact, thousands of lives or deaths."

He stared into Thorlak's glistening eyes. Through the entire sentence, the man had hardly moved a muscle, apart from those that worked his mouth. Gunnar cocked his head. Thorlak never engaged in useless conversation.

"You want to go visit the dead? Just sail back to the Danelaw. You'll find hundreds of people happy to help you. My family, especially. They still think you betrayed them."

"Betrayal is, of course, a matter of perspective. I see myself as a great patriot." His eyes had a stony brilliance. "Vethild was the traitor. She's the one who ran when the Danelaw was under attack."

"That's not the story my family tells. They say she was murdered so she could not use her powers to save them."

"And others say she's still alive. So many strange rumors abound, don't they?"

Gunnar vented a disdainful laugh. "She's dead. Trust me on this. If she weren't dead, she would have killed you long ago."

Thorlak's red brows lifted. "I am more powerful than she ever was or will be. And she knows it."

Gunnar tried to glance at the map again. The Lawspeaker leaned forward to rest his forearms on the parchment sheets.

"I'm bored with your tales of your own grandeur, Thorlak. I've come to ask you why you destroyed the Skraeling village. What happened?"

As though surprised by the question, he said, "It was a misunderstanding. We had set up tables to trade with the Skraelings, and while we were haggling over prices, Godi Dag saw an old woman pick up a string of glass beads—"

"So, Dag is here?"

"Well, not here, but alive. His ship sustained less damage on the journey. Two days ago, he sailed *Valhöll Glory* south in search of thralls, and should return tomorrow. To finish my story, Dag assumed the old woman planned to steal the string, so he drew his sword and chopped off her hand. The Skraelings were outraged. Violence erupted. Five of our settlers were killed. In the flush of the moment, we followed them back to their village and destroyed it. We lost another eight men in the battle."

"Dag is a fool. His penchant to pull his sword over the slightest offense may get us all killed. *Was* the old woman trying to steal the beads? I assume you questioned witnesses."

"I questioned several people who'd been standing nearby. I concluded that the old woman was not bent on theft, but rather examining the unusual colors of the beads. Why? What difference—"

"I'll tell you what difference it makes." Gunnar's voice had gone low and threatening. "We made landfall to the north near a place called Soapstone Village, and the chief paid me an unpleasant visit. He was on his way here with a war party to avenge the murders of his relatives by slaughtering all of you. When he saw us loading *Thor's Dragon* he decided to approach us first. I suspect he wished to start his slaughter with us, but—"

"Are they still on their way here?" A hint of panic touched Thorlak's voice.

"Let me finish. One of my leysingi, Kiran the Kristni, speaks the Skraeling tongue, which he learned from a thrall who was born in the village *you* destroyed. Kiran—"

"Leysingi? You freed your Anchorite thrall?" Thorlak asked in astonishment.

"I freed two of my thralls. As I was saying, Kiran translated while I did my best to talk Chief Drona out of killing us, and then trotting down here to ambush you."

Thorlak smiled with genuine delight. A rare sight. "I'm stunned. How will you maintain the respect of the other godar when they learn you freed an Anchorite?"

"Thorlak, don't you care what I had to promise Drona in exchange for our lives?"

"You may tell me, if you wish."

"Oh, thank you for your permission." Gunnar's gaze locked with Thorlak's. "They have blood feuds, same as we do. We can fix this debacle, if we're of a mind to, but we have to do it quick. I assured Drona that we want nothing but peace with his people, who call themselves the People of the Songtrail. Further—" Gunnar inhaled to ease the blow of what he was about to say. "—I gave Drona my oath that I would hold the people who destroyed the village accountable for their actions. I told him I would meet him at the burned village and act a judge in the matter of recompense."

Gunnar had expected an explosive outburst. Thorlak hated the fact that ignorant godar acted as both judges and Lawspeakers in the remote regions of Greenland. Instead, Thorlak sat perfectly still, waiting for Gunnar to flinch or squirm beneath his hot black gaze. Gunnar just stared back.

"So, you plan to turn over Godi Dag? Or all of our people who participated in the battle? Will you just stand by while we are tortured to death by the barbarian Skraelings?"

"Of course not. I'm hoping I can bargain the offense down to goods, but I anticipate that it will require quite a lot of goods. After all, we're no longer just speaking of an old woman's lost hand. Now we're talking about the murder of an entire village. If Dag was responsible for the act that caused the battle, I expect him to pay the bulk of the recompense."

Thorlak seemed to be mulling that over. "And if Dag refuses?"

Gunnar rose and stood with his legs spread, looking down at Thorlak. The man's expression resembled that of a wolf, a creature that feels neither gladness nor remorse at killing, for it is simply the way of things. "Well . . . the godar will deal with such disobedience when, and if, it happens."

"The godar? What makes you think they'll agree to force Dag to turn over everything he owns? Your forest-walking troupe of criminals is far away, Godi Gunnar. And now you have two fewer thralls to call to your defense. If the godar do not support you, how will you enforce your judicial decisions? Or protect yourself afterward?"

Gunnar had been wondering that same thing. He suspected that, regardless of the findings of his court, Dag would not turn over everything he owned to the Skraelings. Dag had many thralls to guard the goods aboard his ship, and he could afford to hire plenty of murderers. Without the support of Thorlak, Gunnar's life wouldn't be worth a wooden earwax spoon.

"I'll figure out something." Gunnar bowed at the waist. "Good day, Thorlak."

Gunnar turned and walked to the door. Just as he shoved it open and daylight poured into the lamplit silence Thorlak called, "I will sanction your court, if I may serve as Lawspeaker."

Gunnar turned around. Thorlak had risen and stood behind his table with his long arms at his sides. Lamplight flickered over hollows of Thorlak's face.

Gunnar said, "I'd rather not have anyone present who was involved in the battle. I don't wish to give the Skraelings a chance at revenge."

"If you agree to allow me to be present as Lawspeaker, I will vow to do everything in my power to carry out the court's decisions."

Gunnar exhaled while he considered it. Without Thorlak's backing he was almost certainly doomed. With it he had a small chance of success.

"Will you simply repeat the Konungsbók? No slippery Lawspeaker interpretations. I want justice, nothing more."

"For both sides, Godi Gunnar?"

"Of course for both sides."

Thorlak bowed his head and smiled. "For more than twelve years, I have been responsible for the preservation and clarification of the Konungsbók. My duties require that I report the laws, Gunnar. I do not 'interpret' them. That is the judge's duty."

Gunnar nodded. "Then I will welcome having you attend the proceedings as Lawspeaker. I plan to walk to the village tomorrow. Will you join me?"

"What if Godi Dag has not returned by the time we leave?"

"As you well know, it's not necessary for the accused to appear at court. If Dag is not here, I assume you can find witnesses to serve on the panel. Testimony requires enough information to determine whether the alleged incidents did, in fact, take place. That's all." Once the facts had been established, Gunnar alone would pass a ruling. If his understanding of the Konungsbók was in error, it would be Thorlak's duty to inform Gunnar that he was mistaken. His real worry at this point was whether or not Drona had managed to convince his Village Council to allow Gunnar to serve as judge. He decided not to mention the possibility to Thorlak. He'd cross that bridge when the time came.

"I will find witnesses for Godi Dag, yes."

"We're agreed, then. I'll see you tomorrow at dawn. But before I go, I need to inform you that Thyra has not returned from her journey to Helheim. She's lying in a trance aboard my ship."

Thorlak lurched forward as though genuinely concerned. "Is she well?"

"So far as any man can tell with such things, she seems to be. Her heartbeat is slow, but there."

"Ah, then"—Thorlak nodded as though he understood—"don't worry. She'll wake when she returns."

"It's been five days, Thorlak. Why would she still be there if Sokkolf is here? Is such a long journey normal?"

"Not normal, but not unusual, either. If she isn't back in another two days, I'll take action."

"Very well. She's your thrall."

Gunnar exited into the warm sunlight, and stopped for a moment just to check the positions of the guards. They stood in the same place, talking.

Kiran strode toward Gunnar. The sixteen-year-old had a grave look on his handsome face. Had he heard the entire conversation? Probably.

Gunnar pulled the door closed behind him and held up a hand to calm Kiran. As he walked toward him, Gunnar said, "Don't fret. This will work. You heard his words about Thyra?"

"Yes, I'm much relieved." Kiran hesitated before he said, "Godi, I'm not sure the People of the Songtrail will abide by the Lawspeaker's—"

"Nor am I." Gunnar cast a glance at Thorlak's closed door. "But it's the best I could do. We're going to have to figure it out as we go along. Which is, to be truthful, the way I usually hold court, so it won't be anything unusual for me. I just wish I knew for sure that Drona's Council . . ." His voice faded when he saw Alfdis the Lig-lodin striding up the hillside toward him.

A heady mixture of relief and happiness rushed through Gunnar's veins. "Forgive me, Kiran. I'll return shortly."

"Yes, Godi."

Gunnar hurried down the hill to meet Alfdis halfway. As he did, he scanned the surrounding area, noting who was watching them. When they stood facing each other, Gunnar said, "Gods, I'm glad to see you alive, Alfdis. But we need to speak quickly. Too many are watching."

"Yes, I know."

"What of Dala and Hoskuld?"

"Both dead. One at sea, one in the battle."

Gunnar bowed his head for a moment. "And our quest?"

Alfdis shoved aside the pitch-black hair that had fallen over his blue eyes. "Thorlak kept his cabin door locked at all times, and posted two guards. They never left. I couldn't get inside."

"Dag?"

"I searched his . . ." Alfdis closed his mouth.

Gunnar didn't need an explanation. He heard Thorlak's leather door hinges squeal as the man stepped outside. Gunnar murmured, "Try to search the chest in the Lawspeaker's booth tomorrow. Just now he had a map on his table, but since he left it out just for me to see, it isn't *the* map."

Alfdis said, "Be well, Godi," and bowed, as though paying his respects to a member of the godar in passing. Then Alfdis headed straight to Thorlak, where Alfdis proceeded to report on the status of the newly made ropes that would replace the *Logmadur's* snapped rigging.

Gunnar did not turn to watch them but let his gaze drift down to the three vessels rocking in the ocean below. *Thor's Dragon* looked small and squat beside the long, sleek *Logmadur*. So, the colonizing expedition had lost four vessels. Half. *Gods.* He could hear rigging snapping and clanging. After a short time, Kiran walked up behind Gunnar.

"What's wrong?" Kiran asked in a blunt voice.

Gunnar shifted to study the young man. Kiran was an observant sort. He'd probably taken in every nuanced expression on Gunnar's and Alfdis' faces, heard their tones, and noted how they parted when Thorlak's door swung open.

"I'd take it as a favor if you didn't mention what you just witnessed, Kiran."

Kiran stared at him with alert green eyes. The breeze tousled his black hair. "Does this have anything to do with Chief Avaldamon or the woman named Vethild?"

Gunnar gripped Kiran's arm and led him another thirty paces away, where they could not possibly be overhead. He'd been too careless already. "I promise, at some point, I'll explain. In the meantime, if you hear anyone speak of the Land of the White Men—"

Kiran sucked in a breath. "Tir na bhFear bhFionn?" he asked in astonishment. "I heard tales of it as a child. It's supposed to be a wondrous land six days' sailing west from Ireland."

Gunnar's heart thundered. "What tales? Do you remember them?"

"Yes. Well, some of them."

Gunnar hissed, "Do you recall anything about islands or the shapes of coastlines? Any landmarks?"

Kiran shrugged his broad shoulders. "A few things."

"Later, I want you to tell me everything you recall."

"I'll be happy to, Godi."

Gunnar tightened his grip on Kiran's arm until it must have hurt. "You have my thanks. But now listen well, Kiran." Gunnar scanned the hills. "There are men—*men here*—who will kill you for that information."

A swallow bobbed as it went down the Kristni's throat. "Why? The stories were common in the Hebrides."

Gunnar released Kiran's arm. For a time, he debated what he could and could not say. "But only there. More than two centuries ago, when Norsemen first landed in Iceland, they found Irish monks already living upon the shores. They were called *papar*. As soon as their glorious spiritual exiles were disturbed by Norse invaders, they left." He stared at Kiran. "They got in their boats and went west, carrying books, bells, and croziers. And they established churches in mythical lands far to the west. Some returned to tell of their perilous journey and what they found there."

"Did they find Tir na bhFear bhFionn and Chief Avaldamon and Vethild?"

Gunnar licked his dry lips, weighing every word now against what he might learn from Kiran. "Yes."

Kiran seemed to sense that the conversation was over. "I don't understand, Godi, but I'll trust you that if I wish to continuing breathing, I'd best speak of none of this."

"I'm mounding secrets upon your shoulders, Kiran, for which I apologize. If we succeed, however, you will be rewarded many times—"

"Godi," Kiran said, and tipped his chin to something behind Gunnar. "Ketil the Fair-hair is coming up the hill."

# Twenty-Four

Ketil the Fair-hair walked over to stand beside Thorlak where both men observed the Skoggangur and the loathsome Anchorite conversing in low tones, obviously concerned about being overhead. As if anything Gunnar had to say would interest Ketil.

"He's an arrogant noddy," Ketil said.

Thorlak didn't turn. He was watching Gunnar with an alert expression. "It would be a grave mistake to underestimate him. And, if you spend some time considering his possible uses, he could work to our advantage."

"Maybe." Ketil's mouth puckered as though he'd eaten a sour lemon. Gunnar had propped his hands on his hips and seemed to be listening intently to something the black-haired Anchorite was telling him. "What do you think they're talking about so secretly?"

Thorlak's red beard barely moved when he replied, "The war."

"Which war?"

The question seemed to annoy Thorlak, as though the answer was obvious to anyone with the sense of a goat.

"Are you referring to the civil war in England, between Edmund and his father, that blithering idiot, King Aethelred?"

Thorlak's eyes narrowed as he watched the two men. In the sky above them, dark thunderheads were building.

"Oh, why would he care, Thorlak? It's irrelevant. We're hundreds of miles away. It doesn't matter what happens in that benighted country. If

Edmund succeeds and claims his father's throne, it will have no effect on us whatso—"

"Are you really that much of a fool? Edmund now has family ties to the Danelaw. He married the widow of Sigeferth, one of the leaders of the Danelaw. An act of rebellion against his father, no doubt, but the marriage gives Edmund the leverage he needs to request assistance from the Danelaw."

"I'm aware of all that. Do you think I'm an imbecile? I was trying to make the point that our new colony will be far enough away that no one will care in the slightest what we—"

"King Cnut will care. Unless someone can stop him, when Cnut sees a crack in England's armor he will swoop down with his army and take the country as his own—just as his father, Sweyn Forkbeard, did." Thorlak clenched a fist and lifted it as though to strike Ketil. "Aethelred has been tolerant of the Seidur faith. To secure the support of his Scandinavian allies, all of whom are Anchorites, Cnut has become a hardened Anchorite."

Ketil glared at Thorlak. "And you're afraid Cnut will send missionaries all the way over here to force us to convert? Ludicrous. Why would he? What value—"

"Landnám."

Landnám, the process of land taking, was the heart of colonization. Men claimed land, drove off the original inhabitants, then defended their claims and turned the soil into arable fields to build civilizations. As the gods intended.

Ketil's gaze was drawn toward the towering mountains in the distance, and what legends described as a vast virgin continent beyond. A place called Hvitramannaland, the Land of the White Men. What king would not want to rule such a mythical paradise? . . . And spread his new faith from shore to shore?

Cold fear flooded Ketil's veins. "I hadn't thought of that."

Thorlak's eyes slid to Ketil before he slowly turned to face him. "Then do so. If the Skoggangur is allied with Edmund, he may doom us all. If Edmund wins, he cannot hold the throne for more than a few months. He's a weakling. Cnut *will* be king of England."

Ketil drew a shaky breath. He gave the Skoggangur a long, thoughtful look. Gunnar did have family in the Danelaw; he made no secret of that. Was he allied with Edmund? If so, the godar would have to take care of him immediately.

# Twenty-Five

**W**hen Gunnar saw Godi Ketil the Fair-hair staring at him he said, "Kiran, let's walk up the hill and stare at the smoke rising from the burned village in the distance. Perhaps it will delay him, or even discourage him, from paying us a visit, and give us more time to speak of important things."

Kiran nodded and followed Gunnar along the crest of the hill to a place where they could see the ocean washing against the one-hundred-foot-tall cliffs. Gulls soared and fluttered over the rim. Wet, the cliffs appeared to be black walls of shining obsidian.

Gunnar chanced a backward glance. Ketil and Thorlak had returned to their conversation, but they kept giving him speculative glances.

Gunnar frowned when he spied a pole cage sitting behind Thorlak's booth. A Skraeling boy huddled inside with his bloody hands over his head. The boy wasn't making a sound, but clearly he'd been beaten. Bruises purpled his face.

Kiran said, "I see you noticed the child. I asked Jofrid about him when she brought the boy water. He belongs to Godi Dag. I don't know why he's being held behind the Lawspeaker's booth. Jofrid said—"

"He's an amusement," Gunnar replied in a dark voice.

Kiran shifted his weight to his opposite foot. "What does that mean?"

"It means, if I've any sense about men, the boy doesn't have long to live." Gunnar tore his gaze away, and fixed it upon the strong Hebrides youth. "Kiran, in the versions of the Celtic stories you heard about the Land of the White Men, what was the most important geographic feature?"

Kiran smoothed his black curls behind his ears, then he propped his hands on his hips and frowned down at Gunnar. "I recall that a ship had to leave from the Aran Islands and always keep the polestar to his right."

"From the Aran Islands?" Gunnar had never heard that tidbit before. "That helps me. I . . ."

When Ketil ended his conversation with Thorlak and started up the hill toward Gunnar and Kiran, Gunnar turned with a broad smile on his face. Loudly, he called, "Why, Ketil the Fair-hair! I was sure you were dead and moldering. You're not good enough as a shipmaster to have survived that monstrous storm. How did you manage? Turn command over to one of your thralls, did you?"

Ketil's mouth quirked. His blond hair and beard gleamed as though freshly washed. "You could at least pretend you're happy to see me before you insult me, Gunnar the Skoggangur."

"Nonsense. I have a weak stomach."

Ketil stopped in front of Gunnar. With great dignity he said, "Well, despite your insults, I'm heartened to see you in one piece. Your family in the Danelaw would be happy to know you made it, especially given their new alliance with that traitor, Edmund. They must be desperate to have a place to flee to when he's murdered in his sleep."

Gunnar's eyes narrowed just slightly before he steered the conversation elsewhere. "I assume the Lawspeaker informed you of our predicament *here*? May I count on the fact that, as a member of the godar, you will be present at my court tomorrow?"

"I will not attend a court for savages."

"Are you referring to Dag and his ilk, or the Skraelings?"

"You know very well to whom I'm referring." Ketil looked down his thin nose at Gunnar. "The very thought is ridiculous. I will not abide—"

"So, you'll remain in your booth hiding under your covers until I've decided the matter?"

"I won't be hiding, I assure you. I'll be discussing your impudence and what to do about it with the rest of the godar."

Gunnar reached out and clapped Ketil the Fair-hair on the shoulder hard enough to make the man stumble. "I'd be surprised if you weren't. Now, I've things to do, but I assure you that I will keep you informed of my villainous activities. Good day to you."

As Gunnar and Kiran walked away, Godi Ketil cupped a hand to his mouth and shouted, "If you think I'll agree to give a horde of barbarians a single bolt of fabric, you are mistaken! I won't! Nor will anyone else. The Skraelings deserve destruction. This is landnám! Have you forgotten? We take what we want!"

Gunnar ignored the Fair-hair, but Kiran glanced back and studied the man far longer than he deserved. In the far distance, cloud shadows roamed the hills like hunting ghosts.

"He's a fool, Godi. If the blood feud with the Skraelings isn't resolved to the satisfaction of the People of the Songtrail, he and the godar will be dead."

Gunnar gave Kiran a casual nod. "Yes, but he knows the Skraelings will start with the two of us, Kiran. Which I'm sure makes him gleeful."

"You mean because we will be at hand?"

"At hand, surrounded, and easy targets for their rage. You'd best start praying to your Monk's Tester now. If you pray hard enough, perhaps we'll live through tomorrow."

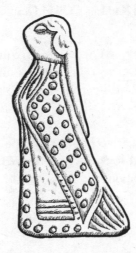

# Twenty-Six

"*What do they want?*" Bjarni shouted.

As though his voice had slapped her awake, Thyra lurched forward, gasping and staring around the cargo hold. The pink gleam of dawn blushed color into the air. Disoriented, she struggled to breathe. Where was she? She reached down and smoothed her hands over her human body, feeling its texture and contours, so alien to her now.

Trembling, she tried to ease her terror by concentrating on the scent of the grass hay and the smell of the wet hull. Sunlight streamed through the open hatch. Where it struck the steps, the damp wood steamed.

Finnbogi answered, "I don't know, but there's a lot of them, and they're Godi Ketil's men. That's Thorbjorn Thistle in the bow of the lead ship."

Thyra inhaled a deep breath and rose on shaky legs. As she walked to the stairs, she brushed the hay from her white tunic. Feet pounded across the deck above, heading toward the bow, and a din of questioning voices broke out.

She didn't hear Kiran's voice.

She ran up the stairs.

When she stepped out onto the deck she found the crew standing near the prow scroll, gazing off the laddebord side at the three boats filled with men that rowed toward them. She did not see Kiran or Godi Gunnar.

Bjarni cupped a hand to his mouth and shouted to the man in the lead boat, "What occasions your visit, Thorbjorn Thistle?"

The man shouted back, "Throw down the ladder, leysingi! We're coming aboard!"

The sensation of foreboding that filled Thyra was overwhelming. From somewhere deep inside her, her Other Mother's voice whispered, *"Run . . . run!"*

Thyra instantly obeyed. She hurried to the steerbord side where the rope ladder lay rolled and kicked it overboard. It fell toward the small boat tethered to the hull below.

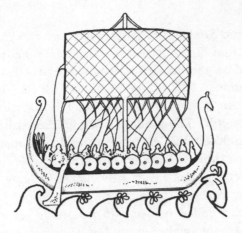

# Twenty-Seven

As he walked the trail to Whale Rib Village Kiran sniffed the air. It had an ashy, fetid odor that overpowered the fragrances of forest and sea. The rain had eased to a whisper, but storm clouds crowded the noon sky. As they blew westward, patches of sunlight fell through the tree branches and striped the trail ahead where Godi Gunnar and the Lawspeaker walked side by side.

Kiran studied their backs. Both had dressed in finery. Thorlak, on the one hand, wore a knee-length red tunic over brown trousers. The tunic shimmered with golden embroidery, which cast sunlit reflections through his tied-back red hair. Around his waist, he'd belted his legendary sword, Skyrmir. He kept his hand propped on the hilt at all times. Given the warmth of the day, he'd rolled up and tied his black cape around his waist. Godi Gunnar, on the other hand, wore pure black. His woolen shirt, sewn across the front with tiny seed pearls, flashed with his movements, as did his belted sword. He was short and skinny, and his blond hair and beard looked almost white in the brilliant midday sun.

Voices sounded behind him, and Kiran turned to glance at the men who followed. The two witnesses would testify on behalf of Godi Dag. Orm Einarsson and Masson the Bellower. Both were built like tree stumps, wide with sturdy limbs, though Orm was taller. They wore leather jerkins and had battle-axes upon their belts. They'd apparently been standing next to Godi Dag when the old woman had lifted the string of beads. Ingolf and Sokkolf brought up the rear, carrying heavy packs on their backs. Gunnar had instructed Kiran to prepare samples of the goods that would be paid to settle the blood feud—just in case the court found Dag at fault.

Kiran glanced uncomfortably at Sokkolf. His bizarre story about being saved from the dead by Thyra had left Kiran deeply disturbed. To make matters worse, Sokkolf had an otherworldly distance in his eyes, as though he couldn't quite believe he was actually here. Everyone had been repeating the story, and with each new version it grew. Only that morning, Kiran had overheard one young woman whisper that Thyra was so powerful Odin had called her soul to Asgard to sit at his right hand. That's why she had not awakened, and why she never would.

*Blessed Lord, give me the strength to make sense of this. I beg you to keep her safe.*

Through the trees ahead, Kiran caught glimpses of the burned lodges. Shattered pots and charred basketry covered the ground, as did children's carved wooden toys and scattered kosweet hides. Crushed shell beads glittered. When the fleeing people had been cut down, their necklaces must have ripped apart and the beads scattered everywhere.

Godi Gunnar entered the meadow first and came to a dead halt. The Lawspeaker walked up behind him and said something low that sounded curious, perhaps even worried.

Godi Gunnar turned. His wrinkled, leathery face shone with sweat. "Kiran?"

Kiran trotted forward. "Yes, Godi?"

Gunnar pointed to the old man moving through the brush at the edge of the meadow. The man's black hair fell around his face, obscuring his features. He kept shoving brush aside, looking around, then continuing to the next clump to search it. His low voice carried, as though he were calling for someone. To the man's right, a large earthen mound stood.

"Is that a fresh burial mound?" Kiran asked.

"I wager it is," Godi Gunnar answered.

Gunnar turned to Thorlak. "I think Kiran and I should go out alone, before the rest of you enter the meadow. Looks less threatening that way."

Thorlak nodded. "Take care. He may have hidden friends."

"I'm sure he does. Come along, Kiran."

Godi Gunnar led the way into the midst of the burned lodges where the acrid scent stung Kiran's eyes, and called, "Hello."

The black-haired elder jerked his head up to stare at them. As he grunted to his feet he said, "Have you seen a small fox? About this big?"

Gunnar glanced up at Kiran, hoping for a translation.

"He's searching for a fox. He probably snared it and it got away." To the elder, Kiran called, "No, Elder. Who are you?"

The elder walked toward them with his bushy black brows lowered. He had a stern oval face with a nose as long and thin as a beak. "Which ship are you from? The long ships or the short ship?"

Gunnar looked at Kiran, and Kiran explained, "He wants to know which ship we're from." To the elder, he replied, "The short ship, Elder. I am Kiran, and this is Chieftain Gunnar."

The old man limped as though his right hip hurt. "Ah, then you did not fight in the battle that killed my relatives."

"No, Elder, we did not."

"I'm happy to hear it. I am Asson. This was my home village. Almost everyone I've ever loved lived here."

Kiran's belly knotted at the sadness in the old man's voice. "That's why we're here, Elder. Godi Gunnar hopes to find out what happened and make things right."

Asson stopped two paces away and scrutinized Kiran and Gunnar for several moments. Then Asson gazed into the trees at the Lawspeaker who stood half-hidden in the shadows. "And the five men in the trees? Did they kill my relatives?"

Kiran spread his arms wide. "Elder, truly, I do not know. Two or three of them may have fought in the battle, but—"

"What are you saying, Kiran?" Gunnar interrupted.

Kiran turned to him. Gunnar's wrinkles cut deep lines around his mouth. "The elder asked if the men in the trees had killed his relatives, and I told him some may have fought in the battle, but I didn't know if they'd killed anyone."

Asson's gaze fixed on Godi Gunnar. "You called him a chieftain. What is his village?"

Kiran turned to Gunnar. "Godi, the elder wishes to know which village you are a chieftain of."

"Tell him I am the chieftain of Skoggangur Farm in Sermilik Fjord."

Kiran turned back to the elder. "Chief Gunnar wishes me to tell you that his village is Skoggangur Village located in Sermilik Fjord in Greenland, which the People of the Songtrail call the Land of the Fallen Star People because you collect iron there."

The elder's gaze shifted to Kiran. "Where did you learn to speak our tongue, Kiran?"

"I was raised with a boy and girl who were born among the People of the Songtrail. Though we are not of the same blood, the boy is my brother. If I understood Chief Drona, his family—"

"Drona? You spoke with Drona?"

"Yes, Elder." Kiran bowed. "Chief Drona told us that Whale Rib Village had been attacked, and we came as soon as we could, to make amends for this tragic misunderstanding."

The elder tucked a windblown lock of black hair behind his ear and his gaze suspiciously slid back and forth between Gunnar and Kiran. "Was it a misunderstanding?"

Kiran held out a hand to Godi Gunnar. "That's why Chieftain Gunnar is here. In his country, he leads his Village Council. He decides who has been wronged and what sort of settlement can be agreed upon so that blood feuds may be ended and people can return to their lives. Today, he will hold a Village Council meeting to determine who was at fault for the destruction of Whale Rib Village. Chief Drona is supposed to meet us here at midday."

As though trying not to startle anyone, Elder Asson slowly reached out to touch Godi Gunnar's black sleeve, feeling the fine wool while his gaze scanned the wealth of pearls that covered the front of the shirt.

Godi Gunnar frowned down at the man's hand but didn't pull away. "What's he doing?"

"I don't think he's ever seen such fine cloth, Godi."

"Tell him I'll trade such cloth in exchange for good narwhal tusks."

Kiran relayed the message, and Elder Asson nodded. "This boy you were raised with, the one who is your brother, what's his name?"

Kiran said to Godi Gunnar, "Godi, Elder Asson wants to know the name of the boy who taught me to speak their language. May I tell him?"

Gunnar spread his feet. "I was hoping to save that bit of information, but yes, Kiran."

"Thank you, Godi. His name is Elrik, and he and I were—"

Asson's eyes flew wide. "Then he's alive? Where is he?"

"He is alive, Elder. At this moment, he's living at Skoggangur Village in the Land of the Fallen Star People."

"And the woman who came here with you, the one who also knows Elrik, what is her name?"

Kiran frowned in confusion, and Gunnar said, "You're looking perplexed, Kristni. Why?"

"Well, I—I don't understand. Elder Asson asked me for the name of the woman who is here with us who also knows Elrik."

Gunnar's blond brows lowered. "How could he know such a woman exists? None of my crew has traipsed off into the woods to converse with Skraelings, have they? Besides, which woman speaks the Skraeling tongue?"

Kiran shook his head. "Elrik taught Thyra some, but she's been in a trance. So there are just three women who might have traipsed off: Arnora, Grettir, and Osk. Arnora does speak some Skraeling language, which she also learned from Elrik."

Kiran could see Asson studying them, assessing their curious tones of voice. He said, "Elder, we're trying to figure out which woman you might mean. Arnora, perhaps, knows Elrik best, and she speaks some of your tongue. She works as Godi Gunnar's maidservant. But Grettir the Weaver and Osk the Potter also know Elrik, though they know none of your tongue. However, all of these women are aboard Godi Gunnar's ship."

"Maidservant, weaver, potter," Asson repeated, then said, "Which has the Spirit Power?"

Kiran's spine tingled. "Spirit Power?"

Gunnar stepped closer to Kiran. "What's he saying? I heard you speak of Arnora, Grettir, and Osk."

"Yes, Godi, then he asked me which one has the Spirit Power, which we would call magic."

"None of them have magic."

"Which leads me to believe he means Thyra. Even though we both know she hasn't been off the ship for an instant."

Gunnar lifted his eyes to Kiran's and they stared at each other for a time. "Well, maybe. I'm no expert on where or how souls can travel. Tell him."

Kiran turned. "Elder Asson, just one of the women with us has Spirit Power. She is a Seidur seeress named Thyra. But she has been in a trance for days, so I doubt she is the woman you—"

"Thyra," Asson replied, and nodded in gratitude. His face took on a soft expression. "And what is this *Seidur*?"

"I—well—I'm not the best person to ask. I barely grasp the concept." Kiran stopped when he heard Thorlak's soft, carefully placed steps coming up behind him.

Asson shifted his gaze to look over Kiran's shoulder, watching the Lawspeaker approach. He must have heard Thyra's name, and the word *Seidur*.

The elder's brown eyes narrowed, as though he saw something that put him on guard. Before Thorlak could speak, Asson said, "I've seen this man before. From a distance. Is he the seeress' teacher?"

Kiran spun around to look at Thorlak. "Yes, Elder."

Asson's face slackened when Thorlak walked to Kiran's right and stood staring at Asson. He had his palm hanging near the hilt of Skyrmir. The runes carved upon the metal flashed in the sunlight. Thorlak looked down at the small, dark-haired elder. Some silent communication passed between the men. As though lightning was about to strike, the hair on Kiran's neck and arms stood up. "Elder, this is Thorl—"

"I know who he is." Asson cocked his head and a faint, dreadful smile came to his lips. "Far better than you do, Kiran."

Kiran watched as Thorlak's amber eyes sparkled, then the depths seemed to recede, falling away forever, and Kiran swore he was falling into them, into a fetid honeyed abyss inside Thorlak. As though in a dream, Kiran felt a gentle hand upon his arm, shaking him, and heard Asson say, "Let him go."

When the Lawspeaker's gaze left him Kiran stumbled. He felt ice-cold, as though the warmth had been sucked from his bones.

Asson reached a hand toward Thorlak and the Lawspeaker backed away, putting distance between himself and Asson. In a stone-dead voice, Thorlak said, "Who is he, Kristni?"

"This is Elder Asson, Lawspeaker."

"Was this his village?"

"Yes, Lawspeaker."

Thorlak's black gaze drifted around at the destroyed lodges, and an expression of melodramatic pity came over his cadaverous face. He turned to Asson. "Old man, where is your family?"

Kiran hesitated to translate the malicious question, and wouldn't have if Asson had not ordered, "You must tell me. We are all in danger."

Kiran said, "It's cruel, Elder. He wants to know where your family is."

When Asson's expression turned brittle, Thorlak smiled as though enjoying a delightful joke. Locks of his red hair had come loose from the knotted cord and darted like serpent tongues around his flat, empty eyes.

Asson bowed his head to Thorlak, which seemed to surprise the Lawspeaker, for his fist tightened around the hilt of his sword. Thorlak shouted, "*Do not—!*"

"Stop this!" Godi Gunnar strode to stand between Asson and Thorlak, looking back and forth between the men with his jaw clenched. "The elder is unarmed, Thorlak, and he's made no move toward you at all. Get your hand off your sword!"

The Lawspeaker's lips quivered at the order, but he removed his hand from Skyrmir's shining hilt and glared at Godi Gunnar. In a too-quiet voice, Thorlak said, "You may think he made no move toward me, but he's a clever little magician. He . . ."

Thorlak's voice trailed away as his face flushed and his gaze jerked toward the tree line to the north, then swept to the west. There was an expectant silence before he murmured, "Great Odin, did you know there would be this many?"

Kiran turned around to see what the Lawspeaker was talking about and shock constricted his throat.

One hundred or more People of the Songtrail stepped out of the forest to surround them. Only the way to the sea cliffs remained open. Exhausted warriors, slick with sweat and carrying weapons in their fists, approached from three sides. Behind them, old gray-haired men hobbled. Many supported themselves on walking sticks. Their headdresses, made from the skinned heads of grizzly bears, kosweet, and deer, streamed ribbons of colored feathers interspersed with shell beads. Two hard-eyed women walked with the old men. All were covered with red ochre from head to toe. The warriors wore only hide aprons. Kiran could smell the scent of the pine resin they mixed with the ochre to keep insects at bay. Chief Drona appeared to Kiran's left. The white rings painted around his eyes gleamed in the sunlight. Around his throat, like a scarf, he wore the red cloth Kiran had given him.

When Ingolf and Sokkolf started glancing over their shoulders at the trees, and it appeared they might flee, Gunnar said, "Hold fast, thralls! You'll be worse off if you bolt than not, for surely they'll chase you down."

Ingolf and Sokkolf seemed to freeze in place, along with the two witnesses, Orm and Masson the Bellower.

Gunnar said, "I want everyone to lift his hands. Under no circumstances are you to reach for a weapon." Turning, Gunnar glowered at Thorlak. "That especially means you, Lawspeaker. I'll not have you giving our friends a reason to kill us."

Thorlak's dark gaze remained on the Skraeling army, but he replied, "*Friends*, Gunnar?"

"For now, yes."

"This is landnám. We are here to take these people's lands. They will never be our friends."

Gunnar's brows lifted in appreciation. "There are times when you actually surprise me, Thorlak, which takes some doing, since I pride myself on my knowledge of men's characters. You are the worst sort of dunderhead. The sort that thinks he knows something he, in fact, does not."

Affronted, Thorlak's tone went low and threatening. "You may boldly insult others, Gunnar, but if you value your life—"

"The Skraelings probably outnumber us ten to one. Only a dunderhead could imagine that we can take what we want. If we intend to establish a colony here, we will have to purchase the right. If you have any wits, you'll leave it to me. Kiran?" Gunnar said. "Follow me with your hands over your head. Don't lower them until I do. We must greet Drona."

"I'll be right behind you, Godi."

A weasel-faced man left Chief Drona's side and trotted over to speak with Asson.

Gunnar ignored him, marching across the burned village with hands held high. He walked at an unhurried but purposeful pace, seemingly unafraid as the Skraeling army closed in around them. Truth be told, even though Kiran knew these people were his best friend's relatives, it made his blood run cold.

Godi Gunnar walked straight to Drona and said, "I'm heartened to see you, Chief Drona. Thank you for the canoe escort you provided my ship, and for meeting me here at the appointed time." Without taking his eyes from Drona's, Gunnar asked, "Who are these other people?"

Kiran translated the words.

Drona's boyish face showed no expression as he answered and made a sweeping gesture to the army.

Kiran said, "Chief Drona says he did not know until a short time ago that nearby villages would be present for today's event, but he wishes you to know that they are not here to slaughter us. There are two women and one man who survived the battle. They will tell their story. The others are here to listen."

The weasel-faced man trotted back and stood just behind Drona.

Godi Gunnar's eyes tightened, but he said, "Tell Chief Drona, I'm glad they're here. And I'm especially glad to have the survivors give testimony. All we want is a fair settlement for the injured. That's why we have come."

As Kiran relayed what Godi Gunnar had said Weasel-Face leaned forward to whisper something in Drona's ear. Drona nodded to him, but his attention remained on Kiran.

When Kiran had finished, Drona tipped his head. "This is Odjet, our village shaman. He told me to believe you—for now. He says he's spoken with Elder Asson and Asson says he was alone when you entered the meadow and you could have killed him at any time, but you did not. Chief Gunnar even stopped the starved man from reaching for his weapon."

"Yes, he did. I think you will find that Chief Gunnar is a good and fair man. He will do his best today to make sure no one leaves here without feeling that justice has been done."

Drona's gaze moved away from Kiran and drifted across the burned lodges and scattered children's toys that littered the meadow. Pain lived in Drona's eyes. "Justice will be a hard thing, do you know that?"

"I . . ."

"What's he saying, Kiran?"

"He says it will not be easy for these people to feel they have received justice for the murder of their relatives."

Godi Gunnar looked Drona straight in the eyes and nodded solemnly. "Please tell him I understand that and, with his permission, will begin the proceedings that I hope will ease the grief of both our peoples, and restore the proper Spirit balance to the world."

Kiran relayed the message, and after a few instants of staring at Godi Gunnar the chief's head dipped in a nod.

# Twenty-Eight

As Alfdis made his way through the spruces and poplars toward the Lawspeaker's booth on the crest of the hill he kept glancing over his shoulder. A flurry of activity encompassed the shore. People dashed about, some shouting Thyra's name, others carrying goods to the water's edge, where small rowboats ferried them to the three ships anchored in the inlet. As the tide came in, the water lifted the ships and set them to rocking like cradles beneath an attentive mother's hand. Alfdis frowned. He'd sneaked away about two hours ago, and so did not know what had caused the flurry, but the master of the *Logmadur*, Olaf the Blue, was undoubtedly looking for him. He'd been assigned to help Olaf. While a free man, Alfdis had obligations, as any settler did. If they were loading something, he should be down there carrying boxes and chests.

Instead, Alfdis moved from tree trunk to tree trunk, hiding long enough to scan the forest and the area around the Lawspeaker's booth. Sunlight gilded the pointed roof of Thorlak's house. Unease stole through Alfdis. When Thorlak was away he always posted two guards. Where were Thorlak's guards?

Alfdis' gaze searched the hilltop, then lifted to the high branches where men might hide. When he glimpsed nothing, his gaze moved on, surveying boulders and any unusual shapes that clung to the shadows. He saw nothing. No one. Even the thrall cage behind the Lawspeaker's booth stood empty. Where, Alfdis wondered, had they taken the boy? And where was Jofrid? As Thorlak's personal maidservant, the Foal's-brow was required to always be at hand.

Shouts went up from the shore.

Alfdis edged out of the trees thirty paces behind Thorlak's booth to watch the rowboats being dragged ashore, whereupon bundles and boxes were loaded into two of the boats and settlers climbed into the remaining boats.

Alfdis looked around again, expecting to be discovered and attacked at any instant.

When no guards emerged from hiding he trotted for Thorlak's booth.

Alfdis opened the door latch, and dodged inside into the darkness. The scents of old books and damp wool wrinkled his nose.

Alfdis slung his bow and shoved his arrow back in his quiver. He left the door ajar and hurried to the big chest in the rear, which sat near the table and two chairs. Before he knelt in front of the chest Alfdis cast a worried glance back at the door.

"Gunnar said the chest bore a lock. There's no lock on this chest," Alfdis whispered to himself. "Has someone been here before me?"

Alfdis lifted the lid, praying the brass hinges wouldn't squeal. The chest was empty.

He moved to the wooden box sitting beside the chest, and opened it. Also empty.

Alfdis squinted at the dimly lit room. In the sliver of sunlight that penetrated around the ajar door, he saw that the Lawspeaker's bed had no blankets and the man's cloak did not hang upon the peg by the door. Fear shot through Alfdis' veins.

As rapidly as he could, he searched the boxes beneath the bed, and also found them empty. He straightened up. That's why there were no guards. Except for a few belongings, there was nothing to protect. Though, if stolen, the magnificent rune-covered chest would be impossible to replace. So why had Thorlak left it? A ruse?

Alfdis swallowed hard when it occurred to him in a moment of sheer panic that he might just be standing in the midst of a trap. He ran hard for the door, threw it open, and leaped outside into the warm sunshine.

When he looked down at the cove below he gasped. All three ships had set sail and were headed south with their sails billowing in the ocean breezes. Too stunned to speak, he just watched until they curved around the distant point and, one by one, vanished from sight.

*Gods, where are they going?*

"Great Thor, Bjarni the Deep-minded would never have sailed *Thor's Dragon* away unless he had a knife to his throat—or unless he and the rest of the crew had been taken prisoner and were shackled in the hold."

Alfdis hit the trail to Whale Rib Village at a run.

F our hours into the journey, Porkell the Elder stood on the deck of *Defense of Asgard* and watched the ship drop anchor. A group of around forty colonists stood near him, murmuring, trying to figure out what was going on.

Helgi the Stout ran his tongue through the gap of his missing front teeth before he said, "Porkell, I thought they told you we had to scurry to board because a Skraeling army had been sighted and they were about to slaughter us all." He hesitated, eyes scanning the coastline. "I don't see a Skraeling in sight."

Porkell rubbed his jaw on his woolen sleeve as he studied the beautiful forested hills. They'd stopped in a shallow cove with broad, sandy beaches. Slowly, he said, "Nor do I."

"Didn't Godi Ketil tell you we were heading for Vinland to get away from them?"

"He did. But I thought it curious that he wanted us aboard his ship, and not back on *Thor's Dragon.*"

Porkell glanced at Godi Gunnar's cargo ship. Though Ketil had sent several men to help Bjarni's crew, no settlers had been assigned to travel aboard *Thor's Dragon.* That meant that both the *Logmadur* and *Defense of Asgard* were overloaded.

The entire confused group of settlers, over one hundred men, women, and children, turned around when men bristling with weapons began gathering on the steerbord sides of both the *Logmadur* and *Defense of Asgard.*

"Are we off-loading warriors to go fight the Skraelings?" Helgi asked.

"Appears so."

"But that's ridiculous if we're headed to Vinland."

Porkell noted that each warrior carried a bow and stuffed quiver, plus a battle-ax and sword. They seemed to be expecting a horde of Skraelings. "I suspect there's mischief afoot."

Helgi's young face contorted. "You mean Godi Ketil lied to us?"

Cool wind tousled Porkell's white hair around his eyes while he thought about the matter. Several people had crowded close to listen to his conversation with Helgi. Porkell's gaze drifted over their worried faces. A few angry voices erupted as their words were relayed back through the assembly.

Porkell turned around and lifted both hands to get their attention before he called, "There's no need for concern, not yet. Godi Gunnar and the Lawspeaker said they'd be back by nightfall. I'm sure they'll answer all our questions when they return!"

Grumbles went through the settlers. Every eye had fixed upon the growing number of warriors assembling on the decks of each ship—except for *Thor's Dragon*. A skeleton crew appeared to be sailing Godi Gunnar's vessel. Porkell counted just ten men on deck. Most of the oar ports were vacant.

Quietly, which was an oddity for Helgi the Stout, he said, "Porkell? It looks like we're off-loading the entire private armies of both the Lawspeaker and Godi Ketil. Doesn't that leave us vulnerable if the Skraelings mount a flotilla of canoes to attack our ships?"

Porkell exhaled a long-drawn-out breath. "We might want to take an inventory of the weapons possessed by each colonist, just in case we have to defend them ourselves. It seems the godar have more important business than protecting us."

# Twenty-Nine

Let's find a place to be seated."

Gunnar gestured to an outcrop of rounded stones that stood knee-high near the tree line. The shadows of the new leaves danced over the rocks, providing shade. As the day warmed, Gunnar suspected that would come as a welcome relief to those engaged in the court.

Gunnar led the way toward the rocks with Kiran walking at his side and Thorlak two paces behind them. The fragrance of the sea was powerful today. It blended with the green scents of the land to perfume the air.

Softly, for Gunnar's ears alone, Kiran said, "Godi, if all these people count themselves as relatives, the goods we may be required to provide in recompense—"

"I've already been running the calculations myself, Kiran. But if it takes every trade item on every ship we have to stop a war and create a safe place for our settlers to establish a place in this new world, then so be it." He cast a glance over his shoulder at where Ingolf and Sokkolf stood. Both had brown hair, though Ingolf stood a full six inches taller than Sokkolf. Overstuffed packs nestled beside them. "If you get the opportunity, Kiran, tell Ingolf to cut the red cloth we brought into smaller strips. That will ease our burden some."

"Yes, Godi, I will."

Gunnar sat down on a boulder and watched the Skraeling circle tighten around him. Kiran and Thorlak took up positions standing just behind his shoulders, as was customary, while Drona and several elderly men stood three paces in front of him. The red ochre smeared over the elders' bodies had sunken into their wrinkles, giving each a webbed appearance.

Only Asson wore no red ochre. As a result, he spent as much time slapping at insects as the Norse did.

It struck Gunnar as peculiar that the old wizard stood off in the distance beyond the circle. His shoulder-length black hair fell forward as he bent to pick up the broken pieces of a small child's bow and examine them. For his people, he was tall—around five and a half feet. It seemed that no one wished to share the elder's company on this difficult day. In fact, anyone whose path veered toward Asson immediately shifted course.

Gunnar glanced over his right shoulder at Thorlak and found the Law-speaker staring at Asson, as though afraid to take his eyes from him. "Are you ready, Thorlak?"

"I am," he said in a clipped voice.

"Kiran?"

"Yes, Godi, I'm prepared."

Gunnar opened his hands and lifted them to the assembly as he called, "I am Chieftain Gunnar of the Fallen Star land, and it is my sacred duty this day to decide who was at fault for the battle that destroyed Whale Rib Village, and to find justice for those who were wronged."

When Kiran translated, murmurs broke out and eddied through the assembly. A group of old men stood off to the side, watching Gunnar. The Soapstone Village Council?

"Kiran, bring forward Godi Dag's defenders. I want you to translate as we go, at least as best you can."

Kiran waved the two men forward, and they shouldered through the Skraelings as though terrified to breathe, lest they be torn to bits. Their chain-mail armor clinked with their movements. When they stood beside Thorlak, both men were breathing hard. Like everyone else, they must have assumed they would be facing a handful of barbarian survivors, not an army painted bright red and gripping lances, clubs, and knives.

Gunnar held out a hand. "This is Orm Einarsson and Masson the Bellower. Both men serve as bodyguards for Godi Dag the Ice-fist. They will tell the story of what they saw the morning of the battle. Orm Einarsson, please begin."

Orm squared his shoulders and swallowed hard. His mousy brown hair stuck to his sweating temples in wisps. Twenty-two, Orm had a wife and three children waiting for him back home near Ocean's End in Finnmark. Because Dag did not trust thralls to guard him, both Orm and Masson were hired men, men with violent reputations. They were paid well for one purpose: to make sure no harm came to Dag.

Gunnar understood such men with perfect clarity, and so was under no illusions as to their coming testimony.

Orm used his sleeve to wipe his forehead. "Masson and me were standing behind Godi Dag at the table filled with strings of glass beads. For over two hours Skraelings had been coming and going from the table, cooing to each other and smiling whilst examining the beads. We had a head-high stack of fine pelts for our efforts, but two strings of fine Venetian beads, sky blue with red bands, ended up missing in the first hour, which displeasured Godi Dag fiercely. He can't abide thievery in any form. Toward the end, a loud argument broke out between the Lawspeaker and a group of Skraeling men. Me and Masson grabbed for our swords, fearing a fight, and prepared to run to the Lawspeaker's aid. An old gray Skraeling woman took the distraction for an opportunity to snatch a string of red beads. But Godi Dag saw the treachery, drew his sword, and cut off the hand holding the string. When it thunked to the ground, she let out a yowl that caused every Skraeling, including those who had been arguing with the Lawspeaker, to rush to her. At the sight of the thief's gushing stump, roars went up. Our men nocked their bows and commenced to let fly. We killed eight barbarian warriors in moments, and they skewered five of us with their lances before hightailing it for the uplands. We followed them, fighting the whole way. When they got to this village, most ran for the longhouse and holed up. We made quick work of those that tried to hide in the skin lodges."

Gunnar waited for Kiran to finish relaying the story, and when cries of outrage rose he called, "Silence! I tolerate no disruptions in my court. I must hear from all witnesses. Masson the Bellower, you were standing beside Orm. Do you agree with the story he just told?"

"I do, Godi!" the big man half-shouted.

"And do you have anything to add to the tale?"

Masson's jaw jutted out as he glared at the assembly. Gunnar straightened his black sleeves while he waited for an answer. He knew from long experience that such squinty-eyed, purse-lipped expressions more often than not meant a man was scared to death.

Masson growled, "I've nothing to add. I agree with Orm's telling. That's just how it happened. The old hag stole the beads and Godi Dag gave her just what she had coming."

Kiran finished and shrill voices erupted as people shifted to speak to one another.

While Gunnar waited for the voices to die down, he watched Asson. The wizard appeared unconcerned by the proceedings. He was ambling around the periphery of the village with a vague smile on his wrinkled face, staring at the ground, as though tracking something. Perhaps the fox he'd been looking for when they'd arrived?

Gunnar turned to Drona and found the chief staring at him. "Chief Drona, please call forth your witnesses."

Drona gestured to two young men and a woman. The short, stocky warrior with a round face took the lead. His oversized ears stuck out through his black hair.

Chief Drona said something, and Kiran translated the chief's words: "This woman is ShiHolder, and the men are Camtac and Gower. All survived the battle. All saw what happened to Obosheen, the elder who lost her hand."

Drona gestured to the stocky warrior, Gower, who drew himself to his full height of around five feet three inches tall. He had a strong voice and looked at Gunnar as he spoke.

Kiran translated in a halting manner, saying a few words at a time: "I was standing . . . just to Elder Obosheen's right. I had picked out a string of green-and-white beads . . . for my wife, and was haggling over the price with the man you call Godi Dag. I offered two beaver hides, but he wanted six. When the argument broke out, I saw Obosheen . . . pick up a string of red beads. She stepped back from the table and turned with the string in her hand to tell Kannabush about the beautiful colors. That's when . . . Godi Dag jerked his sword from its sheath, and hacked off Obosheen's hand. She never tried to steal anything! She was just . . . turning to talk with her friend about the beads."

Gunnar listened, then looked back at Drona. As the sun rose higher in the sky, the white rings around his dark eyes began to run with sweat. Stripes now decorated the red ochre on his cheeks. He showed no emotion whatsoever. "Do the other witnesses wish to add anything to Gower's description of the event?"

Kiran translated and listened to the responses of the two other people before he said, "Godi, young Camtac verifies Gower's story word for word, as does ShiHolder. But ShiHolder is also here for another reason. She says that Godi Dag took her children as thralls and she wants them back. There's an infant girl, and a ten-year-old boy."

*The boy behind Thorlak's booth?*

"Tell her I'll be happy to discuss that after we've come to an agreement about the Obosheen incident."

As Kiran spoke, the woman's eyes tightened, but she nodded.

Gunnar couldn't help but stare at the youth Gower. He had the unblinking eyes of a hunting lion. On trading expeditions to the Black Land, Gunnar had seen many lions. When the big cats fixed upon prey, they never stopped.

They pursued their quarry until it dropped dead in its tracks from thirst or sheer exhaustion. Gunnar had the feeling that Gower planned to hunt the Norse with the same savage diligence. His gaze drifted around the assembly, where he noted similar expressions on the faces of other warriors. If he couldn't find a way to end this hatred, there would no landnám here.

Gunnar shifted upon the rock and scratched his blond beard. Finally, after due thought, he turned back to Orm and Masson. "Let me see if I understand the details of your stories."

Kiran continued to translate.

Orm and Masson faced Gunnar, but both kept glancing out at the Skraeling warriors.

Gunnar was distracted when Alfdis the Lig-lodin stepped out of the trees to the west. Breathing hard, he looked like he'd run the whole way. His black hair framed his face in sweat-damp locks.

Gunnar said, "Orm Einarsson, you said that when a loud argument broke out between the Lawspeaker and a group of Skraeling men, you feared there was going to be a fight, and you and Masson grabbed for your swords and prepared to run to Thorlak's aid. At the same time, the Skraeling woman picked up the string of red beads. Is that correct?"

Orm and Masson nodded. Orm said, "Yes, absolutely. That's right."

Gunnar waited for Kiran to explain the conversation to the Skraeling audience.

"How long did you stare at Thorlak as you prepared to join the fight?" Gunnar asked.

Masson's eyes narrowed, but he said, "Two seconds. Three."

Orm nodded, and Gunnar said, "What drew your attention back to the table?"

Masson grinned with a mouthful of rotted teeth. "The sound of Godi Dag's sword ringing as it cleared his sheath."

Gunnar turned to Orm Einarsson. "And you?"

"I turned back at the meaty sound of iron striking flesh."

"I see." Gunnar blinked out at the crowd. Every eye rested upon him, with the exception of the old wizard who stood bent over, poking at something interesting on the ground. "Then neither of you actually saw the old woman pick up the beads."

"Well," Orm said, "the string was still clutched in her hand when Godi Dag lopped it off. I saw that."

Masson the Bellower gritted his teeth and gave Gunnar a hard look. "Godi Dag said she was stealing it. I'd believe him any instant over a bunch of filthy, conniving barbarians."

As Kiran started to translate, Gunnar interrupted. "Kiran, smooth over that last. We don't want Masson the Bellower to suddenly discover several feathered lances sticking in his guts."

"I'd already planned to do so, Godi."

"You're an apt translator, then. Continue."

Kiran did, and Gunnar studied expressions, judging the feelings of the listeners. The youngest warriors wore disbelieving sneers. Drona and the old men seemed to be doing the same thing Gunnar was, waiting to proceed until he understood the sentiments of the assembly.

Gunnar, at last, said, "Is there any Norseman here who actually saw old Obosheen pick up the beads?"

He caught a glimpse of Thorlak's red sleeve when the wind billowed it out. The Lawspeaker said nothing. That, Gunnar knew, was about to change.

Gunnar leaned forward. "Then, as the judge in this matter, I find there are no Norse witnesses who can verify Godi Dag's claim that the old woman was stealing the string of beads. This court has only Dag's word of what he alone witnessed. However, we have three witnesses from the People of the Songtrail who saw the entire affair, and say without a doubt that Obosheen was not stealing the beads. She'd just picked them up, as any potential buyer would, and turned to speak with her friend about the red colors."

Gunnar paused while Kiran translated.

Conversations broke out among the elders whom Gunnar assumed to be the Soapstone Village Council.

When he lifted his hands, people went quiet. "Since there are three witnesses to verify Obosheen's innocence, and no witnesses to verify her guilt, this court finds her innocent of the accused theft."

Asson, at last, lifted his head to look at Gunnar.

Chief Drona's face showed grudging respect, as though he'd been certain of a reverse ruling and found it laudatory that Gunnar had based his judgment upon the facts presented. The four old men gathered around Drona to talk to him in hushed voices, and Gunnar had the sense they might be making their own rulings.

"I must add, though," Gunnar called out, "that I also judge that Godi Dag's actions were just a mistake made in the haste of misunderstanding! A violent argument had broken out and he, like Orm and Masson, must have been afraid there was going to be a fight. Godi Dag was probably staring at Thorlak, just as Orm and Masson were, and glimpsed Obosheen picking up the beads from the corner of his vision. When she turned away, I suspect he thought she was attempting to take the beads, and he stupidly drew his sword to stop her. He was wrong. This court rules that Godi Dag must pay wergild to all aggrieved parties." He added, "Kiran, after you've translated that, please have Ingolf and Sokkolf display the goods we're offering in compensation. Once we've established a price with Drona and the Council, each person may select—"

Thorlak interrupted, "The Konungsbók requires that wergild be offered for each life lost. What if a man lost ten relatives in the battle? Will you allow him to collect goods for each one? If so, you don't have enough goods here to cover the wergild."

Coal-black curls flipped around Kiran's bearded face when he said, "Worse, Godi, I suspect they each lost thirty relatives."

"You may wish," Thorlak suggested, "to ask the Skraelings to assemble on the shore near our booths to receive their wergild later in the day. That would give us time to gather our resources."

Gunnar rubbed his chin. "You're right. Kiran, can you negotiate the price? We must establish a fair value for each lost relative. If we don't have enough goods here to cover the wergild, we will have to ask people to meet us at the booths at dusk, where I'll pay them from my own stores, and collect from Dag later."

Kiran hesitated, uneasy about the request, but he squared his shoulders. "Yes, Godi, I will negotiate the price."

"Best get started then."

Kiran called to Drona, explained the dilemma, and gestured to Ingolf and Sokkolf, then led the chief and the elders toward the packs.

Drona called something to the crowd, and when he walked toward Ingolf and Sokkolf dozens of people followed him.

As Ingolf rushed to lay out the different pieces of fabric, lances, iron pots, knives, small brooches, and other objects, astonished voices rose. To these people, it must look like an unbelievable collection of riches. He suspected they could trade each item for enough to wealth to live in luxury for months.

Sokkolf drew out a piece of parchment and a chunk of charcoal to write down names and associated objects. His strange empty eyes had an eerie light.

From behind Gunnar, Thorlak said, "You should not give them iron. They'll just hammer every pot into a weapon to kill us."

"Thorlak, if you'll make a careful study of the lance points and knives that prickle all around us, you'll see that they already have enough iron blades to kill us many times over. A few more will make no difference."

The Lawspeaker walked around Gunnar's shoulder to stand in front of him. The breeze fluttered his red hair and beard. "There is another matter you must address. What will you do about the woman's claim that she wants her children back?"

In the distance, Asson stood talking with the woman whose children had been taken as thralls by Godi Dag. And, still at the edge of the trees,

Alfdis looked like he was eager to speak with Gunnar. *What did he find in Thorlak's booth?*

"I haven't heard the facts yet, so I've no idea."

Thorlak's lips pressed into a hard line. "Well, I know both the facts and the law, so let me enlighten you. She did not escape before the battle or during the battle. When the battle was done, and the prisoners had already been rounded up, she ran."

Gunnar shifted uncomfortably on the rock. As he looked around at the almost naked Skraeling army bristling with weapons, his guts went runny. The Norse had strict rules about the three social classes—the jarls, the bondi, and the thralls: nobles, freeborn, and slaves. Because they'd been created by the god Heimdall when he was wandering through Middle Earth lying with women, they were not conveniences but divinely willed realities. Thralls were the first class of humans created by Heimdall. Every Norse child learned the rhyme about their creation:

> *Their daughters were Drudge and Daggle-tail,*
> *Slattern, Serving-Wench, and Cinder-Wench,*
> *Stout-Leg, Shorty, Stumps and Dumps,*
> *Spinkleshanks eke, and Stutterer:*
> *Thence are sprung the breed of thralls.*

Thralls were the most common trade item in existence, and one of the most valuable, especially exotic breeds. Everyone took thralls. They captured them in raids, purchased them at slave markets, or traded for them. Icelanders had Danish thralls. Norse kept Swedes, and Swedes kidnapped Finns. The child of a slave was always a slave. Most slaves could not own property or marry, and if they did their children belonged to the slaves' owner. The one exception was when an owner allowed a thrall to work for a portion of the proceeds of an enterprise, such as farming, or weaving, or, as Gunnar had always done, for a portion of the profits of his shipping business. Thralls could also sell any crafts they created when not at work, and could use the money earned to purchase their freedom. Owners could free thralls, but such thralls were not considered citizens. Indeed, they had no rights in the eyes of the law, which is why most owners who freed their thralls also adopted them into their families, effectively giving them citizenship and awarding the leysingi the rights and duties of any other free person, including testifying and bringing grievances before the court . . . and therein rested Gunnar's problem.

Technically, the instant the survivors of the battle had been rounded up by the victors they'd become the property, the thralls, of the jarls. By law,

ShiHolder's children had been slaves at that point. She could not give them to any man, because they no longer belonged to her. Worse, Shi-Holder was an escaped slave. The woman had no legal right to bring claims in his court. Gunnar exhaled the words, "The jarls should have distributed the spoils equally. Why did Dag get both of her children?"

"The godar negotiated it on the battlefield, just before the woman ran. Dag said he would forego all other spoils from the village if he could have the children. The godar agreed."

"When did the godar decide to slaughter the adult thralls?"

"Toward the end of the battle when our victory became clear. Godi Ketil said, and the others agreed, that the adult Skraelings would be plotting to kill us all in our sleep and we didn't have enough men to guard so many adult barbarians."

Gunnar's life had just been complicated in ways he didn't even want to consider. By all rights, then, the children belonged to Dag the Ice-fist as his share of the spoils.

"I must hear ShiHolder before I rule, Thorlak. She may disagree with your version of the story."

The Lawspeaker's lips formed a hard smile. "Of course, Godi Gunnar."

A disturbance broke out around Kiran when a few people grabbed precious items and ran away with them. Kiran yelled at them, but they kept running, clutching pots and pieces of fabric to their breasts. Kiran must have ordered Ingolf and Sokkolf to pack up the remaining items, because Sokkolf started stuffing brooches back into a pack while Ingolf rushed to roll up the bolts of fabric.

Chief Drona said something to Kiran. Kiran nodded and led Drona and the old men back toward Gunnar. Fifty or more disgruntled people trailed at their heels.

Kiran's sixteen-year-old face had reddened. "Godi, the People of the Songtrail have agreed to accept the wergild, but are upset that most of them cannot claim their recompense now. They don't believe that it will be waiting for them on the shoreline later in the day."

"Please explain to Drona that we had no idea how many people would be here and we need time to carry the goods from our ships and get them organized for distribution to the aggrieved parties. I give him my oath that the goods will be ready to claim by nightfall."

As Kiran relayed his words, Drona listened. The people gathered around them grumbled and shook their heads.

Gunnar looked up at Chief Drona, who stood just behind Kiran with his arms folded over his ochre-painted chest. The elders had formed a knot to his right and murmured to one another.

"Kiran? What value did the chief and elders agree to? What do we owe them for each life lost?"

"One ell of cloth, one iron item, or three pieces of jewelry equal the value of one lost relative. However, I bargained them down to one-half ell for the red cloth, which they especially desire."

Gunnar's brows lifted in admiration. One ell was the measure from a man's armpit to his wrist. "That will do nicely, Kiran. I can meet those demands without Dag—just in case he's recalcitrant over the matter. Please tell Drona that, if he has no objections, we will distribute the goods at dusk, then tomorrow we will address ShiHolder's request for her children." *Which will give me more time to consider the matter.*

Drona listened to Kiran, then nodded to Gunnar. Finally, Drona and the elders walked away toward Asson.

Gunnar heaved a breath. "Well, that was a thing done by a hair's breadth. If we—"

Thorlak vented a deep-throated laugh and stalked away.

Alfdis looked around before he strode forward like a man on a sacred mission. When he got closer, Gunnar could see that his blue eyes had gone as hard and fiery as sapphires from the Black Land.

Thinking that Alfdis wished to discuss his findings in Thorlak's booth, Gunnar said, "Kiran, could you give me a few moments of privacy with Alfdis the Lig-lodin?"

"Of course. I'll be over speaking with Elder Asson." Kiran bowed and walked toward where the little wizard stood with a host of Skraelings, including the two youths, Camtac and Gower, who'd given testimonies.

Alfdis broke into a trot. He was breathing hard when he whispered, "They're gone, Gunnar."

"Who's gone?"

"The ships. All of them. They left this morn—"

"What do you mean *gone*?" As though Gunnar's mind couldn't quite accept the words, he growled, "You mean they sailed away?"

"Yes, someone clearly told the colonists to pack up in a hurry, and they sailed south down the coastline."

Gunnar felt like the bottom had just fallen out of his stomach. A sinking sensation of doom spread through him. "Including *Thor's Dragon*?"

"Yes, and you and I both know that Bjarni wouldn't have gone without a fight, so there's no telling how many of your crew got hurt or killed when they were overrun."

Rage turned Gunnar's blood to lava. He whirled to glare at Thorlak.

The Lawspeaker stood twenty paces away with his red sleeves billowing in the wind. Gunnar couldn't see the man's eyes, for they were focused on Asson, but his thin lips had curled into a subtle smile . . . *as though he knows what news Alfdis just brought me.*

In a low voice, Alfdis said, "It required considerable secret planning to succeed, Gunnar. They must have intended to foil your efforts the whole time."

"Why didn't you get the message that the ships were leaving? They think you're just another settler."

"I sneaked away from the booths very early. That's the one reason I can think of. I was gone before the order came to pack up, and they couldn't find me to tell me."

"Did you see any evidence that they tried to find you? People combing the shore or hills calling your name?" How many people knew that he and Alfdis were allied? And how did they discover that fact?

Alfdis swallowed hard. "No. Though I heard Godi Ketil's men calling for Thyra, as though she was missing."

"Missing?" Gunnar ground his teeth.

"Maybe she woke and left, maybe she vanished into thin air, I don't know."

"And what did you find in Thorlak's chest?"

"Nothing. He must have packed up in the middle of the night and had his belongings carried to the *Logmadur.*"

Gunnar's thoughts were elsewhere, imagining the pandemonium at dusk when none of his promised wergild appeared on the shore.

Old instincts, habits of survival long honed to perfection during his forest-walking years, sprang to life, and his veins throbbed with the almost uncontrollable need to kill.

Gunnar cocked his head to study Thorlak. "Why do you think he hasn't run?"

Alfdis looked at the Lawspeaker. "He's brave. I'll say that for him."

"Is he?"

Alfdis turned to give Gunnar a curious look. "Well, he's going to claim he knew nothing of the treachery. You know that. And if he does, we dare not mention that his booth is empty, or he'll know we searched—"

"He already knows."

As the ramifications sank in, Alfdis looked faint. "That's not possible, Gunnar. How could he?"

"I suspect he knows that you're my man."

Alfdis inhaled a breath and let it out slowly. "Gods, I pray not."

Gunnar scanned the people in the meadow. Most of the Skraelings wandered through the burned lodges, picking up small items, discussing them in forlorn tones. Tears ran down faces.

Gunnar drew his sword. "Let's go ask him."

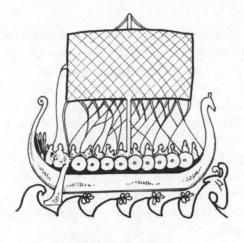

# Thirty

When Kiran saw Godi Gunnar marching headlong toward the Lawspeaker with his sword drawn, Asson reached out and gripped his forearm, pulling him back. The old man's face held a gentleness that could stop the heart. In a deep voice, Asson said, "Please, listen to me. You must not go to him."

"Forgive me, Elder, but truly I must." Kiran pulled away, trying to catch up with Sokkolf and Ingolf, who'd already made it halfway to where Godi Gunnar and Alfdis stood with the Lawspeaker at the edge of the trees.

The godi had a murderous expression on his wrinkled face as he swung his sword up to rest the shining blade upon his shoulder. A provocative position, to say the least.

Kiran heard Godi Gunnar say, "Thorlak, this is your doing, I suppose?"

The icy timbre of Godi Gunnar's voice made Sokkolf and Ingolf run harder. And Kiran, too, broke into a run.

Thorlak's gaze shifted to where Kiran, Ingolf, and Sokkolf dashed toward him. "You would do well to tell your friends to keep their distance, Gunnar."

The godi lifted a hand, a familiar gesture to them all, and Kiran, Ingolf, and Sokkolf halted at the same instant four paces away.

The Lawspeaker took an odd moment to smooth down his red sleeves. It had to be a trick of afternoon light, but Kiran thought he saw sparks glitter beneath the man's fingers. "Gunnar, let me begin this discussion by telling you that I do not possess the authority you imagine. This was not solely my decision. But you do not wish to test my ability to defend myself."

"I think you underestimate your influence, Lawspeaker," Gunnar said with a smile. "When does Ketil plan to return? When I'm dead?"

"I've no idea."

"Indeed? Well, a few days should be adequate to assure that I and anyone who's sided with me have been murdered by the Skraelings."

Thorlak seemed to be assessing Gunnar's posture. His gaze lingered on the sword, which had a fiery edge in the sunlight. He gestured to it. "Do you plan to use that?"

Godi Gunnar bowed his head and shook it. The sword moved as he took a new grip. When Gunnar looked up again, a smile clung to his lips, but his voice held no amusement whatsoever. "What are you looking for in the Land of the White Men, Thorlak? Some great treasure, as I understand it."

"You understand *from whom?*"

"Good men."

The hands hanging at Thorlak's sides flexed open and closed, which set the runes on Skyrmir's hilt to flashing. They appeared to dance in the air above the metal. "I'm looking for a grave, Gunnar. That's all."

"A grave? Why? It contains a treasure?"

Their gazes held.

When Thorlak spoke, his voice had gone quiet, cold: "Whose purpose do you serve, Gunnar?"

"My own, of course."

Thorlak shook his head. "I think not. My sources tell me that before we set sail on this voyage you secretly met with the ealdorman of Northumbria. Is it true?"

Godi Gunnar's smile faded. The expression that replaced it could only be described as lethal. Gunnar canted his body at an angle, his sword poised for a crosscut that would slice the Lawspeaker in half with a single stroke. Like a short statue cut from tanned marble, the thunderous folds of Godi Gunnar's face left no doubt that he intended to take that stroke.

"You should choose your words with more care, Thorlak. Since the ealdorman of Northumbria is allied with the rebellious son of the king of England, it might be construed by lesser men that you're accusing me of treason."

Thorlak's teeth gleamed in the midst of his red beard. "Are you a traitor?"

Godi Gunnar's eyes flared. As his sword lifted from his shoulder . . .

Kiran shouted, "Godi, wait!" and lunged into a run.

He was two paces away when he felt the air change. There was a puff of wind at his back that ruffled his black hair and caused the trees to rustle; then he felt pressure on his chest. Barely noticeable at first, it soon became a leaden weight that squeezed the air from his lungs. As though a gigantic hand had swung out of the heavens, Kiran felt himself knocked backward and slammed to the ground. He saw Gunnar, Sokkolf, Ingolf, and Alfdis topple at the same instant.

Kiran thrashed across the grass, gasping, while his gaze swept the meadow. Whatever was happening to Kiran and the others, neither the People of the Songtrail nor the Lawspeaker had been affected. The Skraelings made no moves to intervene, probably at Elder Asson's insistence. They watched and carried on a discussion about what they saw.

Gray wings fluttered at the edges of Kiran's vision. It took his last ounce of strength to flip to his belly, get to his hands and knees, and struggle to crawl to safety in the one direction he knew, back toward Asson.

When the little elder saw him, he stepped away from his people and walked toward Kiran.

Thorlak shouted, "*Stop!* Come no closer or I'll kill him, and every other man, woman—"

Kiran went deaf. He seemed to be staring down a dark, quiet tunnel with no light at the end.

He must have collapsed and rolled to his back, for he found himself gazing up into Elder Asson's hazy face, backlit by brilliant sunlight, and felt the old man pat his shoulder. Asson's mouth moved, but Kiran couldn't hear him.

More helpless than he had ever been, Kiran's rigid body began relaxing, and he realized in a detached sort of way that he was suffocating, his lungs starving for air.

He was alone, floating in emptiness, when a bolt of silent lightning split the darkness. Fire seemed to spin out of the eternal night and fly away in tongues of flame. Somewhere in the distance, he heard screams. Feet pounded the earth like the flight of giants . . . or maybe it was just his heart thundering to a stop.

Kiran's arms and legs made feeble swimming motions as he fought for life. His eyes opened. He glimpsed Asson standing over him bathed in pale yellowish light. The elder had his feet braced and his open hands extended in front of him, as though holding back the gulf of darkness that threatened to swallow them all.

From some great distance, Kiran heard Thorlak shout in rage: "*Thyra!*"

# Thirty-One

When the rest of the People of the Songtrail fled in terror, Ewinon stood gaping, his gaze moving from Asson to the building thunderheads that roiled across the skies. Massive and dark, they grew taller and taller. Asson seemed to be calling them together. Only Camtac and Gower remained steadfastly at Ewinon's side. Each of them had a weapon in his hand, ready to battle to protect Asson, if necessary, but Ewinon could hear their rapid breathing, and feared that, at any moment, they might bolt to join their relatives racing away in the distance.

The Wobee shaman, Thorlak, roared something at Asson, but the alien words had no effect on the little elder's calm. When Asson threw his arms wide, as though to embrace the entire sky, Thorlak's gaze jerked upward. The clouds swirled like waves in the wake of a gigantic ship, molding themselves into monstrous shapes. When they stopped swirling, Ewinon's chest swelled with wonder.

In the center of the storm, Rainbow Serpent's body slithered out of the bruised thunderheads, his eyes flashing with lightning. At his sides, spiraling down, colossal herds thundered. They ran in dazzling white silence, neither gods nor men nor beasts, but combinations of all three. Mute with reverence, Ewinon's gaze drifted across the antlered humans, winged wolves, and ethereal blue caribou, their pointed forelegs stabbing down the clouds. Glimmering curtains of iridescent color wavered around them as they all rushed earthward. . . .

Asson clapped his hands together.

High above, foxfire streamed, exploding through the herds and drizzling down, glimmering, dancing, filling the destroyed village with stunning brilliance. Those few instants of magnificence seemed to last forever.

Then Thorlak shouted, drew his sword from its scabbard, and aimed it at Asson. The air itself seemed to gasp. As though gathering strength, the sword glowed with a bluish fire. The man bellowed, "Thyra!"

From deep in the forest, Ewinon heard a woman's hoarse cry . . . and the sky exploded with lightning. Lightning everywhere! A slender bolt crackled down and struck Thorlak's sword. Brilliant metallic fragments cartwheeled through the air. Ewinon, Camtac, and Gower simultaneously dove for the ground and covered their heads. Camtac gibbered in terror. Only when Asson cried out did Ewinon lift his eyes to look. One of the sword fragments had sliced open the elder's leg. Blood gushed through the rent in his pants.

When Asson finally straightened and lifted his hands to the sky gods again, Thorlak let out an enraged roar, turned, and charged into the forest.

Ewinon got to his feet and stood shaking. Chief Gunnar and his men remained sprawled on the ground. Unconscious or dead. *They didn't have Asson to protect them.*

Ewinon staggered to Asson and picked up the fragment of sword that had sliced open the elder's leg. "Are you all right, Asson?"

Asson gasped for breath as he looked out into the forest, apparently searching for Thorlak. "Did you see where he went? Did he catch Thyra?"

For an instant, Ewinon didn't know how to answer. He turned to look at Camtac and Gower. Both were on their feet, staring around like clubbed ducks. "I didn't see anything, did you?"

Gower called back, "No. He just vanished!"

When Asson walked away to rest upon a rock, Ewinon studied the shards of broken sword. They glittered.

He couldn't help it. He walked across the dead village, collecting every fragment he could find and tucking them into his belt pouch. The sword had shot out blue flame. It had to be magical.

"Ewinon?" Camtac called in an unnaturally high voice. "Let's get out of here! Now!"

Asson said, "Please, wait. I need your help. I must find the little fox."

"*Are you insane?*" Ewinon shouted. "I hope it was trampled to death beneath a hundred boots! Now, come with us. Thorlak may return!"

Asson hung his head, vented a deep sigh, and said, "I can't go with you. She needs me now more than ever."

Thyra shoved brush out of her way as she fled through the forest like a hunted animal. She could feel Thorlak's dark, malignant presence. Out in the trees, twigs cracked beneath his heavy boots.

He was coming for her. . . .

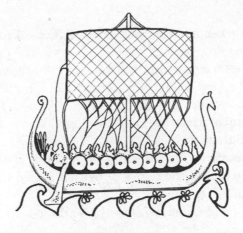

# Thirty-Two

When Kiran woke, he found Godi Gunnar kneeling at his side, looking down at him worriedly.

Sick to his stomach, he did not attempt to speak or stand up. The People of the Songtrail had vanished from the meadow, and Kiran didn't have the strength yet to turn to see what had happened to the other Norsemen. A soft, rhythmic flapping sounded as the sea breeze moved through the charred lodges.

"Are you back with me, Kiran?"

"Yes. Where is everyone?"

"I wish I knew. By the time my senses returned, the Skraelings were gone, along with the Lawspeaker, Orm Einarsson, and Masson the Bellower."

"What happened, Godi?" Kiran couldn't remember much.

Gunnar paused to frown out at the skeletal poles of the destroyed long-house. "I'm probably mad, but when I was perched on the precipice of death, I think Thorlak attacked them, or cast some Seidur spell upon them. I saw him draw his sword and point it at Asson. The glimpses I saw while I was fainting away looked like a great battle of light and dark between Thorlak and Asson."

Kiran tried to rise, but his strength failed him.

When he tried again, Gunnar gripped Kiran's elbow to help him to his feet. He fought down the bile that rose into his throat. The smell of the burned village increased his nausea.

"Why am I so weak and you look fine?" Kiran asked, annoyed by his infirmity.

"I've had more time to regain my wits. I woke about an hour ago, as did Sokkolf, Alfdis, and Ingolf. We searched for Thorlak and the others, but to no avail. I instructed them to keep searching. That's where they are now. They'll meet us at the booths at dusk."

"I pray none of them are dead."

Gunnar's lips curled with distaste. "Oh, so do I, especially Thorlak. I very much want to finish the sword stroke I'd begun before the bolts of lightning erupted."

Kiran staggered and Gunnar grabbed his arm to keep him from falling. "My head's spinning."

"It will for a time. Just take things slow."

Kiran blinked at the ocean. Fog clung to the water's surface like a gauzy blanket. In a rush it came back to him that Godi Gunnar had been betrayed by the godar and all the ships were gone.

"Godi, the People of the Songtrail must be waiting on the shore near our booths right now, expecting to receive their promised wergild. What are we going to do? Run?"

Gunnar released Kiran's arm and grimaced. "I've never run in my life . . . well, not from a fight. Just a few overzealous lawmen. No, Kristni, as soon as you're able, we're going to head down there, find Drona, and ask for a meeting with the village elders who were present at court today. If I'm not mistaken they came from several different villages, didn't they?"

"Yes. At least three villages, I think. Possibly four. But if you imagine that they will be forgiving about our failure to—"

"I imagine no such thing."

Kiran studied Gunnar's expression. He could see thoughts moving behind the savage glitter in the man's eyes. Kiran spread his feet to brace his weak knees. "I'm not going to like this plan, am I?"

Gunnar massaged his wrinkled forehead. "I don't like it much myself. It's risky. But I don't think we've a choice. Not if we wish to defeat Thorlak."

The last word sounded like a curse.

"He's going to do everything he can to destroy us now, isn't he?"

Gunnar nodded. "He can't let us find what's he's searching for before he does."

"The Land of the White Men?"

Gunnar paused. "And a grave, apparently."

"Whose grave?"

Gunnar examined Kiran from the corners of his eyes. "I'm genuinely afraid I may know the answer to that question."

When Gunnar said no more, Kiran batted dirt from his pants and shirt. "Are you going to tell me?"

"I haven't decided. Walk with me, Kristni." Gunnar extended a hand to the trail that led down to their booths in Seal Cove.

Kiran fell in beside him and tried to keep pace. Gunnar seemed to be in a great hurry to meet people who by now wanted to slit his throat.

After a good ten or fifteen minutes, Gunnar said, "Thirteen years ago, the Danes were slaughtered by the English in the northern region known as the Danelaw. Speculation was that the ealdorman of Mercia, Eadric, King Aethelred's chief advisor, had told him to do it because the Danes were conspiring against the king. Though I was born in Iceland, my family came from Denmark. I lost many many relatives in the massacre."

Kiran heard the pain in Gunnar's voice. "I'm sorry, Godi. But what does that have to do with us now?"

Gunnar lifted a finger to get Kiran's attention. "Everything, Kristni. King Sweyn Forkbeard's Seidur prophetess lived just a few houses away from my family in the Danelaw. The English told Forkbeard she and her daughter were dead, but our king was never allowed to see the bodies to verify that claim. Instead, he heard whispers that the Prophetess lived, that she and her daughter had been taken captive by Aethelred's forces and were being held to use against him when the time came."

Confused, and still not thinking well, Kiran shook his head. "But King Sweyn died over a year ago. His son, Cnut, is now king of Denmark. Why would it matter—"

"King Aethelred is very ill, Kiran. His son is waging war against him. If the Prophetess does live, and she returns to fight on the side of Edmund—"

"Aethelred fears her powers? After all these years?"

Gunnar hesitated as if carefully selecting his words: "I'm not sure about Aethelred, but Thorlak does."

"Thorlak?"

"Yes. You see, Thorlak was not always a Lawspeaker. For a few years, he was the Seidur seer of the rebel, Pallig, and Vethild's main rival. He—"

"*Vethild?*"

Gunnar nodded. "Yes, Kiran. She and Thorlak despised each other. Vethild had urged Pallig not to listen to Thorlak, and generally Pallig didn't. But when Thorlak claimed he'd had a 'vision' that Pallig would become king of England if he broke his treaty with Aethelred and joined the raiders attacking England's south coast, it was too much for Pallig.

He was an ambitious man. Pallig did as Thorlak suggested, broke the treaty that obliged him to protect England, and defected to join the raiders. That act directly led to Aethelred's slaughter of the Danelaw."

"I'm surprised the Danes didn't murder Thorlak in his sleep."

"Well, for one thing, he made a run for it. He fled through half of Europe, then caught a ship to Greenland, where he became a Lawspeaker."

Almost violently, Gunnar batted a spruce branch out of his way. "I'm sure Vethild is dead, but there are those who disagree with me."

Kiran's gaze flitted over the forest and rocks as he pieced the details together. "Why would it matter if she were alive?"

Gunnar held his tongue for a time, then replied, "Well, it's complicated. Aethelred's son by his first wife, Edmund, has claimed the right of succession. But his claim is being challenged by Aethelred's second wife, Queen Emma, who has two sons of her own. She, naturally, wants them to be king after Aethelred dies."

"Do you still have relatives in the Danelaw?"

"Plenty, and they're desperately afraid of another slaughter. That's why the Danelaw recently allied with Edmund. He's their only hope."

Kiran licked his lips as he thought. "But if Edmund fails, won't every man, woman, and child in the Danelaw be considered a traitor?"

Gunnar's stride quickened as the trail descended a steep slope. Towering birches lined the way, their windblown leaves glittering in the fading rays of sunset. "My fears are about what happens before that."

"What do you mean?"

"I'm afraid that in the end Edmund and Aethelred will be forced to ally to keep King Cnut from reconquering England. Which means Edmund will have to yield to his father."

"Where will that leave the Danelaw?"

Gunnar gave him an agonized glance. "In the depths of treason, considered traitors by both Aethelred and Cnut. That's why Edmund must win."

Kiran spent a few minutes trying to sift through the information he'd gathered over the past few days.

"Godi, I need to ask you a personal question."

"Go on."

"You're not involved with the Danelaw's plot to place Edmund on the throne, are you?"

The godi went silent. Kiran walked and waited.

As Sol disappeared below the western horizon, twilight settled over the rolling hills like a smoke-colored veil, and the first stars sprinkled the heavens.

Finally, Gunnar said, "Keep your voice down, Kristni. Even way out here there are hidden murderers just waiting to fulfill a king's orders."

"Which king?"

When the path curved around an outcrop of gray boulders, the scent of moss rose into the air, and Kiran saw the pools of water shining at the bases of the rocks. Moss covered the entire western side of the outcrop.

Gunnar tilted his head to give Kiran an amused look. "All three, I suspect."

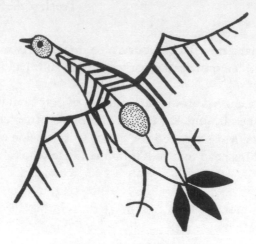

# Thirty-Three

**W**ounded and stunned, Asson kept limping along the caribou trail, forcing his shaking legs to carry him deeper into the darkening forest.

Everywhere he looked the white trunks of birches and aspens slatted the hills. Starlight had begun to shimmer in the gauzy tendrils of fog that twined through the canopy. It was so silent. Not a breath of wind stirred the leaves. Silence always seemed to magnify fragrances, especially at night. He breathed in the pungency of damp bark and earth.

Memories of the battle kept accosting him. His chest felt like a hollowed-out log. He had witnessed unbelievable Spirit Power before, with Neechwa, but nothing like this. Even now, seven hands of time later, the sheer vastness of strength displayed shocked him.

He stumbled, and righted himself. Crusted blood from his thigh wound had stiffened his leather pant leg, making it even more difficult to walk.

A snowy owl watched him from where it perched upon a branch. The big bird blinked its yellow eyes but made no move to fly away. It had its head cocked, as though listening to the sound that seeped through the mist like the breathing of an animal. Asson had been hearing the faint panting since the end of the battle. It appeared and disappeared, sometimes to Asson's left, sometimes to his right, but always just ahead of him on the trail.

He struggled to steady his nerves.

The forest was alive with Power. It crawled over his skin on ant feet and flashed through the alder leaves like drifting sparks. He hadn't felt a night like this in over seven winters, and the last time had been devastating for him. On that terrible night, he'd lost a cherished friend. For a few instants, old grief came to breathe in his heart, stilling every other pain.

Panting. Very faint.

Asson turned around in a full circle, looking for the source.

When he faced eastward, through the filigree of branches, supper fires glittered on the shoreline like a swath of golden stars. The People had obviously gone down to receive their promised goods. Had they received them? He had no idea. The villages seemed to have separated into different camps, some situated far from the central bonfire. Perhaps some of the People even had grown tired of waiting and were already headed home.

He expelled a pained breath. Not a single person had offered to come with him when he'd left the charred remains of Whale Rib Village. Instead, they'd backed away from him. Some had even run, including Ewinon.

Asson groaned as he started forward along the trail, and a snowy owl's head swiveled, as though watching something to Asson's left.

He turned and spied a gray wolf moving through the darkness twenty hands away, so quiet it might have been a trick of shadow rather than an animal hunting the earth-scented twilight.

Asson watched the wolf slide through the trees with ghostly stillness. Taller than any wolf Asson had ever seen, the big male licked his gray muzzle and watched Asson with glittering eyes.

Oddly, the spectral panting grew louder, coming from Asson's right, but he feared to turn his gaze from the wolf. A furred ear twitched, apparently also listening to the panting. Perhaps hunting it, just as Asson was. Or the wolf could have been drawn by the scent of Asson's blood.

"Go on about your hunt, brother. You don't want me. I'm old and tough."

The wolf remained for a time, listening. When the panting did not return, he slipped through the trees like a blaze of moonlight and was gone.

Asson exhaled in relief. He braced his wounded leg and struggled against the pain. The lightning had just grazed him, but it had been like a searing blue knife in his flesh. Though it was a clean cut, he needed to care for it soon, before the feeding tunghaks grew too numerous. He couldn't afford to be sprawled in his bedding hides for days.

He bent over and picked up a branch from the forest floor to use as a walking stick. When he leaned on it, the pain in his leg eased some.

The fog, dyed by nightfall, had turned soot colored and cold. As it thickened, the dark slither of the caribou trail began to vanish and a soft, glistening cocoon enveloped Asson.

To his right, he heard it again. He looked around.

In a heap of deadfall, odd flutters of light drew his attention. The Spirits of the Dead sprang to life, filling the night sky with green fire. Their gleams reflected in the mist like rainbows dreaming. But . . . there was also something in the deadfall.

Asson propped his walking stick and stepped closer.

Only slowly did he become aware of her. She appeared and disappeared, first there, then not, as though flickering in and out of this world. His breath caught.

Asson couldn't take his eyes from her.

The young woman lay sound asleep, hidden in the nest of deadfall with her head pillowed upon her slender arm. She wore a white tunic with a magical creature painted on the front. As the fluttering Dance of the Dead reflected from the fabric, it shivered light upon the wet wood. For a time, he just stared in disbelief.

When the truth began to seep through his astonishment, his wits returned. Asson whispered, "Oh, there you are. I've been worried about you."

She stirred at the familiar sound of his voice, and a faint smile turned her lips.

Asson eased down just outside her hiding place. "You must be exhausted."

Her fingers twitched.

"The youth named Kiran told me your name is Thyra. Is it?"

As Asson had done with the fox's fur, he slid his arm through the tangle of branches and tenderly stroked her long ivory-colored hair where it spread across the twigs. When he drew his hand back, it smelled fragrant, as though she'd slept for days in a bed of grass.

He desperately wished he could speak with her but didn't wish to wake her, so he just leaned back against the largest log thrusting out from the deadfall and contemplated the night.

"Well, you'll be interested to know that my reputation as a Kutsitualit has soared. Everyone is talking about the Spirit Power that engulfed Whale Rib Village this afternoon. My people say I am the greatest Kutsitualit ever born."

His wrinkled face rearranged into thoughtful lines. "When it ended, everyone ran away. No one wanted to wait with me. Not even Ewinon, Camtac, or Gower. I thought at least they would help me. . . ." He waved a hand to dismiss it. "But it doesn't matter now, does it?"

He studied the shape of her young body. She couldn't have seen more than ten-and-five winters. She looked very thin and frail curled on her side, sheathed in the wavering reflections of the ancestors. He longed to pick her up and hold her in his arms, as he'd done with the fox.

"Yes," he said with a proud nod, "you missed something terrifying today, Thyra Little Fox. The greatest Kutsitualit alive blasted the evil Thorlak's sword to bits, and sent him running into the forest."

She remained fast asleep, oblivious to Asson's grand story.

Asson frowned at her. "How did you call down the lightning, my friend? I've always wanted to do that."

Asson pulled his wolfhide hood closed beneath his chin and gazed up at the night sky where the fog flickered green. A knot of fear was growing in his belly.

"I must admit, though, you frightened me today."

No response.

Asson heaved a deep sigh. "When you are well and strong again, you must teach me that lightning trick."

It might have been his voice that woke her, or the dancing green lights or the feel of the mist on her face, perhaps just the fact that she was in her own body again. Asson didn't know why she blinked her blue eyes. When she lifted her head, her long ivory hair slurred across the twigs. Her innocence stilled his heart.

"Is your name Thyra?"

Nothing in her expression conveyed understanding. She didn't seem to know his language.

Then, with a strange accent, she replied, "We must go, Asson. He knows it was me. He'll do anything to kill me, or those who helped me."

# Thirty-Four

**W**e are all miserable cowards!" Ewinon shouted at Gower and Camtac, who sat on the opposite side of the fire. "Gods, what kind of warriors abandon an injured old man? He asked us for help and we ran away. I'm ashamed of myself. And especially of you two. You're braver than I am."

Ewinon dropped into a crouch before the fire, and went back to ferociously grinding the broken sword on a coarse piece of sandstone. The weapon had shattered into seven pieces. He'd collected each one and tucked it into his belt pouch, but the only useful piece was the hilt and the piece of iron attached to it. Barely two hands long, if reshaped the thick blade would still be a useful tool. But, gods, it was almost impossible to grind this metal! A constant *rasp, rasp* erupted as he worked at it. Strangely, the symbols etched into the blade never went away. He couldn't grind them off. It made no sense.

Camtac said, "But, my brother, everyone was afraid of Asson. Not just the three of us. No one has witnessed a Spirit battle like that in more than a generation."

"Not since the legendary heroes Rumbler the Dwarf and Little Wren lived in this country," Gower added. He had a sheepish look.

Camtac said, "And why didn't Asson come with us? Walking away into the forest alone was madness. What if Thorlak was waiting for him out there? He could be—"

"You're making my guilt worse."

To avoid Ewinon's hot gaze, Gower lifted his wooden cup and took a long drink of spruce needle tea while he frowned out at the camp.

Mist had started to roll in off the ocean. The campfires flickering across the beach grew gauzy halos. While they'd all come down here to await the goods promised them by Chief Gunnar, the camp's main conversation was about the stunning Spirit battle they had witnessed that afternoon. Even now, five hands of time later, awed voices echoed across the sand. Gower's gaze kept straying to where his dead wife's family knelt before their supper fire. Each time he saw them, agony twisted his features. Ewinon knew that Camtac had spoken with them earlier. Had Gower spoken with them since the battle?

"People are leaving," Gower said, and used his cup to gesture to the group of eight people walking away up the trail that led to the terrace.

"It's late. They should wait until morning," Camtac said with a worried shake of his head.

Ewinon pressed harder, forcing the broken sword blade down upon the sandstone, grinding it with a vengeance, taking out his anger at himself on the stone. When a sharp chunk of sandstone shot across the fire and struck Gower, he let out a yip.

"Blessed Anguta, Ewinon! That hurt." Gower lifted his forearm and sucked at the blood that had welled.

"It was an accident. Sorry. I'm just . . . I shouldn't be here. I should be out in the forest trying to find Asson." Ewinon growled in frustration, slammed the grinding stone to the ground, and shoved the broken sword in his belt.

Camtac and Gower exchanged knowing looks and Ewinon sharply said, "What?"

"Nothing, Brother," Camtac replied. "We understand. We feel the same way."

"Then get up right now and come with me to find him." Ewinon lurched to his feet.

"That's ridiculous, Ewinon," Gower said. "It's night. Even if you find his trail, you can't track him at night. Do you just plan to wander aimlessly through the forest calling his name? I'm sure the evil Thorlak would appreciate that. It'll make it much easier to find you."

Ewinon sat back down and glumly frowned at the people nearby. Many were listening to their conversation and muttering soft comments.

Old Woman Eshimut, who sat at the closest fire, called, "Son of Badisut, you should think on the giant sky beasts you saw rampaging today! What if they reappear and chase you across the hills like a dog? Better to stay close to camp tonight where we can defend you if they come to get you."

"Why would they come to get me, Grandmother? What have I done?"

The snarly-haired old woman cupped a hand to her mouth to call, "They were Asson's Spirit Helpers and you acted like a miserable coward and abandoned him!"

"Blessed Ancestors," Ewinon choked on the soft words. "Everyone knows!"

Gower's lips twisted. "Well, there's nothing we can do tonight, my friend. At dawn we will head back, pick up his trail, and find him."

Camtac timidly glanced between them. "And it shouldn't be difficult. Asson was hurt. He can't have gone far."

Ewinon glared. "Yes, Brother, thank you. I know. He was hurt, and I ran away."

Camtac's shoulders hunched in defense. "I only meant that you shouldn't worry. We will find him. Tomorrow we will help him, just as he asked us to."

"If he lives through the night."

The scent of roasting salmon drifted to Camtac, sweet and delicious, along with the fragrance of maple and birch fires.

"Brother, don't forget how powerful he was today, more powerful than anyone ever believed possible," Camtac said. "If he has to fight Thorlak again tonight, he will win."

Old Woman Eshimut yelled, "Except, of course, he's injured and not as strong as he was this afternoon!"

Ewinon groaned.

Gower frowned down into his tea, then glanced at Abidish's family again. Was he worried about seeing them? After a few moments of thought, Gower tossed the dregs of his tea into the fire. An explosion of steam rose into the gathering mist. "Ewinon's right. We should go find him tonight."

"Yes, finally!" Ewinon got to his feet again. "At least we can make it back to the village tonight, and start looking at first light. Get your packs. Let's get started." He slung his quiver and bow over his shoulder.

Reluctantly, Camtac started stuffing things into his pack. He only had his hatchet, which he tucked into his belt. Shoulder-length black hair swung around his face as he rose to his feet. "I'm ready, Brother."

Gower slipped his quiver over his shoulder and started to rise but turned suddenly to stare at the three people walking in their direction. As they passed by the beach fires, their faces flashed: man, woman, and boy. Gower's expression slackened. "It's Abidish's family."

Ewinon stiffened. *They will wish Gower to tell them of the deaths of their daughter and grandchildren.* "Oh, Gower. I've been so occupied with my own guilt, I . . . Forgive me. I've been keeping you, and I—I should have gone with you when we first got here."

Gower shook his head weakly. "No, my friend. This is my duty and mine alone." As he lifted a hand to his dead wife's mother, brother, and father, he said, "Don't wait for me. I will meet you at Whale Rib Village at dawn tomorrow. I need privacy to do this well."

Ewinon nodded in respect. "I understand."

He couldn't imagine what Gower must be feeling. Abidish's family would want to know every detail of the battle. Ewinon tried to put himself in Gower's place, but it hurt too much to contemplate. "Be careful on the journey. We'll see you at dawn."

Gower gave him a firm nod. "You will."

"Come on, Camtac. Let's get started."

"Yes, Brother."

As they turned and strode away, he saw Abidish's father walk forward with a frail smile on his face. "Son-in-law, we know you are a warrior and have responsibilities, but when you have the opportunity, if you could come to our fire, we would be grateful."

Gower bowed slightly. "I need to grab my pack and I'll be right there, Father-in-law."

"Thank you. We'll be waiting."

Ewinon led the way up the trail at a brisk run. When he reached the terrace, he glanced back and saw Gower still milling around their fire, as though the last thing he wished to do was face Abidish's family.

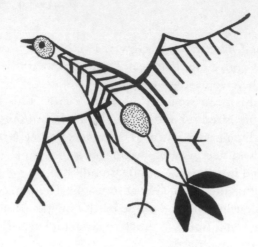

# Thirty-Five

As Thyra Little Fox strode down the caribou trail, Asson did his best to keep up. The way she moved fascinated him, so graceful she might have been a ghost floating above the trail. When South Wind Woman gusted and flattened Thyra's white tunic against her body, Asson stared. She had a boyish figure, the breasts still small, her legs too long for her torso. But the wisdom in her eyes was ancient.

What horrors had she endured to gain such insights into life?

Things that made her afraid to be still for too long. Things that kept her running.

"Thyra Little Fox, forgive me," he groaned, "but I must rest for just a few moments."

As Asson hobbled off the trail and sank down upon a flat boulder, she walked back to sit upon the stone beside him. Long ivory hair fell around her hips, appearing very bright against the black rock.

Asson massaged his leg. He'd broken open the wound. Tunghaks must have smelled the blood and flocked to feed. He untied his Healing pouch from his belt, rested it upon the rock between them, and drew out his iron knife. "When I slice the leather it will ease some of the pressure. I'm sure I'll be able to walk again."

She watched in concern as he sawed through the leather. His legging had stretched so tight over the swollen flesh that he had trouble not cutting his skin. The instant his knife had created a rent, torn muscle swelled through the opening, along with a gush of fresh blood. The relief was almost overpowering. Asson inhaled a deep breath. "Oh, that's better."

Her eyes widened at the sight of the fevered flesh. "Please tell me how to help, Asson. What can I do?"

"That's very kind of you. If you will pull out the small bags in my Healing pouch and lay them out across the stone, I'll instruct you."

Thyra Little Fox leaned forward over his Healing pouch, and her pale hair fell over the dark stone like cobwebs caught in a bonfire of green light. As she sorted through his herbs, laying bags out in a line across the boulder, he watched her with an embarrassing tenderness of heart. She was so young, yet everything about her spoke of a woman far older.

It touched him. Eventually a person saw too much, understood too much, and the result was a clarity that wounded the soul.

"The yellow bag contains powdered willow bark." Asson pointed to it. "If you mix it with water, then sprinkle in half as much redbud bark—in the white bag—it will help my fever and reduce the swelling."

Without a word, she picked up the two bags, found a wooden cup in his pack, and hurried to a pool of water that had collected in a spruce tree hollow. After she'd filled the cup, she poured in the powdered barks and mixed them with a twig. "This smells bitter."

"Yes, and tastes much worse."

She carried the cup back and handed it to him. Asson took his time drinking it while he gazed out at the fog blowing through the smoke-colored tree trunks.

"Asson?" She stared at him with shining eyes. "I will never be able to thank you enough—"

"You don't have to."

She lightly touched his arm. "Yes, I do." Tears beaded her lashes. "I am in your debt."

He waved it away. "Where did you learn our language?"

"Some from Elrik, some from my—my mother, but mostly from you over the past few days."

Asson shifted his aching leg to a more comfortable position. Everything about her was familiar to him, the way she cocked her head, clasped her hands, and squinted her eyes. "Can you answer some questions for me?"

"I'll try."

He hesitated before asking, "Who is the woman who calls to you? Do you know?"

Thyra Little Fox blinked. She did not ask what he meant, or appear surprised that he heard the cries, too. "My mother, I think. My Other Mother."

"Other?"

"Yes. I was raised by a family in Denmark, but I think I was born in England."

Asson's bushy brows drew together. "I don't know those places, but I assume they exist beyond the sea to the east, far from the Fallen Star land?"

"They do, yes. Many days' sea voyage away."

She tipped her head back to look up at the green glow dancing through the roof of fog. When she exhaled, her breath condensed into a luminous cloud. "I've heard her calling to me for as long as I remember. There were times when her soft voice was the one thing that kept me sane."

Asson swallowed the lump in his throat. "What does she say to you?"

"Usually she sings me to sleep. Sometimes she tells me stories of Asgard, the City of the Gods. She was a great seeress, I think."

"Did you ever tell your adopted family about your Other Mother?"

As though uncomfortable, she looked away from him. "I tried once. My father told me I was very creative, and I knew from the way he said the word that it was bad to be creative. For years, I believed him. I did try to be what my mother and father wanted me to be. I didn't want to be creative." She knotted her fists in her lap. "Then they died, and Thorlak the Lawspeaker purchased me as his thrall. He ordered me to forget all my Anchorite teachings, and trained me in the ways of Odin magic."

"You are his student, then?"

"Yes."

Her gaze moved away from Asson to the forest, but she didn't seem to see the fog twining up the tree trunks, or the flickering shadows. Instead, the sudden tightening of her mouth told him guilt or perhaps regret had possessed her heart.

"Are you sorry you turned against him today?"

Thyra shook her head, but sadness filled her voice. "No. I just don't know what's going to happen. In the past few moons I've found a new home and made friends. That's gone now. When he finds me, he'll—"

"I won't let him hurt you."

"He's enraged, Asson, and far more powerful than either you or I. There's no telling what he will do. I humiliated him today. But only because I surprised him. He did not know I was there in the forest. We've forced his hand. When the word goes round that he ran, he'll have to do something spectacular to restore his reputation."

"Something bad, you mean?"

"Something horrifying."

Asson remained silent. The fear in that melodic voice made him clench a fist. He had a momentary glimpse of a skinny child moving obediently in her master's monstrous shadow, trying to please him, and it reminded him of his own years of striving to be a great Kutsitualit and never quite managing. He'd always been "not good enough," according to Neechwa. Words he'd never resented, for he knew them to be true.

He tipped his cup up and drank every drop of the healing tea; then he tucked the cup back in his open pack. "Are you sure he knows it was you?"

"Yes. When he realized it, he screamed my name. And every moment since I ran away, I've felt him searching for me in my thoughts."

"Can he find you that way?"

She hesitated for a long time, her young face tense with concentration, as if she were hunting him in his thoughts and didn't much like it. "Not if I keep running."

"Well, let's do that." A moan escaped his lips as he shoved to his feet and reached for his makeshift walking stick. The bark bore a wet sheath of mist.

Thyra Little Fox rose beside him. "Asson?" The magical eight-legged creature on her dress seemed to break into a run when the wind fluttered the fabric. "He's hunting you, too, you know."

"We'll be safe as soon as we reach my people. They're camped on the shore where your ships were anchored."

"He won't let you reach your people. Don't you understand? You don't know what he's capable of! What you saw this afternoon was a mere whisper of his power."

She started shaking. Asson wondered if she'd ever seen the full extent of Thorlak's power and, if so, what might have occasioned such a display by her master! A lesson?

Asson vented a deep sigh and tipped his head far back to peer up at the fog meandering around the treetops. "Yes, a whisper we must silence forever."

A short distance away, Thorlak watched them walking together through the dripping trees and fluttering light. Neither knew he was there, hidden among the forest shadows.

As they traveled, he paralleled their course. Quiet. Utterly quiet.

No longer human, he had become his purpose, lean and lethal, less than a shadow. When he breathed, every scent in the forest burned through him like liquid fire.

He had seen this over and over, the Norns parceling out fragments of fate until they all came together like a crashing blow to the heart. He was about to give Thyra the thing she most desired. Though she would not understand his gesture.

"Wait!" she hissed.

She seemed to sense his presence. She stepped forward, away from Asson, and looked at Thorlak where he stood in the trees.

"What is it?" Asson asked as he searched the mist.

"I—I thought . . ."

Thorlak cocked his head and looked straight into her eyes, but she did not see him. She might have seen a wisp of light or maybe the fog shift. Sometimes people saw the darkness ripple when he moved.

"It's nothing," Thyra said. "I'm sorry. Let's keep going."

When they left, his nostrils quivered. He sprang forward, trotting through the trees less than three paces from them, watching, listening. The scent of wet pine needles grew stronger as the mist soaked them.

*Yes, you're right, Thyra. Horror is coming. . . .*

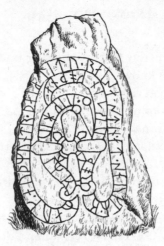

# Thirty-Six

Gower tramped across the firelit camp with his fists clenched, heading for the small fire where his dead wife's parents and younger brother sat eating fish stew. Blessed Anguta, he dreaded this. It had taken him almost a full hand of time to prepare himself, and he still wasn't ready. He'd secretly been hoping he would find them all asleep when he arrived.

As he wove between fires, voices drifted to him. A few warriors spoke angrily, saying they'd been betrayed by Chief Gunnar, but most of the voices brimmed with reverence. The Spirit battle at Whale Rib Village that afternoon had already become the stuff of legend. Several versions circulated the camp. As each person described what he or she had witnessed, and listened to what others had seen, the story blossomed.

From Gowen's right, a woman said, "Who would have ever believed it? When he lifted his arms and called out to the Thunderbirds, I expected nothing to happen, as usual. Then the entire sky ripped apart, and so many lightning bolts blasted the village that I couldn't see for all the sand thrown into the air." She hesitated as though out of breath. "I thought Asson was just an old fake."

"We all did, my wife. How many times have we seen him fail?" The dark-haired man beside her put his arm around her shoulders and hugged her.

"More than I can count. Why didn't the old loon reveal himself winters ago? He is surely the greatest Kutsitualit ever born among our people. It would have been nice to know."

"Perhaps he had a good reason."

"Do you think he's coming here? To this camp? Maybe we can get him to offer a blessing for our new grandchild."

"I'm surprised you're not afraid to be here in this Wobee village."

"Don't be ridiculous. The Wobee can't hurt us. No matter where he is, if the Wobee attack, Asson will call upon the Spirits to protect us. If only I'd known before . . ."

As Gower passed on, their conversation faded, but he heard virtually the same words at every fire. He looked up and down the beach. Half the people had already gone home, some angry, some afraid to stay in a Wobee camp, even an empty one. Those who remained agreed with the old woman. So long as Asson lived, nothing could ever hurt them again.

Gower didn't know what to think. Before Drona's flotilla of canoes left, escorting the elders home to Soapstone Village, Drona had wisely posted guards on every high point around the camp. He seemed the only man whose senses had not been numbed by awe. Where was he now? If the currents had favored him, he might have made it to Asson's old beach camp where Camtac and Gower, running up the shore, had seen Ewinon.

As he walked, Gower scanned the dozens of fires. Many people lay rolled in hides, fast asleep, as Gower longed to be. But he had this one last duty to perform.

He picked up his pace, marching purposefully toward his wife's family. Every step made his heart beat harder.

When his father-in-law, Debine, saw Gower, he smiled his love and lifted a hand to him. "Gower, thank you for coming, I know all of our warriors have duties tonight. Are Ewinon and Camtac off on their journey?"

"Yes, off to hunt for Asson."

"I hope they find him well. He surprised all of us today—"

"Forgive me, Father-in-law, I mean no disrespect, but I must tell you how your daughter and grandchildren died, and I must do it swiftly or I fear I won't be able to."

"Don't apologize. We understand. Abidish's soul is nearby. I've felt her. She's proud of you for all you've done to protect your people. As we are."

Abidish's mother and brother, Hadalaet and Yeech, smiled at Gower and nodded.

Gower's throat went tight. Images of his wife and children flashed behind his eyes and he almost couldn't bear it. Gower reached out to grip

Yeech's shoulder. The boy had seen eight summers. He'd loved Abidish perhaps as much as Gower had. Would he understand Gower's next words?

"My family," he began with difficulty. "Your daughter and grandchildren died because I failed them. I was not there when they needed me. I—"

Hadalaet reached out to take his hand. "Let us judge, Son-in-law. Just tell us the story."

Gower knelt between Hadalaet and Yeech. The stunning Dance of the ancestors reflected brilliantly from the faces of his relatives and sent shimmering strings of light across the sand. In all his life, Gower had never seen such a night sky. He couldn't decide whether the ancestors were just deliriously happy about Asson's victory this afternoon or trying to warn the People of the Songtrail of impending doom. But Gower had the vague feeling it was the latter.

He began again, his voice a little stronger. "The battle started here, in this village. We ran away with the Wobee right behind us, shooting arrows. Chief Badisut ordered me, and most of our warriors, to guard the rear to protect the women and children. When we reached the outskirts of Whale Rib Village, the chief yelled for everyone to follow him to the longhouse, but some people were terrified senseless and ran to the closest lodge instead." On the canvas of his soul, Gower watched Abidish dashing across the village, carrying their two children in her arms. . . . "Your daughter ran for our lodge. She and our children were cut down by Wobee arrows. That's how they died. That's the story."

Yeech started weeping softly, and Debine reached over to silently clasp his son's hand. After a few moments of silence, Debine said, "I don't think that's the whole story, Gower. We heard that you went back for them. Camtac said you acted like an insane man. You ran through a shower of arrows and dragged all three back to the longhouse."

"Yes, but if I'd been beside Abidish when we entered the village, I . . . I could have protected—"

"No, my son-in-law," Debine said gently. "No, you could not have. Don't think that. Camtac told us that Abidish and your son were already dead when you dragged them into the longhouse and you held your two-winters-old daughter in your arms until she died."

Gower squeezed his eyes closed, trying not to see it again. He never wanted to see the look in Jiggamint's eyes again. Despite the arrow in her tiny chest, she'd looked up at him with love and smiled. And he'd known that his daughter believed in her heart that she was in her father's arms now and that he would save her.

Debine's soft voice made Gower open his eyes. "Camtac said that after your daughter died Badisut ordered you to get to your feet to fight for your people. He said the look on your face when you placed your baby girl on the floor and nocked your bow . . . Well, he said he hoped he never saw such an expression ever again."

Yeech peered up at Gower with his mouth quivering. "Thank you, my brother, for trying to save them."

As one, Hadalaet, Yeech, and Debine gathered around Gower, wrapped their arms around him, and held him in a tight embrace. Gower tried to be strong. He needed to be strong for them, but after thirty heart-beats silent sobs racked his chest. His family just held him tighter and murmured soft words, which he barely heard.

When at last they released him and began to back away, Gower got to his feet and forced a deep breath into his lungs. "I must go. But I . . . I want you to know that you will always be my family, even if I am no longer married to—"

"You will always be our son and brother," Debine said to spare Gower from having to say the names of the dead again.

As Debine rose to say good-bye, he suddenly frowned. Then he tilted his head as though listening to something. "Do you hear that? It sounds like moose bellowing."

Gower turned, and an eerie crawling sensation ran up his spine.

All across the beach, people rose to their feet with their faces shining in the light of the dancing ancestors.

"Or bears roaring?" Hadalaet asked.

"Maybe."

When the sound grew louder, shocked people began to back away; some fled. Oddly, many sleeping people barely moved. A few grumbled, rolled over, and pulled their hides over their heads. Two infants wailed angrily at being disturbed.

Gower said, "Father-in-law, it's probably nothing, but I think it might be wise to—"

"Yes, I—I think you're right. We'll see you when this is over." He grabbed Yeech's hand and he and Hadalaet ran for the trees.

A man's voice suddenly rose above the roar. *"Nock your bows. Everyone prepare to fight!"*

"Fight?" Gower said in confusion. "Fight what?"

All around him, warriors muttered to one another, trying to decipher the order. But the hiss of bowstrings being pulled back eddied across camp.

Twenty or so warriors sprinted for the terrace with their bows up, ready to do battle with whatever rushed out of the night. When they lined up out on the lip of the terrace, they ceased being men and became black statues silhouetted against a stunning wave of light. He'd never seen the ancestors kick up so much light. And . . . it didn't flutter or twist into serpentine patterns.

No shouts went up. No warnings.

Gower broke into a trot, heading up to join them. As he got closer, he could see the men's faces. Each stood staring, his mouth open, as though he couldn't believe his eyes.

The strange glow expanded higher into the sky.

Just before Gower reached the crest, screams broke loose and men staggered, falling back as the glow billowed upward like building thunderheads, then seemed to burst. Copper-colored light exploded across the heavens and poured down, flooding the land in a gigantic frothing wave that rolled straight for them. Screaming men fled into the trees.

G unnar stopped dead in the middle of the shadow-striped trail. "What is that?"

Kiran shook his head. "The northern lights. Isn't it?"

"I've never seen them look like that."

"No, but what else could it be?"

"Forest fire? Or . . ." Gunnar paused when he saw two people ahead of them. Quietly, he said to Kiran, "Am I mad, or is that Thyra?"

Kiran took a quick step forward and frowned at the dark shapes moving through the forest. "Are you sure it's people, and not caribou?"

Gunnar didn't answer. The trail wound through the trees toward a clearing. When the strangers stepped out of the shadows, the answer was obvious.

Kiran gasped, "*Thyra?*" and charged ahead.

Gunnar didn't move. The blaze of light had faded, and the northern lights were back as spritely and green as ever. But he heard something. Footsteps. Faint voices. Out in the trees.

He backed up and stood in the shadow cast by the white spruce, letting his gaze search for the origin of the sounds. When Kiran and Thyra met, they leaped into each other's arms and excited whispers rose. Asson's eyes had focused on Gunnar, watching him, as though he sensed Gunnar's unease.

Out in the willows, three other men appeared, but Gunnar could tell little more than that. Thorlak, Einarsson, and the Bellower? It took another minute before Gunnar heaved a sigh of relief and called, "Alfdis? Bring Ingolf and Sokkolf. We've plans to make before we get back to the booths."

Alfdis led the way, smiling, clearly glad to see Gunnar. "Did you see the fiery heavens? What was it? I was beginning to fear—"

Sokkolf let out a shocked cry and stumbled backward when he saw Thyra. "Y-you," he stammered. "It's you. I saw you . . . in Helheim. You c-came for me."

"Don't be afraid." Thyra separated from Kiran and walked toward Sokkolf.

Sokkolf glanced at the other men. "She rode in on an eight-legged horse, and led me out of the Banquet Hall of the Dead in the form of a little white fox. I swear to you!"

Thyra stopped two paces away from him, as though not to frighten him further. "I'm glad you made it back, Sokkolf. I told you you would."

Sokkolf fell to his knees at her feet, and sobbed, "Thank you, Seeress. May the gods protect you, thank you for helping me to live again!"

Gunnar glanced at Kiran. The struggle showed on his face. Gunnar wondered how his Anchorite soul would ever make peace with this.

# Thirty-Seven

Most of the fog had blown away, but patches continued to cling to the forest and out over the ocean. Ewinon had been pushing hard to get to the last place he'd seen Asson. He longed to find the old Kutsitualit, find him and apologize for being a miserable coward.

"Could you slow down?" Camtac panted behind Ewinon. "My legs feel like earthquakes."

"What if he's in danger, my brother? We must find him before something happens to him." Ewinon clutched his bow so tightly the quiver of arrows rattled upon his left shoulder.

Camtac trotted up beside Ewinon. Sweat drenched his face and glued black hair to his cheeks. "You are *not* a coward, Brother."

The consoling words did not make Ewinon feel better. Intensely conscious of how vulnerable he and Camtac were in this dark forest, Ewinon kept looking around, expecting to see Wobee warriors leap from the shadows, or even Thorlak appear and kill them with a wave of his hand.

As the wind picked up, the Fog Spirits vanished into thin air, leaving the vast bowl of the night sky clean and magnificent.

Ewinon pushed harder, running up the beaten trail that flickered with eerie bars of green light. He could sense the remnants of old Spirit Power that clung to this place, the legacy of a time when hundreds of Kutsitualits, including Rumbler and Little Wren, had walked these hills. On occasion,

Ewinon caught sight of a small animal, its fur glimmering in the gleam of the ancestors' sky dance.

"Besides, Asson is partly to blame," Camtac said, breathing hard. "He should have come with us. I'll never understand why he decided to wander off into the forest alone. It was madness. He could have—"

"He went hunting for that wretched fox, Camtac. I wish that creature had never dragged its bleeding body into our camp. I swear it's cursed."

Camtac glanced at Ewinon and blinked his too-wide eyes. "Please don't say that, Brother. You didn't see her when she bravely dashed out of the trees to attack Thorlak."

Ewinon's self-loathing deepened. He longed to shout that Camtac was a fool. *The fox could not possibly be the same, and anyway, she wasn't a Kutsitualit or she would have already changed back into human form.* But Ewinon kept that appalling impulse locked inside him, and said, "I know you think she did, Brother. I'm just not as sure as you are."

"Asson thinks I'm right."

Ewinon expelled a breath. "Yes. He does."

When Ewinon reached the top of the hill, he stopped to study the mist that fluttered and flashed with fantastic colors. Several trails came together here, radiating outward like the spokes of a spiderweb. Some of the rutted paths were so old they were barely visible in broad daylight. No one knew what they were or even where they'd gone, for if a man followed them today they led nowhere. Holy people whispered that the paths were dangerous because they were still traveled by witches and ghosts. Ewinon didn't really believe it . . . but he stepped onto the well-traveled, if rough, path that followed the sea cliff to Whale Rib Village. It required less time, because a man did not have to curve through trees and careen over hills. However, if a gust of wind hit you just right on the Cliff Trail, you'd topple over the edge to your death far below. These days only strong warriors took this trail. It was too risky and difficult for elders or children.

"Be cautious, Camtac. The rocks are slick and—"

Camtac scoffed, "You think this is slick? You should have seen the Shaman's Trail when we ran away from the battle. Gower made me hold on to the back of his shirt so I wouldn't get washed off the ledge by the rivers of rain."

The tightness in Ewinon's chest eased as pride swelled his heart. "Did he?"

"He saved my life at least twice that day, Brother."

Love for his best friend filled him. Ewinon had to swallow before he could say, "He's the bravest man I've ever known."

A gust of wind whipped his hair around his face, and he spun around to make sure that Camtac hadn't gone over the precipice. Ewinon found his younger brother standing with his feet braced like a seasoned veteran of many such trails. "You all right?"

"Yes. I just needed a short rest. I can run again. My legs are feeling stronger."

Ewinon broke into a trot, leaping rocks and skirting the scraggly trees living a tortured existence on the cliff edge.

For some strange reason, their conversation had made him remember Asson's story of the Lost People. . . *because they have learned to feed one another, to care for one another.*

Ewinon tried to imagine how it could ever be possible for someone like Gower to make peace with the Wobee. It would be hard enough for Ewinon, but if he'd held Mapet and their son in his arms as they'd died . . .

Tears of hatred burned his eyes.

*Never.*

From behind him, Camtac half-shouted, "Brother! Do you see them?"

Ewinon started to swing around, but when he lifted his gaze from the trail he spied the five Wobee ships anchored in the ocean just ahead, hulls engulfed in the green flames cast by the night sky.

Ewinon halted. Camtac trotted up beside him, and they both stood, breathing hard, staring.

"What are they doing here?"

"Apparently, they are not gone. Four of them just sailed a short distance to White Dove Shoals. The fifth must have just arrived. I've never seen the one on the far right before. That's a sleek, fast vessel, isn't it?"

Camtac rubbed his nose on his buckskin sleeve. "Does that mean we can come here to get the goods promised to us by Chief Gunnar?"

Ewinon toyed with the bow in his left hand, thinking about it. "I have no idea, Brother."

"Should we go tell our elders of this?"

The sudden sting of guilt tormented Ewinon. This was more important than finding one old Kutsitualit. If Ewinon's people ran to their canoes now, they might be able to capture those ships, or kill enough Wobee that the desperate survivors would leave these shores and never return.

"Yes, Brother. We're going back. The joint Village Council must know of this immediately."

Just as Ewinon began to turn, he heard Camtac gasp.

In one terrified motion, Ewinon pulled an arrow from his quiver, nocked it, and dropped to a knee with his bow aimed at the dark figure standing on the trail.

*Gods, how did he get so close to us without making a single . . .*

For a few moments, Ewinon was so stunned he could only gape at the man. Wind whipped his cape around his tall body like black flames. Ewinon couldn't see his face because he was staring off across the ocean to the east, as though dreaming of distant lands.

"Sh-shoot!" Camtac cried as he jerked his hatchet from his belt. "Shoot him!"

Ewinon's eyes narrowed, studying the black silhouette.

*"You should, you know."*

Ewinon frowned. The words had been uttered with slow patience, as though those of a teacher lecturing a dim-witted child, but Ewinon wasn't sure if the man had actually spoken or he'd just heard the deep voice in his head.

"Camtac, run."

"What? No!"

"Run now, blast you! Obey me! I'm your older brother. Get to the elders. Tell them about the ships!"

"Brother, I don't want to—"

*"Go on!"*

Camtac backed away, glancing between the dark figure and Ewinon. Finally, Camtac sprinted down the trail with his legs pumping, and Ewinon exhaled in relief.

An expectant silence held the cliff.

Ewinon rose with his bow still aimed. "Turn around. I want to see your face."

*"Then you're a fool."*

As the man's head slowly tilted back to look up at the fluttering heavens, the subtle texture of the wind changed, growing heavier, colder.

"You have five heartbeats to turn around."

A low laugh.

The man turned.

Ewinon went perfectly still. The face of a tunghak. The eyes bottomless holes. A half-moon of white teeth.

Ewinon loosed his arrow, and watched the feathered shaft as it sailed past his target and continued out over the cliff, arcing downward into the surf like a slender flame.

*I can't possibly have missed. He stands barely five paces away.*

In shock, Ewinon staggered backward and grabbed to pull another arrow from his quiver.

The smiling man quietly walked toward him.

Like a dog struck in the head with a club, Ewinon's senses had left him. He struggled to nock the arrow in his bow, but it kept slipping . . .

Then the nightmare got worse. From out in the darkness, another form appeared. All Ewinon saw were starlit eyes.

"Run, Lawspeaker!" the man cried, and rushed Ewinon.

The Lawspeaker shouted, "You fool, get back! Get out of my way!"

Ewinon threw down his bow, drew the broken sword from his belt, and aimed it at the Lawspeaker. In less than a heartbeat it had warmed in Ewinon's fist until he almost couldn't hold it. Ice-blue color engulfed the blade. . . .

The dark figure's scream resembled the roar of a dying bear.

# Thirty-Eight

By the time Camtac reached the last hill, his wobbling legs felt like boiled grass stems. He forced his shaking knees to climb the slope.

Gods, he should have stayed with Ewinon, no matter what he ordered! Was he all right?

A surge of fear carried Camtac to the high point overlooking Seal Cove where he blinked, trying to fathom what he was seeing. North Wind Man had chased the Fog Spirits from the shore. In their place, the world seemed to have wings. Everywhere Camtac looked flutters and flashes of light reflected from cliffs, ocean, and the shapes of trees.

Camtac rubbed his eyes to clear them. He sniffed again. Rather than smoke, the air was heavy with the scent of violent Thunderbirds, as though the sky should be shuddering from their powerful wing beats.

No fires or whale-oil lamps lit the shore, which wasn't that unusual. People probably slept, but with the wind the coals in dozens of firepots should have been fanned to life, creating a mosaic of red dots. The large communal bonfire, especially, should be a gleaming beacon. He sniffed the air. Why didn't he smell smoke? Had the wind changed direction and blown the scent away from him?

Hesitantly, Camtac broke into a trot and headed down the trail. Gravel crackled beneath his boots. He had to wake each chief and elder and tell them about the five ships; then he could go back for Ewinon.

For another finger of time, Camtac kept his knees from collapsing.

Finally, he hit the outskirts of the camp. And stopped.

His lungs heaving for air, he looked around. Hides lay rolled across the shore, but they looked empty. He heard no sounds. No infants cried; no one snored or coughed.

A sensation of incomprehension filtered through him.

He walked to the first hide and kicked it. Empty, as though the people had left the rolled hides there to fool intruders. Had they gotten word that Wobee warriors were coming and fled? No, the hides would have been thrown open and tangled, not rolled as though invisible people still slept in them.

"Hello? *Is anyone here? Someone answer me!*"

South Wind Woman whimpered in his ears, as if trying to force him to run away.

Instead, he walked to slump down in front of the dead coals of the bonfire. Not even a trace of heat remained. The fire had been large and hot. What could have sucked the warmth away so completely?

An iron pot hung on a tripod at the edge of the fire pit. He was suddenly desperately thirsty. Did it contain tea or soup? He reached over to tip the pot to look inside and a sound like ice shattering erupted as the iron broke apart and crumbled onto the hearthstones.

Too confused to even gasp, he just stared at the rusty chunks of metal.

Then twigs cracked out in the darkness.

*"Camtac?"*

Camtac scrambled to his feet with his heart racing. "Who's there?"

Asson hobbled out of the night. In the gleam, the Kutsitualit's wrinkled face might have been sculpted of green mud, the hollows shaded with charcoal.

"Oh, Blessed Spirits, Elder! I'm relieved to see you alive. Ewinon and I went back for you. We thought—"

"Come. Join us. There's much we need to discuss." Asson waved to Camtac. "We're over here at the foot of the hill."

"We?" Camtac squinted into the night. Behind Asson, Camtac saw several dark figures, but he couldn't tell how many. "Who . . . who is that? Is Gower—"

"I don't know who, or how many, survived. We were on our way here when, around midnight, we saw the light fill the heavens. We got here as quickly as we could."

Camtac forced his weak legs to take him closer to the elder, where he blurted, "Asson, what happened to our people? Where are they?"

Asson put a gentle hand on Camtac's shoulder. "That's what we're trying to figure out. Why don't you help us? Come—"

"No, I have to get back to Ewinon! I should never have left him. He ordered me to come back and tell the elders that there are five Wobee ships anchored just off White Dove Shoals, but I shouldn't have listened, I—"

"Camtac," Asson said in a soothing voice. "Look at me. Slow down, and tell me where Ewinon is?"

Camtac flung an arm toward the Cliff Trail. "He was going back to Whale Rib Village to find you. He was worried about you. We were about halfway there when a man in a long cape appeared on the cliff behind us, and—"

"What man?"

Camtac shook his head. "I don't know! Ewinon ordered me to run. I—I didn't want to, Elder. I knew I should stay—"

"You obeyed your older brother, exactly as you should have. Did the man say anything to you?"

"I didn't hear anything, but I think Ewinon did. That's when he told me to run."

Asson stared at Camtac for a time, as though judging his emotions, then put an arm around Camtac's shoulders, and held him so long Camtac wanted to weep. "Can you help me, Camtac? My wounded leg hurts. I'm afraid I won't make it back to our friends unless I can lean on you."

"Yes, Elder, of course, but then I have to go."

"I understand. Just help me back up the hill."

Camtac pulled Asson's arm over his shoulders and supported him for the ten paces it took to climb to where three people waited. As Camtac expected to see someone he knew, his heart lurched when six Wobee appeared: the youth with odd curly black hair, the old blond chief, three other men whom he couldn't see very well, and a young woman.

Camtac shoved away from Asson, and ripped his hatchet from his belt. "What are they doing here?"

"Camtac, wait," Asson said. "Put away your hatchet. Give me a chance to explain."

"They just did something to our people. You know they did! They held a false council meeting and promised us wealth to get us all down here in one place so they could slaughter us! I just . . . I don't know where the bodies are! Why weren't you here to protect our people?"

Kiran was translating his words for Chief Gunnar, and the elder's eyes narrowed.

"I should have been," Asson said. "Please, forgive me. If we hadn't stopped to care for my wounded leg—"

"You should never have gone looking for that miserable fox, Asson!"

Camtac looked at the Wobee and backed away with a mixture of fear and hatred surging through him.

Chief Gunnar said something soft, and he and Kiran, and the other men, spread their arms, as though to show Camtac they held no weapons and meant him no harm.

Kiran said, "Camtac, we did not do this. Please—"

"Who else could have?"

Chief Gunnar spoke to Kiran, and the youth whispered an answer, then listened for a time longer before he blinked thoughtfully at the ground. When he looked up, he said to Camtac, "Chief Gunnar thinks you are right, Camtac. Something awful happened here."

Camtac shook his head to dislodge the words from his brain. Hearing them admit it made it worse. Clearly, they wanted him to know that they, personally, had not been involved, but he didn't care. He wanted them all dead!

His gaze swept to the young woman standing a few paces to the left. She was about his age, and long ivory hair blew around her narrow shoulders. She wore an agonized expression as though the empty hides and dead fires terrified her as much as they did Camtac.

"Who are you?" he shouted.

She clenched her fists, apparently gathering her courage, before she walked toward him. "Your brother Elrik asked me to tell you that he still loves you and hasn't forgotten you."

Disbelief left Camtac feeling weightless. The hatchet trembled in his fist. *I know that voice. . . .*

He stammered, "You-y-you're a Kutsitualit. You tried to speak to me in the longhouse. You helped us. You f-fought for us. I saw you!"

She took another step toward him and looked up into his eyes. Blessed Spirits, what eyes. In the dancing gleam they shone an unearthly shade of azure. "My name is Thyra. I heard you talking about seeing a man in a long cape. Where is he?"

Kiran repeated what she'd said to Chief Gunnar, and the elder called her name. She turned slightly to listen to him, responded, then turned back to face Asson and Camtac. "I told Chief Gunnar that we are wasting precious time standing here talking. Our only hope is to find Thorlak as soon as possible, while he's still recovering."

"Recovering? From what?"

"Wielding light," Asson said, "takes great strength."

Camtac swallowed hard. Not sure he understood. "We must find Ewinon first."

"I'm not sure we can afford to find Ewinon. We—"

"I don't care what you do!" Camtac shouted. "I'm going after my brother!"

"*We*," Asson said, and turned to Thyra. "We are going after your brother."

"Then let's hurry. If Ewinon is in the same place, the five ships are there, as well. Maybe that's where Thorlak was headed."

Chief Gunnar listened to Kiran translate. When the youth reached the part about the five ships, the man grabbed Kiran's arm hard and a rapid string of words poured from Gunnar's mouth.

Kiran said, "Chief Gunnar says Thorlak was almost certainly headed for those ships. He would want to—"

"Does he think Thorlak did this?" Camtac asked.

Kiran asked Gunnar. "Maybe. Chief Gunnar says Thorlak is searching for a grave, and will do anything to—"

Thyra's windblown dress flattened against her slender body as she turned to Asson. "What grave?"

Asson's expression slackened. "I'm not sure; I—"

"Please tell me, Asson."

The elder expelled a long breath. "Maybe the Wobee fire grave." Asson stared at her with his eyes slightly squinted.

Gunnar marched to Thyra, and Kiran translated their soft conversation: "What's he talking about, Thyra? What is a fire grave?"

A veil of mist blew in off the ocean and settled over them like a shimmering blanket.

Thyra seemed hesitant to answer. "Among his people, fire graves are places where great Spirit Power lives."

"Is Spirit Power like magic?"

"Yes."

When Chief Gunnar propped his hands upon his hips, wind filled his shirt, ballooning the fabric; the necklace he wore was lifted by South Wind Woman and laid upon his chest.

Camtac glanced at Kiran's pendant, then at Gunnar's pendant. To Camtac, the pendants looked very similar, just anchors of different varieties. One iron. One gold. Camtac gestured to Chief Gunnar's necklace. "Is that another anchor?"

"Hmm?" Gunnar looked down. "It's Thor's hammer, Mjölnir."

Camtac silently formed the name, *Mjölnir*. "What does it do?"

Gunnar spread his arms, then flapped them against his sides. "Well, it's a tool. A tool of the god Thor. It's his power."

"Spirit Power lives in that piece of gold?" Frightened, Camtac took a step backward.

"No, no, not in this little . . ." Gunnar stopped and appeared to think about that. As Kiran waited to translate more, Gunnar reached up to clasp his pendant and an expression of calm came over him. He continued, "The truth is, I do believe Thor's power resides in this piece of metal. That's why I wear it, to protect me, my crew, my ship."

Asson stepped forward and drew out his own pendant. Carved from whalebone and yellowed with age, it was an image of a long-haired woman, probably his Spirit Helper, Sea Woman. "We all carry Spirit Power with us, and perhaps that's the answer."

"What do you mean?"

Asson fixed his gaze upon Thyra. They stared at each other for what seemed a long time. "Little fox, what Spirit objects does Thorlak value?"

Thyra inhaled a deep breath, and shook her head. "His sword, Skyrmir, was his most cherished tool."

Camtac threw up his hands. *This is useless.* He had no idea what they were talking about, nor did he care. Obviously, none of them knew what had actually happened to his relatives.

He clutched his hatchet and walked away from Asson and the Wobee to slump to the ground and let his gaze drift over the empty shore.

Camtac tried to force himself to think. He had to think! *Had there been a fight? If so, there should be dead bodies. Maybe people just left and went home?*

Camtac got to his feet and forced his legs to climb the slope to search more carefully. He had to know what had happened. When he found Ewinon, he would want to know every detail.

As Camtac struggled up the rocky path, something caught his eye. He turned to frown at it. The fletching of an arrow flashed in the wavering gleam, distinctive black and white. It looked somehow famil—

In a sudden burst of strength, he lunged for the quiver, crying, *"This is Gower's quiver!"*

For several moments, Camtac turned it over and over in his hand, listening to the arrows rattle. "Asson, where is he? He would never have thrown down his quiver."

Asson hobbled forward and gingerly lowered himself to the ground beside Camtac. He rubbed his wounded leg for a long time before he said, "I'm afraid he's gone. I'm afraid they are all gone."

Thyra walked away from the men.

Like fine old communion wine, numbness had begun to filter through her veins. Months ago, Thorlak had tried to teach her how to do this, to pull shreds of light from the sky and weave them into a smothering blanket of brilliance that vanquished everything with any darkness in it.

She looked down at her hands: dark lumps in the night.

He'd started her with a herd of deer. She'd tried to gather the light, but it hurt so much it had been difficult. Then, when she'd cast her pathetic wave, everything it touched died. The deer hadn't vanished—they'd been murdered where they stood. Too horrified to attempt it again, she'd run to her chamber. Thorlak had been livid and disappointed.

Her knees felt weak, shaky.

By the time she reached the edge of the water and stood gazing out into the mist, fear had eaten away her insides, leaving a hollow, thumping shell behind. She sank down upon the sand.

Her powers were a pale imitation of his.

If he could make a hundred people vanish into the mist, how could she ever fight him?

# Thirty-Nine

Godi Dag the Ice-fist clamped his embroidered cloak across his throat to block the wind, and looked at Ketil the Fair-hair, and Wulf the White, the master of the recently arrived ship, the *Maldon*. It had taken the *Maldon* a mere eight days to get here from England bearing its criticial message. The men sat staring contemplatively at the fire, which they'd built on the beach to avoid being overheard.

As though to swallow them, light mist enveloped the shore, glittering with an eerie brilliance in the wavering curtains of the northern lights that lit the sky. All passengers and crews had been forbidden to leave the ships. There were too many slaves and prisoners to guard. Ketil had already lost three good men to a fight aboard *Thor's Dragon*. He would have to tend to Bjarni the Deep-minded in the near future. The man's crew respected him far too much. They did whatever he told them to, including murdering their captors at the first opportunity.

"No, it's not so simple," Wulf the White said as he shoved tangled brown hair away from his weathered face. "Thorkell the Tall, in charge of the king's mercenary army, betrayed Aethelred, took his ships, and returned to Denmark, where he prostrated himself before King Cnut."

Dag laughed out loud. "Thorkell is such an ingenious swine. I am in awe of his ability to save his own hide." Dag clapped his hands in joy. "The value of my new thralls ought to go sky-high!"

Ketil leaned toward Wulf. "Aethelred must be terrified. The war has just escalated out of his control. He'll demand to know the fate of the Prophetess immediately. What of Uhtred, the ealdorman of Northumbria? Is he still alive?"

"So far, but if rumors can be believed, not for long." Wulf added with a chuckle, "To make matters more interesting, the day we set sail we heard that Edmund was in London trying to make amends with his father."

Dag's eyes widened. "Edmund is allying with King Aethelred?"

"Well, perhaps. You know how rumors are."

Ketil the Fair-hair sat up straighter. Firelight glittered through the golden threads decorating his sleeves. "Then Edmund, Eadric, and Aethelred expect King Cnut and Thorkell to invade London without delay?"

"They'd be fools not to. England is vulnerable."

"Oh, they must invade." Dag leaned back on his blanket and laughed until tears rolled down his cheeks. "This is better than we could have hoped for. What a comedy!"

"If you had any wits, you'd not be so gleeful, Dag," Ketil scolded. "They are all Anchorites. Aethelred, Edmund, and Cnut. What good does any of this do us? They've already forced us to flee two nations to avoid persecution and now—"

"I'm not so certain that King Cnut is an Anchorite," Dag said, "though he pretends to be. After all, he's his father's son, and Sweyn the Forkbeard never used his Anchorite name a single day of his life. Besides, I didn't say it benefited us, Ketil. Only that I found it amusing."

"Well, I find it disturbing. If any of the three factions win, the victor will force Greenland to convert to the Anchorite faith, just like they did Iceland, and then they'll come for us!"

Dag reached over to slap Ketil's knee. "You're being too grim, my friend. No matter what transpires in the rest of the world, we will hold fast to our Seidur faith here in this wild country. Even if it means we must declare our independence from Greenland."

Shocked, Ketil glanced around as though to make sure no one stood close by, then whispered, "I wouldn't say such treasonous things so loudly, if I were you. Someone might feel it necessary to report your disloyal statements to Cnut's allies in Greenland."

"There's no one else out here tonight!" Dag said, but sobered immediately. Several of their people were missing, so they *could* be out there listening. The thought that someone might repeat his statement soured his stomach. He forced a swallow down his throat to ease the tightness, and turned back to Wulf the White. "And if Edmund allies with Aethelred to defend London, what of the king's advisor, Eadric, ealdorman of Mercia? He despises Edmund and his claim to the throne."

"Oh, who knows? Eadric is really loyal only to himself. Though I suspect he'll support Edmund for a time before he betrays him. How long?" he waved a hand. "Your conjecture is as good as any."

Ketil the Fair-hair did not appear consoled. He picked up a stick of driftwood and stabbed the fire. Sparks burst into the darkness and winked out in mist. "This is unexpected. I'm worried. You may think that Thorkell fled to Cnut to save himself, but I fear it was a strategic move."

"How so?" Wulf the White asked.

"Queen Emma is good friends with Thorkell. She will do anything to assure that one of her sons becomes king of England instead of Edmund. Perhaps . . . perhaps . . ." Ketil twisted the driftwood in his hands as though to wring the life from it. "Just imagine what would happen if Aethelred died tomorrow and Thorkell helped Emma to gain access to Cnut? What if she offered to marry him?"

Dag's eyes narrowed. "Gods, what a thought. In a single stroke she could defeat Edmund, while retaining her title and authority as queen of England, and thereby assuring her sons' ascendance to the throne."

"The marriage would also make Cnut the king of all England."

"Well, yes, obviously," Ketil agreed, annoyed. "The point is, Aethelred was somewhat tolerant of other religions. Will Emma coerce Cnut into declaring all of England Anchorite? Even the Danelaw? The Danes will almost certainly convert in exchange for their lives."

"Who cares?" Dag said. "If it—"

"I care, you imbecile. As more and more rulers become Anchorites, the assault on the Seidur faith grows. They're intent upon wiping our beliefs from the earth. Do you wish to live in a world where no one knows the story of Lif and Lifthrasir, the man and woman who repopulated the earth after the Twilight of the Gods? I cannot bear to think of a future where no one dreams of Asgard, or knows the names of the goddesses Freya, Nanna, and Iduna. In fact, I would not live in such a world. If some king ordered me never again to practice my faith, to forget my gods, I'd rather be dead." Angry, Ketil threw the driftwood into the fire and watched as flames leaped up to consume it.

Feeling chastened, Dag apologized, "Yes, forgive me. You're right. I hadn't thought of that."

"Consider this: I may want to establish a colony where I can believe as I wish, but Thorlak wants to wipe Anchorites from the face of the earth." Ketil glared at Dag. "When he hears of this—"

The sound of boots moving rapidly across sand came from Dag's left. He jumped to his feet and drew his sword with a ringing whine, preparing to kill whatever emerged from the misty darkness. Ketil and Wulf leaped up, as well, their swords in hand.

Three seconds later, Masson the Bellower stumbled out of the night with his clothing in shreds, and cried, "Thank the gods, I found you! I've been fleeing aimlessly along the cliffs for hours . . . then I glimpsed the ships."

He staggered forward and threw himself at Dag's feet. "Godi, we have to go home! The stories are true! This land is filled with colossal creatures, evil beyond anything we—"

"Get on your feet!" Dag ordered, and sheathed his sword. "Tell me what happened."

Ketil and Wulf the White did not sheath their swords but moved closer to listen.

Masson clenched his jaw. As he rose on shaking legs, he said, "Godi, I swear to you, it was like standing in the middle of Ragnarök watching the gods destroy themselves. Great beasts thundered across the sky, hissing and spitting lightning. I could feel the heat of their breath scorching me. And—"

"What are you talking about? It sounds like a violent thunderstorm."

Masson continued as though Dag had not spoken, "And the old Skraeling wizard held the wind in his hands, wielding it like a gigantic club! When he struck the clouds, they burst into flame, and the earth roared like a dying lion, then—"

Ketil shouted, "You're babbling senselessly! Where's Thorlak?"

Masson turned to stare wide-eyed at Ketil. "Dead, maybe. I don't know. When a bolt of lightning crackled out of the blue and blasted his sword to splinters, he screamed Thyra's name, and ran away into the forest. Orm said that Thorlak was a—a coward. Did you know that? I never knew that. All my life, I've been so afraid of him, I thought—"

Dag grabbed Masson's filthy sleeve and swung him around to face him. "Where's Orm Einarsson? I heard he went with you to testify in my defense."

Masson cast a glance over his shoulder. "He was right behind me."

"How long ago?"

The Bellower swiveled his head to look back along his own trail. "Well, a while ago. I—I don't know when I lost him. I'm sure he'll be along. He can't be too far away. Unless . . . you don't think they found him, do you?"

"Who? Were you being pursued by Skraelings?"

"I don't know what they were. Giants, maybe. They breathed fire across the sky. Didn't you see it? Didn't you feel heat?"

When wind whipped across the ocean in the distance, Dag caught the alert look on Masson's face, as though he expected Thor himself to walk out of the surf. The tension built to such extremes that Ketil lurched when waves slammed the shore, pushed by the coming gale, and they heard men shouting on the ships, ordering the crew to take down the sails.

"You're as jumpy as a chased hare, Ketil. Sit down, before your nerves cause you to soil your britch—"

"Hush!" Ketil's head went up sharply, glaring at something in the mist behind Dag.

Before Dag could whirl around to look, Ketil ran past him with his sword extended as though to do battle.

Wulf cried, "It's the Lawspeaker!"

Dag turned and saw Thorlak standing at the edge of the firelight with his hood thrown back, the wind whipping his long cape about him in snapping folds. He possessed a cold-eyed look of madness. He stood motionless and silent, staring at the ships rocking on the waves.

Ketil shouted, "What happened?," and used his sword to point at the object in Thorlak's hand. Ketil's shadow fell over it, blocking the firelight, so Dag couldn't tell what it was, but Ketil seemed to be in a paralysis of fear.

"Thorlak?" Dag called. "It's good to see you alive. After hearing the Bellower's bizarre tales of alien sky beasts—"

Thorlak tossed the heavy object at Dag, forcing him to skip sideways to avoid being struck. When it rolled to a stop, he tried to identify the mousy brown hair clinging to the scalp. Then it dawned on him that the sand-coated eyes of Orm Einarsson gazed blindly up from the severed head. "Great Odin! Why did you kill him?"

Only Thorlak's eyes moved, looking at each man on the beach. "I didn't kill him."

Dag made a shooing-away gesture toward the head. "Why did you bring it to me?"

"I thought you might want to know he was dead."

Thorlak walked past Dag to stand at the edge of the surf. Cloaked in shadows, Thorlak seemed to be watching the dark shapes of men rush around the decks, taking down sails and securing anything that might be blown off when the storm rolled in. Faint voices carried.

A feeling of being watched haunted Dag. He glanced at every swirl or shift in the mist, glad for anything that would relieve the tension.

"Thorlak, are you well?" Dag asked with trepidation.

"Where is Thyra?"

"I haven't seen her." Dag glanced at Ketil.

Ketil shrugged. "No one knows her whereabouts. We searched everywhere for her before we sailed away. My guess is that she must have wakened and wandered off—"

"How did she get off the ship? Who's responsible?"

A sudden gust of wind set the fire to crackling. The flames fluttered back and forth, but their light came nowhere close to Thorlak. His tall body might have been sculpted of midnight.

"Well, Thorlak," Ketil said uneasily, "I'd sent most of my crew to capture *Thor's Dragon*, and the rest was rushing about trying to get settlers, livestock, and belongings loaded so we could leave before noon."

"Did she leave with Alfdis the Lig-lodin?"

Ketil didn't answer, apparently because the possibility had never occurred to him and he needed to consider the matter. "Truly, I don't know, though Alfdis did disappear at about the same time."

In a low, icy voice, Thorlak said, "You displease me, Ketil. You and the entire godar."

Wulf the White laughed, attempting to make light of the situation, and walked out across the sand toward Thorlak. "Lawspeaker, we must speak soon. Our mutual friend is very concerned that you haven't sent—"

Five paces from Thorlak, the man convulsed and shrieked like a wounded animal as he crumpled to his knees.

Ketil ran to him. "Are you all right? What's wrong?"

Wulf moaned, holding his shaking arms over his midsection and rocking back and forth in pain.

Dag tried to swallow the lump in his throat without much success. Thorlak's black gaze had fallen upon him, and he felt it like a knife suspended above his heart. Thorlak grew perfectly still.

Dag just stared, waiting for Thorlak to do or say something. "Don't forget, Thorlak, that I am your ally here. I know everything there is to know about you, and this mission."

The cool threat seemed to amuse Thorlak. A smile touched his lips. "I must get to *Thor's Dragon*."

# Forty

Gasping for breath, Chief Drona and twenty warriors stumbled into Whale Rib Village. It had taken them two hands of hard canoeing to get back to the place where they'd first seen the large halo of firelight. He'd suspected the halo was spawned by a massive Wobee army. But what he saw confused him.

The wavering gleam of the ancestors shot eerie shadows through the mist.

Shocked, he just stared. His warriors seemed to have gone just as mute. The destroyed village had been . . . wiped away. For what purpose? Just the need to destroy every vestige of their enemies' lives?

The trees in the distance—at the edge of the devastation—were little more than dark, skeletal arms. The few leaves clinging to the branches were stone dead and created a constant, serpent-like *shish*ing in the breeze.

"Why would the Wobee do this?" an unknown warrior asked.

"You should be asking *how* the Wobee did this."

"They're animals," someone else whispered.

"No, they're tunghaks in human bodies."

As Drona listened to his worried warriors, he walked toward where the longhouse had been. Just yesterday, the roof poles had created a lattice-like weave visible from across the village. Tonight, he saw nothing. When he reached the location, he found only a hole in the ground filled with old blankets and roof fall.

"Chief?" Seventeen-winters-old Shootak trotted up to Drona. Still breathing hard, Shootak said, "Some people are saying it couldn't have been the Wobee. It must have been the ancestors casting fire from the sky—"

"It was the Wobee. But we won't know anything else until morning when we can study the tracks."

Shootak shifted his weight to his other foot, uneasy as he looked around. "The elders are discussing what we should do now. One thinks we should return to our canoes and hurry back to Soapstone Village to make sure our families are safe."

Drona shook his head. "Please, tell the elders I recommend we make camp on the rim where we can watch for passing canoes or Wobee ships. We are all tired. At dawn, if it meets with their approval, we'll hold a council meeting to discuss this . . . this event."

"Yes, Chief."

Shootak trotted away, and Drona listened to the wavering groan that shuddered the air. Almost beyond his ability to hear, it seemed to spring from within Earth Mother, like an earthquake being born in the depths of her heart. Or, perhaps, somewhere far beneath his feet, she was roaring in outrage.

He folded his arms tightly over his chest and listened to his heart beating in his ears.

# Forty-One

W hile Dag waited for the men aboard *Thor's Dragon* to unroll the ladder and drop it over the side, he tied the towrope of his boat to the ring on the ship's keel. Wulf the White, still reeling with sickness, had chosen to remain onshore. Dag had promised to send the boat back for him. His gaze shifted to where Thorlak crouched in the bow like a jumping spider poised to leap upon prey. The man's curious behavior unnerved Dag.

"Godi!" Masson the Bellower called from where he sat next to Ketil in the rear of the rowboat. "They're dropping the ladder now. I see them."

"And long past time," Dag grumbled.

The instant the rope ladder cascaded down the side of the ship Thorlak snatched it out of the air and began scaling the rungs with inhuman quickness.

"Gods," Ketil said. The boat rocked as he worked his way to Dag's side. Pale blond hair blew around his head. "I've never seen him act this bizarre. What's the matter with him?"

Dag waited to answer until the Lawspeaker had made it to the top of the ladder, and been helped off onto the deck, before he replied, "I'm beginning to think he's not human, at least not in his soul."

Ketil had a distraught expression. "You think he changed his soul into an animal? Can Seidur magicians do that? Change just their souls, and not their bodies?"

"I suspect that, with the help of Odin, the good ones can do anything they please."

Ketil gestured to the rope ladder. "You climb up next, Dag. I'll follow."

Dag caught the swaying ladder, and began his ascent. Two of Ketil's men, both with yellow rotted teeth, waited at the top. As Dag took their hands and let them pull him onto the deck, a gust of wind lashed the ship. He flipped up his hood and waited for Ketil and Masson. When they'd both made it safely onto the ladder, he searched the deck for Thorlak, and didn't see him. He turned to the dark-haired man. "Where did the Lawspeaker go?"

The man shouted against the gale, "He said he wanted to speak with Bjarni, so we sent him to the hold where the slaves are being held."

Dag helped Ketil aboard. When Masson stepped onto the deck, he staggered to catch his balance, then both gathered around Dag.

The storm struck with a vengeance. Rain battered Dag, trying to shove him over the edge and into the ocean. Staggering, he leaned into the gale. "We have to get below quickly."

Ketil strode across the deck. Dag naturally expected Masson to follow, but when he turned he found his personal guard hanging on to the mast with a sheepish look on his face.

"What are you doing? Come on!" Dag yelled.

The Bellower shook his head. "I'm not going down there, not with the Lawspeaker in such a mood. At least up here I can jump overboard if need be."

Dag despised insubordination. He considered ordering Ketil's men to give the Bellower his wish and throw him overboard but relented. "Very well, but I want you standing at the top of the stairs in case I shout for you!"

Masson wiped rain from his terrified face and walked to the stairs that led down below. "Thank you, Godi. Truly. Thank you. I'm sure he's going to kill someone down there."

Ketil peered down the stairs with wide eyes. "I suspect he's right. Do you want to go down first, Dag?"

"Great Odin, I'm surrounded by sniveling cowards." Dag shouldered past Ketil and trotted down the stairs into the stinking hold.

The odors of sweat, urine, and feces—both human and animal—thickened the lamplit air. A cow mooed. Dag saw the beast tied to the steerbord wall, along with several sheep, goats, three other milk cows, and a big evil-eyed bull. Dag's child thralls, including the six new thralls he'd captured in the south, huddled together in the stern, beside the last cow, their chains rattling. The oldest child, Podebeek, was shaking badly, but they all looked petrified. To the laddebord, the Skoggangur's crew watched Thorlak, who was pacing before them in such a threatening manner, all they dared to do was stare at him.

"How did Thyra get off this ship?" Thorlak asked.

Bjarni the Deep-minded, who sat in the middle, chained between Arnora and Osk, answered, "None of us know." Bjarni's long, wavy red hair stuck to his blood-soaked shirt, and his wedge-shaped face had swollen up so hideously from the beatings that he was almost unrecognizable.

Thorlak paced to the next man in line, Finnbogi the Skull-splitter. The big Norwegian looked almost as bad as Bjarni, but not quite. "When did she leave the ship?"

"How would I know, Lawspeaker? The last time I checked on her it was barely past dawn, and we were attacked right after that." Finnbogi tilted his head to the guards. "Ask Godi Ketil's henchmen. Maybe they saw her leave."

Ketil quickly called out, "None of my people saw her leave the ship."

Thorlak's gaze returned to Bjarni. "Not one of you saw her wake or leave?"

Bjarni looked up and down the line before replying, "We've discussed this, and we are not sure she walked off this ship of her own free will, Lawspeaker."

"What do you mean?"

"Has it occurred to you that one of the godar might have spirited Thyra off this boat for his own purposes?"

Thorlak's dark gaze slid to Ketil, and when the Fair-hair fiercely shook his head his gaze moved to Dag.

"Of course not, Thorlak!" Dag threw up his arms. "Great gods. Why would I do that?"

Thorlak started taking slow, measured steps across the deck. "Bjarni, did anyone search the hay where she'd been sleeping?"

"No, Lawspeaker, but Godi Ketil's thralls have been forking hay to feed the animals all day. What are you looking for?"

"She owned a Seidur sword. I want it."

Arnora said, "She lost her sword fighting that terrible storm on the way here. It was swept from her hand by a gigantic wave. At least . . . that's what I heard. I—I wasn't up there on deck."

"Did anyone else see that happen?"

The prisoners muttered to one another and looked up and down the line at their comrades.

Finally, Bjarni said, "I saw her come up from the hold and lift her sword to do battle with Thor. Great Freya, it was nothing less than a miracle. She cried out and Thor's fire swallowed the entire ship. The mast snapped and fell. Then—"

"What happened to her sword?"

"I never saw it again. I'm sure she lost it when she was swept overboard."

Thorlak stared at Bjarni for an uncomfortable period, then turned and went to the hay, where he started kicking through the dry shocks. The sweet scent of sun-dried grass rose to compete with the stench.

As the keel rolled beneath Dag, he spread his legs to steady himself. The storm was getting worse. "For the sake of the gods, Thorlak, why do you care about Thyra's belongings? If she had a Seidur sword, she likely took it with her when she left the ship."

"No, she didn't."

"How do you know that?"

"I know everything about that sword: how it hefts, how it sings, how it *feels* when she's using it. I gave it to her. It belonged to me once, a long time ago, before I acquired Skyrmir."

"Truly, Lawspeaker, I'm certain she lost her sword in the storm," Bjarni said.

Thorlak got down on his hands and knees and continued searching the hay by hand, violently brushing the grass away until he found bare floor beneath.

*Gods, with* Skyrmir *gone, he must need another Seidur sword badly.*

Ketil eased up beside Dag and whispered, "I'm really worried now."

"Now? What took you so long?"

Ketil obsessively smoothed his blond beard while he watched the Lawspeaker. "Thorlak, let's discuss this matter in Gunnar's chamber, where we can speak in private." He held out a hand to the small door in the bow just behind the haystack.

"Yes," Dag said. "We need to hear what really happened at Gunnar's court. The stories thus far are ludicrous. What imbecile would ever believe that an old Skraeling wizard could conjure gigantic sky beasts so powerful they'd hurl lightning bolts that blasted your magical sword to bits? Skyrmir was invincible! Completely unbelievable."

As shocked whispers and muttering broke out among the prisoners, Thorlak slowly rose to his feet.

For a time, he stood with his back to Dag, swaying with the movement of the ship. When at last Thorlak turned, his eyes resembled glittering yellow jewels. "Who told you about my sword?"

"Masson the Bellower, of course."

"Did he?"

Thorlak regarded Dag without a shred of emotion, but Dag could see indignation building behind his eyes, and it made Dag slightly nauseous.

"Thorlak, really, we shouldn't be talking in front of the thralls. Let's—"

Dag staggered when an earth-shattering crack split the air at the same instant that thunder battered the ship, shaking it violently.

A commotion broke out on deck. Boots thudded as men ran around shouting at one another, then a thrall leaned over the hold and yelled, "Godi Dag, you'd best get up here!"

"What's the matter now?" In irritation, Dag turned and trotted up the stairs onto the rainy deck. Lightning flickered through the clouds like a vast blue-white web.

"Over here, Godi. Hurry!"

Dag strode across the deck to where the man leaned over a body that sprawled near the mast. "What—"

"Godi, it was a freak accident! Masson had been kneeling by the stairs listening to the conversation below when suddenly he jumped up and charged across the deck. An instant later, Thor cast a bolt of lightning that lanced clear through him. He didn't even have time to make a sound. Just collapsed, dead as a wedge."

Every other member of the crew stood a good three paces away, afraid to get any closer to the body.

A tight sensation constricted Dag's chest. He turned and found Thorlak standing on deck. The white flashes gave his face a cadaverous look, all sharp angles and dark hollows, here one instant, gone the next.

*He can call down the lightning without a Seidur sword. . . .*

His belly in knots, Dag turned back to the deckhand. In a loud ringing voice, he ordered, "Shove his body over the side, and be done with it. The man was a liar and a coward. If he told you any outlandish stories, you are never to repeat them. Do you understand?"

Stunned men nodded, but as they bent to grasp the body every head turned toward Thorlak.

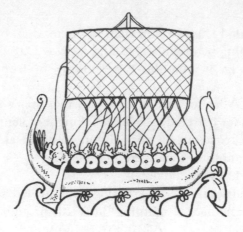

# Forty-Two

As the leading edge of the storm passed, the wind died down, and rain fell in a steady stream from the sky. Kiran could barely see the line of people following behind him on the Cliff Trail, though he could hear their feet rasping upon the stones.

Godi Gunnar came next, followed by Alfdis, then Ingolf and Sokkolf. Far in the rear, Camtac and Elder Asson stumbled along together. If Kiran squinted, he could see them. Camtac appeared to be holding Asson up . . . or maybe it was the reverse. Thyra walked a few paces in front of them, but she kept glancing back, probably monitoring their progress.

Kiran ought to be walking beside her, but . . . she frightened him. A strange transformation had come over her. Only a few days ago, she had been an insecure and lighthearted girl. Now she moved with an air of power, and her slender body, once so fragile to him, had become somehow latently dangerous. Just the sweeping of her arms held threat. He felt it in the air, but he did not understand it. And, especially, he did not know how to react to it. Deep inside him, he had the feeling that her soul, like a butterfly, had unfurled its magnificent wings and was preparing to take flight into a vast unknown, leaving him far behind.

And stories about her changing into a fox . . .

"Godi?" Thyra called. *Even her voice sounds deeper.* "Could we stop for a time? Camtac and Elder Asson must rest."

Gunnar turned and frowned. "Gods, I had no idea they'd fallen so far behind." As he held his hands up to the line of people, murmuring started. "Let's rest. Catch our breaths!"

Thyra trotted back to help Camtac lower Asson to the ground. The elder's injured leg had swollen grotesquely.

Kiran trotted back to help her. Alfdis, Ingolf, and Sokkolf gathered around Godi Gunnar and started a quiet conversation.

Asson said, "I'm all right. Sit down, both of you, and rest for as long as you can. Thyra Little Fox? Stop fussing over me. I'm fine."

"We need to change your bandage, Asson."

Asson glanced up as Kiran approached. "I can do that myself. Camtac will help me. Go and spend time with your friend."

Thyra stared down at Asson lovingly, then walked to meet Kiran.

When she stopped in front of him and looked up, Kiran forced a smile. "Is Elder Asson all right?"

"No. He needs to sleep for days, Kiran." Thyra glanced back at the old Kutsitualit, and her eyes tightened. "I'm very worried about him. He told me that his cave isn't far from here. I'm wondering if we shouldn't take him home, and leave him, while we search for the fire grave. He can give us directions. There's no reason for him to die in the fight that's coming."

"We are *not* going to die, Thyra."

Brusquely, Thyra took his hand and led him across the wet rocks to a promontory overlooking the rainy ocean. "Sit with me, Kiran. We must speak honestly."

Kiran cast a glance at where Godi Gunnar and the other men stood talking. "I don't think we have long."

She pulled him down to the ledge beside her. "Then let's get started."

Reluctantly, he sat down and watched as she drew up her knees and propped her elbows atop them. "Kiran, please tell me what you know of this grave that Thorlak is trying to find."

Kiran considered the request. Softly, he said, "I've promised Godi Gunnar that I will not repeat the things he's told me—"

"You must tell me. I need to know everything I can."

A curious sensation invaded Kiran's chest. Something frightening hid in her eyes, something that compelled him to say, "I know very little, truthfully. Just that Thorlak is desperate to find it, and the grave has something to do with the civil war going on in England."

"Whose grave is it?"

Kiran shrugged. "At one point, I thought Godi Gunnar was going to tell me, but he didn't. From what I've gathered, though, it has something to do with an old battle between Thorlak and the renowned Seidur prophetess who served Sweyn Forkbeard, King Cnut's father."

"Seidur prophetess?" Thyra's eyes narrowed and the raindrops falling around her changed their descent, bending around her as if afraid.

*I'm dreaming. Being foolish.*

"Yes. Gunnar thinks she was killed along with her daughter in the slaughter of the Danelaw."

"What slaughter?"

Kiran blinked. Everyone knew of the 1002 slaughter of the Danes. Even thralls in Greenland. It was infamous, and the main reason King Aethelred was so hated by the Danish. How was it possible that Thyra did not know? Gently, Kiran said, "You've never heard of the St. Brice Day Massacre?"

She shook her head. "No."

"I'm surprised your Danish parents never mentioned it. It happened thirteen years ago, Thyra. Apparently, Thorlak served as the Seidur seer for the rebel, Pallig, and there was a rivalry between Thorlak and Vethild. She—"

*"Vethild? Vet . . . Vethild?"*

"The Forkbeard's prophetess, yes. She was his most cherished asset. Just before the massacre, as a result of a vision, Thorlak told Pallig to break the treaty he'd signed with Aethelred to protect England, and advised him to join raiders attacking England's south coast. King Aethelred's chief advisor, Ealdorman Eadric of Mercia—"

Thyra grabbed his arm hard. She stammered, "The e-e-ealdorman . . . of Mercia?"

"Yes. Why?"

"I'm sorry. I'm just . . . I'm probably wrong. Please, go on." She propped her elbows on her knees again and massaged her temples, as though she had a headache building.

"So, Eadric told the king that Pallig's betrayal meant the Danelaw was plotting to overthrow him and take his kingdom. The idea that they, and Pallig, had betrayed him enraged the king. Aethelred sent his army to kill them. As I understand it, the slaughter led directly to King Sweyn Forkbeard's invasion of England a short time later, and his ascension to the throne, though the Forkbeard ruled as king of England for only a few weeks before he and son, Cnut, were driven out again by Aethelred's mercenary army, which was led by Thorkell the Tall."

Thyra was staring at Kiran, but distance filled her gaze, as though she could see the slaughter taking place right behind her eyes. A barely visible shiver went through her.

"Are you cold?" Kiran took off his cape and wrapped it around her shoulders. "Forgive me, I should have thought—"

"Is the grave Vethild's?" Thyra almost choked on the words, as though it was hard for her to say them.

He gently tied the cape beneath her chin. "It could be anyone's, Thyra. I don't understand Danish royal politics very well."

"But what if he's really looking for Vethild's grave?"

Kiran tenderly pulled wet hair away from her eyes so he could see her freckled face. The northern lights had briefly appeared in a rent in the clouds, and set her eyes afire with reflections. "Why does it matter so much to you?"

"I think . . ." A hard swallow went down her throat. "Kiran, I may have been there."

Momentarily confused, he had to think about it before he asked, "At the slaughter? But I heard that every man, woman, and child was murdered."

"Maybe. Except for those that were kidnapped and taken far away."

Kiran leaned back, and took a long, deep breath. "Are you saying that you were—"

"No, I—I don't know. But I have memories. . . ." She paused. "I have memories, Kiran. I know you won't believe—"

She left the sentence hanging while she fumbled to pull the hem of his cape over her feet.

With simple honesty, he said, "I will, Thyra. I will believe anything you tell me." With difficulty, he added, "Including that you rode into Helheim on an eight-legged horse, found Sokkolf, then turned into a white fox to lead his soul back to the land of the living. It frightens me. I won't lie about that. But I'll still love you with all my heart." She touched his hand and, like an earthquake in his Anchorite bones, he felt a shiver go through his soul. "I just . . . I need time to find a place for this in my beliefs. Maybe the Fisherman allows such things. I mean, he must."

Kiran reached up to clasp his anchor pendant, for it comforted him.

She licked her lips, clearly preparing herself. "Kiran, I think I know the name of my Other Mother."

Kiran's brows lowered as he tried to figure out what Thyra might be trying to tell him. She had reacted with shock at the name Vethild, and believed that she had memories of the slaughter. "Are you trying to tell me that you think your mother was Thorlak's archenemy Vethild?"

Thyra tipped her face up to Kiran and raindrops pearled over her pale cheeks. "I'm almost sure of it."

Kiran laid a gentle hand against her dripping hair, anxiously studying her expression. "If she was, or is, it brings up a whole new series of questions, none of which I like."

"I know," she whispered fiercely. "Like who captured me that day, and why? Who took me in secret to Denmark and paid my new family to care for me? Who took my mother, and where did they take her?"

"How do you know your family in Denmark was paid to take care of you?"

"I saw money exchange hands. They were paid. Believe me."

"I do. But, Thyra, if that's true they were, in effect, conspirators in keeping you captive for most of your life."

In a tight voice, she said, "No, Kiran, no. They thought they were protecting me."

"Did they say that?"

"No, but . . . they loved me, Kiran. I swear they did."

At the pain on her face, he quickly said, "Of course they did, Thyra. Who wouldn't?" He smoothed the long hair that fell down her back and smiled at her. His love for her right now was so intense it was a physical ache. "I only meant that they must have believed they were protecting you for a reason—"

"Yes, because I'll be useful to keep my mother in line."

As he lowered his hand, his brows knitted together. "Useful?"

She violently shook her head. "Both Edmund and Cnut are committed to finding her. Or were nine months ago."

"Edmund? . . . King Aethelred's son? And King Cnut?"

Thyra turned slowly to look at Kiran, and it felt as though she dragged the rain with her. For a few moments, streamers swirled around them in tiny tornadoes. "Edmund is King Aethelred's son?"

"Well, I—I can't be certain, many men bear that name, but I suspect so. When you mention his name in the same sentence with Cnut's, I think your Edmund must be King Aethelred's son. Did someone tell you that? That Edmund and Cnut were hunting for your mother?"

She bowed her head and he saw tears glaze her eyes. "Yes."

"Then you must tell Godi Gunnar, Thyra. He needs to know this."

Thyra's gaze shifted to Gunnar and the group of men surrounding him. "Does Godi Gunnar know the king's son?"

Kiran blanched. "He's never told me that. Not once. But I feel he does. And Edmund is currently allied with the Danelaw to fight against his father, Aethelred. They've partitioned England—"

"Was Edmund allied with Eadric a year ago? Or . . . or even longer?"

"All I know is that the ealdorman of Mercia is currently on Aethelred's side, or seems to be, and Edmund and Aethelred have partitioned the country. Edmund and the leaders of the Danelaw hold the north, while Aethelred holds the south."

Thyra rose on shaking legs. His cape, much too long for her, dragged across the wet stone. She swiftly turned to Asson, as though she'd heard him call her name.

When Kiran swung around, he found Asson looking straight at Thyra. They appeared to be engaged in some silent conversation. The Skraeling youth stared at Asson in the same confused manner that Kiran was staring at Thyra.

"Kiran?" Thyra asked without turning to face him.

"Yes?"

"Thorlak plans to use me as a hostage to draw my mother in." Almost too low to hear, Thyra added, "Great Odin, that's why he had to kill everyone aboard the ship. I'd been speaking openly with the other thralls. The master, crew, and thralls all knew I'd come from Denmark, and when they saw me with him . . . someone might have suspected? He couldn't take any chances. Gods, I must look very much like my mother."

"What are you talking about?" Uneasy, Kiran shoved to his feet to stand beside her.

She used both hands to wipe rain from her freckled face. Staring straight into Asson's eyes, she quietly said, "No, there must be . . . there's another reason, Asson." A pause. She shook her head. "I think he wants to kill her."

Though Asson could not possibly hear Thyra from this distance, the elder gave her a solemn nod.

Thyra paced back and forth across the cliff top for a time, then finally placed her hands on either side of her head and pressed hard, as though trying to force the answer from her memories. "I can't find it, Asson!"

Asson lifted his voice, and called, "But it's there, Thyra Little Fox. Hidden right before your eyes. Keep looking."

Kiran hesitantly reached out to touch her shoulder and she jumped. "Sorry." He jerked his hand back. "Thyra, I don't understand all this"—he glanced at Asson—"but we don't have nearly enough information yet to answer these questions."

Before he knew what was happening, she'd stepped forward, wrapped her arms around his waist, and clutched him so tightly against her, he could barely breathe. Kiran hugged her, holding her up as her knees shook. He was aware of her warm breath on his throat, and her body pressed against his. He longed to stand like this forever. As he stroked her hair, he said, "Everything's going to be all right, Thyra. If Vethild is here, we'll find her. I promise you. We'll hunt for her until we know for sure whether she's alive or dead. Then we'll warn her that Thorlak is here and hunting her."

Thyra went still in Kiran's arms, and cold.

He just held her. They stood like that for a blessed eternity, until she pushed away from him. "She already knows he's hunting her."

Kiran glanced at Asson again before he quietly asked, "May I—may I ask you a question?"

"Yes, of course."

He whispered, "Tell me how to help you. I'll do anything you ask of me."

"Thank you for loving me," she said in a half-agonized voice. "Thank you, Kiran. You're the only thing in the world that matters to me."

"Well," he corrected, teasing her, "me and the quest to find your mother." When he noticed Thyra had started crying, he gasped, "What did I say? I'm sorry; I didn't mean—"

"Yes. The two of you."

Thyra reached up to clasp his anchor pendant and held it for a few moments. "Do you think he can still punish me?"

"The Fisherman wouldn't—"

"The Lawspeaker."

Kiran hesitated, trying to understand. "Why would he wish to punish you? You've done nothing to deserve—"

"Listen to me, please. Once Asson has taken us to the fire grave—"

She abruptly turned toward the ocean, and seemed to be listening to something. "We must prepare ourselves. I . . . I'll be fighting him alone. I'll need—"

"You won't be alone," Asson called, and reached for the branch he'd been using as a walking stick. "Help me up, Camtac."

"Yes, Elder."

The youth helped Asson to his feet. The old man groaned and stood for a time just leaning on his walking stick. Finally, he hobbled forward.

He stopped in front of Thyra and tenderness warmed his face. "You have never been alone. She wouldn't have allowed it. She loves you too much. And *I* will be there, too."

# Forty-Three

Podebeek huddled with the twelve other children, watching the blazing-eyed tunghak that loomed over them with his fists clenched, as though about to strike them. Standing just behind the tunghak, its servant Dag carried a whale-oil lamp. The flickering gleam played through the belly of the ship, dancing over the struts, animals, and stark faces of Wobee prisoners.

The tunghak called something to the man named Bjarni, who turned and spoke to the woman beside him. She nodded and sat forward.

After a short conversation, the woman said, "Podebeek, I Arnora. Who child know Asson?"

Podebeek whispered to the child next to him, Moosin, a nine-winters-old boy who'd been captured from a far southern village, "She speaks our language poorly."

Moosin whispered back, "Why does the tunghak want to know about Elder Asson?"

Podebeek shook his head, uncertain. He and the other children had been plotting their escape. One of the little girls, Kuis, had already managed to slip her small hands from the manacles, and she'd been working to free the hands of other children.

To give her more time, Podebeek said, "I know Asson."

When the tunghak crouched before Podebeek, he couldn't help it; he yelped in terror as he scrambled backward. The other children started wailing and the strong scent of urine rose. Dag's nose wrinkled.

The tunghak seemed barely aware that several of the children, including Podebeek, had wet themselves. It spoke to Arnora.

She asked, "Where Asson lives?"

Podebeek tightened his muscles to control his shuddering. "He—he lives in a cave. A sea cave."

"Where cave?"

"Near my home. My—my old home."

The tunghak turned to listen to Arnora and the lines of its starved face deepened, especially those at the corners of its eyes. They might have been cut into the desiccated hide by a master leather worker. Its voice went low and menacing.

Arnora swallowed hard before she asked, "Thorlak want know if you take there?"

A quivering mixture of horror and hope twined through Podebeek. Maybe he could run away when the creature wasn't watching? Though his village had been destroyed, his mother lived. He'd seen her escape. He could find her.

The village elders never allowed children to go near the Shaman's Trail for fear that they'd fall to their deaths, but Podebeek knew it better than any of these people did. He would not lead them to Asson's cave, though. What if Asson was home? They'd kill him. Instead, Podebeek would lead them to Asson's Spirit Cave, the dangerous place where the elder communed with the two Lightning Spirits. Would Thorlak the tunghak have any idea Podebeek was leading it in the wrong direction? No, Podebeek decided, the tunghak would never know. He could lead Thorlak around in circles for days and it wouldn't know.

*Probably.*

Podebeek's voice shook when he said, "Yes, I'll take it there. But the Shaman's Trail is very dangerous. It's narrow and chunks often crack and fall off. If it takes too many people the trail will crumble apart from the weight."

As Arnora translated, the tunghak's yellow glistening eyes bored into Podebeek, searching for deception. Finally, it rose to its feet and lifted its fist, ready to bring it down on someone's head with all the strength it could muster.

Podebeek squeezed his eyes closed, waiting for the attack. By now, he knew the creature's blow rhythms by heart. When they didn't come, Podebeek opened one eye. Thorlak gave Arnora some command. She answered in a trembling voice and nodded.

Apparently satisfied, it stalked away.

When Thorlak and Dag disappeared up the stairs, and Podebeek heard their boots on the deck above, he slumped back against the hull panting. Blessed Anguta, could he do this? Could he lead them in the wrong direction long enough that the children could escape, and Podebeek might have a chance . . .

Moosin edged closer and bumped shoulders with him. "Thank you, Podebeek."

Podebeek blinked. "For what?"

Moosin chewed his lower lip for a time, watching Arnora, who was quietly speaking to Bjarni, maybe translating their conversation. "When you lead him away from us, I will find a way, I-I don't know how yet, but I'll find a way to set the other children free and escape."

Podebeek anxiously wet his lips. "I know you will, Moosin. Before you leap over the side, make sure you know who can swim and who can't."

"I will."

"The good swimmers will have to help the bad swimmers."

"We won't let anyone drown."

"And when you reach the shore, don't run along the cliff. They will see you. Get into the forest as fast as you can. Remember your hunting lessons. Walk in water and on rocks, so that you don't leave tracks. It'll be harder for them to find you."

Moosin jerked his head in a frightened nod. "Yes, I won't forget. I promise."

"Good." Podebeek straightened up, took a deep breath, and stared at Bjarni. The redhead wore a frown as he spoke with Arnora. Podebeek called, "Bjarni?"

The man turned to stare at Podebeek. Bjarni had a wedge-shaped face and looked to have seen around twenty-five winters.

"If we help you escape, will you help us?"

Arnora translated, and Bjarni's eyes narrowed. He spoke softly with several of his friends before Arnora translated his words: "How could help us?"

"First, you must give me your oath that if we help you, you will help us."

Bjarni listened to Arnora, gave Podebeek a skeptical look, but finally nodded.

Arnora said, "We give oaths."

Podebeek was shaking badly, afraid that once these Wobee were free they might just hurt him and the other children more, but he said, "Kuis?

Please walk over to Bjarni and take him any tools he asks you for, so that he can get out of his chains."

When six-winters-old Kuis rose and trotted over to stand before Bjarni, waiting for instructions, the man's eyes flew wide.

Arnora translated Podebeek's last words and Bjarni frantically began pointing to boxes stacked behind the hay bin.

Kuis marched over, shoved off the lids, and started carrying armloads of tools to the Wobee slaves. Some looked like hammers; others resembled deerbone stilettos, except made of iron. The big man on the far end was the first to free himself. He quickly began picking at the chunk of metal that held the person next to him. Chains rattled.

As more and more Wobee slaves stood up, Podebeek began to wonder if Bjarni ever planned to help him and the other children. He waited, and worried.

Finally, when most of Bjarni's people were free, he grabbed the stiletto tool, and he and Arnora hurried over to kneel before Podebeek. The brilliant red color of Bjarni's hair fascinated Podebeek. Bjarni stabbed the iron stiletto into the metal around Moosin's wrists, and worked it around, while Arnora translated his words:

"We free, but can children pretend still chained?"

Podebeek blinked. "Yes."

Bjarni gave Podebeek a nod, but then Arnora said, "Can't free you. Understand?"

Tears burned Podebeek's eyes. The tunghak would be coming soon and if it found Podebeek free . . . "Yes. I understand."

It would take them time to make their plan to take over the ship, which meant Podebeek would not be among the children to go home, for he would be with Thorlak, but it didn't matter. As he looked into the wide eyes of the other children, happiness left him breathless.

Arnora translated Bjarni's words: "Soon, we make plan. Then free children."

A wave of relief flooded Podebeek's veins. "Thank you, Bjarni."

# Forty-Four

**B**oth Gunnar and Kiran were bareheaded, and resembled drowned rats.

Ingolf and Sokkolf walked a few paces back with Elder Asson's arms over their shoulders, helping him along the trail, while the youth Camtac wearily trudged beside them. Gunnar was certain the boy would collapse at any moment. They were all exhausted. Gunnar would have to make camp soon so everyone could get a few hours of sleep.

Far back in the darkness, he saw Thyra. If there was any light, even the faintest amount, her ivory hair shone. Kiran had given her his cape. In the oval frame of the hood, her young face had a pale gleam.

Gunnar looked up at the clouds. They'd started to gray with the coming of morning, as had the sea, but rain and darkness still held the world. As the tide rushed in, he could hear its distinct roar and the fiercer waves splashing the cliff below.

Gunnar slowed to study the high point thirty paces ahead. In the falling rain, all he could make out was a darker shade of gray sprawled on the promontory in the middle of the trail, but it appeared vaguely human shaped. Kiran and Alfdis walked up beside him.

"What is it?" Alfdis asked, squinting at the dark patch. Rain poured from his hood. His hair and beard created a pitch-black ring around his eyes.

Gunnar turned back to Alfdis. "I'm of a mind to think it's human."

Kiran frowned at it. "Alive? Maybe asleep?"

Alfdis shook his head. "If it's sprawled like I think it is, the arms akimbo . . . dead."

Gunnar glanced back at Camtac and his mouth pinched into a tight line. "Well, I hope not. This is about the right place, isn't it? The place where he and his brother met the black-caped man?"

Kiran looked around at the faint swath of trees undulating across the hills, then out at the ocean. "I think so."

Gunnar called, "Camtac?"

Camtac came at a shambling trot. He was short and thin, and the storm had pasted his leather shirt to his chest. Bars of ribs showed through. "Yes?"

Kiran translated.

Gunnar examined Camtac. His slanting eyes and very high cheekbones gave his face a pointed, angular symmetry. "Is this where you left your brother?"

Camtac jerked a nod. "Yes. Somewhere in here."

Gunnar stepped slightly to the left so that Camtac could see the dark form lying on the trail ahead.

Camtac's eyes widened, but he didn't move. He just blinked against the falling rain and frowned, trying to . . .

As though he suddenly understood, Camtac braced his feet to steady himself, but Gunnar could see the fear glinting in his eyes. The youth lifted his chin and stoically walked forward to face the truth.

When Kiran and Alfdis started to follow, Gunnar said, "Wait. Give him a moment."

Gunnar stood watching. He knew well the sensation of shock and horror at first seeing a loved one dead. The sight shredded the heart. And afterward, as the person tried to feel his way forward into a world where the beloved would never exist again, never smile at you or love you, the pain became unbearable. It was something a man never got over. Camtac deserved a few moments alone before others shattered his—

Camtac turned around in the rain. Kiran translated his words: "I don't know who this is. He is one of your men, Chief Gunnar."

"*My* men?"

Gunnar sprinted across the wet rock.

As he neared the corpse, he could tell from the woolen clothing that Camtac was correct. Norse. And headless. Gunnar instinctively looked around for the head. Headless bodies were almost impossible to identify. You'd think a friend ought to be able to know from a man's height, or the breadth of the shoulders, maybe a person's hands, but that was rarely the case. He frowned down at the corpse. He had no idea who this was. Not Bjarni, however; too tall, and for that Gunnar felt deeply grateful.

Kiran and Alfdis arrived. Kiran gasped at the sight of the headless body, but Alfdis just walked around to the opposite side to get a different view. As they mulled the corpse's identity, Camtac wandered a short distance away, and began searching the ground, maybe for the head, maybe for a sign of his brother.

Alfdis scratched his black beard. "The corpse is sopping wet. In this gloom, I can't tell the color of his clothing. But he's tall. Do you think it's Thorlak?"

"Much as that would delight me, I doubt it. He's not tall enough, and his boots have holes in the bottom, something Thorlak's vanity would never tolerate."

Alfdis bent down to study the bottoms of the man's boots.

Kiran quietly said, "Godi? I think it's Orm Einarsson."

"Really? Why?"

Kiran gestured to the man's shirt. "Thorlak was wearing a long red tunic. This man's shirt reaches only to his waist."

"So did Masson the Bellower's. Could just as easily be that scoundrel."

Alfdis methodically searched his way up the dead body to the neck, where he crouched. "It's too clean and narrow to be an ax wound. Sword cut. He wasn't killed by a Skraeling."

Gunnar knelt to examine the throat. "Nice stroke, too. Severed the spine like a hot knife through butter. Whoever swung the weapon had powerful arms."

Pools of blood clotted around the shoulders. Animals hadn't been at it yet but would when the day arrived.

"If this is Orm Einarsson, could have been Masson that killed him," Alfdis suggested. "He's built like a bull ox."

"The Bellower is no swordsman, though. He's more handy with a battle-ax. The fellow who did this knew his way around a sword."

Ingolf and Sokkolf caught up with them, and left Asson propped on his walking stick while they rushed forward to gawk. Thyra slowly climbed the trail, as if deep in thought.

"Norns below!" Ingolf's mouth hung ajar. "He's not one of our crew, is he?"

"We're still musing on that. More likely it's Einarsson or the Bellower."

"Oh," Ingolf breathed, and stepped back. "What a relief."

Sokkolf leaned over the corpse with his eyes narrowed. Soaked hair dangled around his face. "Either way, the killer deserves accolades."

Gunnar rubbed his jaw. "Yes, he certainly did us all a service, I'll say that for him."

Ingolf and Alfdis laughed.

Gunnar noted with mild amusement that Kiran appeared shocked by their calm assessment of the corpse's possible identity.

"Don't let us dismay you, Kiran. We're just pragmatists, that's all."

Kiran gave Gunnar an askance look. "Yes, Godi."

From two paces distant, Thyra suddenly stopped. "Who is he?"

Gunnar shook his head. "It's not Thorlak, if that's what you're hoping. We're well on our way to believing he's one of Dag's men, Einarsson or Masson the Bellower."

Thyra bravely walked forward for a better look. In Kiran's oversized cape, her skinny frame resembled that of a frail little girl playing at being a woman . . . until she turned; then all impressions of helplessness evaporated into thin air. Gunnar slitted his eyes in defense. Was she really just fifteen? Gods, her manner had changed in the past few days.

Asson hobbled to stand between Thyra and Gunnar. His bushy black brows knitted over his long beak of a nose. "Do you smell it?" Asson softly asked her.

"I do."

Gunnar glanced between them. "Smell what? The coppery odor of the blood?"

The clouds briefly parted, and when Máni's face appeared a wave of silver dusted the ocean and made the rain look like falling pearls.

Thyra hitched up her hem to kneel beyond the pool of congealed gore where she could gaze at the neck stump. Kiran's cape spread around her in sculpted folds. "This is Seidur magic, Godi."

"Like the wave of light? How can you tell?"

Thyra waved a hand over the severed neck. "A faint resin-like scent clings to the body."

"Well, since I know for a fact that you didn't kill this man that leaves Thorlak."

Alfdis propped his bearded chin in his fist while he contemplated the mystery. "Why would Thorlak kill one of Dag's guards?"

Sokkolf shrugged. "Maybe the brute attacked him?"

"More likely annoyed him," Ingolf said. "What imbecile would attack Thorlak?"

Gunnar's brows lowered thunderously, since he'd been about to do exactly that just before the lightning war erupted between Asson and Thorlak.

When Ingolf noticed Gunnar's expression, he gave him a weak smile. "Unless, of course, you're the bravest man alive."

Gunnar's mouth quirked.

A sharp cry split the night, wavering through the storm as though coming in waves. Directionless, it seemed to come out of nowhere.

Everyone stood frozen for a few heartbeats.

"That's Camtac!" Thyra lifted her long cape hem, and ran over the jutting promontory, disappearing down the other side.

"Thyra, wait! It's too dangerous!" Kiran dashed after her.

"Ingolf? Sokkolf? Help Asson," Gunnar ordered. "Alfdis, you come with me."

Gunnar hurried over the rise to find Kiran, Camtac, and Thyra encircling a man seated on the ground. A warrior. He carried a quiver of arrows over his left shoulder, but Gunnar saw no bow. Long black hair sleeked down the man's back.

A downpour swept over them, pounding the rim so hard that drops bounced across the rimrock like dancing sprites, and utter darkness reclaimed the world.

Gunnar and Alfdis marched through it, and into the circle around Camtac and his brother. Kiran turned to avoid the brunt of the gusting rain but translated the boy's words:

"Ewinon?" Camtac waved his hand in front of Ewinon's eyes. "Brother? Answer me. What happened?"

Ewinon blinked as if he barely heard. His gaze remained steadfastly upon the chunks of rain-shiny metal that lay in a curious line on the ground.

Alfdis said, "That's a sword, Gunnar. A broken sword."

When the dim fragments took form in his mind, Gunnar said, "It certainly is. What was he doing? Piecing it together?"

"Maybe Ewinon is our murderer?"

"Perhaps, but it would take more than Einarsson's thick neck to break a well-tempered sword into seven pieces."

Alfdis folded his arms over his chest. "That's certain."

As the squall passed over and the rain lessened to a constant drizzle, thin light penetrated the clouds. The sword reacted as though brilliant sunlight had just struck its blade. It glowed to life.

Camtac lurched to his feet and staggered backward. "What's happening?"

Thyra said, "Be calm. The sword doesn't know it's broken. Its power is intact." To Ewinon, she said, "You must have kept the pieces very close together, Elrik's brother."

"All I did was point it."

As though somewhat coming back to himself, Ewinon reached out and grabbed Camtac's shoulder. "He came at me out of nowhere, Brother. I just . . . I couldn't get my bow nocked. When I drew the broken sword from my belt, Thorlak screamed and grabbed"—his head swiveled to look at the headless body—"grabbed that man to use him as a shield."

Ewinon started to reach for the piece of sword with the hilt and hand guard intact, but his fingers hovered over the object. He pulled them back. "All I did was point it. That's all I did."

Gunnar scowled at Kiran. "What's he talking about? I don't understand what he means."

Kiran questioned Ewinon for a time, then turned to Gunnar. "He says that when he pointed the sword, his attacker's head was severed, but he never swung the sword. The blade never touched his opponent."

"He's daft, then. And, frankly, looks it. His eyes won't stop rolling."

Asson hobbled closer and spoke gently to Ewinon.

Kiran said, "Godi, Elder Asson is suggesting that perhaps the severing of the head had nothing to do with the sword. He says Thorlak probably slit the man's throat at the same instant that Ewinon pointed the sword—"

Ewinon shook his head but then seemed to consider the idea. He spoke to Asson.

Kiran said, "Ewinon thinks maybe Asson is right, because Thorlak did run away with the head, which made no sense to Ewinon."

"He took the head?" Gunnar wondered what Thorlak planned to do with it. He'd have some devious plan for its use. "Why would Thorlak behead Einarsson or the Bellower?"

Kiran started to reply but stopped to watch Thyra.

The seeress shouldered through the men to get to the sword. She knelt, and a small, almost inaudible cry escaped her lips. Disbelief slackened her face, but some monumental realization was seeping across her features, tightening her eyes. "This—no. No, it's my imagination. It . . . It can't be."

"You mean you've seen this sword before?"

Thyra violently shook her head. "No, no. I *must* be wrong."

For a time, only the evening answered her—the *shish*ing of rain falling across the ocean, the sleepy calls of owls hunting the cliffs, and the strange, half-heard whispering of grass in the wind. Gunnar felt, in his own small way, the earth all around him murmuring of things to come, and he wasn't sure he liked the tone.

He scrutinized Thyra's tormented expression. "Seeress, why don't you tell me, and let me be the judge?"

Thyra looked up at him with wet eyes. "I think this is—it's Hel."

She spoke the name softly, on this continent that knew nothing of Helheim, within earshot of shore Spirits who might not take kindly to being invaded by the giant goddess of the Norse underworld.

Asson, nearly invisible in the storm, sighed, and a fleeting lance of moonlight caught upon his shell pendant. "Her soul is only partly in this world. Why, little fox?"

"Her heart lives in the underworld, Asson, in a hall sprayed with snowstorms." Thyra gently stroked the sword. "Everything in the hall is alive. Her bed is named Sick Bed, and her curtains are Gleaming Disaster. Her dish is Hunger." When Thyra drew her fingers back, she closed them as though to keep hold of the sword's strength.

Asson leaned heavily upon his walking stick. "Ewinon, are these the fragments of Thorlak's sword that you—"

"*Thorlak's* sword?" Thyra whispered, as though afraid he might hear her.

"Yes, my young friend," Asson said. "When the Thunderbirds heard your call and blasted Thorlak's sword, chunks of the blade cartwheeled across the destroyed village. Ewinon collected them."

Gunnar turned to Kiran. "When *she* called to the Thunderbirds? Are you sure you translated that right?"

"Yes, Godi." Kiran gazed at her and swallowed hard. As though to stave off his own emotions, he clenched his fists.

*She called the lightning that blasted the sword from Thorlak's hand?* Gunnar turned away. Every hour she frightened him more.

Thyra said, "But this is not Thorlak's sword."

Camtac touched his brother's arm. "Brother, *are* these the fragments of Thorlak's broken sword you picked up in Whale Rib Village?"

While Kiran translated the words, Ewinon shoved to his feet and spread his legs to brace his knees. Gods, the warrior looked haunted. His eyes kept darting around, as though he expected the Lawspeaker to step out of the shadows and strike him down with the flick of his hand.

Kiran repeated Ewinon's answer: "Yes, this is Thorlak's sword."

Thyra's eyes narrowed as she stared at the broken sword.

"I should have known," she said in a shaking voice. "If only I'd known, I . . ."

Thyra gracefully rose to her feet, and walked away to stand with her back to them, staring off into the wet distances.

Gunnar looked around the circle. "I have no idea what she's talking about."

Kiran was so focused on Thyra, he forgot to translate for the Skraeling's benefit. A gust of wind had blown Thyra's hood back and, in the faint light, her long hair shone like sunlit snow. Kiran's face was tense with an expression of struggle, as if he were debating Thyra's words within himself. Or perhaps he was so afraid of her he didn't know what to think.

Gunnar felt the same way. "Kiran, I need you—"

"Vethild," he said simply. "The sword belonged to Vethild. Her mother. Thorlak must have stolen it."

"Her *mother*? Her mother was Vethild?" Gunnar shouted in shock. He felt like he'd just been punched in the belly.

Asson said, "Vethild?," pointed to the sword, and studied Kiran, waiting for a translation.

Kiran did not oblige. Instead, he stepped to Thyra's side and took her in his arms. They just stood there holding each other, drenched in rain. Silent. Her shoulders were shaking, in tears, probably.

The odd curves of Asson's mouth tightened. He said something to Ewinon. The warrior nodded and bent down to collect the small pieces of the broken sword. He tucked them into his belt pouch, then handed it to Asson. The large piece with the hilt and hand guard gave Ewinon pause. He flexed his fingers above the object, then hesitantly picked it up with two fingers and handed it to Asson, as well.

When Asson touched it, the runes on the blade shimmered faintly green.

Gunnar looked up at the sky, searching for the northern lights, for surely that must be the source of the reflections.

Asson lovingly repeated, "Vethild," followed by a string of soft unknown words as he curiously eyed the runes.

Alfdis gave Gunnar a sidelong glance. "Are you thinking what I am?"

"If you're trying to imagine the circumstances under which Vethild would have allowed Thorlak to steal her precious Seidur sword, then yes."

"Must have happened just before the slaughter. Maybe when they kidnapped her. Maybe when they kidnapped Vethild *and her daughter*."

"Which makes me wonder if Thorlak was there."

Alfdis' hand unconsciously lowered to his belted sword. "I was wondering the same thing."

The political ramifications were stunning. First, it meant that Thorlak had not been on Pallig's ship. At some point after advising Pallig to join the raiders attacking the south coast of England, Thorlak had returned to the Danelaw. Why? To lead the conspirators who'd kidnapped his archenemy? Had someone in the Danelaw assisted him? Gods, *who*?

The odd tang of resin-scented smoke encircled them, blowing down from somewhere to the north. Gunnar extended his arm. "You see those trees over there?"

Alfdis looked. "The grove of alders?"

"We're going to camp there so people can get some sleep, and I can ask Thyra some pointed questions."

"Give her some time first, Gunnar. She looks lost."

When Asson murmured, Gunnar's gaze moved back to him. The little elder petted the sword as though to soothe its broken heart.

Finally, the elder nodded to himself, smiled, and carried the sword and belt pouch over to where Thyra stood in Kiran's arms.

Thyra and Asson spoke softly. Then Thyra stepped away from Kiran.

Asson firmly placed the sword in Thyra's hand and strapped Ewinon's belt pouch, containing the broken pieces, around her waist.

# Forty-Five

Podebeek lay on his back beside Moosin, struggling to sleep. The ship rocked as it sailed southward. Occasionally, when the door to the deck above was thrown open, gusts of wind swept the hold, temporarily clearing away the stench of animals and humans, and Podebeek could hear men calling in alien tongues, and the faint bell-like jingle of the rigging on the sail.

Though the others slept, Bjarni and the big man named Finnbogi sat with their heads together, talking. For a time, they'd quietly argued, Finnbogi shaking his head while Bjarni nodded sternly, but now they both seemed content with the plan they were making. Their voices had dropped to confident whispers. Though, at every odd sound, Finnbogi jumped up and rushed back to the end of the chain of prisoners to shove his hands into his iron cuffs.

One of the oddly malformed Wobee buffalo blew through her nostrils, and irritably stamped her feet.

Podebeek smiled at the animal. She stood in her stall chewing her hay with her eyes half-closed. He wished he could touch her. It would make him feel better. Every morning, a man came down and drained her milk into a pot. Though he never got to taste it, Podebeek liked the sweet smell of the milk.

He kept thinking about his family and village. He wanted them to live again. Wanted it so badly. More than anything, he feared for his baby sister. He asked every new slave about her, but no one had seen her. Had Dag already sold or traded her? Was she dead? Where was Mother? Probably at a nearby village, but she could be hiding in the forest around Whale Rib Village waiting for Podebeek to return.

And, soon, he would be home again, standing at the head of the Shaman's Trail with a vicious tunghak beside him. All Podebeek had ever wanted was to be a good warrior. To protect his people. Now most of them were dead.

But these children were alive.

When boots thudded on the deck above, Finnbogi lunged to his feet and ran back to his place. Metal clanked as he fitted the cuffs around his wrists, then curled on his side next to the other prisoners, pretending to be asleep.

Several of the children stirred. Podebeek whispered, "Quiet! Keep your hands in your cuffs."

When the door flung open, faint gray light flooded the hold. It had to be about one hand of time before dawn.

Podebeek sat up and placed his chained hands out in front of him, waiting with his heart slamming against his ribs.

Thorlak the tunghak and its servant Dag came down the stairs. The tunghak had thrown its black cape back over its shoulders, revealing the red clothing it wore beneath. As always, Podebeek stared at the strange color. His people did not know how to make that shade. What did the Wobee use for their brilliant dye? Some rare flower or mineral from the Fallen Star land?

Dag turned to scan Bjarni's group. Many of the prisoners watched Dag and Thorlak with hateful eyes. Some refused to look at him.

As Thorlak walked forward, it took great effort for Podebeek not to wet himself again. He forced himself to sit up straighter. The tunghak knelt and unlocked the heavy iron cuffs around Podebeek's wrists. He heaved a sigh of relief.

Without a word, Thorlak gripped Podebeek's bloody left wrist, hauled him to his feet, and roughly dragged him across the ship toward the stairs. Dag kept his hand on his sword, but his gaze remained on Bjarni until Podebeek and Thorlak passed; then he heard Arnora speaking as her chains rattled, and Podebeek heard two sets of steps on the stairs behind them.

Was Arnora coming with them? He turned and saw her.

Just before the tunghak yanked Podebeek out onto the deck, he glimpsed Moosin staring at him with tears in his eyes. Podebeek gave his friend a confident nod. No matter what, Moosin would save the other children, or he would die trying. Podebeek silently hurt for him.

On deck, Podebeek tipped his face into the wind and sucked fresh air into his lungs as though he couldn't get enough. Dag dragged Arnora up and shoved her next to Podebeek.

The tunghak spun Podebeek around to face the dark sea cliffs and said something harsh.

Arnora translated, "Where Asson cave?"

Podebeek bit his lip while he searched the cliffs. When he spotted the distinctive tree line behind Whale Rib Village, his chest spasmed. He swallowed the sob, and pointed. "There."

Thorlak listened to Arnora, then replied.

Arnora repeated, "How get there? Out of sight village."

"Without being seen from the village?" Podebeek chewed his lower lip for a few moments as he thought, then he pointed to the canoe landing north of Whale Rib Village. "We can take the northern ledge trail that starts at the canoe landing, and cut across the cliff just below Whale Rib Village. It connects to the Shaman's Trail. But we'll have to wait until Brother Moon carries the tide out. When the tide is high, most of the northern ledge trail is under water."

The tunghak gave Podebeek a threatening look as Arnora translated, then lifted its hand to one of the crew.

A brown-haired man sprinted over and bowed deeply. He listened to Thorlak's orders, bowed again, and raced away.

Podebeek saw the man unroll a rope ladder and toss it over the side. Was the small boat already down there waiting for them?

Thorlak walked toward the ladder.

"Move," Dag said, and pushed Podebeek to make him follow.

While Podebeek stood on the edge beside Arnora, waiting for the tunghak to climb into the small boat below, Arnora reached out and gave Podebeek's hand a squeeze as she whispered in his tongue, "We kill soon."

Podebeek breathlessly looked up at her. It occurred to him for the first time that she wasn't just along to translate; she was on his side. He gave her a brave nod.

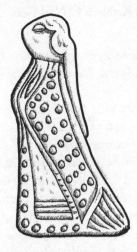

# Forty-Six

**W**here she sat on the rim overlooking the ocean, Thyra's white hem blew around her legs. She'd tied Kiran's cape beneath her chin, and shoved it over her shoulders, letting it billow in the gusts that swept the cliff. The damp chill helped to keep her awake.

Godi Gunnar stood guard thirty paces away, his sword propped on his shoulder. The rest of the group slept soundly in the alder grove to Thyra's left.

"He was there," she whispered to herself. "Thorlak was there that day."

A frightening sensation possessed her, an unfathomable blend of terror and rage that stung every fiber of her muscles.

Thyra struggled to focus on the sword propped atop her drawn-up knees. She was almost too tired and hungry to think of anything but impending death. She kept seeing her mother's eyes that last day, looking down at her with so much love.

"Mother was afraid. Afraid of Thorlak."

At that moment, Mother must have known that Thorlak had won. Every person in the Danelaw was about to be slaughtered, because she had failed to protect them.

"You were so much more powerful than I will ever be, Mother. If you couldn't stop him from stealing me and slaughtering the people you loved in the Danelaw, how can I ever hope to face him?"

Thyra stiffened when she heard Hel's voice whispering to her. She remembered that voice, the sweet high tones that lilted like music being played in her own heart. Gently, she stroked the blade. "I've missed you so much, Hel."

The black form of an owl sailed over the treetops behind where Kiran slept. Silent. Deadly. The perfect night creature.

. . . *a darkness-rider. Something I will never be.*

When a powerful gust of wind assaulted her, Thyra shivered. Death lived in the air she breathed and the water in the distance, and she knew she had no strength to confront it, to drive it back. Mother must have felt the same way when she first saw Thorlak step into their home that day.

Thyra squeezed her eyes closed. She longed to have someone stronger and older there to fight the battle until she could rest and prepare herself for the inevitable. But she couldn't ask Asson to hold back the fiery tide when it began. He was injured and elderly. And not strong enough.

*I can't let Thorlak find Mother.*

Thyra braced her forearms on her knees to support them while she examined the sword. Ripples of light surged across the blade as she turned it in the faint gray of coming dawn. The rune for "gleaming disaster" kept flashing, trying to get her attention.

"I'm sorry I didn't know you when I first saw you at Thorlak's side. I should have. If I'd seen your blade, I would have known."

Thyra clutched the sword while tears filled her eyes.

How could she not have known?

So many things . . .

When she'd first heard Thorlak's voice, she'd recognized it, though she hadn't been able to place it. She should have made the connection instantly, but the heart protected itself in the strangest ways. Her ears hadn't been able to place Thorlak's voice, and her eyes hadn't *seen* the runes on Hel's guard and hilt.

Hel suddenly warmed in her hands, sending a jolt through Thyra. She instinctively looked down at Ewinon's belt pouch, tied around her waist. The other pieces of the sword had warmed, as well.

"Gods, even shattered you're powerful."

Thyra's brows drew together. The northern lights had died, but as dawn neared, the last stars seemed to flare more brilliantly. The fragment of blade below the hand guard was only about one foot long, but it quaked in her fingers at the brightening gleam. Had Thorlak felt this rush of power every morning for the past thirteen years?

She suddenly hated him with all the strength in her body, hated that he had felt this and she had not, she who was the rightful owner of her mother's Seidur sword.

*"She's a* myrkrida, *a darkness-rider. Don't let her touch her sword or staff. Grab them from the wall."*

How could that memory bring so much pain after so long?

Thyra looked out at the ocean. The whitecaps glittered as though sprinkled with handfuls of frost. The scent of the air was changing, growing mossy, signaling that Máni was taking the tide out.

Mother had been Thorlak's archenemy. He must have felt exultant when he'd stepped into that room and seen her without her sword in her hand.

Thyra had never in her life felt authentic rage, and it stunned her, blotting out every other emotion, sharpening her vision and her purpose. She petted Hel and whispered, "You're home now. He'll never touch you again so long as I live. I promise you, he won't."

It startled her when she heard Godi Gunnar's distinctively soft tread coming across the rim toward her.

He knelt at Thyra's side and gave her a faint smile. Blond hair tousled around his leathery face. For the short time that she'd known him, he'd been good to her, allowing her freedoms Thorlak never would have. It was so hard to believe the things people muttered behind Godi Gunnar's back. Could any living man have single-handedly cut such a murderous swath across Iceland? It didn't seem possible.

"You've been staring at the broken sword all night, Seeress. You should try to sleep. There's no telling how awful the rest of the day is going to be."

"I can't sleep, Godi."

"Well, I'm sorry to hear it, for I suspect that before nightfall we're going to need your strength badly." Gunnar stared out at the glistening ocean. The lingering blueness of night still shaded the waves. "But if you won't sleep, are you up to speaking with me for a bit?"

Thyra quietly wrapped Hel in her cape hem so the sword could rest while she and Gunnar talked. Gunnar watched her with a studied nonchalance, as though he didn't understand the act but respected it just the same.

Thyra started the conversation: "Godi, please tell me about my mother?"

He frowned, then spread his hands, and hesitantly responded, "Seeress, are you sure your mother was Vethild? I must tell you that it seems unlikely. She—"

"Tell me, please?"

His bushy brows lowered. "Very well, but keep in mind that I didn't know Vethild personally. My family has no noble blood. We're just generations of peasants. But everyone in the Danelaw knew her reputation. She was supposed to have been generous and kind, and somewhat shy."

"And very powerful."

"Immensely powerful. No man injured those under her protection without feeling the brunt of that power. Apparently, once riled, her temper could sear the world." He glanced at Thyra, as though he knew the emotion that marauded through her heart. "She loved her daughter and Avaldamon very much. In fact, the relationship between Avaldamon and Vethild was the great love story of the time."

Thyra's heartbeat sped up, as though that ought to mean something to her. Did she know that name? "Avaldamon?"

Gunnar shifted to face her and the pendant of Thor's hammer resting on his black shirt winked in the ghostly light. "Your father. If Vethild is your mother. They had only one child."

Thyra searched inside her. "I have no memories of him at all. His name was Avaldamon?"

Sympathy tightened the lines in Gunnar's face. "It was."

"What happened to him?"

"Ah, well, that's a long story for another time. Suffice to say, he lived through the war that followed the slaughter of the Danelaw, and when he heard the rumor that Vethild and his daughter had been hauled away in chains and taken to Albania-Land for safekeeping, he mounted a flotilla of ships to go find them."

"He looked for us?"

"Of course he did."

For many years, Thyra had dreamed of her Other Mother arriving like a miracle, stepping through the doorway, and opening her arms for Thyra to run into them. She'd never even considered that her real father might be missing her, loving her, and doing everything he could to find her. Thyra tried to imagine what he must have gone through. While Avaldamon had been out fighting a war, both his wife and his two-year-old daughter had been taken from him. It must have torn him apart: first when he thought they'd been killed in the slaughter and again when he heard the rumors that they'd been kidnapped and taken to the Land of the White Men.

"Did he find Mother?"

Gunnar stared out at the luminous turquoise beams that spiked over the eastern horizon like a crown. "No one knows. Not for certain. Many years later, rumors filtered back to Iceland and Denmark that Avaldamon was hunting for Vethild in Hvitramannaland. Supposedly, he'd sent word back that he would never stop until he found her, and his daughter. Few believed the stories, however. There were so many different versions, and there was no evidence. Everyone just assumed it was the latest account of their legendary love story."

Unbearable longing filled Thyra. "Did you believe it, Godi?"

"There was one version I favored, but I suspect you won't appreciate it."

"I want to know every version. Please tell me."

He smiled. "I particularly liked the story that a shipwrecked crew had found Avaldamon's body in a sea cave, sitting upright, with Vethild's necklace clutched in his skeletal hand. The story claimed that Avaldamon was still searching for Vethild through the golden hall of the slain in Valhöll."

As Sol ascended closer to the eastern horizon, the seabirds awakened in a fluttering, diving horde and soared over the water in search of breakfast. A melodious riot of chirps and squawks serenaded them.

"Where were my parents born?"

"She was born in Denmark, Avaldamon in Norway; at least that's what my family told me. At one point, I know for a fact that Pallig sent Avaldamon to Norway to intercede with King Olaf on behalf of the Danelaw— the plea of one Norwegian to another to help the Danelaw fight against the king of England. Olaf refused, of course. He was too—"

"Thorlak was there, Godi."

". . . Where?"

"The day my mother and I were kidnapped. He led the men who broke into our home in the Danelaw. He told his servants to grab her sword and staff before she could get to them."

Gunnar gave Thyra a faintly skeptical look. "You would have been around two years old, Thyra; how could you remember such a thing?"

"I remember every detail. Thorlak said, '*She's a myrkrida, a darkness-rider. Don't let her touch her sword or staff. Grab them from the wall. And make no mistake, I want her alive.*"

Gunnar rubbed his bearded chin with the back of his hand. "Well, if it's a child's imaginative story, it's a detailed one. You remember his exact words?"

"I'll never forget them."

As though to help him think, Gunnar reached down to pick up a pebble from the rim and seemed to be examining it. "You're sure it was Thorlak's voice?"

"I am. I—I don't know why I never made the connection before, but I'm sure now."

Gunnar tossed the pebble out over the cliff and watched it fall into the surf below. "Who was the man who wanted Vethild alive?"

"I don't know. Maybe the ealdorman."

Gunnar's head jerked around. "Which ealdorman?"

"He came to our home, nine months ago, just before the deaths of my family. I watched the ealdorman ride up the fjord with twenty soldiers. He paid my father a heavy sack of coins to continue taking care of me. The ealdorman told my father that he had to keep me safe, because I would be useful to keep my mother in line. He added that personally he thought it was a cruel myth, but that both Edmund and Cnut were committed to finding her."

Beneath his shirt, she saw Godi Gunnar's arm muscles swell, as though they'd suddenly contracted.

When a fierce gust of wind swept over them, Thyra reached down to clamp her white tunic around her legs until it passed. Morning had blushed color into the ocean, painting the surface with a faint lavender gleam and flashing though the wings of the diving gulls.

"Listen to me, now," Godi Gunnar said in a dreadful voice. "This is not child's play. What was the ealdorman's name?"

Thyra lifted her shoulders in a shrug. "I never heard his name, but he came to tell my parents that someone was dead and had been buried at the Roskilde Church."

"Roskilde?" Even in the dimness she could see that Gunnar's face had flushed. "Did he mean King Sweyn Forkbeard? That happened months before—"

"Yes, the ealdorman said Sweyn's son, Harald, had made the decision to bury the king as a Christian, though the ealdorman doubted the king would have chosen that for himself."

"I suspect your ealdorman was correct. Sweyn Forkbeard was baptized as Otto, but every coin he ever had struck used the name Sweyn, as though he'd disavowed his Christian name, and maybe the whole religion. What else did the ealdorman say?"

Thyra tried to run a hand through her long hair, to shove the ivory strands behind her ears, but it was such a tangled mass, she gave up. "He said that on Michaelmas Eve a great tide had risen up from the sea, higher than any tide known before, and flooded England."

The wind flattened Gunnar's shirt against his ribs. The eyes beneath his lowered brows were as cold and hard as flint. He violently hurled another pebble at the ocean.

"I'm liking this less and less. If Sweyn or Cnut was responsible for kidnapping you and your mother, it was a great betrayal. Sweyn vowed that he trusted Vethild with his life." Gunnar paused. "And there's no doubt but that Cnut longs for the same thing his father achieved . . . the throne of England." Gunnar glanced at her but lowered his voice and seemed to be speaking to himself: "Surely, he does not believe Vethild will help him after what she's been through."

Thyra considered the ramifications of the new information. "I'm not sure the ealdorman was Sweyn or Cnut's servant."

"Nor am I, but why do you say that?"

"If Sweyn had wanted to keep us safe, he could have lodged us in his own household in Denmark. That would have been the safest place, wouldn't it? No, someone wanted my mother and me safe, but out of the way."

"Aethelred?"

Thyra wondered but asked, "Is this Thorlak's first trip to Vinland?"

"Yes, or so he says. Why?"

"If my mother is alive, would she be a threat to Edmund?"

Godi Gunnar mulled the possibilities for a few moments before he answered his own question. "She'd be a threat to anyone who controlled her. . . ." The sentence faded as his eyes slowly widened. "Dear Thor Above." He pointed a finger at Thyra. "Tell me what the ealdorman looked like?"

"He was about Kiran's height, with black hair, a braided beard, and blue eyes."

Godi Gunnar's gaze quietly slid to the ocean, where he glared, as though not happy about that description.

"Godi, do you know Edmund?"

Gunnar's head jerked around and he gave her a long look. "The atheling Edmund? I've met him. I don't think anyone knows him."

"If Thorlak is searching for my mother's grave, then he must believe she's dead, and he's seeking something in the grave. The ealdorman said Edmund was convinced that I am the only one who can identify *it*. What is it? Why is no one brave enough to name it? Is it a sword, a staff, or some other Seidur artifact?"

"I don't know what you're talking about. Truly."

With too much desperation in her voice, she said, "Maybe not, but you do know the identity of the ealdorman. I can see it on your face. Who is he?"

Deep loneliness suddenly seeped up from inside her, a loneliness born from being torn from her mother as an infant. To ease her fears, she reached down and placed her hand on Hel.

The sword sang to her in an achingly beautiful voice.

"Even if I have a suspicion, it would be irresponsible to give you a name, Thyra, because I really do not know."

She refused to look at him.

His boots grated as he shifted upon the rock. "You've changed in the past few days. Do you know that? It's like something has awakened in you. I don't understand what it means, but it has a lethal edge to it that, frankly, worries me."

"Does it?"

"Yes, and don't think you're fooling me. I know all about that look in your eyes and that weak-kneed rage in your gut. I've felt it in my own too many times to count, and it's always resulted in mayhem. Be wiser than me."

"Godi, in the near future I will be engaged in a fight to the death to protect the people I care about. I lost my Seidur sword in the storm. All I have is a broken blade that once belonged to my mother. I don't even know if Hel will allow me to use her Power, but the price of losing is too much to bear."

He gave her a sober look. "Well, you won't be fighting alone. You know that, don't you?" He panned an arm across the people sleeping at the edge of the alder grove. "I'll grant that the largest share of the burden will be borne by you and Elder Asson, but there's always something decisive that hidden people can do. Shoulder your share, but don't take up mine. I'm looking forward to chopping Thorlak into little pieces."

As the alder limbs flailed back and forth in the wind, a faint tracery of shadows fell across Kiran's sleeping body. They'd had so little time together, surely Odin wouldn't let him die when Thyra loved and needed him so much?

"Is Thorlak working with Edmund, Godi? Why? What does it have to do with me and my mother?"

Gunnar reached over to place a friendly hand on her shoulder. "Calm down. You've no idea what you're saying. I guarantee you that Thorlak and Edmund are not allies. For one thing . . ." He briefly hesitated, as though suddenly uncertain. "For one thing, Edmund is an Anchorite, and Thorlak hates all Anchorites. As you know."

"Doesn't mean they can't be allies."

"No, it doesn't, but—"

"Godi, after my family died from the plague, I think Thorlak sent men to capture me and bring me to Greenland. If he wasn't working with the ealdorman, how did he know where I was?"

Gunnar scratched his blond beard and gave her a sidelong look. "Maybe he caught the ealdorman and tortured it out of him. That's what I would have done."

Thyra's brows drew together. That possibility had never occurred to her. For a moment, she didn't know what to say. "Really?"

"Certainly. If I'd gotten wind that Vethild's daughter was being held on a farm in Denmark, I'd have hired enough knaves to follow every man or woman who might know something about it. When I was fairly certain it was your ealdorman, I would have offered him money for the information. If that didn't work, I'd have gotten the information anyway."

Thyra listened to his matter-of-fact description. "It's so hard to believe you're as evil as people say."

"I'm far worse. It's just that those who know the full truth are dead."

A small tendril of fear went through her. Thyra lifted Hel and gripped her in both hands.

Godi Gunnar's mouth quirked, as though suppressing a smile.

"Well, if it wasn't Edmund working with Thorlak, who was it?"

"Someone who thinks he may need you."

"For what? As a hostage to use against my mother?"

A gust of wind blasted the rim. They both turned away to wait for it to pass; then Gunnar shoved blond hair out of his eyes.

"Regardless of his reason, Thyra, he's done a good job. You're alive, safe, and you've become powerful, haven't you?"

"Powerful?" She gave him a desperate laugh. "No, Godi. Not at all. I am a novice, at best."

Gunnar smiled. "I thought the battle yesterday was between Asson and Thorlak, but after listening to Asson, it seems that you were actually the one who defeated Thorlak. If you're a novice, you've considerable in-born skills. Which I'm sure surprised and displeased the Lawspeaker." He flipped a hand at Hel. "Don't forget, you did it when your mother's sword was in Thorlak's hand."

Thyra clutched the sword. The runes shimmered in the morning light. "Why does Edmund want to find Vethild's grave, Godi?"

Gunnar ground his teeth, as though deciding whether or not to answer that question. "It isn't Edmund who wishes to find it, Thyra. But . . ."

"Please tell me."

"I'm about to. But if you repeat a single word, you will certainly seal my death warrant, and probably your own."

She drew herself up straight. "I won't."

"Edmund doesn't want to find Vethild's grave. He wants to find Vethild. I've a lockbox filled with gold hidden in my quarters aboard *Thor's Dragon* to pay her to return to help him and the Danelaw."

"You mean . . . Edmund believes she's alive?"

"He does. Edmund wants Vethild to help him defeat Aethelred. The leaders of the Danelaw want that, too, but they have an additional motive. The leaders believe she's the one person who can protect them if Edmund fails."

"But Godi, what role would I play in any of that? I'm just—"

He held up a hand to stop her. "I've been thinking about it since you said

Vethild was your mother. Thyra, if it becomes apparent that your mother is dead, I'm absolutely sure Edmund would pay you well to use your Seidur powers to help win the civil war, and keep Cnut out of England."

"Me? Godi, Thorlak is going to kill me. I cannot stand against him! What use would I be to Edmund or—"

"Just place it in the back of your mind. Don't think about it until all this is over. I believe in you, and I think the Danelaw would throw itself at your feet in gratitude."

"Oh, Godi, I can't—"

He abruptly rose to his feet and narrowed his eyes at something in the distance. "Gods, that's *Thor's Dragon*. She's coming this way."

Thyra stood up and saw the wide-bodied cargo vessel in the lead. "There are ships behind her, Godi. With the light mist, I can't tell how—"

"Four. There are four ships behind her." Gunnar gripped the hilt of his sheathed sword, as though it made him feel better. "Apparently, another ship has arrived."

Thyra's heart beat faster. "From where?"

"A more important question is, 'Bringing what message . . . and to whom?'" Gunnar gave her a cynical look. "I'm most concerned with *whom*, and what he's supposed to do with the information once he has it."

Almost as clearly as if that awful day had returned, Thyra could feel the fire-warmed air, the hunger gnawing at her empty belly, and remembered her mother's screams, and her terror when the unknown man grabbed her and mounted the horse to ride through the icy flaming world. A haunted sensation of certainty possessed her.

She whispered, "The shipmaster is the ealdorman's messenger."

Gunnar stepped closer to her, as though she'd spoken too softly for him to hear her. "What did you say?"

Thyra inhaled a deep breath, took stock of what lay ahead . . . and heard a faint sweet voice whispering from the air around her. "Godi, the ealdorman sent the ship. He will want to know if his contact here has found *it* yet, or my mother."

Gunnar's brows lowered. "How do you know that?"

Thyra looked down at the sword she held so lovingly in her hand. "I just do."

The longer Gunnar looked at the sword, the shallower his breathing became. "If you're right, the situation in England is desperate. We must succeed before the ealdorman's hired lackey has a chance to act upon the new information."

# Forty-Seven

The morning smelled of wet earth and spring leaves.

Camtac took a moment to appreciate the sunlight that shot through the clouds before he turned to look at camp. Only about one hand of time's travel from Whale Rib Village, which perched on the high point to the north, the land here was considerably more rocky. Boulders, polished to a shine by the legendary Ice Giants, studded the meadow, interspersed with alders and willows.

Soft alien voices drifted on the sea breeze. He turned to watch Chief Gunnar and Thyra Little Fox as they passed through the camp, bending down, waking the other Wobee. Half-asleep men rose and shook beads of dew from their capes.

Camtac didn't like this new alliance. He didn't trust any of them . . . except maybe Thyra Little Fox, and even after all she'd done to help his village during the battle, he was afraid of her.

Ewinon muttered something in his sleep, and Camtac quietly walked to him. Long black hair framed Ewinon's sleeping face. Camtac hadn't told him about Gower or the empty camp yet. He was terrified the information would so devastate Ewinon that he wouldn't be able to think or fight.

Camtac knelt and shook his brother.

Ewinon woke with a wild-eyed start, then heaved a relieved breath when he saw Camtac.

"Blessed Sea Woman, Brother, call my name before you shake me like that."

"It's dawn," Camtac said. "The others are up. We should be going."

Ewinon used his fingers to comb tangled hair away from his face. The whites of his eyes resembled bloody spiderwebs. He rubbed his face hard. "Yes, we should."

As Ewinon shoved to his feet, Camtac noticed that flecks of blood dotted his brother's cheeks and throat. Had Thorlak really killed Masson, or had it happened exactly as Ewinon claimed? He'd just pointed the broken sword and the man's head had instantly been lopped from his shoulders?

Asson still lay sound asleep in his seal-gut rain slicker with his arm over his eyes. When Camtac had helped him change his bandage last night, the fevered flesh reeked of feasting tunghaks. Asson shouldn't walk at all for several days.

"Ewinon? I want to talk with you about Elder Asson."

"Hmm?" Ewinon's gaze had riveted on the Wobee. The five men had gathered in a knot to talk while Thyra Little Fox knelt before the low fire. Long hair, the color of old walrus tusk, hung down the back of her cape. Occasionally, she lifted her hand to stir contents of the hide bag suspended on the tripod over the flames.

Camtac sniffed the air. The rich fragrance of kosweet jerky soup wafted on the breeze.

"What about Asson?" Ewinon finally asked.

Camtac motioned for his brother to follow him a few paces away. He didn't want their conversation to be overhead, especially by Asson.

Softly, Camtac said, "I just walked the Shaman's Trail. There is no way that Asson can navigate the slippery twists and turns with his wounded leg. He'll fall to his death."

Ewinon glanced at Asson, and affection warmed his face. "I've been worried about that same thing. What about the tunnel you took from the cave to the beach? If, that is, there are still canoes at the landing."

"There should be, but if that's our choice, we don't have much time. Even with a canoe, when the tide returns, the tunnel will flood in a stunning rush of water."

Camtac tried to calculate the amount of time it was going to take to walk to the canoe landing north of their destroyed village—at least three hands of time with Asson's leg—then canoe along the cliff face until they arrived at the place where the tunnel opened on to the beach at low tide: another one-half hand of time if nothing, absolutely nothing, intervened to delay them.

Ewinon said, "If we make a sled for Asson, it will cut the time in half. We can take turns towing him."

"A sled might work on the sand, but it will be too bumpy over rocks. He would be in agony. If we can recruit the Wobee to help us carry a litter, it would help."

Camtac's gaze sought out the young woman, and the sword that she wore tucked into a cord around her waist. Some crazy part of him longed to touch it, to point it as his brother had done, just to see what happened. *Foolishness, but I always dreamed of becoming a Kutsitualit, of holding the winds and lightning in my hands.*

"If we're going to build a litter, we should start soon," Ewinon said.

Asson moved, shifting his arm to a different position over his eyes.

"Brother, one last thing," Camtac whispered. "There is another way that I wish you to consider. Maybe we should do this thing alone."

"You mean without Asson or the Wobee?"

"Yes. Why can't Asson simply tell us what we're looking for and where to find it? You and I could go in, get it, and get out quickly. At a hard run, it will only take us two hands of time. Then if Asson told us the location of the fire grave, we could—"

"The Wobee will be upset. They think they're part of this quest."

"They will just slow us down. You know I'm right."

Ewinon seemed to be considering it as he watched the knot of Wobee near the breakfast fire. The blond chief, Gunnar, was pointing fingers at certain men, apparently issuing orders.

Camtac pressed, "There's no reason to risk anyone else, Brother. You and I can do this by ourselves."

"No," Asson said with a deep sigh, "you can't."

They both turned to look at him.

Ewinon grimaced. "You have the ears of a lynx. If you'll just tell us what we need to know, we *can* do it by ourselves."

Asson sat up and winced. "I must be there."

"You're sick, Asson! You shouldn't be walking at all. Why can't you just tell us what to look for, and let us bring it to you?"

In the pale amber gleam, Asson's wrinkles cast crisscrossing shadows over his cheeks. "Because if you so much as reach for it, it will kill you. And the Spirits may kill you just for entering the cave."

Afraid, Camtac asked, "What is *it*?"

Black hair straggled around Asson's face as he stretched his back muscles. "It's a walking stick."

"A walking stick?"

Camtac considered that. To Ewinon he murmured, "I saw many walking sticks in his sea cave, stacked against the back wall."

As the old Kutsitualit braced a hand on the ground and pushed to try to stand up, water, collected during the night, cascaded from his seal-gut slicker and created a shimmering ring around him. "I'm the only one here who can touch it."

Ewinon scowled. "Tell us what it looks like."

At his commanding tone, Asson's brows lifted. He pointed to Thyra Little Fox. "That broken sword you're so afraid of is a pale reflection of the Power that lives in that rusty stick. Its owner is the most powerful shaman I've ever known. She breathed a universe of light into that walking stick."

Ewinon's scowl deepened. "We don't have to touch it. Can't we just wrap it in hide so it doesn't—?"

"No."

Ewinon threw up his hands in exasperation. "All right, I know how stubborn you are. I guess we have to find a way to haul you to your Spirit Cave."

Asson grabbed the branch he'd been using as a walking stick, propped it firmly on the ground, and managed to wobble to his feet, where he stood grunting breathlessly. "Yes, but neither of you can enter my cave. Only Chief Gunnar and Thyra Little Fox may accompany me inside."

"What!" Camtac said plaintively. "I've already been there once! Why not?"

"I don't know why they let you live, but consider yourself fortunate. You can't come. That's all."

Camtac could tell from the concerned tone of the old man's voice that he was trying to protect them.

One word at a time, Ewinon stubbornly enunciated, "You. Need. Us." He gestured to Asson's wounded leg. "You can't make it without us."

Asson moved his walking stick forward and took a step. When he eased his bad leg down, he flinched as though at the flick of a whip. For a time, he just stood with his eyes squeezed closed against the pain; then he managed to take a deep breath. "I would be grateful if you could build your proposed litter and get me to the tunnel. That would help me greatly. After that, it would also be helpful if you could stand guard at the tunnel entrance." He mocked Ewinon with: "Can. You. Do. That?"

Ewinon said, "What are you afraid of us seeing in your cave? Whatever it is, Camtac has already seen it. He was just there. He and Gower slept in your hides and ate the dried fish from your baskets."

"Hides and dried fish can't bite back. Spirits can. Especially these two Spirits."

Ewinon made a deep-throated sound of disgust. "Gods, it annoys me when you try to scare us!" He grabbed Camtac's shoulder. "Come on. Let's get started building a litter."

Camtac nodded but quickly said, "Brother? While we cut poles, there's something I must tell you. I . . . I should have told you last night, but you looked so stunned that I didn't think—"

"Tell me what?" Ewinon's face had slackened with dread.

Camtac stared into his eyes for several moments before he found the strength to say, "The entire camp at Seal Cove vanished last night."

Ewinon shook his head in confusion. "Vanished? What are you talking about?"

Camtac extended a hand toward his brother in a "listen" gesture. "When I got there, I found Asson standing with Chief Gunnar and his Wobee near the terrace, but everyone else, everyone who'd stayed at that camp for the night—"

"Y-y-you mean they were attacked?" he stammered.

"I don't know. Maybe."

Owls hooted out in the forest and Ewinon seemed to pause to listen to them. "Start at the beginning."

"It was dark. I found rolled blankets where people had been sleeping, but they were empty. All of them. The bonfire was icy to the touch. Any metal that I touched fell to pieces. I searched, Ewinon, but I found nothing. No bodies, no blood, no evidence of enemy arrows lost in the heat of battle." He locked gazes with his brother. "Our people were just . . . gone."

"Maybe they went home?"

Camtac shook his head. "No. Asson saw a wave of light, like a fire in the sky. It swept over them."

Ewinon's jaw slackened. The name was almost inaudible: "Gower?"

"No sign of him."

"You're positive?" Ewinon grabbed his arm and squeezed hard enough to hurt.

"Yes, my brother. Asson said it was Spirit Power. Thyra Little Fox suspects that Thorlak wielded it."

Ewinon stood as though paralyzed by a blow to the head. "Spirit Power? You mean Asson believes they are all dead?"

Asson gently called, "Yes."

Ewinon didn't look like he believed it. He turned on his heel and strode to the alder grove, where he pulled his iron-bladed knife and began noisily chopping down poles for the litter.

Asson told Camtac, "Go to him. He needs you."

Asson gingerly turned around on his walking stick and saw Thyra Little Fox, Chief Gunnar, and Kiran coming toward him.

Kiran arrived two steps ahead of the others. "May we speak with you, Elder?"

"About our destination?"

Kiran nodded. Lines of exhaustion etched the corners of his green eyes. He extended a hand to his chief. "Chief Gunnar needs to understand exactly where we are going."

"To a sea cave. It isn't far. We should arrive by midday."

Gunnar propped his hands on his hips, and the seed pearls on his black shirt glimmered, reflecting the pale yellow gleam of dawn. While the chief spoke to Kiran, Asson turned to Thyra Little Fox.

He reached out to pat her shoulder. "Don't worry."

She bowed her head. For his ears alone, she said, "He's coming, Asson."

"I know. There is darkness in the wind."

When she looked up, Spirit Power lived and breathed in her sky-colored eyes, roiling the depths like a submerged ocean current. He knew now that Vethild was her mother, and because of that, Thyra meant even more to Asson. If only he had the time, he would so love to teach her the sacred ways of his People.

When Gunnar stopped speaking, Kiran said, "Elder, Chief Gunnar needs to know everything you can tell him about the location of your cave. If possible, he wants to post sentinels above and below the cave to call out warnings, and post guards on all the approaches. There are other chiefs, men who came with us, who have their own private armies. We need to be prepared in case they—"

"Please tell Chief Gunnar that I will show him the best places when we arrive."

Kiran relayed the message to Chief Gunnar, who nodded, and turned to stare at Ewinon and Camtac. Ewinon hacked poles with his knife while Camtac sliced strips of leather from the bottom of his shirt. When they laid out the poles, Camtac would use the strips to tie them together to form the litter.

"What are they doing?" Kiran asked.

"Building a litter for me. That means it will take us perhaps three hands of time to reach the canoe landing, then, if we can find a canoe, another one-half hand of time to reach the tunnel to the sea cave."

Kiran translated for Chief Gunnar.

Gunnar seemed disturbed. He said something lengthy, then asked Kiran a terse question.

Kiran did not translate. He kept his eyes downcast, refusing to face Asson as he answered the chief in a low voice.

The exchange made Thyra Little Fox turn to Asson. "Asson, Chief Gunnar doesn't trust you. He hopes that we are not walking into a trap."

Kiran murmured to Gunnar, probably telling the chief that Thyra had translated their conversation. The chief heaved an annoyed breath.

Asson walked closer to Chief Gunnar and gave him a pleasant nod. "Please tell your chief that I fear the same thing."

# Forty-Eight

Podebeek stood at Arnora's side. His knees were shaking. He listened to Thorlak speak to the four warriors who had rowed the boat to the landing. Each carried a sword and ax. Podebeek found it curious that the tunghak did not. It must think it didn't need weapons. Podebeek tried not to look at the tunghak's fierce face. Instead, his eyes sought out all the places he loved.

Podebeek knew every rock and tree on these shoals. He and the other Whale Rib Village boys played here almost every day during the summers, running races, throwing lances to see who could cast the farthest, fishing and hunting to their hearts' content. Usually seals sunned themselves on the flat rocks to the north, and just beyond Seal Rocks grizzly bears hunted salmon at the mouth of the creek that ran into the sea. A weather-gray pile of fallen trees, blown down many winters ago, lay beside the creek. Next moon, short-tailed weasels would mate. As part of their courtship, they would frolic and chase each other, leaping through the hollow logs in utter joy.

Podebeek's lungs labored.

As Father Sun's milky light penetrated the clouds, it fell in swaths and streaks of gold across the canoes that rested in a neat line on the terrace just above high tide.

Podebeek kept his teeth locked to keep his head from shaking. Father's canoe rested in the middle. The red image of a bearded seal decorated the bow. Behind his eyes, far back, Podebeek saw Father smiling at him.

Father hadn't made it back for the great battle in Whale Rib Village. He had died on the shore near the strange Wobee houses. Podebeek had seen Father fall, shot through the chest. When Podebeek had screamed and whirled around to run back, Mother had grabbed his hand and ferociously dragged him away, following Chief Badisut, heading home to the safety of the longhouse. Even though Podebeek knew now that Mother had saved his life, at the time he'd been insanely angry that she hadn't let him go back for Father. If the situation had been reversed, if Podebeek had been shot, Father would have come back for him.

No tears burned Podebeek's eyes. He stared clear eyed at the trail that led to Whale Rib Village, a trail he'd taken hundreds of times. He desperately wished he could go home. To the home he remembered. He imagined the village as it had been just a few days ago, filled with laughing people going about their duties. Drying racks of freshly harvested kosweet meat smoked over low fires while the young women and girls used stone scrapers to clean the kosweet hides staked out upon the ground, readying them for tanning. The old men gathered in their usual place. Every morning they sat before Chief Badisut's fire outside the longhouse and knapped stone tools while they discussed the political situation among neighboring nations.

When Podebeek could, he tried to listen to their conversations. He longed to understand what was happening with the Masks People or the Glacier People. Father said that someday Podebeek would need to know their enemies better than their enemies knew themselves. He didn't understand what that meant, but he had planned to learn as much as he could, so that when the time came he could help Father defend their People.

Podebeek looked up at Arnora. "What happened to the tunghak's servant Dag? Why isn't he here?"

She seemed to have some trouble understanding the question but finally whispered, "Dag brings warriors."

"To the cave?"

Reddish-brown hair whipped around her pretty face as she shook her head. "Maybe."

Thorlak the tunghak turned away from its servants and strode toward them. Podebeek watched it with burning eyes. The Masks People were no longer his enemy. They were human. His new enemy was not.

Sweat darkened the tunghak's red knee-length shirt beneath the arms and in the middle of the chest. It must not feel the morning chill as people did.

It spoke harshly to Arnora. She flinched.

"Where trail, Podebeek?"

Podebeek wet his lips nervously. He glanced at Arnora, then at the tunghak. Its red hair and beard looked like old blood in the morning light.

"Just up there."

Sucking in a breath, Podebeek walked toward it.

Before he reached the ledge, he cast one last look at the ships anchored a short distance from shore. He tried to imagine what Moosin was doing. He must be organizing the children, getting everyone ready for the moment when Bjarni and Finnbogi made their move to take over the ship. In the midst of the fight, Moosin would lead everyone onto the deck and they'd leap overboard and swim for shore.

Podebeek was shaking badly when he reached the trail and stepped up onto the narrow ledge that cut across the face of the cliff, but he knew exactly what he was doing and why.

# Forty-Nine

Drona lifted a hand in warning, motioning for his men to take cover. Twenty-six warriors vanished behind trees and boulders.

Drona tried to peer through the weave of branches to the canoe landing faintly visible below, but he didn't see anything moving, though the Wobee voices were unmistakable now.

They'd seen the ships shortly after dawn. When the rowboat left the smallest ship and headed for shore, Drona had gathered the Village Council to discuss what to do.

ShiHolder and ten warriors took the elders to hide in the dense grove of birches and spruces while Drona and the rest of his warriors had worked their way to the high point overlooking the canoe landing.

On his hands and knees, Drona crawled along the rim just out of view of the man who stood guard beside the Wobee boat. The other six people, four men, one woman, and a boy, walked in a line for the northern ledge trail.

Drona studied the boy. He had shoulder-length black hair and wore a caribouhide shirt decorated with faded blue images. ShiHolder's son? He was about the right age.

Drona eased back and gestured to Odjet to come forward.

The weasel-faced shaman trotted forward bent over. When he got close, he flattened out on his belly and slid forward to lie beside Drona and gaze over the edge to the canoe landing where he frowned at the two guards.

"Yes, Chief?"

"I want you to go back and get ShiHolder. I think that's her son down there leading the Wobee across the ledge trail."

Odjet cautiously slid forward to look down at the narrow trail that cut along the cliff face five tens of hands below. "I do, too, but she'll know for certain. I'll right back."

While he waited, Drona scanned the five ships rocking in the surf. How many warriors could each ship carry? Depending upon the size of the vessel, he guessed at least three tens. The two longships, however, could carry twice as many, and maybe more.

Feet scrambled on stone as ShiHolder and Odjet crawled toward Drona. He turned to look. ShiHolder's long black hair dragged through the puddles of water that filled the dips in the rimrock.

In a desperate voice, she said, "Where is he? Do you still see him?"

"Quiet. Do not call out to him, or you'll get him killed. Slide forward on your belly. When you stretch out beside me, you'll see them on the ledge trail below."

She slid up beside him and peered over the cliff at the five Wobee and the boy walking the ledge. Tears filled her eyes. She had to clap a hand to her mouth to keep her cries locked in her throat. She nodded to Drona, and finally managed to say, "Yes, that's Podebeek."

"Where is he leading the Wobee?"

ShiHolder hastily shook her head. "I don't know."

Many trails cut upward from the northern ledge trail, leading travelers to the rim, but all were nearby, and all dropped travelers at Whale Rib Village. Why would they be going back to the village they'd destroyed?

Drona focused on the tall red-haired man in the black cape. Thorlak. The enemy shaman Asson had sent fleeing into the forest. Thorlak seemed to be in charge. He kept turning around and speaking to the others, who nodded obediently.

"Thorlak has more courage than I do," Odjet whispered. "What if Asson sees him? I doubt he'll survive his next encounter with the greatest Kutsitualit that has ever lived."

ShiHolder touched Odjet's arm. "Maybe that's it."

Drona and Odjet swiveled to give her questioning looks.

"Maybe he's looking for Asson, for another chance to defeat him. The northern ledge trail connects to the Shaman's Trail in another hand of time, at least if they can keep up this pace. Maybe he's trying to find Asson's Spirit Cave? He could think Asson is there."

Drona's brows plunged down. "I only know one person who's ever seen it, and he's long dead. Does your son know where it is?"

"No. I guarantee you. None of the village children are allowed on the Shaman's Trail. But . . ." She swallowed hard. "He knows it's up there somewhere, and if the Wobee are forcing him to take them to Asson, this is the way he'd come."

Drona nodded to himself. "Then let's get back to our people. I need to send out scouts. Once we find the perfect locations on the rim where we can shoot down at them, we'll pick them off like ducks in a pond."

"But, what of my son, Chief?" ShiHolder asked in alarm. "If we shoot any of them, the first thing Thorlak will do is grab Podebeek."

On the ledge below, the boy was wasting no time. He'd picked up his pace, rushing along the precarious twists as though he knew the trail like his own lodge. The Wobee woman next in line couldn't keep up. She fell behind. Two paces, then three. Four.

A curse rang out. Thorlak grasped the woman by the hair and growled something in her face. She let out a cry of terror, but she moved faster after that.

Drona studied the situation, trying to place his soul inside Podebeek. If he was there right now, he would have one goal.

At last, Drona replied, "I think your son may be waiting for his chance to escape. We need to give him that chance, ShiHolder. He's no longer your little boy. He's a warrior now. We must treat him as such."

# Fifty

Podebeek braced a hand against the sun-warmed cliff and took a moment to steady his legs. Waves crashed against the rock below, shooting spray up. His soaked caribouhide shirt clung to his body. As the trail continued, it sloped upward. They'd be out of the spray in another finger of time.

Podebeek shook wet hair out of his eyes and started walking again. Arnora was three paces behind him, with the tunghak practically hanging over the top of her, ordering her to go faster. The trail was too narrow for it to step past her, so it had no choice but to walk behind Arnora. Podebeek felt sorry for her. She kept slipping and grabbing for rocks. Her boots, made of cow leather, didn't grip the rock as well as sealhide boots.

But it also occurred to Podebeek that she might be trying to slow down their captors, maybe to give Podebeek a chance to escape.

The trail curved around a protruding part of the cliff and sloped upward for about ten paces. Podebeek sprinted up the stretch, searching every moment for a place to lose them. He was terrified that if he didn't escape before they realized that he had no idea where Asson's cave was the tunghak would just shove him over the edge and keep looking by himself.

Podebeek glanced out at the five ships in the ocean. What were Bjarni and Finnbogi doing? Had they attacked the other Wobee yet? Their ship remained in the same place with its sail down. When would they attack?

Podebeek suspected that when the tunghak saw Bjarni's ship leaving he'd be shocked, and maybe distracted for long enough that Podebeek could make a run for it.

The tunghak shouted.

Arnora called, "Slow, Podebeek!"

He turned his head to watch her. The trail spread three hand-lengths across here. Arnora edged along with her head turned toward the cliff, as though afraid to look down.

The tunghak and its three servants looked angry.

As the ledge trail rose and dipped, Podebeek spied the Shaman's Trail ahead. His jaw trembled before he clamped it tight. Because they weren't allowed on the Shaman's Trail, that's the place where he and the other boys used to trot to the top of the cliff, then race home across Whale Rib Village.

A small portion of the ledge had cracked off, leaving a gap about one pace across. Podebeek leaped it and ran on.

Arnora let out a small cry, and when he turned Podebeek saw the tunghak shaking her so hard he feared her neck might snap. She must have been afraid to jump.

Podebeek chewed his lip while he thought about it; then he trotted back and called, "Arnora, just jump! I'll catch your arms and pull you across!" As he grabbed a handhold on the cliff, he extended one hand to her.

She looked at him with terrified eyes. "No, no."

"You have to! If you don't, the tunghak will throw you out of his way."

She looked down at the angular chunks of rock thrusting up from the surf. Finally, she wiped her nose on her sleeve.

"I come," she called.

Podebeek braced his feet. When she took a flying leap, he caught her forearm and dragged her onto the ledge. She hugged him tightly for a few moments, breathing, "Thank you, Podebeek. Thank you."

"Let's hurry."

"Yes."

Podebeek held her hand as he hiked along the ledge. Her trembling fingers felt warm in his grasp. What would happen to her if he escaped? She'd be all right, wouldn't she? They had no reason to hurt her. Arnora hadn't done anything wrong. . . . *Unless they think she's helping me.*

Podebeek craned his neck to look straight up at the cliff rim high over his head. Cloud People billowed in the blue sky and, for the briefest of instants, he thought he saw movement. But when he looked right at it, he saw nothing. Remembering Father's hunting lessons, Podebeek shifted his gaze slightly to the side and waited.

Nothing.

But he *had* seen something. Probably an animal looking over the edge, or a flash of birds' wings.

But maybe not. He couldn't let himself think about it or the hope would crumble his resolve. Even if someone was up there, Podebeek had no way of knowing if they were a friend or an enemy. The only person he could count on was himself.

He glanced out at the ocean when he saw men hoisting the sail on Bjarni's ship. It might mean nothing, but—

The tunghak asked Arnora something.

She said, "Where Asson cave?"

Podebeek frowned at the crisscrossing ledges formed by the eroded layers of limestone. Strangers often got lost on these ledges, not realizing that few were actually trails. Two winters ago during the Ptarmigan Moon, the elders had gathered all the children around the winter fires and told them stories about these trails. Old Teehonee had scared their hearts loose by telling tales about the trail that led to Asson's Spirit Cave. She said it was haunted by gigantic mist creatures that strangled disobedient children and threw them over the edge.

Old Teehonee had also said that a person just had to follow the main ledge that cut across the cliff and he'd find the cave at the end.

Podebeek pointed to the place where the Shaman's Trail intersected with the northern ledge trail. "That's the Shaman's Trail right up there. It leads to the cave."

Arnora relayed the message to the tunghak.

Podebeek kept walking.

Each time the trail bent back and Podebeek could see the tunghak's bony face, he found the malevolent Spirit staring at him with burning amber eyes.

With each step, Podebeek tried to piece together some alternative to the plan he'd already set in motion while he watched the deck of Bjarni's ship. Moosin and the other children would be ready. When the chance arose, they would flood up onto the deck and leap over the edge into the water to swim for shore.

*Please, Sea Woman, let them be safe.*

# Fifty-One

Asson clung to the sides of the litter as Camtac and Ewinon carried him up the trail to Whale Rib Village. This portion of the path climbed a steep slope that required negotiating around broken uplifted slabs. They were struggling to be careful, but the jostling affected his wounded leg like fiery sticks thrust into the flesh. To take his mind off the pain, he surveyed the faces of the people around him. Camtac carried the front of the litter, so Asson couldn't see his face, but everyone else walked behind.

The probable slaughter of the villagers had left all of them numb. Most hiked along the trail in silence, seeing things inside their own souls, barely aware of the brilliant afternoon sunlight that played among the rocks, or shimmered across the sea. The magnificent cloud-strewn sky might have been painted by the Thunderbirds themselves.

*Thorlak's magic is strong, maybe too strong, even if Thyra and I combine our power.*

He would call out to his Spirit Helpers, begging their aid, but he did not know if they would hear him.

Alfdis turned to Chief Gunnar and said something. The chief shook his blond head vehemently, and said, "No."

That was the only word Asson understood, but the low, dire tones of their conversation seemed to haunt the day. Were they plotting to take back their ship? Discussing how to defeat Thorlak? Perhaps commenting on the wave of light that had filled the world last night?

Asson kept seeing the faces of people he'd loved, especially the missing children. For many winters, he had tried to fathom how warriors could justify killing children. Designed to break the heart of the enemy, in reality it broke the heart of the world. Neither side escaped such horrors, and certainly not the warriors who had committed the acts. Murdering innocents was a knife that cut both ways.

Thorlak must have been drunk with Spirit Power, focused only upon hurting Asson, and probably Thyra.

Far back on the trail, Thyra Little Fox walked with long ivory locks whipping about her shoulders. When she saw him watching her, she lifted a hand. He smiled in return, and she trotted forward to walk beside Asson's litter. The freckles that sprinkled her nose and cheeks looked larger and darker against her pale face.

Asson said, "We're almost there. The canoe landing is just up and over the Whale Rib Village promontory, then another one-half hand of time down the trail on the other side."

"How is your leg?"

"Well enough to climb through the tunnel to the cave. After that, I give no assurances."

"What's in your Spirit Cave, Asson?"

Asson gave her a sidelong look. "What makes you think it's *my* cave?"

"That's what Camtac and Ewinon call it. You mean, it isn't?"

Asson smiled faintly. "The cave belongs to the Spirits who inhabit it, not me."

Thyra seemed to be thinking about that.

Ewinon, who carried the rear of the litter, said, "How close is it?" Black hair hung in stringy locks over his flushed cheeks.

Asson sank back onto the litter. "Close enough. How are you, son of Badisut?"

Ewinon just shook his head, refusing to answer, but his red-rimmed eyes told Asson everything he needed to know. Gower's probable death had stunned Ewinon. On top of the deaths of his parents and sisters, he could barely keep his head above the ocean of grief that was trying to suck him under. When all this was over, the youth needed to find a place where he could grant himself time to hurt.

"Have I ever told you about my grandfather?" Asson asked.

Ewinon glanced down. "I don't have time for a lesson, Asson."

"No one ever has time for lessons, my friend, which is exactly why I teach them."

"I thought it was just to annoy people."

"No, not always," he answered with a smile. "As I was saying, my grandfather died long before you were born, but he was a wise man, an old war chief who had lost many cherished friends."

"Asson, I'd rather not—"

"I asked him once how he dealt with the deaths of so many people he'd cared about. He had to think about it a long time before he answered, but he said that when we live the death of someone we love, we do not live one death, but two."

Ewinon frowned. "What?"

"He meant that we live the death of the human being we lost and the death of a friendship that has given us hope and meaning. In my long life, I have found that the first is easier to bear than the second."

The litter tipped sideways as Ewinon shifted to step over a dip in the rimrock. "Can I tell you a story back? One my father told me?"

Asson smiled. "Please do."

Thyra listened to them intently, her brow furrowed, probably struggling with the language.

"In the first battle I ever fought, Elder, I lost a good friend. I had seen just twelve winters. I sank down beside him on the battlefield and refused to leave him. As the battle continued to rage around me, I threw my body over his and closed my eyes. Even though I knew he was dead, I thought he still needed me to protect him."

Asson ached at the tenderness of youth, and softly asked, "What was his name?"

"Tapatook."

"Ah, from the bear clan. Yes, I remember him well. He was always smiling."

Old pain tightened Ewinon's expression. "When Father found me, he hauled me to my feet, dragged me into the forest, and forced me to sit down on a log. He told me that if I allowed grief to make a cocoon inside me, the creature would eat all of my strength and devour every shred of love in my heart, leaving nothing more than a pale shell of rage behind. He pointed a finger in my face and told me that by collapsing and leaving the rest of my relatives to fight for me I had not honored Tapatook's sacrifice." Sunlight glinted in his wet eyes. "I have not forgotten his words. You're right, and I appreciate your concern. I am grieving, not just for Gower, but for all the people I've lost in the past few days. But I will not let the weight of it force me to collapse. Not ever again. I know my living relatives need me to fight for them."

Asson nodded solemnly. "Badisut was a good father."

Gray streamers of rain fell from the clouds, but not a drop touched the ground.

Camtac cast a glance over his shoulder, surveying each of their faces, before he said, "Asson, the air smells of rain. What happens at the cave entrance if there's a storm at sea when the tide comes in?"

"The waves will be ferocious. But, hopefully, we will be gone long before—"

"Ewinon?" Camtac called in a worried voice.

Ewinon's face slackened. He must see something ahead of them on the trail. "I see him. I don't recognize him. Do you?"

"No."

Asson twisted around on his litter and saw the warrior dashing down the trail toward them.

"We're going to set you down, Asson."

"Yes, hurry."

Ewinon and Camtac lowered the litter and trotted forward to meet the runner. The three men spoke for less than two tens of heartbeats before Camtac ran back.

"Elder, Chief Drona's scouts saw us coming and ask that we wait here. Drona is about to spring a trap and fears—"

"What trap?" Asson grunted to a sitting position.

"Apparently, ShiHolder's son, Podebeek, is leading several Wobee, including one woman, along the Shaman's Trail. When they get to the right place, Drona has warriors positioned to shower them with arrows. Hopefully, they'll kill all the Wobee, but at least he wants to create enough of a diversion that Podebeek can escape."

Asson had traveled that trail for more than forty winters. If any of the Wobee survived, the boy would not escape.

Asson slapped the sides of his litter. "Lift me up! Carry me to Drona. I must stop this."

"Why?"

"Just do it!"

Ewinon and Camtac lifted the litter and prepared to obey, but Chief Gunnar and Kiran trotted forward to find out what was going on.

Gunnar studied the runner.

Kiran turned to Asson. "Who is the runner? What's wrong?"

Camtac answered, "Just ahead, Chief Drona has a trap set up. He asks that we wait here until he's sprung it."

"What is he trapping?"

Camtac gave Kiran a suspicious look, obviously wondering what orders Chief Gunnar might give if he knew Wobee were about to be killed.

When Camtac didn't answer, Kiran turned to Thyra and asked the same question.

She answered.

Chief Gunnar's eyes widened. He spoke rapidly to her.

Thyra said, "Camtac, Chief Gunnar needs to see *who* the Wobee are. They may be friends, not enemies! Hurry. Both Asson and Chief Gunnar need to speak with Drona immediately."

Camtac and Ewinon broke into a run, which forced Asson to frantically grab for the litter poles.

# Fifty-Two

Podebeek searched for the trail. It was gone—just gone. He stood on the lip of a gigantic rockshelter, a place where the cliff had been undercut by waves. Squealing gulls filled the hollow, fluttering and diving.

"Blessed Anguta," he whispered. "This must be Spirit Hollow. Asson's cave *is* here somewhere."

From behind him, Arnora called, "What wrong, Podebeek?"

He didn't answer for a time. "I need just a few moments. I can't see the trail."

Arnora came forward and looked over his shoulder, whispering, "Stay brave, Podebeek. We find way."

Blood surged in Podebeek's ears as he frantically searched for it. He shook his head and looked upward. On the rim above him, twisted trees hung out over the edge. They couldn't climb up. Far below, gigantic chunks of cliff fall thrust up from the surf. If they couldn't go straight ahead or up, could they go down?

Swallowing hard, Podebeek sat on the ledge and leaned out. A thrill went through him. A gaping crack split the rock just steps below. The scents of moss and spruce needles breathed from the dark maw. *The cave. It must be! Gods, if I can get inside before they do, maybe I can see a way to escape.*

When the tunghak quietly came to stand beside Arnora, its face was completely expressionless, its amber eyes empty, as though its soul had flown. Red hair blew around its face.

Podebeek gestured. "Arnora, tell it the trail cracked off last winter. We must find a new way. I'm going to climb down to look in that crack. There may be a path through there."

The tunghak instantly got down on its hands and knees and looked over the edge. When it saw the opening, it spoke to Arnora with deadly softness.

"Thorlak say, you stay. He go."

"But, no, I need to go first! Tell him it may be dangerous!"

Without waiting for the translation, the tunghak climbed over the edge, found a foothold, and descended toward the crack.

Tears burned Podebeek's eyes. He longed to sob. If only he'd climbed down first . . .

A soft grunt sounded, and the man at the end of the line toppled over the cliff's edge. Podebeek gasped as he watched him fall. "What . . . ?"

The next man staggered when an arrow lanced through the top of his skull and burst out beneath his chin.

Then arrows began clattering all around Podebeek, and his gaze jerked upward to the rim where he saw a hail of arrows glittering as they sailed down toward him.

"Arnora!" He lunged to his feet to slam her body back against the cliff. "Don't move!" he shouted. *"Stay flat against the cliff!"*

Father had taught him well. Shooting straight down was very hard.

The last Wobee let out a roar of defiance and foolishly tried to race back along the ledge. Three arrows lanced through him almost simultaneously. A ragged scream burst from his lips as he stepped right over the edge. Sickening thuds erupted as his body bashed every ledge on the way down.

"Let's go, Podebeek!" Arnora tried to slip out of his grasp.

"No, don't move. Not yet! Just wait."

Gods, if he released her and she stepped away from him, would they shoot her, too? The warriors could not know she was Podebeek's friend. They must think she was one of the tunghak's servants.

When the arrows ceased to fly, Podebeek bravely stepped away from Arnora, raised his hands over his head, and looked straight up at the archers with tears in his eyes. More to himself than to her, he whispered, "It . . . it's Chief Drona. Arnora, it's Drona."

The chief waved to Podebeek. It took him a moment to understand that the chief was telling him to run back along the Shaman's Trail, to get as far away from the tunghak as he possibly could.

Podebeek understood suddenly that if the tunghak dared to climb back up through the crack the archers would loose another volley of arrows.

"Arnora, come on. We have to run." He gripped her hand and held it up for Drona to see that she was his friend, and dragged her back along the trail.

# Fifty-Three

Thorlak ignored the sound of screams on the ledge above. Those people were no longer important. Silently, one step at time, he descended the wet stairs cut into the rock. A bulge of stone blocked most of his view of the lower cave, but fluttering orange light coated the walls. Somewhere below, a lamp burned.

He sniffed the odd, spicy air.

As he descended, the cave seemed to swell around him, fifty feet deep and maybe one hundred feet wide. Tufts of moss draped every ledge. Like dark beards, they swayed in the breeze swirling up from deep within the cave.

Thorlak's gaze slowly moved over every possible hiding place. He saw no one.

He stopped when he heard hooves clattering over stones in the bottom of the cave. A dark shape moved. Hooves clattered again. Then they were gone, as though the animal had found a way out and taken it.

Thorlak placed a hand against the wall to steady his steps as he continued his descent. Water soaked his fingers. He wiped them on his cape in irritation, and noticed that the walls wept. Tiny rivulets cascaded down the stone ledges and streamed across the floor below, where they poured into a shining firelit pool. The surface seemed to be in constant motion, giving the illusion that the pool was filled with wavering white sticks.

His brow furrowed when he saw the magnificent Norway spruce that grew at the edge of the pool. The lamp rested in the fork of the branches. Its gleam played through the drooping twigs and branchlets like slips of fire. *What's a Norway spruce doing here?* Did they grow this far west?

He sniffed the air again.

Smoke rose from a soapstone bowl resting at the base of the spruce. He knew that spicy smell. When he finally identified it, his shoulder muscles contracted. Henbane. A plant used by the myrkrida when seeking a vision.

He was alert now, really alert. Blood began to surge in his ears.

His gaze darted around the cave. Only the lamplight seemed alive.

Stepping down to the moss-covered floor, he stood transfixed. For several moments, he just stared in awe at the magnificent rune-covered walls. The inscriptions were deeply carved, as though the writer had been desperate to have them last for thousands of years. Some were pleas to legendary *volur*, prophetesses of extraordinary power: Huld, Groa, Heidur. They were so skilled, it was said that Odin himself consulted the volur to learn the future of the gods.

But most of the inscriptions were commemorations of the dead. One particularly deep carving read: *And Eyjolf the Grey took in England two gelds. The first was paid by Toste. Then Thorkell paid.*

Thorlak shook his head in amazement. The runic inscription clearly documented that Eyjolf the Grey had taken part in the Norse raids of England and received his share of the *geld*, the money paid to the Norse by England to keep them from attacking their villages, which ranged from ten thousand pounds in 991 to forty-eight thousand pounds most recently, in 1012.

Another inscription simply read: *Gullog had a road made for her daughter Thorunn's soul, who was the wife of Sven.*

There were hundreds of such inscriptions, and from this position he could only read the largest. Why were they here? Ordinarily such commemorations were written on standing stones and raised in prominent places, near bridges, along roadways, or on the farms of relatives.

When he took another step toward the pool, the first things he noticed were the skulls. They'd been deliberately laid out around the water to define the shape of a ship, just like the burials of nobles in Sweden, Norway, and Denmark.

. . . Then he saw the bones. Dozens of hands and feet, leg bones and ribs.

"It's a grave."

He walked closer.

As the lamp flickered, embers seemed to fly like wisps of fire through the shining scraps of metal in the bottom of the pool. The iron objects had rusted beyond recognition, but the gold remained lustrous. He knelt beside the ship burial to examine the artifacts. Fragments of helmets, chain mail, and common iron bracelets created rusty patches among the bones, but it was the miniature chairs, cast in silver and tarnished black, that drew his attention. The loops that had suspended the pendants around throats were long gone, but their symbolism remained. They represented the high seat in Valhöll from which Odin surveyed the worlds. But why would Asson have collected so many of the high-seat pendants? What was he looking for?

"This *must* be Avaldamon's grave. He was lig-lodin for years."

When Thorlak saw two metal rings resting beneath a shoulder blade, excitement filled him. He rose and walked to peer down into the water. His reflection stared back, his bushy red hair and beard glittering with fiery light.

Carefully, he reached down into the water and pulled up the closest ring to study it more closely. Broken from the end of a Seidur staff, the ring contained the perfectly cast head of a roaring lion. Thorlak threw it back into the water. It was just a common staff. Concentric rings bobbed away from the splash, making the bones appear to move in serpentine patterns, like hundreds of crawling white snakes.

He turned. At the base of the protruding rock was a scooped-out place almost five feet high and ten deep. Rolled hides, soapstone pots, and baskets stuffed the rear.

Asson must sleep there. Was he the guardian of this burial? Why would a Skraeling guard a Norse mass grave? On the other hand, Thorlak had no way of knowing that all of these bones belonged to Norse dead. After all, among the runes carved into the walls he also saw the crude images of running caribou, seals, and bears.

Just as he started to turn away, he glimpsed the collection of walking sticks that leaned against the wall near the rolled hides.

His eyes flashed with excitement.

Only one held his interest: the iron staff. The central rod was plain, but the tips ended in eight-sided knobs. He entered the sleeping shelter and duckwalked to the rear, where he crouched before the sticks.

He reached for the Seidur staff.

As he turned it in the lamplight, examining the knob, he tried to keep his hands from shaking. "Is it . . . it's the key . . . I—I'm almost certain."

Weak-kneed, Thorlak slumped to the floor with the staff across his lap. He just sat there, stunned, running his hands over the irregularly shaped key. "But where's the high-seat pendant? Avaldamon was supposed to have carried both."

Didn't matter.

If this was the legendary Eyr, when placed into the lock and turned it opened the door to the greatest Seidur seers ever known, and the chamber of the knowledge of the ages.

The day of the massacre, thirteen years ago, Thorlak thought he'd found Eyr hanging on the wall beneath Vethild's sword. But that staff had been virtually worthless, and he'd had no time to question her before Aethelred ordered her shipped her off for safekeeping in the wilds of Albania-Land. What a triumph that had been for the king. By capturing Sweyn Forkbeard's legendary prophetess, Aethelred had neutered his foe in a heartbeat, which had allowed him to slaughter the Forkbeard's family and everyone else living in the Danelaw, eliminating in a single stroke one of England's greatest problems—and setting the stage for war.

Thorlak had been well rewarded for convincing Pallig to side with the wretched raiders, which had given Aethelred just the excuse he needed, but Thorlak's true goal had been far more than wealth. He'd been desperate to acquire *the key*. With it, he could gain the knowledge to become the most powerful man in existence. Indispensable to the king of Denmark, who Thorlak felt certain would soon be Cnut. As Cnut's Seidur prophet, Thorlak could cleanse the world of the Anchorite madness forever—starting with England.

And now . . .

Thorlak lifted the staff and pressed it to his forehead. Power surged through him, leaving him breathless.

His lips formed her name, *Eyr.*

As he lowered the staff to study the key's intricate octagonal shape, very faintly he heard feet scuff stone.

A soft voice said, "*Hello, old enemy.*"

Thorlak stiffened.

Time seemed to die around him.

He'd been hearing that voice in his dreams for thirteen years.

He clutched Eyr as he slowly rose to his feet. When he turned, his breath caught.

"Blessed Odin, you are even more beautiful than I recall."

Vethild's eyes glistened like blue diamonds. Tall, slender, with flowing ice-colored hair, she stood near the Norway spruce. Her white dress might have been sculpted of snow.

When she took a step toward him, Thorlak lifted the staff and aimed it at her chest.

She stopped.

Chuckling, he said, "I always get to your weapons before you do. First your sword, now your—"

"Bait."

"Bait?" He laughed. "I didn't just come for this, you know." He gripped the staff. "Aethelred must deny his enemies, Edmund and Cnut, the treasure they most desire. You."

She walked toward him so gracefully she might have been a floating ghost. Her white hem whispered across the moss. "You're still a fool, Thorlak."

Thorlak's gaze lingered upon the swell of her breasts and hips. It pleased him when she glared. "Me? I always find you alone. Poor planning on your part. Especially if you knew I was coming. And you did, didn't you?"

She tilted her head slightly, and a smile came to her lips.

Against the back wall of the cave, an elusive wink of lamplight flashed on polished metal.

A man said, "She's not alone. Not this time."

Thorlak's shoulder muscles contracted. *"Baldur."*

"I'm honored you remember me, you traitorous filth."

When Thorlak turned and saw the sword in Baldur's hand, an incoherent cry broke from his throat.

Baldur rushed him, swinging his sword for the killing blow. As Thorlak watched the silver blade arc toward him, he lifted Eyr. Blinding light flashed from the staff. Baldur was struck in the chest and thrown backward into the stone wall like a rag doll. His sword clattered across the floor.

Gasping and whimpering, *"No, no,"* Baldur frantically crawled for the weapon.

Thorlak kicked the sword aside. Wild exultation filled him. Gods, he had never felt such power surging through his body. Baldur was still alive, gasping for breath. "I'll finish you later."

He turned. In the lingering flickers of light, Thorlak saw the tears streaking Vethild's cheeks.

"Now, we end it," he said, and leveled Eyr at his archenemy. "Finally, after all these years, it will be over."

"Yes," Vethild said. "It will."

As a final affront, Thorlak said, "You know, don't you, that your daughter is not as powerful as you. She has no chance against me."

"She's not as powerful *yet*. She doesn't have the tools she needs, but she will. In the Helgafell of my ancestors is the chamber that contains the magical knowledge of the ages. The greatest seers of all time have shown me her future, Thorlak. Thyra will shake the world."

"Yes, well"—he nonchalantly twirled the staff—"very soon, I will also visit that chamber, and when I do—"

"Do you really think my ancestors will allow you entry, even if you have the key?"

The comment startled him. As she'd intended. He could sense her power growing; the air hummed with it. He had to disarm her to disrupt it. "I'm not going to give Thyra the chance to shake the world. If she has the courage to fight me, I'll simply kill her."

"She's not going to fight you, Thorlak." Vethild's head tilted, and ivory hair tumbled down her back. "I am."

The legendary Prophetess lifted her hands high into the air, and the room, the runes on the walls, the lamps down the tunnel, all simultaneously burst into flame. . . .

# Fifty-Four

**F**ear raced through Ewinon when Drona's warriors erupted in cheers and victorious clan war cries.

"Hurry!" Asson commanded. "Get me there!"

"We're trying, Asson."

He and Camrac carried the litter up the slope as fast as they could, but it was steep, and the footing unpredictable.

Asson said, "I must speak with Drona briefly; then we must hurry to the Spirit Cave."

"Yes, Elder, of course."

Kiran translated for Gunnar, and the man nodded. Thyra Little Fox seemed only vaguely aware of the conversation. As though she heard or saw something terrifying far out in the ocean, and moving their way, her eyes had gone glassy.

Ewinon focused on the warriors who danced and shook their bows in the air. Three men still bravely stretched out on the limbs of twisted trees that hung over the edge of the cliff, their bows aimed down, probably to protect Podebeek as he escaped along the trail.

Ewinon said, "Drona must have had to act when he had the chance."

He watched Drona trot back on the trail with a sober expression.

"Is it over?" Ewinon called.

"It's over."

"How many died?"

"Three Wobee warriors. Podebeek and the Wobee woman escaped, as did Chief Thorlak."

"Thorlak escaped?" Asson's voice shook. "Where did he go?"

Drona used his sleeve to wipe sweat from his forehead. His boyish face was flushed. "Down into some crack. I couldn't see—"

"No!" Asson cried. "Move, Ewinon! Get me to a boat!"

# Fifty-Five

ait, Asson! Just for a few moments. I need to understand—"

Camtac said, "Brother, Gower and I climbed down into Asson's Spirit Cave through a crack in the rock. If it's the same crack, Thorlak may be inside right now."

"Blessed Spirits."

Ewinon set the litter down and trotted to Drona.

When the chief saw him coming, he called, "Be quick, my daughter's husband. I haven't much—"

"Father-in-law, have you seen any of our people? Gower or any of the villagers who were at the beach camp last night?"

Drona appeared confused by the question. He shook his head. "No. I assume they rose early and headed home. Why?"

Ewinon propped his hands on his hips. How did he explain this? "Last night, there was a—a wave of light. It—"

"Yes, we saw it." Drona expelled a breath. He gestured to the scorched trees in the distance. "We saw it swell to life. It started here, in this village."

"Here?"

"Yes. We canoed back as quickly as we could. We assumed it came from the supper fires cast by a huge Wobee encampment. I had to find out." Drona's eyes narrowed in pain as he looked out across the dead village and burned trees. "This is what we found. I don't know how to explain—"

"Asson says it was great Spirit Power, probably wielded by Thorlak."

Drona's boyish face slackened. "By Thorlak?"

"Yes. Our people in the beach camp vanished."

"Vanished? What do you mean?"

"Asson thinks they're dead. Killed by the light, and if Thorlak escaped, he may be planning something even more terrifying."

Pebbles and alder leaves abruptly swirled over them, engulfing them. Somewhere in the chaos, metal whined. Then strange horns blew, and the sound of ten tens of feet moving through the forest rose.

Drona swung around, and fear blazed in his eyes. "Blessed Sea Woman, there are too many!" He charged back to his warriors.

Ewinon stared, frozen in shock, at the massive Wobee army that emerged from the trees, wielding swords, longbows, and broadaxes. Their weapons glowed with sunlight.

Drona and his warriors charged out to meet them, and Gunnar called, "Men, let's get into this fight!"

He waved his friends forward to support Drona, and they rushed into the chaos.

"Ewinon?" Camtac blurted, "What should we—"

Ewinon grabbed Camtac's shoulder hard. "The Wobee army outnumbers us three to one. Grab Asson and find a place to take cover! Protect him!"

When the first line of Drona's warriors was cut down, Ewinon dragged a hatchet from a dead man's hand, and ran to join the battle.

A burly blond leaped at Ewinon. The sword sliced the air a hair's breadth from his eyes. He spun, and slammed the hatchet into the man's spine, and jumped out of the way as his enemy toppled to the ground roaring like a dying bear.

The next Wobee came at Ewinon from his left, swinging a heavy broadax. He ducked under the stroke, then lunged, slamming his shoulder into the Wobee's chest. The man let out a deep-throated bellow as he stumbled backward. Ewinon was instantly upon him, leaping forward with his hatchet in midarc, cutting down for a death blow. The instant before the blow connected with flesh, he heard the shocked voices of the men on the battlefield and glimpsed Thyra Little Fox walking out into the midst of the worst fighting. Ewinon buried his hatchet in his opponent's skull, jerked the broadax from his dead hand, and moved on.

Gunnar shouted, "Thyra, what are you doing? Take cover!"

She either didn't hear him or didn't care to listen to him. With men dying all around her, she stared northward as though at some great mystery.

Ewinon didn't have time to save her. Two Wobee with swords charged him. Both wore huge grins. Ewinon stood his ground, his feet braced, waiting. . . .

Somewhere close by he heard a warrior gasp, "What is that? I've never seen Father Sun throw off such light."

Ewinon dared not look.

But he didn't have to. The amber gleam seemed to be born in the charred lodge frames. It ran up the poles and seeped out into the air like yellow dye filtering through water.

Ewinon ducked the first sword, and hit the ground rolling. When he came up on his knees within a reach of one man's ankle, Ewinon hefted the broadax and chopped it apart. He was already on his feet before the man even toppled, and brought the ax down across the man's throat, then whirled to face his next opponent.

But the redhead had lowered his weapon. He stood a short distance away, his mouth open, watching the amber light flicker through the ruins of Whale Rib Village, diving like falcons between the destroyed lodges, playing among the skeletal poles of the longhouse. Every angular object flared. It looked eerie and beautiful.

The Wobee began chattering. Several, including his opponent, threw down their swords and ran for the forest.

Those who remained stood with their weapons hanging in limp hands, just staring in astonishment to the north.

Ewinon turned.

All across the village, the faces of warriors shone in the swelling amber gleam.

"Fire?" someone called.

Drona answered, "It can't be. We've had rain almost every day."

A far-off roar shook the ground as the fiery halo expanded to fill the day, blotting out Father Sun's pale yellow radiance.

When the village gleamed as brilliantly as flames, the weapons of the shocked warriors fell from their hands to thud upon the ground. Oddly, many couldn't seem to move. They stood as if made of stone, gaping. Godi Gunnar and his men had gathered together ten paces away, their eyes wide with dread.

Chief Drona shouted, "This is some sort of Wobee trick. Just like last night. Get ready to do battle with whatever comes out of that fire!"

Ewinon glanced around. The Wobee appeared as surprised as the People of the Songtrail.

"Ewinon?" Camtac called. "Help me!"

He saw Camtac lifting Asson to his feet, where the old Kutsitualit leaned precariously on his walking stick, and Ewinon sprinted toward them. Asson kept shaking his head, as though he had no idea what was happening.

When Ewinon arrived, Asson sternly pointed a finger at him. "Do nothing. Just stand here."

"Are you crazy? They're coming back. We have to take cover!" Ewinon shouted back.

As the fiery glow approached, Thyra Little Fox began walking northward with tears streaming down her face.

Ewinon shouted, "Asson, get down!" and dove for the ground.

When the glow passed over in a rumbling torrent of sparks, Ewinon's skin felt as though it were on fire. Then the wave rolled on, down the slope, and out over the ocean.

"Gods, what was that?" Camtac cried.

Ewinon sat up. Gunnar and his men stood with weapons in their fists, staring wide-eyed across the battlefield.

Ewinon blinked. "What . . . ?" He couldn't believe what his eyes saw.

The Wobee lay dead, leaving their swords, longbows, and axes scattered across the battlefield.

Ewinon whirled around to look at Camtac and found Camtac looking at him with watery eyes.

"I—I don't know," Camtac said.

"What do you mean, you don't know? Is this the same light that swallowed our people last night?"

"There were no bodies last night! I don't know!" Camtac lowered his clenched fists to his sides and his blurry gaze moved across the land, then slowly lifted to Thyra where she stood with her head tilted back, as though absorbing sunlight like a sponge.

Struggling to stay on his feet, Asson said, "I'm going to my cave. If you won't carry me there, I'll walk."

"Wait, Asson. We'll carry you."

Asson eased down upon the litter again, and slapped the litter poles. "Then let's go."

As Ewinon reached for the litter, he glimpsed Thyra running headlong down the rim trail toward the canoe landing with her long ivory hair flying out behind her.

"Where's she going?"

"The canoe landing," Asson said. "And, I fear, her destiny."

# Fifty-Six

Massive storm clouds rumbled in the wake of the dissipating wash of light. As Gunnar studied the golden glow, a sickening mixture of awe and terror pumped through his veins. No one, not even Asson, seemed to know what it was, or where it had come from. But Gunnar felt certain Thyra had called it.

As he and Ewinon shoved the canoe into the water, Gunnar watched Thyra. She sat in the middle of the canoe, staring straight ahead, perhaps watching Asson and Camtac paddling in the bow.

"Where is the Spirit Cave?" Gunnar called.

Asson pointed, and spoke to Thyra.

She translated, "Up there, Godi, at the base of the cliff."

"Well, that will be cutting it close. The tide's coming. I can already smell it in the air."

As tides surged and retreated, the currents churned up earthy new fragrances. Gunnar flared his nostrils, scenting the wind, and dug his paddle deep, driving the canoe south along the face of the towering cliff.

Thyra gripped the gunwale as they bucked waves, heading out into deeper water; then she craned her neck to look back at Kiran, Ingolf, Sokkolf, and Alfdis, who stood onshore with Chief Drona and several of his warriors. Gunnar had left them with Drona to help fight off Dag's men if they returned. Thyra's gaze clung to Kiran. He seemed to be translating a conversation between Alfdis and Drona, but his head kept turning, watching their canoe as it pulled farther and farther away. Thyra's young eyes never left him.

"You'll see him again soon, Thyra."

Almost too low to hear, she replied, "No, I won't."

"You don't know that."

She grabbed a handful of windblown hair and held it while she stared at him. "Gods, how could I have been so dull witted?"

Gunnar's thoughts were racing. Who had Thorlak been working for thirteen years ago when the Danelaw was slaughtered? Certainly not Pallig. Thorlak's advice to join the raiders had benefited only one man: the king.

Asson turned around and called something to Ewinon. The tall youth nodded and dragged his paddle, steering the canoe closer to shore.

Gunnar tried to see what they saw. The cliffs soared for more than one hundred feet over the water here, but a narrow strip of white sand glittered between the rock and waves.

Thyra said, "Do you see it, Godi?"

He squinted, searching the cliff face, and finally saw what appeared to be a black dot perched upon the white sand, maybe ten minutes away, if the currents didn't drag them out to sea again.

"I do." Gunnar paddled harder.

They waged a constant battle against the waves for what seemed like far longer than a few minutes. Finally, they got close enough for one final push to drive the canoe up onto the beach. When the bow grounded on the sand, Gunnar leaped into the water, and helped Camtac and Ewinon drag the craft completely up onto the shore.

Gunnar examined the entry to the tunnel. It looked like a small cave, five feet across and about as high. He strode toward it and cautiously bent down to look inside. The thick odor of resin filled the air. But even more interesting, lamplight reflected from the walls, which made Gunnar's heart rate climb. When he bent down and stepped inside, he saw the string of seal-oil lamps arranged at regular intervals for as far as he could see up the throat of the tunnel, maybe twenty feet. Their amber gleams cast every limestone ledge into shadow, creating a dramatic flickering interplay of light and dark. Near the top, pale blue coated the walls.

Gunnar backed out of the opening and said, "Who keeps the lamps lit in the tunnel?"

Thyra asked Asson.

Asson hobbled forward on his walking stick. He reached the opening and sniffed the air.

Thyra translated, "Asson says there are never lamps in the tunnel. Apparently someone is expecting us."

Gunnar's hand tightened around the hilt of his sheathed sword. *Thorlak?* "All right, what now?"

Asson called to Camtac and Ewinon, and both men took up guard positions on either side of the cave entrance. Then Asson ducked into the tunnel and vanished.

When Thyra started to follow, Gunnar grasped her arm. "Please tell Camtac and Ewinon that I'm worried about the thunderheads massing out there. This looks to be one monstrous storm. If we get a storm surge at the same time as the tide rolls in, they're liable to be drowned before they know what struck them. At the first sign of trouble, they should get in the canoe and paddle away from shore."

Thyra turned and relayed his message. Camtac nodded, but Ewinon gave Gunnar a disdainful look, as though he already knew that. Gunnar said, "If that happens, tell them not to wait for us."

Thyra did, then squared her shoulders and stared at the cave entrance. She was trembling.

Gunnar drew his sword. "Let me lead the way."

"No, Godi. I must lead." Thyra marched forward like a woman going to the gallows.

Gunnar followed. He could hear Asson's walking stick clattering on stone somewhere above them but couldn't see him.

Thyra turned slightly to whisper, "Do you feel it?"

Gunnar *did* feel something, filament-like, delicate against his skin. "What is that?"

Thyra braced a hand against the dripping wall before she said, "A Seidur cry for help."

"From whom?"

"I wish I knew, Godi." She reached down to pull up the hem of Kiran's cape and continued up the tunnel.

Gunnar kept pace with her while his gaze scanned every shadowed niche. When they rounded a curve in the tunnel and he saw a smaller tunnel jutting off to the left, he halted to search it for hidden enemies. That last thing they needed was to have some foe close this exit, trapping them in the cave above.

He picked up the closest lamp and extended it into the cave. Instead of living threats, the pale orange gleam reflected in a cache of baskets and rolled hides. Soapstone jars of oil stood on the stone ledges. There was something else in back, a bundle of white cloth—

When he heard someone gasp, Gunnar lurched to his feet and rushed up the tunnel with his boots slipping on the wet floor. He passed the last oil lamp and the blue gleam intensified. Just above him, he saw the cave.

Gunnar set his oil lamp down and scrambled up the steep slope. He could hear Asson and Thyra talking, their voices low and filled with fear.

Gunnar staggered into the upper cave and a hollow sensation expanded his chest.

Thor's fire flickered upon the ledges and danced through the drooping needles of the gigantic spruce to Gunnar's left. The cave walls seemed to ooze azure honey. His gaze moved over the stunning rune-covered walls, then seemed to be drawn upward by some magnetic pull to the massive bulge of stone that intruded into the cave. It was the only thing in the chamber that remained cloaked by darkness. But above it, a crack split the roof and the sky visible through the rent flickered with lightning.

"Is the cave always like this?" Gunnar's voice had gone hoarse with wonder.

Asson spoke to Thyra. When he finished, Thyra turned halfway around and anxiously licked her lips. "No, Godi. There's been a battle here. A Seidur battle of great power."

"I hope that means Thorlak is dead."

Asson heaved a deep sigh and shook his head as he continued to explain something to Thyra.

In the recesses of the cave to Gunnar's right, something moved.

He spun with his sword up, but as his eyes struggled to filter the shapes he realized the faint outline was a human being, hiding, hunched over in one of the many hollows that dented the walls.

"Who is that?"

Thyra instinctively grabbed for the hilt of the broken sword tucked into her belt but did not draw it.

"The loser, maybe?"

Gunnar quietly walked over, and knelt.

"I'm Godi Gunnar the Skoggangur," Gunnar said softly. "I'm not going to hurt you. I need to pull you out of there so I can help you."

The figure had its knees cramped against its chest, and its head had fallen forward, so that all Gunnar could see was gore-encrusted hair. His gaze was drawn to the floor. What Gunnar had taken for water in the blue gleam was probably blood, and there was a lot of it.

"Can you hear me?" Gunnar asked.

When he received no answer, he sheathed his sword and reached into the hollow to drag the person out. As he laid the body across the floor, Thyra tried to walk forward, but Asson spoke to her, telling her something that made her let out a small agonized cry.

*"I know him!"*

"Him?" Gunnar said. "Are you sure it's male? I can't tell."

Thyra ran forward to fall to her knees. Breathing hard, she stared at the victim with wide, wet eyes.

"If it is a man, he's been beaten badly." Gunnar struggled to distinguish anything from the bloody pulp of his face. "Ask Asson if he knows who this is."

Thyra said, "His name is Baldur."

"Well," Gunnar said through a taut exhale. "I don't recognize the name, so I didn't know him. But you might want to say your good-byes. I think he probably already hears the valkyries calling him to Valhöll."

Asson moved closer. He eased down to the floor and pulled Baldur's head onto his lap. As he stroked the dying man's hair, Asson whispered to him in the voice of an old and dear friend. "I'm sorry I wasn't here, my friend. Forgive me."

Hail suddenly thundered upon the rock over their heads, and Gunnar's gaze jerked upward in time to see the brilliant flash of lightning that silhouetted the dark form standing upon the rock high above them.

His heart stopped.

"Gods . . ." Gunnar rose to his feet and drew his sword, expecting the worst.

Almost too low to hear, Thyra said, "Who—who is that?"

Lightning threaded her ivory hair with quicksilver flashes and webbed her blue eyes. They widened and riveted upon Thorlak as he descended the steps one at a time.

"Keep your wits about you," Gunnar whispered to her. "This is life or death, not a Seidur game. Let's move away from Baldur."

Thyra drew the broken sword from her belt and held it before her as though it were whole and shining and brimming with her mother's strength. She followed Gunnar to the edge of the pool, and Gunnar noticed for the first time that it was filled with bones.

Gunnar heard Asson speaking softly, and thought he saw Baldur's mouth move in response.

Thorlak had descended halfway down the steps. He stopped to look at them. Though his right hand held a short iron staff, his left was pressed hard against his belly, and he seemed to be having trouble breathing.

In a friendly voice, Gunnar inquired, "Are you hurt, Thorlak?" He took a new grip on his sword. "If you'll come down here, I'll end the struggle for you."

Thorlak lifted the staff, but for several moments he hesitated. "Where is she?"

Gunnar's eyes narrowed. "Who?"

Thorlak's gaze searched the chamber. "You're a poor liar, Gunnar. I know she's still here."

Gunnar glimpsed Thyra. She was shaking, shaking badly. She walked around the pool and stood at the foot of the stone staircase, looking up at Thorlak with her face glittering in the blue gleam.

"Lawspeaker?" she called. "Before I die, I need to know what happened thirteen years ago."

Thorlak winced in pain and pressed his belly harder. "Put away your swords, both of you."

Thyra hesitated. Then she tucked her broken sword into her belt.

Gunnar shook his head. "No, I don't think so, Thorlak."

"Put it away or I'll kill you all!"

"You could have done that when you first saw us. You didn't. I assume there's a reason. And I want to—"

Thyra interrupted, "Was it you who paid my adopted family to keep me safe in Denmark?"

Thorlak started down the stairs again, one agonizing step at a time. "It doesn't matter now. You are no longer of any use to me."

Thyra kept shifting to face him as he descended. "Men came to make sure I was alive after the plague devastated our region. You sent the men for me, didn't you?"

"You were valuable then. I thought you would help me find your mother. What I did not understand at the time was that your mother would pull our ships here so she could find you."

"She—she found me?"

Thorlak glared at her. "I'm not surprised you didn't feel her hand in the storm that drove us off course. You've always been pathetically weak."

Thorlak stepped off onto the moss-covered floor and staggered past Thyra to the pool. He glared at it for a time before he gestured to the bones. "Your father was known as Avaldamon Lig-lodin, did you know that? I kept track of him. As he searched the world for your mother, he came upon dozens of shipwrecks, or survivors of wrecks who'd taken shelter in caves and perished when winter set in. He brought their remains here, to this cave, to give them proper burial."

"So, Mother and Father were together for a time?" The thought seemed to comfort Thyra.

"A brief time."

Thorlak pulled his bloody left hand from his belly wound and lovingly smoothed it over the iron staff, then he took a step closer to Thyra and held it out. "Do you remember Eyr?"

Thyra glanced at the staff, then at him. "You're too far away. I can't tell."

The Lawspeaker walked closer, holding the staff out so she could see it better. When Thyra reached for it, he pulled it back. "You've no idea what I've gone through to find this. This is why I could never match her powers. She had access to the greatest magical knowledge in history, while I . . ." He grunted and bent over in pain.

"Did King Aethelred send you to find my mother?"

Thorlak searched the cave as though in panic. "Is she alive?"

Gunnar imperceptibly edged toward Thyra, holding his breath until he could see the staff in Thorlak's hands. The ends had been cast into haphazard octagons, no side the same length or depth. The key?

Finally, Thorlak responded, "Did Aethelred send me? Aethelred makes no decisions these days. He's ill, he—"

"The ealdorman of Mercia, then?" Thyra asked.

Thorlak's lips twisted into a cold smile. "I'm not surprised you figured that out. I told him he was a fool for delivering the money himself nine months ago, but he trusted no one, not even me. He knew the end was in sight."

Gunnar's grip on his sword had gone slippery. He clutched it tighter as he tried to piece the plot together. Had Thorlak, Eadric, and Aethelred hatched the plot to kidnap Vethild before the massacre began so she couldn't protect the Danelaw? Just as his family claimed?

Gunnar gestured to the staff. "You and the ealdorman spent a good deal of gold just to steal an ugly key to Vethild's mountain of the dead."

Thorlak shook his head. "Eadric could care less about Eyr. Ten years ago, Aethelred dispatched a ship to Albania-Land to find Vethild. He wanted to use her as a bargaining chip with King Sweyn, who'd been ravaging England for two awful years, and had left the country in the worst famine ever seen. But the ship found no traces of her. None."

Thyra's chest was rising and falling swiftly, listening as though her life depended upon it.

Thorlak paused to suck in a shuddering breath. "Aethelred can't risk having her return to side with his wayward son, Edmund. It isn't just her powers the king is worried about. If Vethild sides with Edmund, it will hearten his army, make them feel invincible. And the king's spies have told him that the Danelaw, at Edmund's behest, is actively searching for her." Thorlak smiled faintly. "Is that true, Gunnar?"

"How would I know?"

"How much are they paying you? I'm sure the other side will give you ten times more."

Gunnar shifted his weight to his other foot and slowly, so as not to startle anyone, casually lifted his sword and propped it on his shoulder. "What does all this nonsense have to do with Thyra?"

"Ah," Thorlak breathed the word. "Thyra. There were only two things Vethild ever loved. Thyra and Avaldamon." He gestured to the bone-filled pool. "This is Avaldamon's grave. I'm sure of it. Though I did not find the necklace he supposedly possessed. But it must be here somewhere."

Distance suddenly filled Thyra's eyes. As though remembering something that happened long ago, she stared blankly at the rune-covered walls. "Necklace?"

Thorlak jerked forward in pain, and blood gushed from beneath his fingers to pour down his leg. He choked out the words, "Vethild wore a very distinctive Seidur pendant that few people ever saw. She supposedly sent it, and Eyr, to Avaldamon. I thought Thyra was the only one alive who could identify it."

Gunnar gestured to the staff. "Why do you need a pendant? You have Eyr."

"Because, you fool, the pendant works in combination with the staff, magnifying its power many times over."

The faint scrape of metal across stone came from near Asson. Gunnar glanced at him. The little Skraeling reached for his walking stick. He grunted as he got to his feet and hobbled toward them.

"Stop!" Thorlak pointed the staff at the injured old man and Asson halted. "Surely you know that I can kill everyone in this room with a single wave of this staff."

Asson murmured something to Thyra. Her head moved in a bare nod.

Gunnar pointed at the staff. "If that staff is so powerful, how did Baldur manage to stick his sword in your guts?"

Thorlak grimaced at the dying man. "He—he didn't. She surprised me."

Gunnar shook his head in confusion, but he had more pressing concerns than Thorlak's misuse of words. For example, they should all be dead. Gunnar wanted to know why they weren't.

"What do you want, Thorlak?"

Thorlak pressed his hand to his belly wound again and a shiver went through him. "I need to get to the healer on my ship, Skoggangur."

Gunnar rubbed his bearded jaw, considering the possibilities. If that wound was as bad as it looked, Thorlak would soon bleed to death, but with Gunnar's luck not soon enough.

From the corner of his vision, he saw Asson turn and, with great difficulty, head for the tunnel that led down to the sea.

"All right, Thorlak, I'll take you to your healer aboard the *Logmadur*, but first we need to negotiate the price. After all, I'm a merchant—"

"I'll let you all live, you old thief!"

"Well, that's lovely, but you're in a bad way. I want more."

Thorlak had to brace his feet to keep standing. "I'll also pay you a vast sum of gold if you can get me there quickly."

Thyra shifted toward Asson and, to keep Thorlak busy, Gunnar said, "How vast a sum? Are we discussing vast by your standards, or vast by mine? I'm sure they're a tad bit different."

Thorlak pointed his staff squarely at Gunnar's chest, and as though all the blood had drained from her head, Thyra's face paled.

Gunnar's grip on his sword went rock hard.

"I'm tired of this, Gunnar. I—"

A groan came from somewhere in the depths of the tunnel. Was that Asson? It didn't sound like him. But Asson was in agony, dragging his bad leg forward. When he finally reached the tunnel's mouth, he peered down at the lamplit gleam.

Less than a heartbeat later, he lifted his hand and caught something. It swung in his fist.

"What's that?" Thorlak shouted. "Where did you get that?"

Asson didn't respond. He seemed to be turning the object in his hand. Finally, he shifted and tossed it to Thyra.

She caught it.

"What is that?" Gunnar asked.

Thyra didn't answer. Instead, she subtly reached beneath her cape, putting her hand on the broken sword. Then she held up the necklace so Thorlak could see it. "I think this is what you're really looking for."

When Gunnar's gaze shot back to Thorlak, he found the Lawspeaker staring breathlessly at the object Thyra held suspended from a chain. The tiny silver chair swung beneath her fingers.

Gunnar had seen such objects before. The pendant represented Odin's high seat in Valhöll, but this one had an added feature. The bottom of the chair was jagged, like a saw, or—

"Where did you get that?" Thorlak roared. "I killed her! Vethild is dead. It cannot have come from—"

"Look at me, Thorlak," Thyra ordered.

He pulled his gaze from the tiny chair, and riveted it upon her.

As Thyra lifted the pendant higher, a halo of flaming light pulsed around her, growing larger, expanding, until it filled the cave with a blazing ocean of light. Thyra jerked when the chair shot out beams of light, and the bone-pool responded by exploding in a blaze of glory that made Gunnar throw up his arm to shield his eyes.

Every tiny high seat beneath the pool fluoresced as though made of pearlescent fire. An intricate web of fire connected them, pulsing as though it had a heartbeat.

*Gods, this must be the fire grave. Why didn't the old Skraeling tell us it was here?*

As though she'd lost her wits, Thyra tossed the necklace at Thorlak's face. "Here, the key is yours."

When Thorlak gasped and flung out his bloody hand to catch it, Thyra lunged forward with her sword and thrust the broken blade through Thorlak's ribs.

Thorlak roared, "You little fool!"

Thyra stumbled. As if stunned by what she'd done, she swallowed convulsively.

For several moments, Thorlak seemed dazed, maybe in shock. Then he blinked at the tiny chair, and laughed. The action seemed to unbalance him; he staggered sideways. With difficulty, Thorlak braced his legs, aimed the staff at Thyra, and pressed the silver pendant to his forehead.

Thyra screamed, "*No!*" and lunged. Swinging Hel with all the strength in her body, she cut his head off.

As the body fell, the head rolled across the floor with its eyes blinking.

The web of light died like a flame being snuffed out, leaving them with only the lamplight seeping up from the tunnel. The pool had gone utterly dark. It might have been a black well that descended straight to the underworld of the Norns.

Thyra let out a small cry.

Gunnar whirled to look at her.

Thyra's hand was over her heart, pressing it as though it hurt, and he saw the veins in her throat throbbing wildly. She was staring at the tunnel with enormous dilated eyes.

He followed her gaze.

A woman leaned against the wall a short distance down the tunnel. Her head had fallen forward, so that her bloody hair covered her face completely.

Thyra tried to run to her, but Asson caught her arm on the way past, and spoke gently to her, "She's dying, little fox. Be gentle with her."

"Asson, turn me loose!" Thyra threw off his hand, and ran, her cape streaming behind her, her arms outstretched. "Mother? *Mother!*"

The woman struggled to lift her head. She smiled when she saw Thyra running toward her. "Knew I'd find you. Been calling . . . so long."

Just as Thyra reached her, Vethild collapsed to the floor in a flutter of her white dress.

Thyra fell to her knees. "Mother?"

A weary smile came to Vethild's face. "Always . . . loved you. More than anything."

Thyra grabbed her mother's hand. "Don't die. Mother, please, don't die! I need you."

Vethild's eyes opened a slit, and closed. After a pause, she sucked in a breath and whispered, "Give me your oath."

"I'll promise you anything. What is it?"

Vethild's head tilted slightly, to look up the tunnel at Gunnar. Dread crossed her face. "Run . . . my daughter. They will try . . . to take you back. Don't . . . don't let them."

Thyra seemed to be strangling on tears. She only nodded and squeezed her mother's hand.

Vethild managed a faint smile, and then her somber gaze went past Thyra. As though she saw a ghost passing through the room, she stared hard at something invisible. But, slowly, her gaze began to drift, her jaw to slacken.

Gunnar waited before he walked down the tunnel.

*"Mother, no!"* Thyra's shoulders heaved. She pressed her mother's limp hand against her heart.

Far below, from the bottom of the tunnel, Ewinon had started to shout. It sounded like a warning to Gunnar, like the youth wanted them to hurry.

But Thyra did not rise.

It took another ten heartbeats until Vethild's dead eyes stared up at Thyra with no awareness at all.

Asson called, "We must leave."

Thyra tenderly placed her mother's hand on the floor and rose to her feet. "We must take her with us, to bury her, Godi."

"I give you my oath that we'll come back for her," Gunnar replied. "But if the tide hasn't already come in, it's moments away. We have to get out of here right now, or I fear I'll never be able to save my ship and those aboard."

He gripped Thyra's arm and guided her down the tunnel. She didn't fight him.

Asson braced his walking stick, and moved across the room, picking up the staff and pendant. Vethild had let him use the staff a few times over the years, but it had been far too powerful for him to control.

He turned and struggled to make his way to the tunnel. As he walked, he looked at Baldur and, when he could see her, Vethild. Grief wrenched his heart. His friends were dead. This cave would never be the same without them. He wasn't sure he could bear to ever return here.

Before he turned away for good, his gaze drifted over the magical Spirit Cave, lingering upon the largest runes, and deeply carved images of animals. In the fluttering light, the legs of the caribou seemed to flash forward and back, running wild and free across the stone walls.

# Fifty-Seven

Only moments ago, Ewinon and Camtac had been standing on sand. Now the water reached their knees. Holding fast to the gunwale of the canoe, Ewinon watched the fight going on aboard the cargo vessel in the distance. Shouts and screams undulated with the wind. Several people had been thrown overboard.

"Brother?" Camtac said. "I hear voices in the tunnel."

Ewinon bent down to shout, "Asson, come on!"

Chief Gunnar emerged first, pulling Thyra by the hand. "Camtac, help Chief Gunnar get Thyra Little Fox into the canoe."

Camtac waded forward and together he and the chief helped Thyra into the boat. Then Gunnar supported Asson as the elder emerged from the tunnel and climbed in. Their expressions were haunted, almost eerily so.

"Camtac, we're going to have to move away from the cliff quickly, before the tide dashes us against the rocks."

Gunnar extended a hand and pulled Camtac into the canoe. Finally, Ewinon heaved himself up over the side, grabbed a paddle, and started frantically stroking, trying to help Gunnar and Camtac get them away from the cliff.

It wasn't until they were well out into the ocean that Ewinon noticed Asson's pants and shirt were soaked with blood.

"Asson? Are you hurt?"

"My leg—"

"Not your leg. You have blood all over you."

Asson blinked down at his clothing. With deep sadness, he said, "It's not my blood."

Ewinon instantly searched Gunnar and Thyra. No one else seemed to be wounded, but they'd been in a fight. Blood spattered Chief Gunnar's right sleeve.

The canoe rolled on a big wave, and when Ewinon glanced back over his shoulder he saw the entrance to the tunnel sink beneath the water.

At the crest of the swell, when they could see far out across the ocean, Gunnar at last noticed the struggle going on aboard the cargo ship, and shouted something to Thyra. She got on her knees in the bow to watch.

The canoe shot down the side of the wave. When they soared upward again, Camtac called, "Brother? Look! Are those children jumping overboard?"

"What?"

While Ewinon paddled to steer the canoe straight into the wave, he watched a group of young children leap from the side of the ship and splash into the sea below, where they began frantically swimming against the storm waves.

"Those aren't Wobee children," Asson called. "Look at the way they're dressed. They are ours, probably captured during the Whale Rib Village battle."

Sick dread filled Ewinon as he watched the children floundering, holding on to one another. "The sea is too rough for them to swim for shore!"

Asson cried, "They'll drown if we don't help them."

Ewinon and Camtac stroked hard for the cargo ship. When Thyra explained their actions to Chief Gunnar, he started paddling like a madman.

As they got closer, they saw not only the children but also the dead Norse bodies floating on the surface, as well as some Norsemen in the distance, who were stroking for shore.

Asson shouted at the children, "Swim to us! We'll take you to shore!"

Several of the children frantically veered toward them. When it became clear that many couldn't make it, Camtac dove into the water, and rescued the most desperate. Ewinon, Asson, Thyra, and Gunnar dragged the others aboard. Ewinon guessed that none of them had seen more than ten winters. They sat huddled together like half-drowned rats, coughing, some weeping, and others smiling.

Three of the men on deck ran to the gunwale to watch them, and when the red-haired man recognized Gunnar he shouted, "Godi! Godi Gunnar!"

Gunnar shouted back, "Bjarni, throw the rope ladder down! I'm coming aboard." Then he turned, said something to Thyra, and dove into the sea to swim for the ship.

Thyra looked at Asson and Ewinon. "Godi Gunnar asked us to meet him at the booths in Seal Cove."

After Ewinon and Camtac had the canoe headed toward shore, Ewinon called over his shoulder. "I will tell the elders, but if they agree, expect them to bring warriors."

# Fifty-Eight

When Gunnar reached the top rung of the ladder, Finnbogi extended hands to help pull him aboard. Drenched and desperate, Gunnar demanded to know, "Is *Thor's Dragon* fully ours?"

"Blessed gods, it's good to see you, Godi," Finnbogi said. "Yes, she's ours. Though it was a fierce fracas to take her back."

Gunnar tried to absorb what he was seeing. Two of Ketil's men sat bound and gagged, tied to the mast. Vilfil stood guard over them, clutching a bearded ax in his fist. Four other men dragged dead bodies toward the bow, where they unceremoniously dumped them overboard. Bjarni sat dutifully at his tiller's position, guiding the ship. He lifted a hand to Gunnar, and Gunnar gave him a lifted fist of victory in return, which made Bjarni smile.

Finnbogi said, "Godi, Bjarni ordered that I immediately take you below to see our prisoners."

Gunnar just nodded. *Probably more of Ketil's men.* "All right. On the way, tell me what happened."

As they walked toward the stairs that led down to the second deck, Finnbogi explained, "They took us by complete surprise, Godi. We were scrubbing the deck when Godi Ketil and twenty of his men rowed over and told Bjarni they were coming aboard. We threw down the ladders, and the instant they stood on deck, Ketil ordered his men to take the ship. It all happened so fast, he must have carefully laid his plans."

Gunnar strode toward the stairs with anger roiling his belly. "Only Ketil's men?"

"Yes, Godi. And after they took the ship, Godi Ketil said that he claimed the *Dragon* and all of her property as his own, including the thralls."

Gunnar nodded to himself. By all rights, his thralls should have yielded and obeyed their new owner. They were thralls. They had no stake in any disagreement between Gunnar and Ketil the Fair-hair. Instead, they'd not only remained loyal to Gunnar; they'd also fought to take his ship back for him. He clamped his jaw against the rising tide of emotion that tingled his veins.

When he reached the entry to the hold, he took the stairs down two at a time. Whale-oil lamps cast a fluttering orange gleam over the walls. It took his eyes a few moments to adjust to the dimness. Past the stalls filled with livestock placidly munching hay, he saw two men. Shackled and chained to the hull, they looked at Gunnar with wide, worried eyes.

Finnbogi said, "We didn't know what to do with them, Godi. We know they're members of the godar, but Bjarni said they were both pirates and deserved to be hanged."

"Quite right."

Gunnar spread his feet as the ship rolled, and glowered at both men. Ketil had his shoulders hunched as if expecting to be beaten to within an inch of his life, while Dag looked very eager to talk to Gunnar.

"Gunnar!" Dag called. "Let me explain!"

Gunnar rubbed his bearded jaw on the back of his hand. His anger was building, and it must show on his face. "There's nothing to explain, Dag. I've heard the story already."

Dag wet his lips nervously. "Listen to me. I wasn't even here when he worked out his scheme with Thorlak! Anyone will tell you that. I had nothing to do with Ketil's piracy!"

Gunnar slowly walked forward to stand glaring down at both men. Quietly, he asked, "No? Nothing at all?"

"Nothing! I swear it!"

Gunnar turned to Finnbogi. "How many did we lose in the fight to take the ship back?"

Grief twisted Finnbogi's features. "Five, Godi."

Gunnar flexed his fists at his sides. Ketil had started to shake, but Dag continued to stare wide-eyed at him. All Gunnar wanted was one hour of privacy with each man. After which, he would throw their mutilated corpses into the sea.

Restraining his urges was not something Gunnar excelled at. But he said, "For the sake of the colony, I must, unfortunately, try you properly. Finnbogi? Please tell Bjarni to steer south for Seal Cove. I want to hold court in the midst of the Skraelings. I suspect the proceedings will last all day."

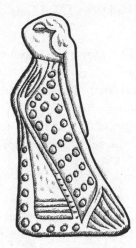

# Fifty-Nine

Thyra sat at the council fire with Kiran's arm wrapped around her back, sheltering her against the cold wind that buffeted the shore, while he translated the discussion going on between the godar. Ketil kept wriggling in his chains and glancing uneasily at where Asson and Chief Drona sat to his left. Gunnar and Dag had shouted at each other for a time but now had settled down to a quiet, if deadly, conversation. Godi Gunnar was the only man standing, and he paced on the opposite side of the fire, behind Ketil and Dag.

Just outside the ruins of Whale Rib Village, two armies camped facing each other: the remains of Ketil's and the Lawspeaker's armies, and an enormous Skraeling army five times the size. The stunning shock wave of light had drawn warriors from every village within a day's run, and more people kept filtering in as time went by. After consulting with the village elders, Drona and Asson had been selected to represent the People of the Songtrail at Godi Gunnar's court.

Thyra blinked tiredly. No sign of the missing villagers had appeared. She was certain now that they were, in fact, all dead.

Occasionally, faces appeared, then melted away. Her mother's beautiful face kept returning to smile at her, and the ache was so intense Thyra couldn't breathe. Losing her a second time was more than Thyra could bear.

Dag thrust a hand at the Fair-hair. "I agree with you, Gunnar! Stealing your ship and crew *was* an act of piracy. But the fool notion was concocted by Ketil and the Lawspeaker. I don't see why I should have to pay wergild for the crime."

Kiran translated. Asson just listened with his head down. Grief seemed to weight his shoulders, for they hunched forward.

Godi Gunnar coolly responded, "When you returned, did you call a council meeting to hear all sides and take actions to give me back my ship or free my crew?"

"No, but—"

"Why not?"

"Well . . ." Dag lifted his shoulders. "It was too late, for one thing, and—"

"As a member of the godar, you should have taken immediate action to establish the facts and punish the crime. Since you did not, you're just as guilty as they are."

"But, Gunnar! I've already agreed to pay the Skraelings for the 'misunderstanding' at Whale Rib Village. If I agree to pay you wergild as well, I'll have nothing left to start a new life in Vinland. Besides, you've already stripped *Defense of Asgard* and the *Logmadur* of their wealth to pay wergild for the mysterious disappearance of the Skraelings on this shore. What more can you possibly—"

"I'm about to tell you," Gunnar said as he propped his hand on the hilt of his belted sword. His wrinkled face had gone stony. "I personally lay claim to both ships, and every thrall possessed by Ketil or Thorlak."

Ketil and Dag exchanged looks, and Dag's mouth pinched into a sour expression.

Thyra now belonged to Godi Gunnar. Her gaze drifted to where Bjarni and the crew of *Thor's Dragon* stood talking a few paces away. They'd given their testimony around noon, as had the two prisoners, Ketil's men, who'd been captured when Bjarni had taken the ship back.

Dag said, "Oh, very well, Gunnar."

As Gunnar turned to look at Thyra, blond hair whipped around his face. He'd lost half the seed pearls from his black shirt and the other half hung by threads, about to fall off at any moment.

"Now that we've settled that, my first act is to free Thyra and award all of Thorlak's personal objects, his Seidur tools, boxes of gold or jewels, to her."

Thyra sat up straighter. "Me? Why me?"

"After all he did to you and your family it is the least he owes you. Besides, who else would know how to use the Seidur objects? Now, I wish to return to the matter of the wergild Dag owes me."

Dag groaned. "Gunnar, I'm telling you . . ."

Thyra leaned her head against Kiran's shoulder and whispered, "I give you my gold."

He tenderly stroked the hair that hung down her back. "It's yours, not mine. You should think about it before—"

"I give it to you to help you start your trading company. I wouldn't know what to do with it."

Kiran smiled down at her. His green eyes glistened in the firelight. "I will accept only if you agree to be my wife."

She tipped her face up. "Are you sure, Kiran? I am a Seidur seer. I'm not going to stop riding Sleipnir, or trotting across the land in the form of—"

"I . . ." He swallowed hard. He'd interrupted because he obviously did not want to hear her say it. "I know, Thyra. It's not going to be easy for me. You'll probably see me praying a lot, but—I love you. Give me the chance to understand?"

She squeezed her eyes closed. A strange mixture of relief and happiness filled her. "I will try to be a good wife to you, Kiran. I vow to—"

"*What?*" Dag blurted. "I will not!"

Thyra looked at Gunnar.

His brows had lowered threateningly. He spread his feet as though bracing for a fight. "That is the very least I'll agree to, Ice-fist. I'll leave you your ship, and crew, so you can make it home to Greenland, but I want all your thralls, including the Skraeling thralls. I want your vow that you will never return to Helluland, Markland, or Vinland."

Dag miserably kicked the pile of driftwood resting beside the fire, sending sticks tumbling across the sand. "It's robbery. Have I no right to religious freedom?"

"Of course. You just have to find it somewhere else."

Dag made a deep-throated sound of disgust. "All right! I agree."

Drona's gaze went back and forth, as he did not understand their words but he probably knew their meaning. His gaze finally focused on Gunnar, as though waiting.

Gunnar turned to Kiran. "Translate for me, Kiran."

"Yes, Godi."

"I return to the matter of Dag's thralls. Chief Drona and the other chiefs have enough warriors here to take what they want, and we all know it. But for the benefit of the Norse, it is the ruling of this court that the boy known as Podebeek and his sister are to be returned to the woman known as ShiHolder—and all the other Skraeling thralls will be returned to their rightful homes. I request the help of the People of the Songtrail to make sure the other children get home."

Kiran told Drona, and Drona said, "Tell Chief Gunnar we will take the children home to their proper villages."

Gunnar nodded his thanks. "Then I dismiss this court."

As Gunnar waved Kiran forward, Kiran said, "I'll be back, Thyra. And, if I have a chance, I'll ask Godi Gunnar to marry us."

Tears filled her eyes. "I'll be waiting for you."

Kiran smiled and followed Gunnar over to where Wulf the White, the master of the *Maldon*, stood.

Drona and Asson were speaking quietly, but Asson glanced up at her when Thyra rose and walked away down the beach, heading out into the firelit darkness.

A merciful numbness filled her, a sensation she knew would soon give way to sharp, prolonged pain, for she'd never get away from the memories of the past thirteen years, or the revelations of the past few days. There was no joy or fear, no emotion that would ever dim her hatred of Thorlak. Already, it had eaten a dark hole inside her, and the monster had just begun to grow. The wars between Denmark and England had set the stage, but it was Thorlak and King Aethelred who had taken everything from her. Her family, her home, her freedom. Because of them, her father had spent years searching blindly across continents, islands, every shore he saw, for the woman he loved.

Thyra stopped and turned to watch the ribbons of foam that washed the sand. She longed so hard for her mother that her whole body hurt.

Godi Gunnar raised his voice.

She turned.

Kiran wore a frown as he listened to Gunnar and Wulf the White talking. Were they discussing the civil war in England? Or perhaps King Cnut's coming invasion? Perhaps they were already at war. It didn't matter any longer, not to her. She was never going back.

All she wanted at this moment was to feel the cool wind on her face and the water gently washing over her boots. Moonlight fell upon the sea like an endless sparkling blanket. Far out in the distance, lightning flickered.

Thyra reached down to touch the high-seat pendant where it rested in the middle of her chest. Otherworldly voices whispered to her from the key. Her mother's voice was the loudest. Where once she had called Thyra to journey across the ocean to the Land of the White Men, now she beckoned Thyra to unlock the sacred doorway and join her and Avaldamon in the Banquet Hall of the Dead.

Thyra had been wondering about the Banquet Hall and the chamber that held the magical knowledge of the ages. What would she find there? Family she'd never known? The greatest Seidur prophets who ever lived? *Maybe a little peace.*

She listened to the soft roar of the waves.

"I'm coming, Mother. *Soon.*"

# Glossary

The foreign words you find in *People of the Songtrail* are either Old Norse, Inuit (Eskimo), or taken from an eighteenth-century Addaboutik dictionary. *Addaboutik*, literally translated, means: "We are red." This is the name the people called themselves, but they are better known as the Beothuk, one of the aboriginal peoples of Canada, found primarily in Newfoundland. The dictionary was dictated by an Addaboutik slave, Ou-bee, who was being held in captivity in England in the year 1760. The last living Addaboutik, Shanawdithit, died of tuberculosis on June 5, 1829.

## Inuit and Addaboutik Terms
### ("I" for Inuit and "A" for Addaboutik)

**Abidish**—(A) Marten.

**Adlivun**—(I) "Those beneath us." The Land of the Dead beneath the sea. Murderers are condemned to Adlivun for eternity, but others eventually pass on to Adliparmiut: the Land of the Dead inhabited by "those farthest below."

**Adliparmiut**—(I) This Land of the Dead is darker and deeper in the earth, but those who go there are allowed to hunt and live in peace.

**Asson**—(A) Gull.

**Badisut**—(A) Dancer.

**Camtac**—(A) Speaker.

**Datyun**—(A) Don't shoot.

**Debine**—(A) Eggs.

**Drona**—(A) Fur.

**Ewinon**—(A) Father.

**Gower**—(A) Scallop.

**Hadalaet**—(A) Ice.

**Inua**—(I) An independent human-like spirit possessed by all things, including humans, plants, animals, mountains, rivers, even the air itself. Inuas make it possible to transform into different physical forms.

**Inugagulligait**—(I) Mysterious dwarfs who roam the hidden reaches of Earth Mother. These dwarfs were discovered by the Inuit-culture hero Atungaq on his journey around the world. He also meets the Kukkia-yuut, humans with claws like a snowy owl who scratch his daughter to death and eat her.

**Jiggamint**—(A) Currents.

**Kannabush**—(A) Long time.

**Kosweet**—(A) Caribou.

**Kuis**—(A) Sun.

**Kutsitualit**—(I) Special kind of holy people who have only one hip bone.

**Moosin**—(A) Moccasins.

**Neechwa**—(A) Tobacco.

**Obosheen**—(A) To warm up.

**Odjet**—(A) Lobster.

**Podebeek**—(A) Paddle.

**Sedna**—(I) Sea woman. She becomes "the one far down there" after her father throws her out of a kayak as a sacrifice to calm a fierce storm and she tries to save herself by clinging to the side. Her father chops off her finger joints one by one, which become the sea mammals, and she drowns. Usually she lives alone, but in some versions of the Sea Woman story a great dog guards her or she is said to live with a magical dwarf.

**Shebin**—(A) River.

**Tapatook**—(A) Birchbark canoe.

**Tarneq**—(I) The soul that appears after a person dies. Early Christians incorrectly identified the tarneq as Satan.

**Tunghaks**—(I) Spirits with the greatest potential for harm. Their home is in the moon. Tunghaks control the fates of human beings, because they control the spirits of animals.

**Washgeesh**—(A) Moon.

**Wobee**—(A) Europeans.

# Old Norse Terms

**Asgard**—The world of the gods. Home to Odin, Thor, Freya, and other deities.

**Booth**—A temporary structure. Booths generally had permanent walls with cloth roofs.

**Draugar**—Ghosts were viewed as corporeal in medieval Scandinavia, which is why the dead were buried with the belongings they would need in the afterlife, such as ships, horses, tools, and food. They were "living ghosts."

**Fetches, or fylgjur**—Personal spirits, usually corporeal, that accompany each person. They were closely associated with individual families. Fetches often appeared in the shapes of animals, as in *The Saga of the People of Vatnsdal* (chapter 36).

**Godar**—Council of local chieftains.

**Godi**—Local chieftain. He had both judicial and religious responsibilities.

**Helgafell**—The holy mountain. Each family or group of Seidur adherents had their own holy mountain. After death, the dead entered the mountain and were welcomed by their kinsmen in a feasting hall. Only very powerful Seidur magicians could enter their Helgafell while alive and return to this world.

**Helluland**—Stone slab land.

**Hvitrammanaland**—Land of the White Men. Corresponds to the English Albania-Land and the Gaelic Tir na BhFear BhFionn. A wondrous but dangerous land far to the west. *The Book of Settlements* records the voyage of Ari Masson and others from Breidafjord to this strange land filled with Unipeds, previously unknown dwarfs, and giants, and encouraged people to sail west in search of this mystical land beyond the sea.

**Jarl**—Earl, a title restricted to men of high rank. Comparable to the rank of an ealdorman in England. Jarls might be servants of a king, or independent rulers.

**Knattleikur**—A game apparently similar to hurling, played with a ball and bat. Rules are unknown.

**Leysingi**—Freed slave.

**Logmadur**—Lawspeaker.

**Mark of gold**—A weight measurement of about eight ounces.

**Markland**—Forest land.

**Mikligardur**—The "Great City" that today we call Istanbul.

**Myrkrida**—Darkness-rider, or night-rider.

**Norns**—Supernatural women who sit in the middle of the earth and spin each person's life thread. They determine the success or failure of both gods and human beings.

**Seidur**—Powerful Odin magic practiced primarily by women. Though the exact nature of the magic is uncertain, archaeologists find many Seidur artifacts at burial sites, including wands, staffs, swords, miniature high-seat chairs, weapons-dancer and valkyrie pendants, detailed images of magical horses (most with eight legs), as well as masks of shape changers, shown as half human and half animal. We know that the primary goal of Seidur magic was prophecy. The magician was supposed to fall into a trance in which his or her soul could shape-shift or travel to other spiritual worlds, including the afterlife. There it would obtain secret wisdom known only to the dead.

**Shootak**—(A) Sharpener.

**Skoggangur**—"Forest-walking" or "forest-man." Term applied to those found guilty of full outlawry and banished from civilized society, as Erik the Red was for the murders he committed in Iceland.

**Sleipnir**—Odin's supernatural many-legged horse. This shamanic horse is depicted on tapestries and picture stones (carved memorials to the dead), throughout the ancient world. Generally the horse has eight legs but sometimes six or seven legs. Similarly, archaeologists find reindeer or elk with six legs depicted across Siberia that do not seem to be representations of Sleipner but rather the mounts of shamans engaged in otherworldly spirit journeys. As well, the Inuit in Alaska tell stories of a ten-legged polar bear, Kukuweaq.

**Tir na BhFear BhFionn**—Gaelic for Land of the White Men.

**Trolls**—Not the dull-witted giants portrayed as trolls today. In A.D. 1000, trolls were nature spirits. They were considered mischievous spirits or even evil spirits. They looked more akin to large, dark elves.

**Vinland**—Wine land, named for the grapes found growing there. Though some scholars argue the term means "meadow" land.

**Wergild**—Compensation established by a court, often to end blood feuds.

**Yggdrassil**—The sacred tree. Yggdrassil connects the worlds below to the worlds above.

# Bibliography

Colum, Padraic.
  *Nordic Gods and Heroes.* New York: Dover, 1996.
Damas, David, ed.
  *Arctic.* Vol. 5, *Handbook of North American Indians.* Washington, D.C.:
  Smithsonian Institution Press, 1984.
Fagan, Brian.
  *Beyond the Blue Horizon: How the Earliest Mariners Unlocked the Secrets of
  the Oceans.* New York: Bloomsbury, 2012.
Fitzhugh, William, and Elizabeth Ward.
  *Vikings: The North Atlantic Saga.* Washington, D.C.: Smithsonian Insti-
  tution Press, 2000.
Gill, Sam, and Irene Sullivan.
  *Dictionary of Native American Mythology.* New York: Oxford University
  Press, 1994.
Goffart, Walter.
  *Barbarian Tides: The Migration Age and the Later Roman Empire.* Phila-
  delphia: University of Pennsylvania, 2006.
Helm, June, ed.
  *Subarctic.* Vol. 6, *Handbook of North American Indians.* Washington,
  D.C.: Smithsonian Institution Press, 1981.
Howard, Ian.
  *Swein Forkbeard's Invasions and the Danish Conquest of England 991—
  1017.* New York: Boydell Press, 2003.
Ingstad, Anne Stine, and Helge Ingstad.
  *The Discovery of a Norse Settlement in America: Excavations at L'Anse aux
  Meadows, Newfoundland, 1961—1968.* Troms: Universites forlaget,
  1977.
Kunz, Keneva, trans.
  *The Vinland Sagas: The Icelandic Sagas About the First Documented Voyages
  Across the North Atlantic. The Saga of the Greenlanders and Eirik the Red's*

*Saga.* With an Introduction and Notes by Gisli Sigurdsson. London: Penguin Books, 2008.

Lewis-Simpson, Shannon, ed.
*Vinland Revisited: The Norse World at the Turn of the First Millennium.* St. John's, Canada: Historic Sites Association of Newfoundland and Labrador, 2000.

McGhee, Robert.
*The Last Imaginary Place: A Human History of the Arctic World.* Chicago: University of Chicago Press, 2005.

Meltzer, David J.
*First Peoples in a New World.* Los Angeles: University of California Press, 2009.

Pálsson, Hermann, and Paul Edwards, trans.
*The Book of Settlements: Landnámabók.* Manitoba: University of Manitoba Press, 1972.

Price, Neil.
"The Archaeology of Seidr: Circumpolar Traditions in Viking Pre-Christian Religion." In *Vinland Revisited: The Norse World at the Turn of the First Millennium,* Shannon Lewis-Simpson, ed. St. John's, Canada: Historic Sites Association of Newfoundland and Labrador 2000, pp. 277—94.

Rasmussen, Knud.
*Eskimo Folk Tales.* Copenhagen: Gyldendal, 1921.

Renouf, M. A. P., ed.
*The Cultural Landscapes of Port au Choix: Precontact Hunter-Gatherers of Northwestern Newfoundland.* New York: Springer, 2011.

Sawyer, Birgit.
"Scandinavia in the Viking Age." In *Vinland Revisited: The Norse World at the Turn of the First Millennium,* Shannon Lewis-Simpson, ed. St. John's, Canada: Historic Sites Association of Newfoundland and Labrador, 2000, pp. 51—64.

Strömbäck, Dag.
*The Conversion of Iceland: A Survey.* London: Viking Society for Northern Research, 1997.

Thorsson, Örnólfur, ed.
*The Sagas of the Icelanders: A Selection.* New York: Penguin Books, 2001.

Tierney, J. J., ed.
*Dicuili: Liber de Mensura Orbis Terrae.* Scriptores Latini Hibernaiae, vol. 6. Dublin: Dublin Institute for Advanced Studies, 1967.

Wahlgren, Erik.
*The Vikings and America.* London: Thames and Hudson, 1986.

Williams, Ann.
    *Aethelred the Unready: The Ill-Counselled King.* London: Hambledon
    and London, 2003.

## For Children

Rice, Earle, Jr.
    *The Life and Times of Erik the Red.* Delaware: Mitchell Lane, 2009.

# About the Authors

W. MICHAEL GEAR holds a master's degree in archaeology and has worked as a professional archaeologist since 1978. He is currently principal investigator for Wind River Archaeological Consultants. KATHLEEN O'NEAL GEAR is a former state historian and archaeologist for Wyoming, Kansas, and Nebraska for the U.S. Department of the Interior. She has twice received the federal government's Special Achievement Award for "outstanding management" of our nation's cultural heritage. Their First North American series hit the international as well as *USA Today* and *New York Times* bestseller lists. They live in Thermopolis, Wyoming.

www.gear-gear.com